Current of Darkness

DESIRE AND DECEIT IN THE GILDED AGE

Also by
ROBERT BRIGHTON

Avenging Angel Detective Agency™ Mysteries

The Unsealing

A Murder in Ashwood

Current of Darkness

The Devil's Business (2025)

OTHER TITLES

The Buffalo Butcher

Winter in the High Sierra (2024)

The Phantom of Forest Lawn (2024)

Current of Darkness

DESIRE AND DECEIT IN THE GILDED AGE

AN AVENGING ANGEL DETECTIVE AGENCY™ MYSTERY

ROBERT BRIGHTON

ASHWOOD PRESS

Current of Darkness: Desire and Deceit in the Gilded Age

An Avenging Angel Detective Agency™ Mystery

A Novel by Robert Brighton

Ashwood Press, the Ashwood Press colophon, Avenging Angel Detective Agency, and the Angel colophon are trademarks of Copper Nickel, LLC.

Cover and Interior Illustrations by Mark Summers

Cover and Interior Design by The Book Cover Whisperer

979-8-9876964-5-3 Paperback
979-8-9876964-4-6 Hardcover
979-8-9876964-6-0 eBook

Library of Congress Control Number: 2023950197

Find out more at
RobertBrightonAuthor.com

For Sarah

CONTENTS

ILLUSTRATIONS

A FEW RANDOM
OBSERVATIONS

IN THIS, THE THIRD AVENGING ANGEL DETECTIVE AGENCY Mystery, we travel to early 1903—this time, to both Buffalo and Niagara Falls, New York. In the early twentieth century, the region was the Silicon Valley of the day—a hive of innovation in the chemical and electric power industries.

Current of Darkness takes us into these two vibrant cities—energetic and hopeful, flush with all the possibilities of youth. Niagara Falls, of course, was already a well-established tourist and honeymoon mecca, and had been since the 1840s. Yet it was the inexhaustible power generated by falling water that remade Niagara Falls into something unique—in a way we can only dimly understand today, when electric-everything is an expectation and not a novelty.

Buffalo, too, was at the top of its game, and would stay there for another forty years or so, before beginning a slow decline. Population is one interesting measure of economic vitality: In 1900, Buffalo's population was 352,000; in 1910, 423,000; and in 1940, 576,000. Yet in 2020, Buffalo's population had declined to 278,000—or about as many people as the city had in 1890. And this while the United States' population grew from 62 million to more than 330 million.

What went wrong? While this is a novel and not a work of history, *Current of Darkness* may give you some idea. Selfishness, corruption, and the human belief that things will always stay the same had something to do with it. But that's not the whole story, either.

As I've mentioned in previous books, I've left prices in dollars as they were then. If you want an idea of what things would be worth today, multiply the dollar values you read here by between thirty and fifty. In 1903, there was no income tax, and most people (other than the middle and upper classes) lived in what we today would consider poverty—without clean water, central heat, or reliable refrigeration.

In that same year, life expectancy for a man was about forty. For women, it was slightly shorter, due to the risks of pregnancy and childbirth. And countless lives were claimed by things that today would shock us. An ingrown toenail could progress to infection and sepsis. Scarlet fever could kill an otherwise healthy adult in a matter of a few days. And in the summer, clouds of flies rising from mountains of manure brought with them all manner of disease (most everything that moved relied on animals to move it).

A hundred and twenty years ago, our predecessors inhabited a very different world, one every bit as complex and confusing as ours—and in some ways, even more so. You'll see some of it firsthand as we journey together into *Current of Darkness*.

Robert Brighton
February 2024

CURRENT

OF

DARKNESS

The Miller Envelope Company

Buffalo, New York
December 25, 1902
Christmas Night

HER HUSBAND'S MURDER, AND HER LOVER'S SUICIDE—BOTH under mysterious circumstances—had made Alicia Miller a free woman, if not an eligible one.

No respectable man was about to marry the tainted Mrs. Miller, and the tidy sum she had amassed from husband Edward's life insurance and lover Arthur Pendle's scandalous death bequest would inevitably run out. And in Ashwood—the fashionable enclave for Buffalo's fast set— what separated the men from the boys and, especially, the men from the women was one thing, and one thing only.

Income.

Men had it, and women had to depend on men who did.

That left the youngish widow with only one option: invest in something that would throw off lots of cash, preferably in some boring business that kept the money flowing in perpetuity. Something everyone needs, like groceries or—

Envelopes!

Fifteen years before his murder—only a few years after his marriage to Alicia—Edward Miller had founded the Miller Envelope Company. The company steadily grew into a thriving concern, the biggest of its kind in Buffalo—and among the largest in the East. Edward was always such a sanctimonious little shit about it, though, Alicia thought, and had tried to make it out to be as strenuous as working in a goddamn coal mine, while in truth the envelope business was as steady and dull and lucrative as a business could be.

Everyone needed envelopes, and like Gillette's safety razor blades, they were used once and then thrown away. It was a humble but brilliant enterprise.

By the time of Ed's demise, Miller Envelope had already given Allie, as most of those who knew her well called her, a very comfortable life. And by right—as her husband's natural heir—it ought to continue to do so. But there was one small fly in the ointment: Ed's will. Near the end of his life, Edward had become quite confident that he would secure a divorce from Alicia—after all her shenanigans with his onetime best friend Arthur Pendle, he felt he deserved one—and he had eagerly amended his will to reflect his soon-to-be-single status.

He had cut Allie out entirely. Ed's will left his wife not a red cent to show for eighteen years of marriage. Miller Envelope, and all of Edward's other assets, would go to their three young daughters, while his wife would be left penniless, now and forever.

And had Edward only lived long enough to secure a divorce, that would have been his right. Unfortunately for his legal scheme to disinherit Alicia, however, at the time of his death, Ed and Allie remained husband and wife. Thus New York State ignored Ed's last will and testament and divided his property as it would have any other deceased husband's: a minimum of one-third to the widow. No lawful wife could be left entirely destitute, even one so thoroughly despised as Allie.

Thus, whether Edward had willed it so or not, Alicia Miller was awarded thirty-three and one-third percent of her husband's estate, and that included an equivalent portion of Miller Envelope. The other two-thirds would be held in trust for the girls, and managed by two trustees until their coming of age.

Since there was no guarantee that Miller Envelope would survive its founder's passing, however, the trustees concluded that the better part of valor was to sell off the girls' share of the business now to someone capable—or gullible—and fund the trust with the cash proceeds.

It didn't take them long to find the perfect buyer. For as much as he'd loved his friend, Ed's junior partner Howard Gaines was smart enough to recognize that the man's untimely death created a golden opportunity—a chance to purchase two-thirds of a thriving business at a discount. When the trustees approached him, Gaines hadn't needed to be asked twice. He quickly offered to purchase the entire envelope business, lock, stock, and barrel. The trustees would extend him a promissory note for the two-thirds that they controlled, and thus there remained only the small matter of the other one-third owned by Alicia.

Bert Hartshorn, Alicia's live-in attorney, counseled her to sell, and live quietly and comfortably on the proceeds. Initially, she had considered this the most reasonable course. Liquidating her shares in Miller Envelope would make life easier, to be sure, and she knew nothing about the envelope business except for the dull shoptalk she'd endured over too many tedious dinners with Ed. But an inconvenient fact remained. Without new money coming in, her pile would inevitably dwindle, and she would end up exactly where Ed had wanted to put her: the poorhouse.

The only sensible thing, it seemed, would be to hold on to her share of the steady, boring, and lucrative Miller Envelope Company. She planned to ask Bert about it—he was a rational man—but that was a formality. Her mind was made up.

Alicia Miller would throw herself into the envelope business.

WHY IS THIS ROOM so goddamn hot? she wondered to herself, staring at the bedroom ceiling.

"Bert," she whispered, and then almost laughed at her own low tone, after all the racket they'd just finished making. No one in *this* house, she thought, has a clear enough conscience to have slept through *that*.

"*What*?" Bert groaned.

Christ, he's already asleep. She gave him an elbow in the ribs.

"Ouch!" he said. "What was that for? Please do *not* tell me you want to go again. I've got to leave for Glen Creek tomorrow."

"You and your crummy little farm," she said, under her breath. "Don't worry—you're not in any danger. And besides, I give you high marks for your performance just now."

"Why, thank you," he murmured, relieved. "I was pretty sure you climaxed."

"How in the world did I land such an incorrigible romantic?"

"Are you going to tell me what's on your mind?"

She pulled her nightdress around her neck and propped herself up against the headboard. "I keep thinking about Howie Gaines."

"*Now?*"

"I think about him all the time."

He opened his eyes reluctantly and sat up, rubbing his temples. "We've already talked this subject to *death*, Alicia. We agreed that you'd sell your interest to Gaines. Holding on to a minority stake when you could liquidate it for cash doesn't make much sense."

"That's what's bothering me," she said.

"But why? *Why?*" he said in a long, exasperated syllable.

"Gaines ought to be working for me, like he worked for Ed."

"He owns two-thirds of the company now. You own one-third."

"You have a talent for the obvious," she hissed. "But I would have inherited a hundred percent, had Edward not cheated me out of it."

"Half a loaf is better than none."

Allie sniffed. "And it's a hell of a lot worse than a whole one. I have to look out for myself now. There's not a man in Buffalo, or any other town with a newspaper, who would marry me after that goddamned police inquest. And you know it."

Bert was silent.

"I notice you're not volunteering for duty," Alicia said.

"Alicia, I'm only recently divorced myself. It would be unseemly for me to remarry so soon."

"Naturally. Yet it's not at all unseemly to live with a murdered man's widow—and at the scene of the crime. I understand, Bert, I really do. No need to explain further."

"My dear," Bert said, with an electric jolt of fear that a change of topic was urgently required, "Gaines is a good man. You can cash out your shares and still retain a little profits interest. If he does a good job running the company, you'll have dividends, on top of your purchase price."

"If," she said. "If, if, if. Ifs don't pay the bills."

"All right, Alicia," Bert said in a weary monotone. "What do you want to do about it?"

"I want you to call Gaines and tell him I'm coming to work with him."

He let out a long sigh. "Do you have any inkling of what you'll be getting yourself into?"

"Do you?"

"This one I think I can predict. It's a crazy idea, if you ask me."

"If I've lost my mind this past year, I earned it fair and square. But I'm done with losing, Bert. I want to start *winning* again."

"May I be honest with you, dear?"

"I should hope so."

"Howie Gaines hates you."

She examined his face. "So? I hate him, too."

"Then how do you think that's going to work out?"

"My mother and I hate each other, and we still find a way to live together."

"You don't."

"Don't what? Hate each other, or find a way to live?"

"You know what I mean. You and Howie are going to be like cats and dogs."

"Maybe so, but I can get it up when I need to."

"Hmm," he said.

"Can *you*?"

"Can I what?"

"Get it up."

"I should think so, as you've seen," he said indignantly.

"Then promise me you'll call Gaines. Tomorrow."

"Will you let me get some sleep if I do?"

"Yes, of course."

"All right, then. I promise."

THE NEXT MORNING, ALICIA'S three daughters woke the house up early, tearing down the staircase, arguing about something stupid. Hot on their heels was Alicia's mother, Mrs. Hall, who—with surprising speed for a woman in her sixties—caught them on the lower landing and began roaring at them to behave like ladies. Allie, trying to enjoy a quiet cup of coffee in the kitchen, was in no mood for drama. She looked at the regulator clock on the wall and considered her options.

The downtown department stores would open early for the New Year's sales, so at promptly 8:30, Allie went to the hall telephone, arranged a carriage for 9:00, and then located her mother, who was now sitting in the front parlor with a sour look on her face.

"Mother," she said, "why don't you take the girls downtown for a little shopping excursion? Some better weather blew in last night, and the streets look quite clear."

"What makes you think I can afford that? Would I be living here like a ward of the state if I possessed the means for a shopping spree?"

Allie was prepared for this objection. "What if I made it a little New Year's present?" she said, producing two crisp ten-dollar bills. "I've been thinking it might be good for you to get out a little more. You've been through so much this past year."

"I *have* been feeling a bit cooped up lately," Mrs. Hall said, eyeing the banknotes.

Alicia gave her mother a flat smile and laid the bills on the reading table. "Have fun," she said, and returned to the kitchen. She heard her mother's footsteps hurrying out of the parlor, presumably to corral the girls, and in a half hour, what sounded like a herd of elephants went thudding down the front porch steps to meet their carriage.

AS HE'D PROMISED, BERT placed a call to Howie Gaines after breakfast, before leaving for his month-long respite at his beloved Glen Creek Farm, the little parcel of land and crumbling farmhouse in Hamburg he'd inherited from his parents.

"Gaines," he said, "I hope I find you well this morning?"

"Well enough, Bert," Gaines said. "But aren't you supposed to be out in the country for the holidays?" Hamburg was less than fifteen miles from Buffalo, but Howie made it sound impossibly remote.

"I'll leave later today. Sorry to disturb you so early, but there's something I wanted to talk with you about before I disappeared into the wilds."

"What can I do for you?"

"I was—talking with Mrs. Miller last evening about her stake in Miller Envelope."

"Good," Howie said. "Is she ready to accept my offer? I'd like to get this wrapped up. It's very fair, as I'm sure you'll agree."

"Oh yes, it's a *very* fair offer," Bert said. "But she wants to take a different tack."

There was a silent, crackling pause on the line. "A different *tack*? What kind of tack?"

"Just a little different. She's decided to take an active hand in Miller Envelope. With you."

"With me how?"

"Helping you run the business. Day to day."

"At the *factory*?" Gaines said, his voice rising in panic.

"Yes. Picking up where Ed left off."

"Holy hell, Bert. You know the trustees warned us both about this."

"And as Mrs. Miller will attest, I underscored those concerns with her. But you know as well as I do—ultimately it is her decision."

"This is horrible," Gaines moaned.

"Don't take such a pessimistic view of it, Howie. Alicia is a very intelligent and capable woman. You might find her quite an asset. It's as much in her interest as it is in yours to make Miller Envelope a success."

"When does she want to start?"

"Monday after the New Year," Bert replied.

There was silence long enough that Bert thought Gaines had keeled over. "Gaines? Are you still there?"

"Yes, I'm here," Howie said slowly. "All right, Monday after New Year's. We start at eight o'clock."

"I'll let her know. Thanks for taking my call, Howie."

"Bert?" Gaines said as Hartshorn was about to hang up the earpiece.

"Yes?"

"Her mind's made up, then? Are you sure?"

"I'm afraid so."

"Bert, I really—"

"Happy New Year, Howie." Bert hung up and looked over at Alicia. "Message delivered. You start at eight o'clock, a week from Monday."

"Eight o'clock?" she said. "Gaines is really keeping bankers' hours these days. Ed was always in the office by seven thirty, and usually earlier than that."

"Well, its eight o'clock now. He'll be expecting you."

"That's good of him."

"I feel morally certain he doesn't have the least idea of what to expect, Alicia."

"That must be the nicest thing you've ever said to me, Bertie boy."

CHARLES KENDALL'S PROBLEM

Niagara Falls, New York
That same morning

"GOOD MORNING, STEFAN," CHARLES KENDALL SAID TO A GIANT, rawboned man standing at attention in the grand entrance foyer of Kendall House. "Has Isadore brought my carriage around?"

"He is waiting outside, sir," Stefan replied, bowing enough that his head came down to something like a normal height.

"Good. I'm in a bit of a hurry." In the hallway mirror, Kendall straightened his tie as the big man swung open the massive door leading to the *porte cochère.*

"Shall I accompany you, Mr. Kendall?"

"No need. Nothing dangerous. Just to the factory."

"Very well, sir."

Stefan—his surname was unpronounceable—had been Kendall's personal bodyguard for more than a year. He was a Slav—or rather, a Cossack, as he reminded anyone who mistook him for a Russian or a Pole. With deep-set eyes, copious dark hair, and sharp cheekbones looming over an enormous mustache—all on top of six and a half feet of solid muscle—he was not a man easily unnoticed, let alone challenged. And, for good measure, he carried a huge Colt revolver in his coat pocket—in case things got out of hand.

"Tell Erin I'll be home in time for luncheon," Kendall said as he climbed into the brougham.

Isadore clucked to his horse, and the carriage followed the circular drive to the stone wall encircling Kendall House. They passed through a looming set of iron gates and turned onto the Lewiston Road for the half-hour ride south to Niagara Falls.

As the walls and turrets of Kendall House receded behind them, Kendall caught himself fidgeting nervously with his watch fob. This won't do, he thought.

The Kendall Electrolytic Abrasives factory was balanced on the very rim of the Niagara Gorge, a towering pair of facing cliffs, squaring off against each other like bookends, one on the Canadian side of the Lower Niagara River—so called after what was the Upper Niagara tumbled over Niagara Falls—and one on the American side, called the High Bank, or the Mill District. Clustered side by side along High Bank was a motley collection of factories, large and small, making everything from silverware to caustic soda.

The mills all had one thing in common—a need for cheap electric power—and an accident of topography provided an elegant and inexhaustible solution. Millions of years of geology and five ice ages had decreed that four of the five Great Lakes would have but one way to find the sea: the Niagara River. And that meant that every last drop of four inland oceans had to fall 150 feet over the Falls to reach the lower river, and thence on to Lake Ontario and the Atlantic.

The industrial pioneers of Niagara Falls grasped that if water could somehow be redirected from the upper river—through tunnels bored under the city itself, bypassing the Falls—it could then be made to fall 150 vertical feet through giant conduits set vertically behind the cliffs of the High Bank. At the bottom of this plunge, called the Long Drop, the eager water had only one remaining task: to spin the turbine wheels of enormous generators huddled against the base of the gorge. Then, spent, it would at last be allowed to rejoin the lower river and find its way to the sea. And thus each and every factory fortunate enough to call the High Bank its home could have its very own miniature Niagara Falls to power its operations.

Falling water had turned mill wheels for centuries, but never at this scale. How much power could be generated was limited only by the amount of water a factory could commandeer. More water meant more power, more product, more profit. Vast sums were bid and gladly paid for nothing more than rights to the most plentiful commodity on earth. A drop more through my factory, a businessman would think, was not only a dollar more in my pocket, it was a drop and a dollar *less* in my competitor's, too.

When Kendall alighted at the unadorned oblong brick building that was his headquarters, he paused and sniffed the air, which reeked of sulfur. Running at full capacity, he thought with satisfaction. But not for long, unless I can get to the bottom of this.

ALEXANDER MACCORMICK HAD COME a long way from his humble beginnings as a dockworker in his native Glasgow. The promise of the Niagara Falls power industry had lured him across the Atlantic, and now—at only thirty years of age—he had been selected by Charles Kendall himself to manage the production of the precious abrasive.

"Mac," Kendall said, rapping on the doorjamb. "A minute?"

"Of course, sir."

"Did you talk with the power company?"

"Aye," he said. "They've found nothing out of whack on their end. Everything checks out."

"If they're telling the truth, you know what that means. The problem's either in our factory, or in the feeder tunnel."

MacCormick rubbed his eyes. "And that puts me at a bit of a loss, sir. I don't know how to investigate the factory without raising suspicion. And worse, we'll never be able to get any of the lads to go in that feeder tunnel."

"Why not?"

"They say it's cursed."

"Cursed? What nonsense."

"Aye, but that tunnel is a wee thing, and black as the Earl of Hell's waistcoat. A torrent of water rushing by like mad, straight for the Long Drop. There isn't a lad in any of our crews that'd go in there. Not for love nor money."

"But what about the Hunkies we brought over? They're brave."

"Ach, they're brave enough, but they're superstitious, those Hunkies. They have all sorts o' mad notions. They refuse to go anywhere a man's been killed. And men died building that tunnel."

"Don't remind me."

"I'm sorry to bring it up," MacCormick said.

Kendall sank into the chair across from his supervisor, exasperated. "Mac, how is it that you and I know more about this business than anyone on the planet, and this is all we can come up with?"

MacCormick was silent for a moment.

"May I be frank with you, sir?"

"Of course."

"If you and I can't figure it out, there's only one thing left to do."

"And that is?"

"Get detectives in here. Pinkertons."

"God, not the Pinkertons. Look what they got up to in Homestead."

"Not the skull-crackin', strikebreaker ones. I mean their under-cover men."

"Their profile is still too high."

"Well, not Pinkertons, then. Some other kind of detective."

Kendall pressed on his temples. "Then we need to get someone no one's ever heard of. And certainly not anyone from Niagara Falls."

"A Buffalo agency, perhaps?"

"That could work," Kendall said. "A small one."

"Aye," MacCormick said. "Would you like me to ask around?"

"No. The less we let on, the better. I'll handle it. I'll look through the Buffalo telephone directory right now."

"But how will you choose?"

Kendall pondered this. "I'm going to call the very first one in the book that I've never heard of."

3

Industrial Espionage

Buffalo, New York
Later that day

THE WELL-WORN FIFTH FLOOR CORRIDOR OF THE HUDSON
Building looked very much like the equally well-worn corridors on each
of the structure's other four floors. Two facing rows of reeded-glass office
doors, all identical, stretched away toward a grimy window at the end of
the hallway. Halfway down on the left was a door that seemed slightly
less battered than the others, as though someone had taken the time to
apply a coat of paste wax and bring out the grain. The window of this
unusually well-tended door was lettered in gold with the words

Avenging Angel Detective Agency, Inc.
Sarah M. Payne, Principal.

with a little set of wings and a halo hovering above.

Inside the door, the space was divided into two—a larger office with
two big oak desks, one occupied and the other apparently vacant, and a
telephone table. There was a smaller private office opening off the larger
one. Both offices boasted large windows, which overlooked the Erie
County Courthouse.

Sarah Payne had chosen the location carefully when she had established her agency half a year before. There was an appealing, slightly
nondescript quality about the threadbare old building, which seemed

appropriate for the work of a sleuth. And, some may have said, which provided an unexpected contrast to Sarah herself, who was generally accepted by men and—more to the point—*women* as the most beautiful young woman in all of Buffalo, and maybe even the state. Blessed with wavy strawberry blonde hair, darting deep-blue eyes that went almost violet in certain lights, a perfect oval face with creamy skin and a pert sprinkle of freckles, all set atop a trim but curvaceous figure dressed in the latest styles by local milliners eager to use her as their movable fashion plate. Sarah Payne was universally admired for her looks, if often with considerable and grudging envy.

Not that most of the good people of Buffalo envied Sarah in other respects. Her miserable decade-long marriage to a local dentist had mercifully expired in spring when the poor man had finally succumbed to his cravings for drink and drugs. And a brief affair with Alicia Miller's husband Edward had ended tragically with Ed's murder in the private den of his home on Ashwood Street and, worse, had left their romance unconsummated.

Following these twin catastrophes, Sarah had become considered something of a jinx—a beautiful specimen, without any doubt but, like a weather vane in a thunderstorm, one best admired from a safe distance. Not everything, though, had gone against Sarah. She had an adorable nine-year-old daughter, Maggie, who was a tiny copy of her mother's looks and plucky, irrepressible personality. And at twenty-eight years of age, the young widow still had plenty of time for her luck to turn.

Her junior partner in the Avenging Angel Detective Agency, Annie Murray, was luckier but also plainer than Sarah, as though the gods had seen fit to balance things out a little. Annie and her sister Ruth had spent years as domestic servants in the Miller household, though Alicia had always considered them too much on Edward's side of things. When, soon after her husband's demise, Mrs. Miller had dismissed them both, Sarah had hired Annie to help with the agency and Ruth to look after little Maggie and everything else at home. Her rescue of the Murray sisters—along with the passionate if ultimately platonic fling with Edward—had not endeared Sarah to Alicia.

Sarah's stylish kid boots were clicking down the fifth-floor corridor toward the office when the door suddenly opened inward and Annie's head poked out.

"I thought I heard you," Annie said. "Did we get the case?"

"Inside," Sarah said, pointing. The two piled into the office and Sarah removed her impossibly ornate hat, a towering mélange of feathers and lace and heaven-knows-what-all. Once she'd hung up her coat, she sat down in the guest chair near the telephone table.

"Well?" Annie said. "Why are you keeping me in suspense?"

Sarah gave her a dazzling smile. "I'm sorry, I was playing with you. We got it!"

Annie clapped. "Thank heavens. I've been worrying a little lately about our finances."

"So have I, but remember—it's my job to worry, not yours. But this case will be a good one for you. It's surveillance."

"I never did think that being plain would be such an asset."

"Stop that," Sarah said. "You are hardly plain. But you can somehow disappear in a way I simply cannot understand. It's a marvel."

"What's the case, then?" Annie said, taking out her notepad.

"It's a divorce case!"

"You're being a little too cheerful. Divorce cases are awful."

"I know they're unpleasant, but they're a big part of the detective business. And you did so well on the last one."

"I just wish we could get some different work."

"I don't disagree with you, but at least we're making ends meet."

Annie sighed. "Well, then, tell me what I—"

She was interrupted by the ringing of the office telephone.

"Avenging Angel Detective Agency," Sarah said, snatching up the earpiece. "May I help you?"

"I'm sorry. I was trying to reach the AA Detective Agency," a man's voice said.

"Yes, sir. You have the correct number. The 'AA' stands for 'Avenging Angel.'"

"That's a curious name for a detective agency."

I don't think it is, Sarah thought, but best not to argue it. "The directory couldn't fit the whole name in our listing. We had to abbreviate it."

"I see. Well, no matter. You're at the very top of the *A*'s, in any case. May I speak with the principal of your agency?"

"You are—I mean, I *am* the principal of the agency, sir. Sarah Payne, at your service. With whom do I have the pleasure of speaking?"

"Did you say your name is Sarah Payne?"

"Yes, that's correct. And to whom am I speaking, sir?"

The caller hesitated a long while, unsure of whether to hang up and go to the next entry in the directory. A lady detective?

"Hello?" Sarah said into the humming silence. "Mr. . . . ?"

"Kendall," he said at last. "Charles Kendall. Kendall Electrolytic Abrasives. I'm calling from Niagara Falls, and I have a matter of some delicacy that requires discreet investigation."

"That's our specialty," Sarah said, a little too brightly. "Divorce, default—"

"This is a matter of *industrial espionage*," Kendall said. "Do you handle that sort of thing?"

What in the world is industrial espionage, Sarah wondered. "Of course," she bluffed. "Although it would be advisable to discuss such a matter in person. The telephone is not secure."

"You're quite right. Can you come to Niagara Falls for a conference with me?"

"I'd be delighted to. When would you like to meet?"

"Is tomorrow too soon?"

"On a Saturday?" Sarah asked.

"Yes, my weekdays are chock-full, I'm afraid," he replied.

"Then that won't be a problem. Tomorrow it is."

"Wonderful. And may we meet at my home? We can discuss the matter over dinner."

Dinner? On a Saturday? Sarah thought. This seems more than a bit irregular. I do hope he hasn't seen me in the newspapers and formulated any *ideas*.

"Mrs. Payne?"

"Yes, I'm sorry. I'm here. You wouldn't prefer that I come to your factory instead?"

"I can't be certain that . . . there's not someone here at my factory who . . . is part of the problem. Our work has to be undertaken in complete secrecy."

Sarah felt a ripple of relief. "Of course."

"Thank you for understanding. How about six o'clock, then?"

"Perfect," she said. "Now, if I may—I note in my Niagara Falls directory here that your address is given only as 'Kendall House, Lewiston.' May I ask your street address, so I may tell the hackman?"

There was the slightest hint of a chuckle on the other end of the line. "Oh, my house doesn't have a street address. But you won't need to worry about any of that. I'll have my driver pick you up at the train or trolley station, as you prefer. It's about forty minutes from downtown Niagara Falls to my house."

"That's very kind, sir," Sarah said. "I'll trolley up to the Falls, then, and plan to arrive at the Prospect Street Station at a quarter after five."

"Perfect. He'll find you there."

"How will he know what I look like?"

"He'll know."

He *has* read the newspapers, she thought.

"Very well. I look forward to meeting you tomorrow, Mr. Kendall."

"Likewise, Mrs. Payne. I've never met a lady detective before."

"You're not the first person who's said that to me," she said, smiling. "But very soon, you'll be able to check that goal off your list."

After she had hung up, Sarah looked over at Annie, who was bubbling over with curiosity.

"Well, how about that?" Sarah said.

"Who was it?"

"Unless it's someone playing a prank on us, that was Charles Kendall."

"*The* Charles Kendall? From Niagara Falls?"

"One and the same."

"What would a man like that want with *us*?" Annie said.

"Now *that's* a confidence builder," Sarah replied.

Mistress of Kendall House

Niagara Falls, New York
December 27, 1902
Saturday

As Kendall had predicted, his driver found her as soon as her foot touched the pavement at the Yellow Car terminus on Prospect Street, in the heart of the tourist district. It was a crisp winter day, the sky a mosaic of delicate blue framed by the bare branches of the trees.

"Mrs. Payne?" the driver said.

"Yes, I am. You must be Mr. Kendall's driver."

"Please call me Isadore," he said.

He helped her into a luxurious brougham, closed the door, and hopped up onto the driver's seat. With a jerk, the pair of horses started the long pull out of the city. It was a slow walk at first, through tree-lined streets of tourist accommodations, which quickly petered out as they approached the High Bank. As they passed the long row of factories, each wrapped in its own cloud of fumes, the air inside the closed carriage quickly became stifling.

When they were safely past the mills, Isadore stopped the coach, set the brake, and hopped down. He came around to the side of the carriage, and Sarah felt in her bag for her revolver, just in case. But all the driver had in mind was to jigger the isinglass window open. He fiddled with a couple of clasps, and slid the window down partway, letting in a welcome surge of fresh, cold air.

"You'll be more comfortable now," he said through the opening. "Sorry about the reek." He then hopped up into his seat again and clucked to his team. He had to encourage them, off and on, for the next thirty minutes of a steady uphill pull along the Lewiston Road, which paralleled the gorge along the American side.

It was nearing six o'clock when Sarah's coach slowed, turned left across the main road, and pulled up outside a pair of gigantic iron gates, flanked by imposing stone gateposts topped with fluttering gas lamps. Sarah craned her neck to see what was beyond the ironwork but couldn't make out anything. Isadore hopped down and pushed a button on one of the gateposts. In a few seconds, the gates slowly opened, revealing a long, curving driveway. Soon, she had a better view of the place.

At the far end of the driveway, seeming to cling to the very edge of the cliff, perched Kendall House. Behind a deep *porte cochère* rose a tall rampart of native stone, covered almost entirely with ivy. Above it hovered three latticework stories of beams, stucco, and leaded glass windows, surmounted by a steeply pitched slate roof whose plane was broken by three dormers and three tall chimneys, one dead center and one at each end. The house glowed like a giant jewel box against the gathering velvet of the sky.

To the right and a little behind the house, off the curved driveway, was what looked to be the carriage house, itself as large as any mansion in Buffalo. The horses seemed to look wistfully at it as Isadore guided them around the drive and under the *porte cochère*. He locked the coach down, opened the door, and offered his hand to Sarah.

Sarah had no sooner smoothed her skirt and steadied her hat when the massive oak front door swung open, spilling yellow light over her and Isadore. Someone must have been watching them come up the drive.

"Welcome, welcome," said a young woman, silhouetted in the doorway. Sarah looked up as the young lady stepped out of her golden halo and under the *porte cochère*.

"I'm Christine Kendall," she said, holding out her hand. Her shapely, still-girlish figure was outlined in a long white gown with

Belgian lace embellishments and a tight-fitting jacket. Her golden hair was tied up in a chignon.

Why, she must be ten years younger than I am, Sarah thought. Rich men certainly do favor young wives.

"Mrs. Kendall," Sarah said, shaking the delicate hand. "It's a pleasure to meet the mistress of Kendall House."

The young woman burst into a peal of laughter. "You think—oh, I can't *wait* to tell Daddy. Charles Kendall's *daughter*, and at present I'm no one's missus, and no one's mistress, either. But you never know what tomorrow will bring."

"I'm terribly sorry, Miss Kendall. I assumed—"

"Never mind that," the young Miss Kendall said. "I think it's funny. And please, call me Christine."

"Then I am Sarah. Has anyone ever told you that you look just like an angel?"

"Now that's something I'll let you tell Daddy. He'd never believe it, coming from me."

"Well, it's true," Sarah said. "And your outfit is divine."

"Thank you very kindly, but I'm a hideous freak compared to *you*," Christine said, looking Sarah up and down. "You're *delectable*. Now do come in out of the cold."

Miss Kendall turned aside for a moment and murmured something to Isadore, who nodded. He then quickly mounted up again and clattered off around the circular drive.

Christine extended her arm to Sarah. Together they stepped into the foyer of Kendall House—if that's what a space so grand could be called. The room was cavernous, larger than an entire floor of Sarah's house in Ashwood. From the Oriental rugs underfoot, chased-walnut paneling led the eye up to a magnificent coffered ceiling, pierced by a huge stained glass skylight, which focused a beam of purple twilight from outside and dashed it into thousands of colored shards on the floor beneath. At the far end was a vast parlor, furnished in the Arts and Crafts style. A grand piano hunkered atop a thick rug in front of a massive stone fireplace. Beyond that was a wide staircase to the upper floors, flanked by corridors leading into the depths of the great house.

"My word," Sarah said, awestruck. "I'd be perfectly content if this were the entire house."

Christine rolled her eyes. "Oh, I've been terribly afraid you'd think it vulgar. When Daddy and I came here from Connecticut, I thought we'd have a nice little frame house like the one I grew up in. But as soon as he became *Charles Kendall* . . . well, you know how that story goes."

Sarah did not know—at least not firsthand—how that story would go, but she nodded amiably. "Well, I think it's simply spectacular."

"Then I humbly thank you," Christine said with a mock curtsy. "Now—here's the plan for the evening. My father had to run down to his smelly factory to see about some stupid emergency. He asked me to send the coach down the hill for him as soon as you got here, instructions which I have now followed to the letter." She laughed. "So we girls have an hour to ourselves."

Sarah smiled. "Then we'll have time for a nice chat."

"Yes, and for a cocktail." Christine Kendall looked barely old enough for a cocktail, but she said the word with such unrestrained glee that Sarah had no doubt that tonight would not be her first.

"We'll take our drinks in the grand parlor," Christine said, hooking Sarah's arm again. "Right this way, my dear."

They walked into the giant parlor with the grand piano. Christine pulled a bell rope near the entrance, flopped down into an overstuffed couch, and patted the seat next to her. Sarah sat down beside her. In no more than a half minute, a young maid arrived.

"Yes, Miss Kendall?"

"My new friend and I would like a cocktail before dinner, Erin," Christine announced. "As I'm sure you already know, Father won't be here for an hour."

"Yes, Miss. The cook told me," the maid said in a pretty Irish accent. "Do you fancy any particular kind of cocktail?"

"I think—one of my *special* cocktails would do nicely. And on second thought—bring us a *pitcher* of them. An hour is a long time."

Erin tried not to smile. "I'll bring them directly, Miss," she said, and disappeared.

Christine turned toward Sarah. "I have a feeling that you are going to be my new friend," she said, patting Sarah's arm. "I want to know all about you. I understand from Daddy that you're a detective, and that you're helping him solve a mystery. How utterly amazing! A woman, with her own detective agency. You must tell me how you managed it."

Sarah found herself liking this brash young woman. "I don't know that I did very much at all. Not too long ago, a very good friend of mine died under mysterious circumstances, and I—"

Christine's eyes were shining. "*Mysterious circumstances*," she whispered. "This is getting better by the second. I want to hear *everything*."

"The reality was less glamorous than it may have sounded. He was murdered."

"Oh God," Christine said, stunned. "I'm terribly sorry."

"I didn't mean—"

"I do hope our cocktails get here soon," Christine said, looking over her shoulder, "so I have something to do with my mouth other than stick my foot in it."

"Really, Christine, it's not—"

"Saved by the bell!" Christine said as Erin came in with a tray holding a crystal pitcher full of something far too dark to be innocent, tumblers, and a silver ice bucket and tongs. The maid set the tray on a table in front of the couch, filled the glasses with ice, and poured the cocktails.

"Even Erin tries to manage me," Christine said, eyeing her drink. "That's half a glassful, at most. Well, here's to lady detectives," she said, holding up her glass.

Sarah sipped her cocktail and winced. Christine took a solid pull and shook her head as though she'd come up for air after a swim underwater.

"Now *that'll* put hair on your chest," the young woman said.

"You can say that again. What makes this your 'special' cocktail, if I may ask?"

Christine leaned toward her. "It's my *code*, for twice the liquor and half the mixer."

"You're funny," Sarah said. "It is certainly special."

"They get better after the first one, I find. Now then—tell me about your adventures as a detective. What is Daddy hiring you to do?"

Sarah set her glass down gently on a little doily Erin had placed on the gleaming tabletop. "I can't say anything about a case in progress."

"Stick-in-the-mud," Christine said, pouting and taking another swig of her drink.

Sarah laughed. "Will you tell me a little about yourself instead?"

"This must be what detectives do—ask questions, but never answer them."

Christine downed the rest of her cocktail. She raised the pitcher and her eyebrows to Sarah, but then noticed that almost none of Sarah's drink was gone. "Don't be a stiff, Sarah dear. Bottoms up," she said, and poured herself a second glass, fuller this time.

She took a big gulp. "You know, even though I can't worm anything out of you, I'm still awfully glad you're here. You have no idea how lonesome it gets up on this cliff sometimes."

"A young lady of your station surely can't possibly lack for friends," Sarah said.

"My station—is *desperation*," Christine whispered.

"Desperation? In such a magnificent home?"

The young woman sighed deeply. "Surely you know the song 'A Bird in a Gilded Cage'? Well, that's me."

"Now, now," Sarah said, looking around. "This is hardly a prison."

"Not in the traditional sense, perhaps, but the effect is the same. Not that I haven't given Daddy plenty of reasons to keep me cooped up." Christine put her hand on Sarah's knee. "Do you want to hear about what got me confined to barracks this time?"

"If you wish to share it."

"Why not? About two or three months ago, my father caught me stealing wine from the cellar and smuggling it up to my room."

"Fathers don't typically like that sort of thing."

"Ha ha, no they do not. Besides, it wasn't the first time he'd caught me out, so he didn't stop with a scolding. He thought it would be a good idea for me to turn back to the church. So he sent me down to Cataract College—below us on the Lewiston Road—and sat me down with a couple of stuffy old priests. They gave me the whole treatment. Just shy of an exorcism."

"And?"

"When I got back home, I marched right down to the cellar to get a bottle of Margaux to help me forget about it."

"You didn't!" Sarah said, smiling in spite of herself.

"Oh, but I did. And careless little me—got caught yet again. This time Daddy decided that the old priests hadn't done the trick. So he arranged for one of the younger seminary students to work me over. And this one happened to be from our hometown. New London."

"That makes quite a bit of sense, I should think. A more personal connection."

"You might call it that," Christine said.

"Perhaps you'd prefer to keep this in confidence?" Sarah said, feeling uneasy.

"What for? We're going to be great friends. So—this fellow—his name was Cornelius, but I called him Neil. He was so prim and proper, at first. But finally he admitted that he wasn't any happier about being confined to a seminary than I was about being confined to this house."

"I am sorry to hear that," Sarah said. "Poor fellow."

"It didn't take much to get him to tell me all about how miserable he was. You know," she said abruptly, "maybe I'd better not—"

"Of course," Sarah said, relieved. "Perhaps instead you can tell me about your educational attainments."

"My *educational attainments*? Have you been reading Jane Austen?"

"I didn't mean to sound like an old fogey. Merely showing interest in what you enjoy learning about."

"I enjoyed learning about Neil," Christine said. "Oh, he was a handsome devil, dark hair and eyes, and very intense. And as I've told you, very unhappy. And full of seething passions that had been kept under wraps. Like a volcano, ready to erupt!"

"I'm a little concerned where this is leading," Sarah said.

"Too late now. In for a penny." She took another big swallow of her cocktail. "I'll spare you all of the details, but suffice it to say that it was easier than I thought to get him to shed his cassock."

"Oh no."

"Oh yes. My big mistake, though, was that we weren't alone in the house when I shoved him over the brink. Daddy had come home early—I swear, he's got a sixth sense for when I'm up to something—and *heard* us." She put her hand over her face. "It was horrible. He came charging up the stairs, and burst into my room just as poor, deprived Neil was about to—"

"I think I get the picture," Sarah said. "How perfectly awful."

"I was afraid you'd think less of me," Christine said, looking crestfallen.

"Oh no, dear—I didn't mean that at all. I meant it's an awful thing that your father happened to barge in on you like that."

"Barge! Good word for it. Daddy was pretty riled up, I can tell you that, and he chased poor Neil down the hill in a state of some disarray. Defrocked, in a manner of speaking."

"How frustrating for both of you," Sarah said, venturing another sip of the special cocktail, which tasted worse than the first sip.

Christine shrugged. "Confined to quarters since. Supervised shopping trips to Niagara Falls is pretty much all I'm allowed to do. Father has his bodyguard, a huge brute called Stefan, keeping an eye on me during the day, so that I can't make a break for it."

"Surely he's only trying to do right by you."

"I love my father tremendously," Christine said, "but I'm nineteen now, almost twenty."

"That's still young. And fathers always see their daughters as little girls, no matter how grown up they are."

"I know you're right. I'm all my father has. My mother died of diphtheria when I was nine years old."

Sarah thought of Maggie, now at that same age, and what it would be like for her if something happened to her mother. "You poor thing. That must have been terribly difficult for you."

Christine looked at her, cocked her head, and swirled her cocktail to make the ice tinkle against the crystal. She set the glass down.

"You know, that's the first time anyone's ever said that to me," she said quietly. "Mostly people tell Daddy that it must have been hard for *him*, raising a daughter on his own."

"And I'm sure it was. But he was a full-grown man, and you were only a little girl. And a girl needs her mother most of all."

All at once Christine leaned forward and gave Sarah a bear hug. "Oh, you are a darling. Thank you. You're the kindest person ever."

Sarah thought she might start to cry. She blinked, looking over Christine's shoulder toward the great fireplace, and hugged her back. "Please, it's nothing," she said, biting her bottom lip.

"It's most assuredly *something*," Christine said, sitting up straight again.

"I'm curious. How did you come to Niagara Falls?"

"When I was little, after my mother died, Daddy and I lived in a wee little house in a part of New London called The Fort, mostly poor Irish people. About the time I turned thirteen, he landed a position with a company that made chemicals.

"Then, about five—no, six—years ago, my father told his employer that they should get into the abrasives business, but they didn't know how. Nor did he, but somehow he bluffed them that he knew something about chemistry, and if they put up some money, he'd come to Niagara Falls and set up a factory. And what do you know? In less than a year, the factory was so successful that Daddy bought out the other investors. He had this place"—she raised her arms—"built, and we moved up here to the cliff about three years ago."

"That's quite a Horatio Alger story," Sarah said. "Rags to riches."

Christine polished off her second special cocktail and refilled her glass. "That father of mine has every right to be proud of himself. But it's different for me, you know. Everyone thinks it must be marvelous to be the daughter of the great Charles Kendall. It's *much* more complicated than that."

"People always think that money makes all one's troubles disappear," Sarah said. "That friend I told you about—the one who died—he had plenty of money and was very successful, but he had become very unhappy. I know he would have been quite content to have a lot less money and a little more joy."

"I hope you don't think I drink too much," Christine said, holding up her tumbler.

"Do you think you do?"

"See, you did it again. Another question, but no answer. I thought you might have an opinion."

"Alcohol can be good or bad. Like nitroglycerine, it's best handled gingerly."

"The problem is," she said, "I like drinking. It makes me feel free."

Sarah put her hand on Christine's arm. "Dear, it's none of my business, but I wish you would do something else with your time. Perhaps you could take up painting?"

Christine giggled. "Or you could hire me on as a detective. That'd keep me out of trouble." She was starting to slur her words slightly. "And I'd like that much better than *painting*. How deadly dull."

"I'll keep that in mind as my agency grows. But in the meantime— is there anything else you would like to do, instead of having so much to drink?"

Christine eyed her. "You're not married," she said, nodding at Sarah's hand.

"Widowed, actually. A year ago. It's just me and Maggie, my little girl."

"I am sorry. So, so sorry."

"Thank you, but it's fine. He was quite ill for some time."

"Still. I thought you were unmarried. See, the other thing that bothers Daddy is that I don't want to marry."

"You don't want children?"

"Heavens no! I find them tedious. Always wanting something. And they do the same things over and over, endlessly. They make the same sound, or the same stupid expression, and you have to laugh every time they do it, or else they start wailing. Which is upsetting."

Sarah laughed. "They do do those things. And I used to think that way, too. It changed when I had one of my own."

"That's what people say. And I'm sure it's so. But aside from wanting children, which I don't, a lot of women get married because otherwise they'd be in the poorhouse. And look at what happens when their husbands die and they're on their own. They must marry again, and again, whether they want to or not."

"That's certainly true," Sarah said. "I've been fortunate in that way."

"Please. Don't make it out to dumb luck. You have your own business, which is what I want one day. But for some reason Daddy doesn't think I ought to. He wants me to mind my manners, and get hitched to some man who will show me off to his friends."

"Marriage is not quite so bad, Christine."

Christine rolled her eyes. "Please don't take any offense, but I think that marriage is little more than a form of prostitution. Men get to have what they want most of all, and in exchange, women get a roof over their heads and a little income."

"I have to confess I've never thought of it quite that way," Sarah said, "but it's an interesting perspective. If a little dark."

Christine drained her cocktail and shrugged. She leaned forward to reach for the pitcher, and Sarah gently took hold of the young woman's hand. Christine nodded and sat back into the couch.

"Thank you," she said quietly, gripping Sarah's hand.

Sarah gave Christine's hand a return squeeze. "Tell me, then, if you weren't married, what would be the use of men at all?"

"Men are useful for lots of things," she said, closing her eyes. "I just don't want one bossing me around. I'd love to have a handsome fellow like Neil who could visit me and—you know."

Sarah listened quietly, still holding Christine's hand. She was about to say something—anything—when Erin reappeared.

"Mr. Kendall has arrived," she said. "He's changing clothes now, and dinner will be served in a quarter of an hour."

The cocktail pitcher was nearly empty, but Sarah's drink was still almost full. Christine was grinning from ear to ear. "This has been so much fun," she said. "I wonder"—she put her lips close to Sarah's ear and whispered boozily into it—"I wonder if I can convince Daddy to marry you. He's only forty-three, you know. Still very much in his prime. And then you'd be here with me all the time."

"I hardly think matrimony is in the cards. I'm looking forward to meeting him, however."

"You'll like him," Christine said. "Everyone does. He's very charming. And handsome. But I will warn you—he's used to having things his own way."

"We all want things our own way. Sometimes even if it's not the best thing for us."

"You really are *beautiful*," Christine said, apropos of nothing. "I wish I could see you sitting at that table tonight. The light in our dining room is so lovely—we've had positively horrid-looking specimens in there— crones!—and it makes them look good."

"Should I take that as a compliment?" Sarah said.

"I don't mean you, silly, and you know it. But the ugliest creatures on earth look good in there, so you'll look like a goddess. There isn't a snowball's chance that Daddy won't fall head over heels for you."

"I'm sure it'll all be very professional. But—won't you be joining us for dinner?"

"Oh no," Christine said. "My job was to entertain you until my father got here. Now he will want to talk business, and that doesn't include me. Now it's up to you to impress the great Charles Kendall. And I have no doubt you will."

"We will see. May I ask if there's somewhere I might powder my nose before dinner?" Sarah asked. She breathed onto her palm. "Perhaps a little mouth rinse would be welcome, too, after your special cocktail."

"Nothing could be easier, dear." Christine stood up, swaying a little. Sarah jumped up and steadied her with an arm.

"Whoa," Christine said. "Those cocktails were a bit stronger than I thought." She held up her index finger. "Now you watch, though, I can and will act sober as a judge around Daddy."

I would be under the table by now, Sarah thought, but this girl hasn't lost any of her charm. She felt a wave of affection for Christine, as though she wanted to hug her again, scoop her up as she did with Maggie.

She didn't have time to act on her impulse, because Christine yanked the bell rope again for Erin, who showed up so quickly Sarah thought she might have been eavesdropping.

"Show Miss Payne to a dressing room so she can freshen up before dinner, if you please," she said. Christine then turned toward the door and brushed by the maid, almost bowling her over. In the doorway, she spun around and blew a kiss in Sarah's direction.

A Woman's Influence

IN THE DRESSING ROOM UPSTAIRS, SARAH MADE A FEW refinements to her coiffure—how did it get so awry, she thought, when I wasn't even drinking?

As soon as she was satisfied that her careful Gibson Girl swirl was no longer a complete disaster, she glided back down the long hallway toward the grand staircase. One side of the wainscoted hallway was a wall of windows, giving a panoramic view over the back of the property and to the gorge beyond. On the other side hung framed Hogarth engravings: *Rake's Progress* and *Gin Lane*—bachelor's choices, she thought.

Humming to herself, she started down the grand staircase, stopping here and there to look out the windows or examine a piece of art. She was so lost in thought that she almost collided with a tall, dark-haired gentleman standing at the foot of the staircase, one hand resting on the newel post. He stepped back just in time.

"Charles Kendall, at your service," he said, giving a crisp bow. "Mrs. Payne, I presume?"

"Mr. Kendall," Sarah said. "I'm sorry, I was daydreaming. I didn't see you there."

"Not at all. I regret I interrupted your reverie. I hope I didn't keep you waiting too long?"

"On the contrary. I had an opportunity to get to know your lovely daughter."

"I saw her only a moment ago, and you seem to have won her over. Though I do hope she didn't tell you any of her *stories*."

"I thoroughly enjoyed her company. I hope I am able to spend more time with her."

"She would profit from a woman's influence," he said.

They stood at the newel post for a moment, Kendall evidently trying to formulate some thought.

"Your house is magnificent," Sarah said, breaking their silence. "And I'm afraid that's a very faint word for it. It really does defy description."

He gave a little sideways smile. "It's kind of you to say so. Christine often tells me that it's overdone, and I suppose there's some truth in that. Once I got started building it, I didn't quite know where to stop."

"And I don't know where to *begin* in saying how lovely it all is. I feel fortunate to see it."

He made another bow. "Since our topic is a very sensitive one, my home is the best place to discuss it securely. With that in mind, we'll be dining in my private dining room tonight. There we can speak freely. If you'll follow me." He gestured down a long hallway.

"Lead on, Mr. Kendall."

At the end of the corridor, they came to a large anteroom, where Christine was leaning languidly against another grand piano situated next to a pair of giant mahogany doors.

"There you are," Christine said. "I was missing you already."

"I missed you, too," Sarah said.

"You did not. You look stunning, of course. Doesn't she, Daddy?"

"Christine," Kendall said. "Behave."

"Will you be joining us, after all?" Sarah said.

"Christine will be dining on her own tonight," Kendall said. "But she importuned me so after meeting you that I told her that she could join us for an aperitif."

"Daddy," Christine said, "will you play for us before supper?"

"Not tonight, dear," he said.

"The pianos are yours, Mr. Kendall? I mean, you play?"

"I do," he said. "It's my one great passion, other than work, I suppose. My mother was a pianist, and she taught me when I was very young."

"Perhaps you would play for us, then?" Sarah said. "Sometime."

"Another time, Mrs. Payne," he said, "it would be my honor." He rapped on the large door.

A butler swung open the door from the inside, and Mr. Kendall motioned Sarah to enter. The private dining room was paneled floor to ceiling, save for a border of leaded clerestory windows set beneath a vaulted ceiling. An immaculate dining table occupied the center of the space, glittering with silver and crystal and looking impossibly large for a private dining room. The butler pulled out a chair for Sarah and then one for Kendall. Christine trailed in after them and plunked herself down in the chair opposite Sarah. "Oh, don't bother about me," she said to no one.

Christine picked up a crystal wine glass. She glanced over her shoulder at one of the butlers, raised her eyebrows, and wiggled the glass. Her father frowned at her.

He motioned to the butler. "Mrs. Payne, you'll join me in a glass of wine? We have a lovely Château Margaux tonight. My favorite. Unless of course you are a temperance advocate. Which I will entirely respect."

"I wouldn't," Christine muttered, earning a second frown.

"I'd love a glass," Sarah said.

"Bravo!" Christine said.

The wine was poured and Kendall raised his glass. "To our new friend, Mrs. Payne."

"And to your continued success, Mr. Kendall."

"God, this wine is good," Christine said. "Daddy, you are really pulling out the stops tonight."

"I really must apologize for my daughter," Kendall said. "She says whatever comes to mind."

"That means that she's thinking," Sarah said.

"Father, do not let this woman leave this house. That's an order."

They enjoyed their Margaux, and Christine prevailed upon the butler to refill her glass, upon which her father told her to shoo.

"Mrs. Payne and I have to talk business now, Christine," he said.

"Guess what? She's *Miss* Payne, Daddy," Christine said on her way out, over her shoulder.

Kendall straightened up in his chair. "My mistake," he said to Sarah. "I seem to recall from—the papers—"

"Ah," Sarah said. "The newspapers."

"It's my custom to do a little homework before I meet people."

"Naturally. I was married when that spectacle was going on. My husband died shortly afterward."

"My condolences," he said. "I was unaware. My wife passed away almost ten years ago."

"My deepest condolences to you, as well," Sarah said.

He raised his eyebrows. "Life is made of such things, isn't it? Fortunately, Christine looks just like her late mother. So I'm reminded of her every day."

"Fate has been kind to both of us, then. I have a nine-year-old daughter of my own."

Kendall nodded and sipped his wine. "Now then, to the business at hand, Mrs.—Miss Payne. I'd like very much if you would tell me the story of what led you to become a detective. I confess I'm really quite fascinated by that."

"I should think your story would be far more interesting. My story is rather humble."

"But I know my story already. So please. If I'm not prying."

"Not in the least. From the time I was a little girl, I was captivated by the notion of becoming a detective. Sherlock Holmes stories made quite an impression on me! But since it's not a thing most girls pursue, I let it go. Instead, I married young, had a child, and then went to secretarial school when my late husband's health failed."

"Something must have caused the penny to drop," Kendall asked.

"It was the murder of Edward Miller—which you know about."

"A terrible tragedy. You and Mr. Miller were friends, as I recall?"

"We were good friends, yes," Sarah said. "To the extent that the police tried to make me out as their prime suspect. That I'd killed him because he jilted me."

"The scoundrels," Kendall said. "They'll do anything they can to call a case closed, even if the wrong person pays the price."

"I'm afraid that's been my experience."

"Yet they never did find the murderer. Though, as I recall, a local fellow was suspected, and then died suddenly."

"Yes, Arthur Pendle. An attorney, a prominent one. And his wife, too. I knew them both quite well. They were killed when a train collided with their automobile, less than two weeks after Mr. Miller's murder. It was never determined whether it was an accident—or suicide."

"It was all so strange," Kendall said.

"And that was what caused me to start my agency. After the Pendles died, the district attorney closed the investigation right away. The whole thing reeked of a rigged game."

"I know all too well the way these people operate. In Niagara Falls, it's the same as it is in Buffalo, if on a smaller scale. Corruption everywhere."

"I would think a man of your consequence would have influence over such men."

"Politicians are fickle creatures," he said. "People like to say you can buy them. But as it turns out, you can only *rent* them. It's a certainty that someone else will eventually come along who's willing to pay higher rent. And that's the end of that."

"It does feel sometimes that I'm David against Goliath," Sarah said.

Mr. Kendall's eyebrows rose. "Then you may be just the right person to solve my little mystery."

"Then tell me: What exactly is the problem we're up against?"

"Yes. I'll try to be brief, if I can."

"Take all the time you wish," Sarah said. She took out her stenographer's pad and pencil. "I will take notes, however, if you don't mind."

"Very well," he said. "As you know, I make abrasives. A particular abrasive called silicon carbide, which happens to be the hardest material known to man. My product is used for finishing metal, polishing glass, making saw blades, cutting gems—anything that requires an abrasive that is harder than the material it's cutting."

"And you invented this substance?" Sarah said, looking around.

He smiled. "Oh no. It was invented about ten years ago by Mr. Edward Acheson. Before he came along, diamond dust was the only alternative. But as you can well imagine, diamonds are too rare and too expensive to supply the growing needs of industry. In inventing silicon carbide, you might say that Mr. Acheson invented a kind of artificial diamond."

"How fascinating," she said. "And is it difficult to manufacture?"

He shook his head. "The process is relatively simple. The challenge is in making enough of it. We're the second-largest manufacturer in the world, we work round the clock, and still we can't keep up with demand."

"Why is that?"

"Because we are running short of the secret ingredient in my product." He held up his water glass. "*This.*"

"Water?"

"Exactly. Water." He tapped gently on the table. "You see, my abrasive is made—baked, you might say—in giant electric ovens. But unlike a domestic oven, mine have to be heated to more than five thousand degrees. And *that* requires an enormous amount of electricity. Which in Niagara Falls is generated—"

"By water power," Sarah said.

"You catch on quickly, Miss Payne. To make more abrasive, I need more electricity. And to make more electricity, I need more water."

"I understand," she said.

"You may have read about the labyrinth of gigantic tunnels bored under the city of Niagara Falls over the past couple years—to bring water from the upper river to the factories along the High Bank. A brand-new one—the biggest one yet—runs deep underground from the American side of the upper river, all the way to the Mill District. While it was still under construction, I signed terms to give me access to fully half of the water it would carry. Twenty thousand horsepower worth of water to spin my generators. Which is a lot of water, and I mean a *lot.*"

"Amazing," she said. "This giant tunnel runs right under the city?"

"It does indeed, and deep enough that not one in a thousand people even knows it's there. City life goes on above an enormous, raging underground river. And then—someplace under the city—the great tunnel divides into two, and I get one of the halves. Several other concerns share the other tributary. Then it goes another little way and makes what's called the Long Drop—a hundred fifty feet straight down, through big iron pipes called penstocks. Those feed into turbines at the bottom, which in turn spin my generators. And voilà! Electric power, created out of nothing more than the force of falling water."

"It boggles the imagination," she said.

"Yes. And I waited for more than a year and a half to get that new supply. Remember, without more water I can't make more abrasive. But things aren't working out quite as planned."

"Why not?"

"Because someone has been stealing my new water, Miss Payne. Every day it dwindles, a little bit at a time. It was hardly noticeable at first, but now it's impossible to overlook. Many millions of gallons of water a day go missing and, with them, untold amounts of potential profit."

"That's a remarkable amount of water," she said.

"Yes, but it's all relative. A million gallons flow over the Falls every *second*, day and night."

"But where is all this missing water going?"

"That's the mystery," he said. "I've talked to the tunnel people, and of course they deny that there's anything amiss. But what my engineers tell me can't be doubted.

"As you now understand, less water means less production, and before the tunnel opened, I hired on dozens of new men to handle my planned expansion. If I can't get to the bottom of this water problem, I'll have to lay them off. Which I've never done before. And if I do, then the next thing is that the unions come in and take over my factory."

"I don't know much about hydraulic tunnels," Sarah said. "Not yet, at least. But other than a giant leak—"

"Which would be impossible to ignore. The whole city of Niagara Falls would disappear into a sinkhole if one of those tunnels started leaking."

"Do you have any theories?"

"Sabotage," Kendall said, sipping his wine. "How or by whom, I don't know. So I need a good detective to get to the bottom of it. My best guess is that someone in my factory is involved."

"I understand," Sarah said, focused on her steno pad. She finished taking notes a few seconds after Kendall stopped talking, looked up, and smiled.

"Now that you've heard my story, Miss Payne, do you think this is something you can help me with?"

"Yes, I believe I can."

"What would you propose?"

"This is why hiring a 'lady detective,' as you called me, is an excellent choice."

"I'm intrigued."

"I suggest you allow me to work in your factory, posing as an office girl. Blend in."

"As much as someone like yourself can."

"Is it difficult to blend in at your factory?"

"That's not what I meant," Kendall said. "I meant that you—look *different*."

"I look *different*?"

"Miss Payne, would you be offended if I said that you are without a doubt the most beautiful woman I have ever met?"

Sarah smiled. "It would be difficult to be offended by that sort of compliment, Mr. Kendall. Though Christine did warn me—"

"She *warned* you? Miss Payne, I assure you, I am not that sort of—"

"No, no," Sarah said, laughing. "She told me that the lighting in this room could make even the ugliest hag look beautiful."

"Of course she said that," he said with a sigh of relief. "I don't know what gets into her sometimes."

"Your daughter has an independent spirit."

"That's an understatement."

"Perhaps, though, I would imagine it could be a very constricting thing to be the daughter and only child of a man so great as yourself."

Kendall sat back in his chair.

"I've overstepped," Sarah said.

"No," he said, "you haven't. Not in the slightest. I'm simply not accustomed to hearing a woman's perspective on such things."

"Obviously, I don't know Christine as well as I'd like to, but I have no doubt that she loves you immensely. And admires you. In fact, I think she would like to model herself along your lines."

"Oh yes," he said. "She's always wanted to work, but I simply don't see the use of it. When I was her age, I hadn't any choice. But she can do anything she wishes."

"And if I may ask—now that you have clearly achieved an independent means, why is it that you continue to work?"

"Work is my life, Miss Payne. Other than Christine, it's the only thing that matters to me."

"And I'm not surprised. The benefits you now receive from work are not material but spiritual, if that's not putting it too strongly. It oughtn't to come as a surprise that your daughter, who has grown into an adult observing the joy you take in your work, might aspire to a similar satisfaction."

"You are a most perceptive woman, Miss Payne."

They sat in silence for a moment, the candles flickering, sending shadows dancing across the chinoiserie wallpaper.

Sarah broke the silence. "Do you favor my idea, Mr. Kendall? About going undercover in your factory?"

"I do," he mused. "You can perhaps pose as the secretary to my superintendent, Mr. MacCormick. He doesn't have a secretary, at present, but everyone knows he's been looking for one. And since he runs the operation, you'd have access to every part of the factory."

"I'd very much like the opportunity to work on your case, Mr. Kendall."

He thought for a moment. "And I'd like you to do it. When can you begin? As I'm sure you've gathered, my need is pressing."

Best not to look too desperate, Sarah thought. "Two weeks?"

"If you'll agree to work on this personally, I will hold on until then."

"Agreed. Thank you for your trust."

"I know it will be well-placed," he said. "Now, perhaps a change of subject is in order? Something more enjoyable, like dessert? Our cook made ice cream today."

"Ice cream is my favorite thing on earth, sir," she said, smiling.

"Mine too," he said.

"WHAT TIME DID YOU let our lovely Sarah out of your clutches, Daddy?" Christine said the following morning in the breakfast parlor. The room was bright and airy, built like a conservatory and full of potted palms and orange trees.

"We talked until almost ten o'clock."

"Why in heaven's name would you let her go at such an hour?"

"I invited her to stay at the house, but she declined. I had Isadore accompany her to Buffalo on the train."

"And what did you think of her?"

"She's clearly very intelligent," Kendall said, studiously buttering his toast. "And determined. I believe she can get to the bottom of things for me."

"I don't mean any of that," she said. "I meant what you thought of *her*?"

"I answered you already."

"Would you agree that she is beautiful?"

"That's obvious, dear. I'm not blind."

"And she's charming?"

"Also obvious."

"Unmarried?"

"Will you stop?"

"If you want my opinion—"

"I don't, really."

"—I think you ought to have married her on the spot. Last night. Dragged some judge out of bed and had him do the honors."

"You're out of your mind."

"You'll see. But I want to see her again, and soon."

"And so you will. She's going to start work in two weeks."

Christine pursed her lips for a moment. "I have another idea," she said.

"Wonderful."

"You ought to ask her to move in here while she's working on the case."

"Move in here?"

"Is there an echo in this room? Yes, move in here. It would make things easier for her, and for you. And we're not exactly short of space."

"It might be awkward, don't you think?"

"You can't fool me, Daddy. I know that smirk."

"I'm not trying to fool you. And I'm not smirking."

"Then you're trying to fool yourself, and I can see right through it. You've fallen for her."

"I have done nothing of the sort," he said, chewing.

"So—what do you think?"

"About what?"

"God, you really are trying sometimes. About Sarah moving in with us."

"I'll think about it."

"You're just afraid the two of you would be married in a month," Christine said. "That's why you're stalling."

"Nonsense," he said. "I'm far too old for her anyway. I'm fifteen years her senior."

"Now *that's* nonsense," she said. "Older men marry younger women every day. Especially rich men. In any event, I'm going to phone her first thing Monday and tell her how much I enjoyed meeting her."

"Oh no you don't. I don't trust you on that telephone with her. Write her a note."

Christine set her cup down gently on the saucer. "That's not very nice, Daddy. I'm going to call her, with or without your permission. But I would much prefer your blessing."

He squinted at her, thinking. "What can I say to that? Fine. Call her, if you insist."

"I *knew* it!" Christine said triumphantly. "You *have* fallen for her. You're tongue-tied, but that's perfectly fine. I'm going to be your Cyrano!"

Charles Kendall popped the last bit of toast into his mouth to cover his smile.

CHANGES OF SCENERY

Buffalo, New York
December 29, 1902
Monday

"MR. CHARLES KENDALL FOR MISS PAYNE," THE BELL OPERATOR said. "Person to person."

"This is Sarah Payne."

"Hold the line for Mr. Kendall."

"Miss Payne," Kendall's voice said after a moment's crackling silence. "I'm sorry to trouble you again so soon."

"Not at all, Mr. Kendall. How may I be of service?"

"Well, actually," he said, "I have a proposition for you."

"A proposition?"

He cleared his throat. "That was perhaps a poor choice of words. Actually it's something my daughter suggested. After you left on Saturday."

"Oh, I see," Sarah said, relieved. "I'm eager to hear it, sir."

"This case of ours . . . it's likely to consume a great deal of your time."

"That's not a problem. I expect to devote myself to it entirely."

"I know that," he said. "But you are in Buffalo. Buffalo's not far, but back and forth on the trolley wastes at least three hours per day. And I would add that, as a practical matter, it will be more difficult for you to blend in here if you are not here full-time."

Sarah tapped her pencil on the desk. "Well, yes, I certainly can't disagree with any of that. But at the same time, I feel that I can compensate for those complications."

"No doubt. My—Christine's—idea, though, eliminates these complications entirely. You and your daughter move in to Kendall House. I'll engage a full-time nanny and tutor for her, at my expense, and you'll have the entire North Wing to yourselves. The view is simply spectacular. You'll be quite safe here—I have a bodyguard—and you and I can discuss the case in complete privacy.

"In addition," he continued, before Sarah could respond, "I'd like to suggest that your being here would be a most welcome—and wholesome—influence on my daughter."

"Mr. Kendall, that's incredibly generous, but I couldn't possibly—"

"Miss Payne. Think about it—that's all I ask. And since you've been so perceptive about *me*, I may have an inkling about one very great benefit to *you* in coming here for a time."

Sarah raised her eyebrows. "And that is?"

"As you know, I have read the newspapers. And while I'm sure at least half of it is lies, even if half is true, in less than a year you have suffered as much heartbreak as many do in a lifetime. I would suggest that Niagara Falls may provide a beneficial change of scenery."

"That it would," Sarah said.

"Then say yes, Miss Payne."

I know I'm too impetuous, Sarah thought, as she tapped her foot. But then again, what is life without risk?

"Mr. Kendall, sir—if you are serious about it, I will gratefully accept your offer."

There was a brief silence. "Wonderful! Christine will be overjoyed. I'll have my secretary make all the arrangements. In the meantime, a very Happy New Year to you, Miss Payne."

"And a Happy New Year to you, too, Mr. Kendall," she said, setting the earpiece back in its cradle with a soft click.

"MAC," KENDALL SAID, LEANING against the doorway of the superintendent's office. "Guess what?"

"What?"

"You're getting a new secretary."

"I am?"

"You are," he said, walking into the office and sitting down across the desk. "I found our detective. She's a lady, and she'll be posing as your secretary. Please give her access to anything she desires."

"A lady detective, sir?" MacCormick said. "I never heard o' such a thing."

"Nor had I. But I have confidence in her."

"That's more than good enough for me, sir."

"Excellent. She'll start in two weeks. Her name is Sarah Payne, but we'll have to give her some other name here. Otherwise people might put two and two together."

"Two and two?"

"When I first spoke with her on the telephone, the name seemed familiar. She was mixed up in that sensational murder case in Buffalo last year. The Miller case."

"Was she a detective on that case?"

"No—a suspect."

"I understand about setting a thief to catch a thief, but don't you think this may be taking the concept a wee bit far?"

"She didn't *do* it. But she was all over the newspapers." He handed a newspaper clipping over to MacCormick, a rotogravure of Sarah entering police court for her testimony at the Miller inquest. "I had the librarian at Cataract College dig this out of the archive."

MacCormick whistled between his teeth.

Kendall nodded.

"Don't you dare let Mrs. MacCormick set so much as a glance of her. The missus figures that all of the women we hire here are plain as a bag of oats." He shook his head slowly, still looking at the clipping. Kendall snatched it out of his grip.

"Don't ogle."

"I'm not oglin'," MacCormick said, reddening.

ALICIA MAKES AN OMELET

Ashwood
January 4, 1903
Sunday

IT WAS AT PARKER'S MARKET THAT SHE BROKE THE NEWS, USING her favorite megaphone—Catherine Stoddard, the busybody who lived across the street from the Millers. Anything Mrs. Stoddard heard, saw, or—not infrequently—imagined, she would repeat throughout the neighborhood, although with the increasing haziness of a mimeograph.

"You'll never guess what I've decided to do, Catherine," Allie said as the two ladies were waiting for the grocer.

"I can't begin to imagine," Mrs. Stoddard said.

"I've decided to take an active part in the envelope business."

"You've what?"

"As I'm sure I told you, I own half of Ed's envelope business—his former business partner bought the rest from me—and I've been mulling over what to do with my share. I was going to sell it for a tidy sum, but now I've decided that I want to keep the business in the family. It's what Ed would have wanted, I feel certain."

"You don't say?" Mrs. Stoddard mused, already thinking of at least a dozen phone calls she planned to make as soon as she could get back home. "I hadn't any idea you were so adept in business."

"Edward shared all of his trade secrets with me," she lied, "and his partner has been *so* welcoming that anything I still do need to learn, I expect he'll very generously teach me."

What a colossal load of horseshit, Allie thought as the words were still dribbling from her mouth. Howie Gaines almost passed a kidney stone when Bert told him I'm joining the business.

"That is so—*commendable*," Mrs. Stoddard said, her mind reeling. "You've never lacked for self-confidence, Alicia. I'm a rather pusillanimous thing by comparison. If I didn't have Mr. Stoddard to make all the decisions, I would be completely at sea."

Poor man, Alicia thought, though the image of Mrs. Stoddard adrift in the trackless ocean dispelled any gloom she might have felt. "Well, I'd love to tell you more, Catherine, but it'll have to wait for another time. It's always such a pleasure to see you." She was almost to the door when the grocer called after her.

"Mrs. Miller!" he said as she put her hand on the doorknob. "You're next."

"I'm terribly sorry, Mr. Parker," she said over her shoulder. "There's something pressing I must attend to."

"I'm sure I'll see you again soon," he called, but she had already gone. "Well, then, Mrs. Stoddard," the grocer said, "how may I help you today? Some fresh eggs, perhaps?"

"Do you know that *she*"—Mrs. Stoddard motioned with her head to the front door—"is going into *business*? She's going to take the helm of her husband's envelope company, and she knows trade secrets that even Mr. Gaines—her husband's former partner—doesn't know."

"You don't say?" Mr. Parker said. "It sure is a modern world we live in, isn't it?"

WHEN ALICIA ARRIVED AT the Miller Envelope Company bright and early the next day, the front door of the office building—which fronted the factory itself—was locked up tight. She rattled it a couple times and cupped her hand against the window glass to see if there were signs of life inside. Nothing.

She consulted her pendant watch. Almost a quarter to eight. Where the hell is everybody? Surely work had commenced in the factory, she thought. Allie walked down Division Street, along the side of the building, and then around to the rear. At last, by the loading docks in the back of the building, she found a couple of men who were loading a large wooden crate onto a buckboard wagon. A third was loafing on the edge of the loading dock, legs dangling, smoking a cigarette.

"Pardon me," Alicia said.

The man on the dock blew out smoke. "Help you?" he said, not very helpfully.

"I'm looking for the way into the office building," she said. "The front door is locked."

"Figures," the man said. "They don't get in until eight or eight thirty."

"Why not?" she asked, to no reply.

The two men loading the crate finished lashing it down to the bed of the wagon. They hopped down and leaned against the loading dock, looking at Alicia. One of them, a tall lanky man wearing a stained leather apron, frowned at her.

"If I were you, lady, I'd go around front and wait. They'll open up soon enough."

Alicia looked back at him. "I don't want to wait. It's cold, if you haven't noticed."

"She's a sassy one, isn't she, boys?" the lanky fellow said.

"Just the way I like 'em," said the one who'd been smoking the cigarette. "You're dynamite, I can tell," he said to Alicia, with a wink.

"And I'm about to blow you all straight to kingdom come if one of you doesn't tell me how to get into the offices."

"Lady, I already told you. Go back around front and wait, like everybody else does."

She put her hands on her hips. "That's your final word on the subject?"

The lanky man didn't reply, but hopped up on the loading dock and walked inside. The other two followed, leaving Alicia standing by herself. She stalked back around the building.

When she got back to the front door, damned if the thing wasn't unlocked. She jerked the door open and saw Howie Gaines with his foot on the first tread of the staircase.

"Howie!" she called.

"Mrs. Miller," he said, turning. "I hope you weren't waiting. I usually get here early."

"We'll talk about that in a minute. But we need to attend to something first."

He returned to the front door. "What's wrong?"

"Follow me," she said, crooking a finger. Together they walked back to the loading dock area, where the cigarette smoker was still sitting, smoking another cigarette. When he spied Gaines, he stubbed it out and jumped down. "Mr. Gaines," he said pleasantly. "Good morning."

"Shevlin," Gaines said. "A good morning to you, too."

"Go get those other two men who were with you," Allie said to Shevlin, waving the back of her hand in his direction. He eyed her and then glanced at Gaines, who nodded. Shevlin hopped up on the loading dock, trailing smoke, and went into the depths of the factory. He reemerged with the lanky man and the other one in tow.

"What is this all about?" Gaines asked Alicia in an undertone.

"Teaching a lesson," she said as the two men shuffled onto the dock with Shevlin. Allie looked up at them. "Who are these men?" she said to Howie, who stood by looking puzzled.

"Utz, on the left, and Kiesler. They're two of our delivery men."

"Mr. Shevlin, Mr. Utz, Mr. Kiesler," Alicia said. "We weren't properly introduced earlier. I'm Alicia Miller. As in *Miller Envelope*."

The three men could almost be heard to swallow audibly. The lanky man, Kiesler, who seemed to occupy a leadership role, cleared his throat. "Mrs. Miller, ma'am," he said. "Sorry we didn't recognize you earlier."

"I see," Alicia said. "You're sorry, then?"

"Yes, ma'am," Kiesler said.

"And you two? Are you sorry, as well?"

Utz and Shevlin nodded, somewhat sheepishly, mumbling assent.

"Apology accepted," she said. "Now, guess what else you are? In addition to 'sorry'?"

The men looked back at her blankly.

"You're *fired*," she said. "All three of you. Right now. Go collect whatever shit you have in your lockers and get out." She looked at her watch. "You have precisely two minutes to leave my property. If you don't, you'll wish you had. The chief of police owes me a favor or ten."

Gaines touched her arm. "Mrs. Miller," he said under his breath, "a word?"

"What do you want?" she said, jerking her arm away. "These men were horrible to me."

"You can't hire and fire people," Howie said quietly, his face quite crimson. "You're a *minority owner.* You don't have the authority to—"

"I won't make a habit of it, Gaines, but I just *did* fire them, and fired they will remain. Now do *not* challenge me on this, or we're going to have a very bad first day together."

The three men were looking at Gaines and Alicia's little sidebar conference. Gaines turned back to them. "You heard her. You're dismissed."

The men muttered a few choice words and disappeared into the building to collect their belongings. Allie and Gaines trudged back to the front entrance.

"Those are—were—three of our best workers, you know," he said to her as they mounted the staircase inside. "Do you know how difficult it is to replace good laborers?"

"You can't make an omelet without breaking a few eggs," she said. "And do you know how difficult it is to replace *customers*? I don't want anyone who represents our company to treat anyone in the way I was treated. Gaines, we need pleasant, polite people meeting our customers, not surly bastards like those three. And they're lazy. Smokers are all lazy. Every last goddamn one of them."

"Fine, fine," Howie said, as they stood on the upper landing, outside their office. "I don't disagree with you, but—"

"Then *don't,*" Alicia said. "Don't say, 'I don't disagree with you,' and then begin disagreeing with me. I absolutely *loathe* that sort of thing. It reminds me of visitors who drop by and, after a few minutes, consult their watches and say, 'Well, I'd better let you get back to your more pressing matters,' or some such horseshit. *They're* the ones with pressing matters, but they want to fob the blame off on me."

Howie seemed perplexed.

"Do you understand, Gaines? It's a simile. A metaphor. I'm drawing a comparison, so that you can understand what your new business partner *hates*." One corner of her mouth rippled up.

"Yes, yes, I understand."

"Then you know what I would like to do? When you introduce me to the company today, I am going to emphasize that every person who works here is going to treat everyone as though he were a customer. Or she. Or they'll be hitting the bricks, just like Shevlin and company."

"People aren't going to like that," he said, working the lock of their office door and putting his hand on the doorknob.

"Isn't that their hard luck. Oh, and by the way"—she put her hand over his on the knob—"these offices open at seven thirty, sharp. Not seven forty-five, not seven thirty-five. We can't expect anyone else to be punctual and attentive to their jobs if we're not. We have excellent street-cars here in Buffalo, and broad sidewalks, and so there's no cause to be late. None. Understand?"

Howie smirked at her. "You will understand, Mrs. Miller, I don't intend to be lectured by a minority owner—"

"It's Alicia. Or just Miller. Like any other business partner. Not *Mrs.* Miller. I'm not calling you *Mr.* Gaines, you can depend on that."

"As you wish, Miller. Now may I please go into my office?"

"It's *our* office, and yes, you may." She removed her hand from his.

Howie swung the door open. Inside was a spacious outer office, with a large secretary's desk, a typewriter table, and two telephones. Adjacent was a sitting area with a couch, presumably for guests. Behind the secretary's desk was another door.

"My—*our*—office is through there," he said, pointing at the door.

"God, you'd think you were showing me the way to El Dorado. You do remember my husband—late husband—occupied this very office for ten years. I know what it looks like. Where's Abby, by the way?"

"She's supposed to get here by eight thirty."

"Whoever heard of a secretary arriving later than her boss?"

Gaines shook his head and threw open the door. Three paneled walls of the office were lined with oak filing cabinets, stuffed to the gills, some of the drawers impossible to close because of the paper crawling out. There were two huge desks in front of the back wall, sitting side by side, about six feet apart, each with a large window behind. On the wall behind the desks, between the windows, hung a calendar from 1901—did no one tell them it's 1903? she thought—and in front of each desk were two oak armchairs. Rays of morning sunlight angled in through the big windows, gilding little eddies of dust motes stirred from slumber.

"My desk is on the right," Gaines said, "as I'm sure you'll recall. Ed's—yours—is the other one."

"Process of elimination," she said. Ed's desk remained the way he'd left it the day before he'd left the earth itself. It was a bit of a mess—miscellaneous clutter scattered about—but in fairness, Alicia thought wryly, he couldn't have known he'd be having visitors.

Gaines's desk, though, made Edward's look like an operating table by comparison. Mountains, heaps, stacks, samples of envelopes of every size, color, and description—some that must surely have gone back to 1901 or before—covered every square inch of the expansive desktop. There was a grey-looking bed pillow on the seat of Howie's desk chair, presumably serving as a cushion atop the unforgiving oak.

"This place looks like a tornado came through," Alicia said, sitting down at her desk chair. "And the dust! My eyes are already starting to itch. How can you abide this unholy mess?"

"You'll get used to it," Howie said.

"I assure you I will not."

"And besides, it may not look like it, but I know where everything is. If you asked me to put my finger on something, whatever you like, I could do it in a matter of seconds."

"Um hmm. We'll see how that works out when I know what to ask you to put your finger on," she said. "For the present, though, let me register a note of skepticism."

"Noted," he said, feeling clever about his retort. He plopped down behind his desk and moved one of the stacks of paper out of his line of sight. "Now what's this about your wanting me to introduce you to the company?"

"That's it, in a nutshell. I would like us to collect everyone, perhaps in the warehouse or someplace there's enough room, and I'd like you to introduce me. And I'll say a few words of my own. Everyone should know who I am and what I am going to be doing here."

"I guess I'd like to know that myself," he said.

"I'm going to be helping you run the place, of course."

"I don't need help. I've been running the place since Ed hired me."

"If you have been handling the entire business all on your own, then please do enlighten me on what my dear departed husband was doing here all those years."

"Ed turned a lot of the daily things over to me," Gaines said, seeming wounded. "He liked selling and being on the road."

"Mostly to get away from me."

Gaines cleared his throat. "He liked his sales trips. He represented us at the Stationers' Guild in New York. He met with, you know, people who matter. I ran things here."

"Then I'll have to pick up things where Ed left off," Alicia said. "And yet I do think that you may need some help in hiring and managing people, if those three cretins we fired—"

"*You* fired."

"Fine. Whom I fired—are any example."

"Like I said, you can't go around hiring and firing. It's not your place. I'm sorry to say it, Mrs. Miller—"

"Alicia, or Miller."

"Then I'm sorry to say it, Miller, but you are a minority owner. It's one thing that you want to be here, and pitch in if there are things you can help with. But you must understand you have no decision-making authority. I've had long discussions about this with the trustees, and with my own attorney. I'm on very solid ground."

"And what are you going to do about it?" she said. "Sue me? I'm here to help, not hurt. My interests are the same as yours—to make as much money as I can. Why would I ever do anything to the detriment of the business?"

"It's not that you would do anything willingly. But you might not— you might not know what you're doing. You could easily make a mistake without realizing it."

"As could you."

Gaines shook his head. "I don't want to argue. All I'm asking is that you let me do what I know how to do. And I'll let you do what you know how to do."

"And what do you think I know how to do?"

Howie was silent for a moment. "I don't really know."

"Then you'll have to trust me, won't you? You're going to find out soon enough that you're lucky to have Alicia Miller here as your partner. That much I will guarantee."

Howie sighed. "Now I do need to be getting down to the factory, to check on production. Every morning I see how far along we are on our various orders. And I give them the new orders."

"How many new orders do we have? Are we running at full capacity?"

Gaines shuffled his feet under his desk. "Well, no, we're not. Things have slowed down since Ed passed on. As I said, he was out there selling and bringing in business. We have quite a few regular customers, and that keeps things going, but we've come down a bit since Ed—left."

"May I see the order books?"

"Why?"

"Why do you think? I'd like to see our orders. That's what's in order books, isn't it?"

"They're right there, on top of that file cabinet."

Allie looked at the row of identical file cabinets, all covered with rows of identical ledgers. "You're going to have to be a little more specific."

Howie got up and pulled down a big ledger book and then dropped it on her desk, sending a plume of dust into the sunlight. "This is the book for the past six months. The new orders."

She opened the book. Sure enough, new orders were sparse. Several fulfilled orders, too, appeared to be well past their payment due dates.

"Gaines, this doesn't look too good to me," she said, looking up. "We don't have much of anything new coming in."

"Well that's what I said!" he replied sharply. "I know. Ed was a great salesman. You think I don't worry about that?"

"Howie, I didn't say you weren't concerned. I'm learning here. Let's set aside the problem of sales for a moment. It seems that—I don't know—a good quarter of our fulfilled orders are past due. Some by two months or more."

"So now you're an expert," Gaines said. "After how long in the business? An hour?"

She squared up the book on her desk. "Howie, I have kept my household accounts for years, and to the penny I might add. And for many of those years, Ed wasn't making much money, so I had to be careful. If I couldn't pay my grocer at the end of the month, as nice as he is, he would very pleasantly tell me that he couldn't extend more credit until I did. And I paid up, pronto, because we had to eat.

"But I can see here"—she ran her finger down the page—"that we have customers who haven't paid for previous orders, and yet we've sent them new orders. And they haven't paid for those, either. I may not have your experience in *business*, but I know enough to know that's not business*like*."

"Well, it's been just me for quite a while," he protested. "There's only so much I can get done each day."

"And that's why I'm here. But we're going to arrive in the office each morning at seven thirty sharp and get right to work. What time do you usually leave in the afternoon?"

"Five."

"Until we get our feet back under us, I would propose we stay until six."

"What difference is one hour going to make?"

"We can use it to catch up on correspondence. Talk about what we need to do the next day. And maybe tidy this place up a little."

"I'll take it under advisement," he said.

"You do that. But I'll be here from seven thirty to six o'clock every day, and unless you want to look bad compared to a *woman*—"

"Fine, I'll do it. Now when do you want to do this introduction, so we can get it over with?"

"Howie. What kind of attitude is that? You ought to be pleased to show off your new partner. If Abby ever decides to show up for work, we can have her round everyone up."

"I'm here," called a voice from the outer office. Alicia got up and walked past Gaines out to Abby's area, where she found the girl hanging up her coat. She looked at Allie and smiled cheerfully.

"Mrs. Miller?"

"Yes, I'm Mrs. Miller. And you're late."

"No, ma'am." The young woman pointed to the clock hanging oppo-site her desk. "It's eight twenty, and I don't start until eight thirty."

"That might have been true before today, but we're changing things. You start ten minutes before I do. Since Mr. Gaines and I will be here at seven thirty each morning, I'll expect you here at seven twenty. You'll open the office building, turn on the lights, and have coffee ready by the time we arrive."

"But, ma'am, that's not what Mr. Gaines—"

"Gaines!" Alicia called. "Oh, *Mister* Gaines! Would you come here for a moment?"

They heard Howie's reluctant, shambling gait toward the outer office.

"For some reason," Alicia said when he came out, "Abby here refuses to believe that we want her here at seven twenty each morning hereafter." She tapped her boot on the floor.

"Um, Abby," Gaines said, hands in his trouser pockets, "Mrs. Miller and I, um, we know that it's earlier than—"

"For God's sake, will you just tell her to mind what I say? I'm not here for my health. Especially with all this dust." She turned toward the secretary. "Don't you ever clean this place?"

"I don't do the cleaning, ma'am. We had a cleaning person," she said.

"She's not doing a very good job of it. It's a pigsty."

"*Had*," Abby repeated. "She left after—around the time your hus-band died, ma'am."

"And why haven't you replaced her? My husband's been gone for a year."

Abby looked down at her shoes. "Mr. Gaines does the hiring," she said quietly.

"I've been too busy to replace the cleaning lady," Gaines said. "Too many other more pressing things."

"I swear to God, this is like watching a goddamn Chinese fire drill," Alicia said. "I'm going to lose my marbles entirely if I have to put up with another minute of it. Gaines, tell Abby here that among my other duties, I'm now personnel manager."

Gaines's eyes bugged out. "We've not discussed this, Mrs. Miller—"

"I fired three people already this morning, so I don't think there's much to discuss," Allie said. "Believe me, you'll thank me for taking this on. You can attend to your more pressing matters, and I'll make sure Abby gets here on time and"—she turned back to the terrified secretary—"picks up a fucking dustrag every once in a blue moon. You won't break a nail, you know that, girl? God, how I hate prima donnas!"

"Fine, have it your way," Gaines said. "Abby, you heard Mrs. Miller. She's going to be personnel manager."

"Effective five minutes ago," Allie said. "Now, Abby. You're going to tell everyone in the company that, two hours from now, I want to say hello and introduce myself. It won't take long, but it's important that I speak to everyone at the same time. Then you and I are going to talk about what kind of cleaning woman we're going to get in here. Once we agree, you'll hire her and take charge of her work. Then you are going to explain to me what you do each day, what is going well, and what isn't. We'll make adjustments together after that. Do you understand all this?"

"I do, ma'am," Abby said, looking less terrified and, indeed, slightly relieved.

"And the other thing we're going to do together is sweep and dust this office. I grew up with a dustrag in my hand, and I expect you did too, so we'll both reminisce while we get things into order. Is that acceptable?"

"It is, ma'am."

"Right answer. Now go on and arrange the meeting. Then we'll get to work."

Abby scampered out of the office and when Allie turned back to Gaines, he was already halfway back to his desk, having apparently forgotten to check on the factory. She followed him and stood in front of his desk.

"Are you happy now?" he said with a squint.

"I know you ought to be. You just found a lot of extra time to run an envelope company."

"You can't come in here and upend everything on a whim," he said, picking up a stray piece of paper from a stack and pretending to review it. "I'm very sorry, but I'm going to have to speak with the trustees about this." He shook his head sadly for effect.

"Let me understand," Allie said. "I arrive and make a few changes that will make this business run more efficiently—and after only grudgingly agreeing to them, you threaten to turn tattletale on me to the very same goddamn trustees who conspired to defraud me of two-thirds of my husband's estate. Do I have that right?"

Gaines looked up. "I'm not a tattletale."

"Then put a smile on your face and be glad that I'm here to help out. God knows we need everyone pulling on the oars right about now. And pretend to be enthusiastic when you introduce me. You'll only embarrass yourself if you look like someone's holding a turd under your nose."

"I certainly shall," he said. "Be enthusiastic, that is."

ON THEIR WAY TO the warehouse for Allie's introduction, Gaines took her on a little cook's tour of the factory. Fifteen years Edward had been in the envelope business, and she'd not once seen how the darned things were made. Paper came into the factory in great bales, and a crew of burly men in aprons sorted and moved it onto the production floor.

The envelope-making machines themselves were large clattering collections of levers and rollers, looking like monstrous mechanical crustaceans. An arm would advance a sheet of paper into the machine, more arms would hold it flat, a die would descend and cut the paper, and then by some impossible choreography—too fast for the eye to analyze—a welter of arms and presses would fold and finish the envelopes, and fire them past three women who sat and checked them all, one by one, as they flashed out of the machine.

It was quite fascinating, Allie thought, the tireless contraptions churning out envelopes by the thousands each day. For the first time, it seemed important, somehow, this business that she'd so often mocked, to Ed's considerable irritation. If I'm being honest with myself, she thought, I think I was mostly jealous. Jealous that he could, without apology, leave home every day and come to this orderly mechanical universe, away from crying, uncomprehending babies and the backbiting women of Ashwood. From his office chair, he could tell other people what to do, and reap the rewards of their effort—money and reputation and slaps on the back.

And while he was doing all that, I was stuck at home, my mother forever chewing on my ear about some stupid nonsensical this or that, worrying about whether the children were learning their lessons well enough, their fucking dance steps or the new piano sonata that sounded like all the old piano sonatas. And my only relief was occasionally to steal away to engage in some momentarily satisfying solitary vice—and even then, half expecting someone to rap on my door just as my head was about to come off.

Ed had so often regaled her with his tales of the titanic struggle of business, the man in the arena, tales of glory won at tremendous cost, as though he had been some gladiator lucky to live to fight another day. What a pile of shit it had all been—or maybe men are a bunch of pussies and don't know how good they have it. The world of business was a world of peace and order when compared to the chaos—pandemonium!—of *home*. Naturally, there was conflict, but it wasn't anything like comforting a sobbing girl through her first menses, or arguing with tedious clubwomen over the hundred meaningless details involved in planning an equally meaningless charity ball.

The world of business was simple, direct, cause-and-effect. You make good things at a good price, and people buy them. Then you make more. You reward people who do good work, and fire the ones who don't. You go home, bitch over drinks and dinner about how hard it had all been, fuck your boring wife, fall asleep with your balls and your head empty. Next day, bright and early, you get to leave it all behind again, for someone else to clean up and make ready for your next triumphant return.

Yes, I could easily get used to this, Allie thought. But the sad fact is that the men won't quietly and willingly open their perfect world to the likes of me. I'm going to have to force myself in, but if I'm to do it, I can't attempt to out*man* them. They're born into it, and I'm not. That's going to mean finding something I *can* do that they *can't*.

Her rumination was interrupted when she and Gaines arrived in the warehouse. The whole of Miller Envelope—perhaps a hundred people—were assembled, standing and leaning and a few sitting on large wooden crates. Probably half women, half men—most of the manufacturing process required a soft touch and sharp eyes, so women were needed for that kind of work—some quite young, and very few very old.

"Go ahead, Gaines," she said. "Throw out the first pitch."

"*What?*"

"I said *pitch*, you idiot. With a 'p.'"

Gaines cleared his throat. "I wanted to bring us all together this morning—" he said.

As though it was your idea, Allie thought.

"—to introduce to you my new business helper, Mrs. Edward Miller. We all have fond memories of dear Mr. Miller, and to her great credit and despite tremendous personal loss, Mrs. Miller simply couldn't leave the envelope business—"

For God's sake, don't say "alone," you moron, she thought.

"—behind. It's in her blood, you might say. So without further ado, let me introduce Mrs. Miller, my new friend and, um, our new personnel manager. I give you—Mrs. Edward Miller."

"Hello and good morning," Alicia said, nodding to Gaines with her flat smile. "My sincere thanks to my *partner* Mr. Gaines for the gracious introduction, though I'll guess most of you already know me rather well—from the newspapers, if nothing else."

There was a ripple of murmuring, a few nervous coughs.

"All I can say about that is—don't believe everything that you read." She paused. "I'm *much* more interesting than the papers made me out to be."

Now there were a few less-guarded laughs, and some nudging of elbows.

"I won't keep you long from the important work we are all doing. I intend to meet each of you and learn what you think is working well, and what isn't. And while I won't dwell on the past, I will say this business was what my late husband was proudest of in his all-too-short life.

"Poor Mr. Gaines here has been toiling away by himself, doing the work of at least two people, and now some of the things he couldn't attend to will get my attention. We are going to be more disciplined, and that may seem like harder work, at first. But as we all become accustomed to it, it will make things easier. And if anyone thinks—and I'm sure *someone* here does—that a woman isn't up to the task"—she paused until the room was utterly quiet—"I can only say to that person:

try raising three young girls, and envelopes will seem rather tame by comparison."

There was open laughter now among the group. "That's all for today. You'll soon see more of me, and don't be afraid if I ask you a question or two. I have a lot to learn, and you will be my teachers. Now, if you don't know the answers, then you may feel free to be afraid."

Silence.

"I'm joking," she said, and there was more laughter, though slightly nervous.

"That went better than I expected," Howie said when they returned to the office.

"You really know how to sweet-talk a girl," Alicia replied.

"I'm only saying that those all-company speeches usually bore people to death."

"Gaines, old chum, may God strike me dead if I ever become boring. Second, who wouldn't want the chance to see the great Jezebel of Buffalo in the flesh? Come on now. I'm famous."

Gaines blushed. "For heaven's sake. What a thing to say about yourself."

She waved her hand. "I don't care. I'd do it all over again. In fact, half of it I'd do twice, but I won't tell you which half." She gave a wicked little laugh. "Don't look so shocked, Howie. You're not a callow youth anymore."

"I like to think of myself as an old-fashioned type of fellow," he said.

"More's the pity. This new century is not going to be very friendly to old-fashioned fellows."

"Maybe, but for all the talk of flying machines and wireless messages, people will always need good old-fashioned envelopes."

"I can see I'm going to have to drag you kicking and screaming into the twentieth century, but I won't mind," Allie said. "But for the present, I intend to immerse myself in these ledger books and see if I can understand how things work around here. I'll be in the boardroom down the hall while I meet everyone, in case you're looking for me."

"I'm sure I'll be fine," Gaines said.

"You might start missing me."

"I'll survive."

"I predict that soon you'll wonder how you did, before I got here."

"I SIMPLY CAN'T UNDERSTAND why you are putting yourself through this," Mrs. Hall said when a weary Alicia walked into the house around a quarter to seven that evening, with two large ledgers held captive under one arm. She set them down with a thud on the entrance table.

"Nice to see you, too, Mother," Allie said. "And how was *your* day? Thank you for asking about mine."

"How *was* your day, then?"

"It was fine. What time is dinner being served?"

"Melissa has been holding it for your arrival."

"I need to look through these order books first," she said. "How about seven thirty?"

"We'll all be half-starved by then," Mrs. Hall said, looking sour.

"Then you and the girls go ahead and eat, and I'll come down later and have something."

"We'll wait," her mother said.

Ever the fucking martyr, Alicia thought as she trooped upstairs with her ledgers. In her bedroom, she peeled off her work clothes. The office must be even dirtier than it looks, she thought, noticing the stained arms of her shirtwaist and the ring of grime inside her collar. She threw on a dressing gown and walked barefoot down the upper hallway to the bathroom, where she took a long hot shower, marveling at the quantity of dirt swirling down the drain.

Back in her room, she sat down naked at her writing desk, in front of the window overlooking Ashwood Street. I hope I give old Mrs. Stoddard a good show, she thought. She opened the first ledger and began to read.

It was far worse than she'd imagined. The ledger's neat columns of dates, names, and numbers revealed the chaos that had engulfed Miller Envelope Company since the murder of its founder. Since Edward's final business trip in December 1901, only one new client had signed on, and a small one at that. Several long-term customers had unaccountably drifted away, presumably poached by the competition. Many others were well in arrears on their outstanding orders. Most troubling of all, Gaines seemed to be bartering the company's envelopes in exchange for money owed to the firms that supplied their machines and paper. That was clearly unsustainable.

The records also revealed that Gaines had taken only tentative steps to respond to the crisis. To his credit, he hadn't drawn a salary since the middle of the preceding year, and the elimination of the cleaning lady had been a tepid effort to economize. But Howie hadn't made any bolder moves, either to reduce expenses or to hire a professional sales corps to replace Ed Miller. Whether through wishful thinking, inexperience, or foul luck, it was clear that Miller Envelope's new owner had allowed the fortunes of the company to ebb dangerously close to insolvency. This, of course, meant that Alicia's one-third stake would soon be worthless, unless something dramatic could be done to right the ship. If it was not already too late.

"Alicia!" Mrs. Hall called from downstairs. "Are you ready for supper *yet*?"

Alicia put her head into her hands. She felt more like throwing up than having whatever it was she smelled percolating up the staircase from the kitchen.

ON THE SECOND DAY

NOW IT'S REAL, ALLIE THOUGHT, AS SHE SWUNG HER LEGS OVER the side of the bed and stared into her lap. My second day. Yesterday, I could have done or said anything, and it would have been passed over. Today I must start conjuring how to pull Gaines out of the hole he's been digging. And a man's pride will keep him digging, all the way to China, if only to maintain appearances. *He's* going to be the biggest challenge to overcome. The envelopes are good—people will buy them—but *Gaines*? He'll trip over his own dick if I don't save him from doing it.

Her head was throbbing, too. She had stayed up very late, poring over the ledgers and drinking whiskey. After dinner, she'd grabbed a glass and a nearly full bottle of Old Overholt Rye from the pantry, stripped down, and worked through half of it, neat, and in the nude. She enjoyed drinking, and enjoyed drinking alone more than in company, where the loss of control might also take with it one's dignity. Sitting naked on her bed, ledgers open and a notepad at hand, she could have as much to drink as she felt like having. It was freeing.

But she was paying for it this morning, and just when she needed her wits about her. At breakfast, she stunned Melissa by having three strong cups of coffee along with her egg and toast, but it sharpened her up. The half-hour trolley ride afterward, bouncing her full bladder over the Buffalo cobblestones, left her in considerable discomfort by the time she stepped down at Division Street. Good God, I need to get upstairs, and fast, she thought. Seven twenty-five. If Abby hasn't arrived on time, I'm done for.

The front door of the Cashton Building was open, though, and she dashed upstairs. Abby was in the front office, and she heard Gaines sneeze from the back.

"Abby," she said breathlessly, hopping back and forth, "I've had too much coffee. Where's the ladies' washroom? It's urgent."

"Oh, ma'am, the only conveniences on this floor are the Executive Washroom, and that's for men only, of course. The ladies' room is on the first floor, in the rear."

"What in hell?" Alicia said, gripping her abdomen. "You mean to say that they make you go all the way downstairs to relieve yourself?"

"Yes, ma'am," Abby said. "It's always been that way."

"Where is it? The Executive Washroom."

"It's just down the hall, past the stair, but—"

"No more time for buts. Do I need a key?"

Abby fished into her desk drawer and took out a large jailer's ring with a single key dangling from it. She held it out tentatively. Like a bird of prey, Allie snatched it from her hand and scurried out the door.

She returned a few minutes later and handed back the key to Abby. "You may well have saved my life. And by the way, that's a pretty fancy washroom for a dump like this."

"I've never seen it, of course," Abby said.

"Hmm. We'll see about that." She passed the girl's desk and went into the big office.

Howie looked up from the newspaper. "Right on time. Seven thirty, on the dot."

"I told you I'd be punctual," she said. "And thank you for being here early, too."

"Quite all right," he muttered into his newspaper.

She settled into her desk and looked around, wondering what to do next. Howie had commandeered the entire paper, gripping all three sections in his fist. That little ritual—like the Executive Washroom—was going to require a change. But first, she thought, I have something else to do.

"Abby?" Alicia called toward the outer office. The secretary poked her head in.

"Yes, Mrs. Miller? Everything all right?"

"Yes, thank you. Can you have one of the men in the warehouse bring up an empty crate?"

"An empty crate?"

"Yes. A crate, without anything in it. A big one."

"Yes, ma'am," Abby said, and vanished.

"Whatever do you want an empty crate for?" Howie asked, putting down his paper.

"Why are you so interested? I thought you were absorbed in the funny pages."

"I like to read the news when I get in. I'm not reading the funnies."

"Sports pages, then."

"I wasn't reading the sports pages, either. I like to know what's happening in the world."

Allie reached over and snatched the paper off his desk and clamped it between her knees.

"All right, then, tell me what is happening in the world this morning. I'd like to learn, too, you know."

"The same things as usual," he said.

She peered at the headlines. "Give me an example."

"I'm not playing this stupid game."

"Come on, you were scrutinizing it like a student before an exam. Fine. I'll give you a hint." She glanced at the paper. "How about this. What's the latest on the treasure found in Peking's Forbidden City? That's bound to have been a compelling read. You can't have missed that."

Gaines was saved when Abby opened the office door and a couple men in stained coveralls maneuvered a large wooden crate through the opening.

"Right over here, boys," Alicia said. "Next to my desk." The men complied, and one of them, a strapping blonde still in his twenties, glanced at the golden torc—a snake eating its own tail—around Allie's neck and let his gaze linger a touch too long and drift a touch too low. She caught his eye, and the man blushed.

"I enjoyed your speech yesterday," he said.

"Why, thank you. Nothing is more satisfying than an appreciative audience."

"Yes, ma'am," he said, and hurried out after the first fellow, who was already almost to Abby's office.

"He's quite a specimen," Allie said after the door closed behind him.

"I wouldn't know," Gaines said.

"Then you may take my word for it."

"Now are you going to tell me what the crate's for?"

"I'm going to do you one better. I'm going to show you."

She lifted the crate's lid and let it bang open on its hinges. Then with both hands she swept everything off Ed's desk—pencils, tablets, even his old sissified Crandall typewriter—and into the empty crate. One by one, she pulled out his desk drawers and dumped their contents into the void, all while Howie watched, slack-jawed. There was a coal foot warmer under the desk, and that went clattering in, too.

Alicia brushed off her hands. "Now we can start over," she said cheerfully, smiling at Gaines. "Abby!" she called again, and again the girl's head appeared.

"Will you have my two new friends come back and haul this away to the dump?" she said. Abby nodded and left. In a few minutes the handsome blonde and the other fellow—a little Italian—showed up, the blonde all smiles for Alicia.

"My dear," she said to the blonde, gesturing at the jumble in the crate, "would you mind carting this stuff off to the dump? I can't be here every day, surrounded by reminders of my dear departed husband. A woman needs a fresh start, you know."

"I'll be happy to help with that," the blonde said. "Taking it to the dump, that is."

"Thank you so much," Alicia said. "I might have something more for you another time."

"I'm in the shipping department whenever you need me," he said. "Anytime."

"How nice to know."

When he and his squatty friend had lugged the crate out and could be heard struggling down the hallway toward the freight elevator, Howie looked over at her.

"And just like that," he said.

"Just like what?"

"You're here for all of two days, and just like that"—he snapped his fingers—"there goes every last trace of Ed. Carted off to the city dump."

"What would you have me do instead? Maintain his desk as a shrine?"

Howie shook his head sadly. "You just don't understand."

"I hear that a lot. But you haven't any idea. I'm not going to be mooning over any mementos of the man who cheated me out of seventy percent of this business. Which, by the by, you bought on the cheap from his other asshole buddies."

"It's sixty-six and two-thirds percent, not seventy," he said. "Your children are set for life. And I had nothing to do with Ed's will."

"Maybe you did, maybe you didn't," she said. "We'll never know, will we?"

"I'm telling you I didn't."

"Um hmm. And by the way, some night I'm going to come in here and take a coal shovel to all that shit on your desk, too," she said, sweeping her hand over the moldering stacks of paper, samples, sandwich wrappers, and miscellany drifted over his desktop. "It makes us look sloppy. Envelopes are neat and tidy little things. Each one carefully folded and glued, perfectly clean until someone writes on it. And people come in here and see the great Majority Owner sitting behind a pile of greasy rubbish. You ought to be ashamed of yourself."

Howie mumbled something about knowing he needed to tidy up, and that he planned to very soon.

"As you pointed out, I've been here for only two days, so I'm not out of patience quite yet. But I'm going to give you one week from today. If I don't see the top of your desk and everything in good order over there by then, it's all going into the incinerator."

"You can't do that. I have some important things here." He placed his hand lovingly on a stack of paper.

"I don't care what's in there. I wouldn't give a good goddamn if you had the Koh-i-Noor Diamond buried under all that. I'd gladly burn it along with all the other garbage."

Howie's face was flushed quite red by now. "You can't talk to me that way, you know," he spluttered.

ON THE SECOND DAY

"And why not? Oh, let me guess—Allie's a minority owner!" she said, mimicking his high-pitched voice.

"Yes, that's right. And there's a pecking order in this as in any business."

"Oh, I see. Well, you may be the sixty-six-what-ever-the-fuck-percent owner now, but until a very little while ago, I was married to the one-hundred-percent owner, and I didn't let him push me around, either."

Gaines sighed deeply. "I was warned," he muttered.

"You were *warned*? About what? And by whom?"

"I'm not divulging any confidences."

"You already have. You divulged that you were warned about something. You can't unring that bell now, Gaines. What were you warned about?"

"I was warned that it would be difficult, working with you."

"Oh, I see. I'm *difficult* because I want us both to have a tidy desk. What a horrible harpy I am! You men are a bunch of nancies, if that's what you're warning other men about."

"That wasn't the only thing."

"Go on," she said.

"No," he said, shaking his head emphatically. "I've said what I'm going to say."

"What a carbuncle you are, Gaines."

"I could come up with—some choice names for you, too, if I tried."

"Then let fly, mister. I can take it."

"I'm too much of a gentleman, thank you."

"Have it your way. May I at least ask you one simple question?" she said, rapping on the bare desk with her knuckles.

"I suppose."

"When are we going to receive payment from those hay-seeds in Ohio?"

"Which ones?"

"The ones who make harness equipment. I saw them on the past due ledger last evening."

"Oh," he said. "You mean Circleville Hame & Harness. They're always late in paying."

"And you find that acceptable?"

"No, but—"

"I'd like to know what Meldrum's would say if I bought a dress, and I wore it out before I paid them for it? Those hicks have had our envelopes for a month, and probably used them all by now, and haven't paid us a dime. I don't know why that doesn't rile you up."

"We've always given them more leeway."

"And I don't think we have that luxury anymore. I recognize it's not my decision, but as your largest shareholder, I would suggest you pick up that phone in front of you and get them to open their wallet."

"I'll call them today. There are so many things—"

"Gaines," she interrupted, "I spent most of last night going over the books. You know—you'd better know, if you don't already—that they do *not* paint a pretty picture of the situation here."

"Every company goes through difficult patches."

"Yes, but if they are to get through them, they need a plan. I'd like to know what ours is."

"Things will turn around," he said. "They always do."

"That's a hope, not a plan. We might as well run down to the nearest church and start praying for God to send us an order."

"It's not that bad. And it's a heck of a lot easier to criticize than it is to do something constructive."

"It most certainly is that bad," she said. "We're losing customers, less and less money is coming in, and our expenses are not declining. You do know where that leads, don't you? They call it bankruptcy, Howie. And I don't intend to be merely critical. I want the two of us to put our heads together and figure out how we are going to get this company humming again."

Gaines suddenly stood up and started toward the door.

"Hey! You can't just walk out on me," Allie said to Gaines's back.

"I'm not walking out." When he reached the door, he closed it with a gentle click. "I know that we have a problem," he said quietly, turning back to her. He sat down in the guest chair in front of Alicia's bare desk. "It's pretty simple, really. It all comes down to one thing. When Ed died, we lost our best and only salesman. And Ed also knew how to sweet-talk the current customers. I've tried to do more of those things, but I don't have his gifts."

"It's not your fault, Howie," she said softly. "I remember when Ed hired you. He said you were the best production manager he'd ever met, and his opinion of you never changed. He said you could make the factory run like a Swiss watch."

Gaines smiled ruefully. "I *am* a very good machine-man," he said, making it sound like a title of honor. "That's what I know. And I love doing it. But I will admit—I can't do what Ed did."

"And he couldn't do what you can, either. Gaines, he needed you and you needed him."

"I guess so."

"Very well, then. We don't have Ed anymore, and that's not going to change. Can't we hire a couple of professional salesmen? Drummers?"

He shook his head. "Naturally, I've considered that. But it's a problem. Big customers want to talk to the owner, not some hired gun. And then even if a salesman is successful, the more successful he becomes, the more leverage he has, and then the demands begin. 'Give me x percent of what I sell, or I'm taking my accounts to your competitor.' And then we're sunk. No, the best salesman is always an owner."

"Then there's only one way out of this," Allie said, running her palms over the naked desk. "We have two owners. One of them—you— is a machine-man, and we most definitely need that. That means that the other one of us must become our salesman. That means me."

He looked up at her. "Well, you'll probably take offense at this—but you're not a salesman."

"Not now," she said after a moment's pause. "But who says I can't be?"

"That's a silly thing to say. Ed was at it for fifteen years."

"And I was with him that whole time, Howie. There was a first sale he made. And then a second, and a third. My name is on the business and—whether you believe it or not—women do have certain advantages that men do not. I'm sure I can do it. And I'm just as sure that I don't have much choice in the matter, if we're going to make a go of this."

Gaines studied her for a few seconds, unsure whether she was goading him somehow. "You're serious about this," he said at last.

"I'm serious about everything, Howie. People refuse to believe it, that's all."

"Then," he said, rubbing his hands together vigorously, "if you're game, I'm game. If you can do even part of what Ed did and bring in some business, I certainly can keep things running smoothly."

"Then that is what we will do." She extended her hand across the wasteland of her desktop and held it there for a long moment. At last he shook it.

"Smile, partner," she said. "Savor the moment. This is our turning point."

"I hope so, Alicia," he said. "This company is my whole life, you know. I'm sorry I—"

"No. No apologies. You and I and this business have been through hell the past year. That's all behind us. We can't do a goddamn thing about any of it now. Except go forward."

"Yes," he said, standing. "Yes, you're right. Thank you."

"Don't mention it, Gaines. Now pick up that phone and call those rubes in Ohio and shake them down for every penny they owe us, plus interest. I'd do it, but it's not a good idea, because I'd tell them how much I detest Ohio."

"What?" he said. "The whole state?"

"Yes, the whole state. Every square inch. When you've finished with them, start calling the others."

"I'll get to it," he said with the first genuine smile he'd had in two days. "And you?"

"I'll start arranging visits to our current customers. To introduce myself. Not that I'll need much introduction, after the year I've had."

He laughed. "You'll have quite a challenge to sweet-talk them the way Ed was able to."

"I sweet-talked Ed for almost twenty years, Gaines. I think I can handle his customers."

ON THE HOMEBOUND STREETCAR, watching the stately houses of Ashwood creep past, Alicia felt—for the first time since she'd resolved to tackle the envelope business—a hollow wave of fear. It was one thing to dream, and bluster a little, and another to *do*. And while she considered herself every bit Edward's equal in natural ability, there was the small matter of experience. He'd been working and learning *how* to work for two decades, while she'd been otherwise occupied: tending house, having children, and hosting neighborhood soirées.

Gaines might be on her side for now, but unless she showed results, that would be temporary. He would want to save face, if things continued along their current trajectory, and that would mean throwing Allie to the wolves—namely, the trustees of Ed's estate, who were no fans of hers to begin with. Howie had paid what he considered a pretty penny for the business, even though Allie was morally certain that the trustees had given him a sweetheart deal. If Edward's smart-ass widow proved an impediment to the business—an impairment of Howie's expected profits—then he could easily claim that his purchase price had been too high and demand additional compensation, which could come only from Allie's remaining one-third.

And perhaps Howie Gaines was smarter than he looked, she thought. Maybe he could read her bluff, and knew he had only to bide his time until she tripped over her own skirts. Surely that's what he most likely was expecting, even if he wasn't admitting it. Yet he had made a very wise and unguarded observation: people who could *sell*, who threw fuel on the fire of business, were the people who mattered, the people who amassed not only money but also *leverage.*

But where to begin? The women and children of Ashwood—her entire world for two decades—weren't buying envelopes by the cartload. Their husbands might be, but she could have no contact with them without their wives' advice and consent, not even in the best of times, and certainly not after having been tarred and feathered publicly for her well-documented dalliance with one such wife's husband. No sane woman would make the same mistake that Cassie Pendle had and allow Alicia Miller within a country mile of her man. Allie might be welcomed back into society, after a fashion—she did have money, after all—but she would always be kept at a safe distance. And yet who else did she know? What other way into the world of men was open to her?

The trolley rumbled down Norwood Avenue, and stopped abruptly to let a passenger off near Sarah Payne's tidy home. Alicia squinted out the window. The house appeared cheerful enough, yet seemed as though the life had gone out of the place since Sarah had told Allie she was taking on a big case in Niagara Falls. Probably just my imagination, she thought, or nostalgia. And nostalgia—lamenting the passage of time—only wastes more time, a circular problem if there ever was one. Furthermore, I'm probably a little jealous—well, more than a little—that Sarah is going off to start life over, away from Buffalo's prying eyes and wagging tongues and, to top it off, seemed well-positioned to land herself a fabulously wealthy man.

The trolley lurched into motion again, jolting itself back into its implacable orbit. Then, just as the creaking car rattled past Sarah's house, the solution to her problem suddenly appeared to her, in a moment of enlightenment—an epiphany so simple and obvious as the moment when she'd first grasped how to read, or do long division, after much futile staring at the blackboard.

She would ask Sarah Payne to put her in front of the great Charles Kendall.

THE TOOLSHED

SARAH PLANNED TO PULL UP STAKES FOR NIAGARA FALLS ON Sunday; Annie and Ruth had agreed to remain behind in the house on Norwood Street. Maggie seemed excited for a new adventure, and especially so when her mother told her that they'd be living in a very grand mansion. Annie had accepted the news stoically, but she was plainly not happy about losing Sarah, even temporarily.

There was only one loose end left—other than Annie's sour mood—and that was one Harry James Price. Harry had been living in the toolshed, back behind Sarah's house, for weeks, and seemed very content to look out for her and her friends in exchange for a roof over his head and minimal creature comforts: a pile of old rugs for a bed and a hot dinner brought to him each evening by Ruth. Harry seemed to find the little shed very homey—it was likely the closest thing he'd had to one since he'd been a boy—and Sarah delayed breaking the news of her move to him for as long as she could.

What made it worse was that—as much as he might try to conceal it—it seemed that Harry was deteriorating. A night's misadventure in his younger days with a hired girl had earned him a death sentence. Nothing could stop the inexorable creep of syphilis through Harry's system except for toxic preparations of mercury, which slowed the progression of the disease but just as often poisoned the patient. In Harry's case, the mercury had caused his teeth to weaken and break, and so the man sported a mouthful of jagged ivory that made him look all the more formidable.

Harry hailed from central Pennsylvania, where he'd been a logger, clear-cutting endless miles of oak and hemlock, until the inexhaustible wood turned out not to be. He'd shown up in Buffalo a few years before, without prospects and without any special skills, except for one that, he learned, was in some demand. He was tough, resistant to cold and pain, and—perhaps because of the effects of the syphilis on his brain—known to be willing and able to mete out punishment for pay. For three years, he'd served as hired muscle, a punisher, for Terence Penrose, then the Erie County district attorney, and his corrupt cops. Their typical enforcers had *limits*. Harry had none, or so it was thought.

Yet Penrose and Bill Roscoe, the assistant DA, had inadvertently found Harry Price's limit. They had paid him handsomely to "have a talk" with Sarah Payne, who had stepped once too many times on powerful toes in city hall. Harry, to Penrose and Roscoe's surprise, didn't kill women, and wouldn't hurt anyone who didn't have it coming to him. Sarah checked off both boxes, and from his first meeting with her, Harry had taken a deep liking to the lady detective. He found her charming but strangely naïve to be working in such a dangerous occupation, and had resolved to serve as her guard dog for whatever time he had left on earth. Ever since the abortive hit ordered by Penrose, from his toolshed Harry had kept a watchful eye on the four ladies.

On Friday, when it couldn't politely be put off any longer, Sarah took a deep breath, pulled on her boots, and crossed the mucky backyard to the toolshed. She rapped tentatively on the door.

"Who's there?" Harry said from inside.

"It's Sarah," she said, and the door opened in an instant.

"Oh, sorry. A fellow can't be too cautious."

"No, I expect not. I won't take much of your time, Harry."

"What's on your mind?"

"I have some news," she said.

"Good or bad?"

"I'm taking on a case in Niagara Falls and I'll be taking Maggie with me and living in our client's house."

"That's a big move," Harry said.

"It's not forever. But for a little while."

"When do you leave?"

"Sunday," she said.

"All right," he said impassively. "I'll find a place to bunk near wherever you are."

"You're under no obligation to come, Harry."

"I don't see it as an obligation."

"Wouldn't you prefer to stay here and look after Annie and Ruth?"

"Those two are tough. They'll do fine. And they don't have the enemies you have."

"I never thought I'd be known for my enemies."

"It's better to be hated than ignored, they say." Harry smiled, showing his mouthful of craggy teeth, and gestured to the small canvas grip that contained all his worldly possessions—shaving gear, a change of clothes, and a dog-eared Bible. "Anyhow, I travel light."

"I'LL TAKE MR. PRICE'S supper out to him now," Ruth said later, passing by the parlor with a heaping tray in her hands. Sarah and Annie exchanged looks.

"She seems pretty cheerful about Harry's meals lately," Sarah said.

From the outset, Ruth had objected to what she called "a horrible man like that" living on the property, let alone ghosting around day and night, keeping an eye on things. Yet it fell to her lot to take Harry's dinner out to him each evening, and before long it seemed that her visits to the toolshed grew longer and longer. Not infrequently, she'd return with a Mona Lisa smile playing across her pretty face, and Annie—who noticed everything—was starting to grow concerned.

"It's one thing to have a hired killer living in our shed," Annie said. "It's quite another that my sister seems to be enjoying his company."

"It's a moot point," Sarah replied. "Harry's going with me to Niagara Falls on Sunday. He won't be persuaded otherwise."

"Finally, something positive about your leaving us," Annie said. "Frankly, he can't leave too soon for my taste."

"You don't mean that, Annie. I know you like Harry."

Annie looked out the window onto Norwood Street.

"Is everything all right?" Sarah asked after a few minutes of uncharacteristic silence.

"Oh yes," Annie said. "Everything's fine."

"I know you well enough to know when something's bothering you."

Annie turned toward her with a flash of anger. "If you can't tell, I'm furious with you."

"About my going to the Falls?"

"Yes, and for making this the shittiest New Year of my life."

Sarah took a long breath. "Annie—"

"Please don't tell me again what's good for me and Ruth. How long ago was it you started this agency? Six, seven months? And you're already breaking it up."

"I'm not doing anything of the sort. It's Niagara Falls, not Timbuktu. I'll be back."

Annie crossed her arms over her chest. "We have such a nice family, the four of us. I never had a real family before, and now you're taking it away from me." Her anger drained away suddenly, like water on sand, and she looked as though she might cry.

Sarah got out of her chair and knelt on the rug in front of Annie, hugging the young woman's knees. Annie stroked Sarah's hair gently, trying to keep herself together.

"I didn't think it would be so hard for you," Sarah said. She could feel Annie's body shaking and looked up to see that her friend was weeping openly now. Annie looked away, out the window, and dabbed her face with her handkerchief.

"I oughtn't to have said anything," Annie said. "It's just that sitting here with you—even Ruth taking food out to horrible Harry Price—this is what I always hoped *home* would feel like. It hurts to think that I'm about to lose the thing I've wanted my whole life."

"It won't be forever," Sarah said, looking up at Annie. "I promise."

Annie wiped her face again and vanished into her private place. "Enough of all that." She looked out of the window toward the toolshed. "What in the world is taking that sister of mine so long?"

Sarah got up from her knees and sat in her chair again. "She's not been gone so very long."

Annie looked worried. "You don't think—"

"Think what?"

"He's—he can be a violent man," she said.

"Harry would never harm a hair on Ruth's head," Sarah said. "But I can go out and check on her, all the same."

"No, I'll go," Annie sniffled, getting up. "I need a change of scenery anyway. I'll only go on wallowing if I sit here." She left the parlor and Sarah heard the front door bang.

ANNIE TROMPED THROUGH THE sodden backyard, not caring that her feet were getting soaked through. She wasn't sure whether she wanted to start sobbing again, or scream, or punch the clapboards on the side of the house. *And now whatever is the matter with Ruth?* Annie thought. *Does she have to make it her profession to worry me all the time?*

When she was ten feet from the toolshed, she stopped, standing in a low spot full of cold muck. From inside the structure she could hear voices, a man's and then a woman's, and laughter.

Laughter?

She crept closer to the toolshed, and sure enough, the voices were those of Harry and Ruth, chattering and laughing. Something about it irritated her, and she closed the distance and rapped hard on the door. She didn't wait for an answer but pushed into the shed. There, propped up against the wall on a pile of old rugs, was Harry, balancing Ruth's tray of food on his lap. His little railroad lantern was flickering on the floor, and Ruth was sitting on the workbench, legs dangling. They both turned toward the door, startled.

"You're either learning a thing or two, Miss Annie, or I'm losing my edge," Harry said. "Didn't even hear you walk up."

"Well, you and Ruth were carrying on so that I doubt you could hear much at all."

Ruth folded her arms. "Harry and I were just talking about old home days. He's got some stories, all right."

"Oh, I'm sure he does," Annie said. "But oughtn't you let the man eat his supper in peace?"

"Miss Annie, Ruth's no bother at all," Harry said. "She's an absolute pistol. Knew it from the first time she came out on that sidewalk and told me to shove off, or else. There's not an ounce of scare in this one."

Ruth laughed again. "*You're* the pistol, Harry."

"Naw, I'm too quiet to be one of them noisemakers," he said, and they both laughed again.

"Come along, Ruth, and let Mr. Price eat," Annie said again.

"You go along yourself," Ruth said. "We're having a nice chitchat. I'll be along soon."

Annie didn't quite know what to say. Her younger sister had always obeyed, even if sometimes under protest, but this time, Ruth was having none of it. Annie pursed her lips and let herself out, closing the shed door quietly as she heard the voices inside resume, softly at first and then, when she was halfway to the house, laughing uproariously again.

On the wooden porch, she took off her wet shoes and carried them and her stockings into the foyer, looking ruefully at their coating of mud. Sarah was still in the parlor, and Annie was going to have to hustle past her and upstairs.

"Is everything all right with Ruth?" Sarah's voice called.

Annie poked her head into the parlor, keeping her bare feet out of the line of sight. "Yes, she was chatting away with Mr. Price while he had his supper."

"Ruth? Chatting with Harry?"

Annie padded into the parlor barefoot, and Sarah refrained from comment. "Yes, and you should have heard the two of them, laughing and carrying on. I could hear them halfway across the yard."

"Now doesn't that beat all?" Sarah said. "Not so long ago, Ruth couldn't stand the sight of the man."

"Something's changed. They're like old friends now. Howling at the dumbest things you ever did hear."

"Could it be that our Ruth has fallen for you-know-who?"

"God help us if she has. A *murderer*, of all things. And on top of it—you know. His *disease*. Of the worst kind."

"He's not really a *murderer*, in the strict sense of the word. For all his—professional exploits, Harry's a decent and honorable man."

"You might think differently, if you'd seen the gleam in his eyes just now."

"Talk to Ruth, Annie. She'll listen to you."

"I'm not so sure. I told her to come along, and she told me to go pound sand. Nicer than that, but that was the theme."

"Then she most definitely has been stung by Cupid's arrow," Sarah said. "It's sweet. There won't be any trouble. It's good for Ruth to feel that she cares for someone other than you and me and Maggie."

"Easy for you to say," Annie said. "You're not losing everyone—I am. First Mr. Miller. Then you and Maggie, and now Ruth—falling for *Harry Price*, of all people. I'll be all alone soon."

"Dear Annie—please don't talk that—"

"No use beating a dead horse," Annie said, waving her hand. "And I had better go and put some dry stockings on, before I catch pneumonia."

"Ruth, may I ask you something?" Annie said, when Ruth finally returned with the tray and empty bowl of stew.

"This sounds serious."

"Only a little. You and Mr. Price—"

"We're friendly, Annie. That's all."

"You seem a little warmer than friendly."

"He's a very interesting man. And he treats me with respect."

"He has been a gentleman?"

"Of course he's been a gentleman."

"Has he told you anything about—has he expressed any interest in—"

"I know about his illness, if that's what you're beating around the bush about."

"And that doesn't trouble you?"

"It makes me sad. He's had some terribly bad luck in his life. He caught that disease many years ago—from a single indiscretion."

"But you know that you mustn't—you know . . ."

"Oh, Annie," Ruth said. "I'm twenty now, but you'd think the way you speak with me that I'm still a girl of twelve or thirteen. Yes, I know about all that. We've no plans of that nature. I do wish it were different, but it's not."

"What does he say—about his health?"

"Only that he doesn't know how much things will change, or how quickly. When things get bad, he has a queer notion that he's going to go home to Pennsylvania, hike up into the mountains, and lie down to die."

"All alone in the woods?"

"That's what he said. Imagine how he must feel, shut out from everything like a normal life, and all because of one misstep. It's very unfair."

Annie nodded. "Yes, it is. And I am sorry for him. But I do want you to be careful. You would not be the first girl who decided to take an unwise risk."

"I won't. And Harry would never allow it. He is that kind of man—which makes it all the sadder. Fortunately, he's here with me now, and that will have to be enough."

"I understand, Sister," Annie said, embracing her. "You're a good girl. Will you write to him in Niagara Falls?"

"Write to him?"

Annie went pale. "Perhaps I have spoken out of turn," she said quietly.

"*Niagara Falls*? Are you telling me he's going to Niagara Falls with Miss Sarah?"

"I thought sure he would have mentioned it to you. I'm—"

Ruth slammed the tray and bowl down on the kitchen table. "I'm marching right back out there now and giving him a piece of my mind."

"Perhaps it's better to sleep on it," Annie said.

"I wouldn't be able to sleep at all if I tried." Ruth stormed down the hall toward the front door.

RUTH MADE A BEELINE for the toolshed, not even trying to avoid the shallow pools of half-frozen slush. She pounded on the door. "Harry!" she yelled. "Open up!"

The door flew open. Harry was standing there in his shirtsleeves. "Ruthie! Is something wrong?"

"You're damn right there's something wrong," she said, brushing by him and into the shed. "Close that door, will you? I'm freezing to death, and I don't want Annie to hear me yelling at you."

"Why *are* you yelling at me?" he said, looking confused.

"Because Annie was asking me about—how you and I have been getting friendly—"

"She loves you, that's all," Harry interrupted. "Don't be angry with her. What kind of sister would want you getting friendly with the likes of me?"

"That's not what she—oh, damn, that's not what, or who, I'm angry about. With. I'm angry with *you*, you dunderhead. Annie told me you're going with Miss Sarah to Niagara Falls."

Harry blushed. "I was going to tell you. But we were having such a good laugh—"

"That you didn't want to spoil it with the truth."

"I was thinking I'd find a better time to tell you."

"*Tell* me? You never thought you might *ask* me?"

"I know what you'd say, Ruth. You'd tell me not to go."

"Exactly. And I'm telling you now. Don't go."

"I have to. I have a duty to Sarah."

"Why?"

"She needs me," he said with a shrug.

"But what about—us? I mean, me and Annie. We need you, too."

Harry smiled, showing his mouthful of broken teeth. "You do like hell. If you'll pardon my French. You and Annie together are tougher than two of me. And you don't have the enemies Sarah has."

"But I don't want you to go," Ruth said. "Doesn't that matter?"

"Yes, it matters," he said. "But what's the point? You and I both know how this has to end. And I'm sure your sister has said as much, too—as is only right. It's much less painful the sooner I get out of here and let you forget about me."

"That's the rudest thing you could have said. I can't, I won't, forget about you, and you can't just tell me to."

"I didn't mean it the way it came out. I don't want to hurt your feelings. But you know—what I *have* doesn't get better."

"At least we'd be together."

"I'm sorry," Harry said.

"Sorry? That's all you have to say?"

"Ruth," he said, holding out his hand, "this ain't easy for me. But I've done a lot of bad things, and now I need to do some good ones, while I still have time to. And keeping an eye on Sarah is a good thing."

"And what if I think it's a good thing for you to stay here with me?" she said, putting her hand in his callused palm.

"It's very sweet," he said, "but it doesn't change anything. I'm luckier than most, in a way, because I know how my life is going to end. But it won't be pretty, and I don't want you around when it does."

"But what if a cure is found? They're working on things all the time."

"It'd be a miracle."

"This book is full of them," she said, picking up his Bible. "You're as entitled to one as much as anyone in here."

"Those were a long time ago," Harry said.

"So what? And anyway, what's a fellow like you doing reading the Bible so much? It's all about forgiveness."

"Some of it is," Harry said. "But God himself strikes plenty of folk dead as a hammer, if they step out of line. He's forever smiting the Philistines. I almost feel sorry for them."

"Jesus didn't smite anyone," she said.

"Maybe not, but I feel a little sorry for Jesus, too. He was too trusting. Always expecting the good out of people. Turning the other cheek. He could have used a bit more sand, if you ask me."

Ruth laughed. "Only you, Harry. Only you."

"Look here, then. How's about you and I make a little deal?"

"What kind of deal?"

"If a cure for what I've got is found, then we'll know we've been given a miracle, and we won't let it go to waste. I'll come back, and if you haven't forgotten old Harry Price by then, and you've still got space on your dance card, we'll pick right up where we left off."

"But—what if the miracle doesn't happen?"

"Don't jinx it," he said.

"Don't think for a second that I'm not still angry with you, Harry Price," she said, pointing at him. "I'm not giving up. I'm going to pester you every day until you change your mind."

"That's my Ruthie."

"You are so frustrating sometimes!"

He squeezed her hand. "I don't mean to be. Especially since it makes me happy when you're happy."

"If that's so," she said, "then why is it that happiness seems so often just out of reach?"

"Might as well ask me why we can't catch our own shadow. Maybe if people didn't have something to chase, they'd have no hope at all."

10

Till Death Do Us Part

"I SURE AM GOING TO MISS YOUR BEEF STEW," HARRY SAID AT suppertime the following day, with his spoon scraping his empty bowl.

Ruth glared at him. "You're leaving me *tomorrow*, and the best you can muster up is that you'll miss my *stew*."

"It's true. But I'll miss you more."

"Saved by the bell," she said. "Just in time before I smacked you, you clod."

"Glad it didn't come to that," he said.

"Harry, do you really have to leave? You know that Kendall has his own security men who can look after Sarah—"

"Never met 'em, don't know 'em, don't trust 'em," Harry said. "There are plenty of bad apples in the security game. Lot of 'em washed-up cops, which tells you something."

"Is there nothing I can do to persuade you to stay?" she said, her eyes welling up.

"Ruthie, we've been over this—"

"Don't lecture me, Harry. And do *not* shake your head at me!"

Harry smiled. "You're a dear thing, you are."

"'Dear' is another word for 'weak.' I ought to have taken a firmer hand with you all along, from the very first time you skulked by this house, spying on us."

He rolled his eyes. "I don't think I'd survive if you get any tougher than you are."

"Very funny. You're trying to change the subject, and I won't let you."

"No, you very likely won't."

"Don't you feel anything for me? That you can up and leave so easily?"

"Of course I feel something for you. I've told you that already."

"What is it? What do you feel?"

"I don't know what you call it," he mumbled.

"You don't know what you feel? I'm supposed to believe that?"

"Ruth," he pleaded.

"Do you love me, Harry?"

His mouth twisted into a wry curve.

"I'm not a man who knows anything about love."

"You'd know it if you loved me. I suppose you don't."

"That's not true."

"Then do you love me? It's a simple question. Yes or no?"

He rubbed the side of his face. "Yes. You might say I do."

"Finally, you say something sensible! And if you didn't already know, I love you, too. And that's why we mustn't be apart. It's not right."

"It won't be forever."

"You're the one saying all the time that you're going to Pennsylvania," she said. "As if you were some wild animal that's going to wander off to die in the forest."

"I'm as close as it comes," he said. "And I want to go away only to spare you."

"If I were unwell," she said, "would you let me go run off to die someplace?"

"Of course not."

"I didn't think so. But you seem to think that I ought to let you do that very thing."

Harry looked puzzled. "I—"

"It'd be different, then, if I were the sick one?"

"But you're not. You are going to live, and I am going to die, and that's the way it's got to be. We don't have a choice."

"That's not what I asked you. I asked you: Would it be different if I were unwell, and told you I was running away from you to die?"

"I said it would be different."

"Then I have a little secret to share," she said in a low voice.

"Something you don't know about me. That I've been keeping from you all this time."

"*What?*" he said. "What have you been keeping from me?"

She crooked a finger at him. "I'll tell you." He leaned toward her.

Ruth came close and put her lips near his ear, but then her right hand snaked behind Harry's head, pulling it toward her. She planted her lips firmly on his and kissed him, hard, and slipped her tongue between his ragged teeth. He pulled back so sharply that he almost fell over backward.

"What in the devil!" he blurted.

"There we go." She stuck out her tongue, which was oozing blood where his teeth had snagged it when he lurched backward. "Now I'm unwell, too."

"Damn fool girl!" he growled, reaching for his handkerchief. "Spit it out! Wipe off your lips!"

"I will *not*," she said, licking her lips and swallowing hard. "It's *my* disease now, too. You don't get to have it all to yourself."

He looked up at the tin roof of the toolshed in frustration, his hands on his head. "Why? *Why?*" he said quietly.

"You said I had no choice," Ruth said. "And I will *not* be told I don't get to choose how I live—or die, for that matter."

Harry stared at her. "It wasn't enough that you knew—that I *told* you—that I've hurt so many people in my life. You had to go and make me your killer, too."

"I love you, Harry. And you love me. We have to be together, and this was the only way."

"Get out," he said softly, his eyes half closing, his voice cold and distant.

"Get out?"

"I won't tell you twice," he said, and now his voice had something else in it, something she had never heard before, a kind of feral menace.

"Don't do this to me, Harry. Don't make me go."

He moved toward her—an inch at most—but there was in his body a resolution, like the tightening of a finger on a trigger, that made her go cold.

"I'm going," she gasped, and ran out of the shed, afraid to look over her shoulder.

"WHAT'S WRONG?" ANNIE SAID, alarmed at her sister's ashen face.

"Nothing," Ruth said.

"I'm not blind, Sister. What has happened?"

"Harry and I had words. About him leaving."

"How many times have I told you? You'd be better off to forget about him. He's not the kind of man you want, whether you think so or not."

"You couldn't possibly know what kind of man I want."

"I know the kind you *ought* to want. And he's not it."

"We'll just have to agree to disagree on that, now won't we?" Ruth said, brushing by Annie.

"You're going to regret it if you don't take my advice," Annie called after her.

Ruth went upstairs to the bathroom and closed the door. She could still taste blood. She leaned over the sink and stuck out her tongue. There, near the very tip, was a tiny rent, seeping red. She looked at it in the mirror for a long moment, wondering that this minuscule tear could truly be large enough for death to enter. She spat into the sink, watched a thread of pink disappear down the drain.

Harry's right, she thought. I *have* been a fool.

THE NEXT MORNING, RUTH took breakfast out to the toolshed, but Harry and his canvas bag were gone. When she got back to the kitchen, she ate his oatmeal herself, if only to pretend that he was still with her. Then she stared at the bowl for a long minute, and started to cry. She was lonely, but afraid, too—afraid of the first sign of her infection appearing, and how she'd tell Annie.

After dressing, she slipped away to the public library and, as surreptitiously as possible, looked for what she could find about syphilis. The accounts diverged as to the likeliest course of treatment, but on one thing they were all in accord: there was no cure, and the progression of the disease was gruesome. In the earliest stages, syphilitics endured periodic sores and ulcers and spreading pink rashes of the skin. After this first flowering, the disease seemed to go to sleep, and remained dormant, sometimes for years. Yet eventually it would reawaken in more virulent and hideous forms, the corruption attacking the skin with painful lesions, and eating away at the bones and the brain. In due course, the afflicted would become bedridden, suffer horrifying seizures and hallucinations, and—ultimately and inevitably—die of what the medical men coolly termed "general paralysis of the insane."

Not that the newspapers weren't full of doctors who, if they couldn't cure the disease, were more than willing to peddle hope, for a price. Salves, creams, unguents, pills, tinctures of mercury, mercury mixed with chalk, salts of mercury—always more and more mercury, until the blood became as badly poisoned with the shiny liquid metal as with the syphilis, and life was snuffed out by the cure rather than the disease.

Yet even then, after so many trials, a syphilitic could find no rest. In a final indignity, many undertakers would refuse to prepare the body for burial, for fear of catching the dreaded malady.

It had all seemed far more romantic to an impulsive twenty-year-old girl. Share all of life with her doomed lover, even take on his disease, nobly wilting away by his side into a young and tragic corpse. But Harry had gone, and Ruth was now left alone with the gnawing certainty that her grand, dramatic gesture had killed not only herself but also the love he had felt for her.

Rooms with a View

CHRISTINE AND CHARLES KENDALL CAME OUT TO GREET THE BIG carriage as Isadore rolled it to a halt under the *porte cochère*. Stefan stood behind and to the side, filling up the doorway. First out of the carriage—before Isadore could even dismount to assist—was little Maggie, who bounded up to the Kendalls with her hand sticking straight out.

"Hello there, I'm Maggie Payne," she said. "Whom do I have the pleasure of addressing?"

Sarah rushed up behind Maggie and hugged her. "I'm terribly sorry," she said to the Kendalls. "She's so excited."

"She's adorable," Mr. Kendall said. "You know, except for the hair and eyes, she reminds me of you, Christine, when you were her age."

"Except for the hair and the eyes and everything else," Christine said. "She is a little doll, though. She looks like a smaller version of you, Sarah."

"This is Mr. Kendall and Miss Kendall," Sarah said.

"Hello, friends," Maggie said, smiling and looking like a tiny copy of her mother, strawberry blonde hair, freckles, and deep blue-violet eyes. "I'm nine years old."

"You're a very big girl, then," Kendall said. "I think you'll have fun here."

Harry Price had quietly stepped down from the carriage, and was standing near the rear wheel, holding his canvas grip.

"And this is Mr. Price," Sarah said, motioning for Harry to come closer. Kendall stuck out his hand. Harry removed his hat and shook Kendall's hand. "Mr. Kendall. Miss Kendall," he said with a little bow.

"Pleasure to have you with us, Mr. Price," Kendall said. "Miss Payne speaks very highly of you."

"Good heavens," Harry said, under his breath. "That's awfully nice of her, sir," he said, louder.

"Your rooms are ready," Christine said. "Erin will see you to them."

Harry leaned over and whispered into Sarah's ear. "They don't mean to put me up in *here*, do they?"

"I assume they do, Harry," Sarah whispered back.

"This place is too grand for me. I'll bunk in the stable and be happier about it."

Kendall overheard. "We can't very well have you sleeping in the stable, Mr. Price."

"Well, sir, while I'm very much in your debt, I'll be just fine."

"Harry has his preferences," Sarah said, shooting Harry a glance. "Even if I sometimes don't understand them."

"Well, then, we have plenty of room in the carriage house," Kendall said. "That's where Isadore and Stefan live, so Mr. Price will be in very good company."

"Thank you, sir," Harry said.

"Isadore, why don't you show Mr. Price to the carriage house, then?" Kendall said.

"Hop in," Isadore said to Harry. "I'll put this up while you get settled in."

"I'll ride up with you," Harry replied. "I don't like being cooped up in that *thing*. Which is first class, of course, Mr. Kendall."

Kendall laughed. "I fully understand, Mr. Price. It took me quite a while to get used to it, myself. I walked most places until a few years ago."

Isadore and Harry mounted up and set off around the circular drive, and then off toward the rear of the property.

"So where do you hail from?" Isadore said as they rattled toward the carriage house.

"Pennsylvania."

"Whereabouts?"

Harry looked at him quizzically. "Little place called Weedville. Jay Township, Elk County. Up in the woods."

Isadore smiled. "Weedville?"

"You've heard of it?"

"No. It's just a funny name, that's all."

"Never seemed funny to me," Harry said.

"What brought you to Buffalo?"

"You ask a lot of questions."

"Trying to be friendly, that's all."

"Well, you don't have to be."

"So what is it you do?" Isadore ventured.

"What do I do?"

"Your trade," the coachman said. "What you do for a living."

"I was a logger."

"Not in Buffalo, you aren't. I mean nowadays."

"Right now my job is looking out for Miss Sarah and Maggie."

"Like a bodyguard?"

"Yeah, I guess you could call it that."

"You know that's Stefan's job," Isadore said. "He might not be too happy about another fellow in the mix."

"Stefan? You mean the big Polak-lookin' fellow?"

"Cossack."

"What-sack?"

"He's a Cossack. That's Russian, not Polish."

"What's the difference?"

"I don't exactly know, but he's sensitive about it. I'd be careful around him."

Harry gave a little snort. "Thanks for the advice."

"Why is it you don't want to stay in the big house?" Isadore asked. "It's pretty grand."

"Maybe I want to keep an eye on you and the nutsack."

"What for?"

"Because no one in *that* house"—Harry pointed to the giant roof of Kendall House—"is a threat to my girls. That leaves the two of you."

"Well, it sure is nice to meet you, too," Isadore said, reining in and setting the handbrake in front of the carriage house.

"Don't take it personally," Harry said, jumping down. "Met a lot of men in my life, and very few of them was worth trusting."

"Maybe so, but Mr. Kendall trusts me and Stefan," he said. "That ought to count for something."

"You don't need to get twitchy about it. If you're trustworthy, I'll trust you. I'm not saying you're not. I'm saying that I don't know yet."

"Hmm," Isadore said. "Well, then I guess we'll see how it goes. Our rooms are upstairs. Pick any one that's not in use, and that'll be yours."

"Will do," Harry said. "And I'm obliged to you for the lift. You know how to handle horses. I can tell how they are with you that you're probably not a bad sort. Horses always know." He ambled off with his grip toward the carriage house.

Isadore stared after him, shaking his head.

INSIDE KENDALL HOUSE, SARAH and Maggie were escorted to a small elevator.

"Just slide the cage shut, and press the top button to go up, and the bottom one to come back down, Miss," Erin said. "I'll meet you at the top." She smiled and trotted off.

"Here goes nothing," Sarah said to Maggie, who was enjoying a piece of cake that the cook had given her. She closed the cage and pushed the button. The wood-and-brass elevator ascended through three floors and then stopped with a gentle jolt. Sarah slid the cage open and she and Maggie stepped out onto the topmost floor of the North Wing, which occupied a jutting prominence of the great house.

Erin was waiting next to the elevator, panting.

"Did you run up the stairs, dear?" Sarah said. "You're out of breath."

"Yes, Miss."

"You could have ridden with us, you know."

"Oh no, Miss. This is your private elevator."

"Well, maybe we can sneak you up and down sometimes," Sarah said, and Erin blushed.

The tiny elevator nook opened out onto a vast open room with a huge stone fireplace on one side. On the far wall, an arc of enormous floor-to-ceiling windows gazed out over the broad back lawn of Kendall House and to the Niagara Gorge beyond. Arching from the fireplace to the other end of the hall—it couldn't properly be called a room, Sarah thought—was a vaulted ceiling of oak. Between the great beams, copper chandeliers directed light upward, ambering the wooden ceiling. Most of the light in the room itself was pouring in through the wall of windows. A large brass telescope on a wooden tripod was aimed out one of the big windows, looking down the gorge toward Lake Ontario.

"Your sitting room is through here," Erin said, sliding open a set of pocket doors. Inside was a cozy nook, with a coffered ceiling and yet another fireplace, shelves full of books, and a long couch. Another big window looked out over the gorge.

"I may never leave this room," Sarah said.

Erin smiled. "There's much more to explore, though. There are six bedrooms in your wing. You can have any you like, but my favorite is the one coming off this sitting room. It has a nursery room adjoining, too, so your daughter can be right next door to you. But you may choose any rooms you like. You'll also find in your suite a billiards room and a small dining room, should you care to take your meals here, or invite guests to dine with you. There are three bathrooms, all complete, and hot and cold water round the clock.

"Anything you need, at any time, Miss, you either pull one of the bell ropes or push the button near the bed or the desk. Either I or another of the staff will attend to you directly, although Mr. Kendall has instructed me to look after you personally, as long as I'm in the house.

"You have your own private telephone line, and Mr. Kendall has a personal switchboard operator in his factory, so all of your calls will be placed through her. Those calls are secure, if you are speaking with Mr. Kendall or Mr. MacCormick. Otherwise, of course, they go over the public Bell lines. Mr. Kendall has also instructed the staff to connect a direct line to Mr. Price, who as I understand is staying in the carriage house."

"I don't know what to say," Sarah said. "I'm not accustomed to living in such a style."

"Nor was I," Erin said, "but I will say, it's not difficult to get used to." She giggled. "And as for you, little lady," Erin said to Maggie, who was staring out the wall of windows, "your schoolteacher will be here tomorrow. You'll like her. She's *French*."

"A French schoolteacher, Mama!" Maggie said.

"Yes, dear, Mr. Kendall is very happy you're here," Sarah said. "He wants you to feel at home."

"It will be a breath of fresh air to have a child around," Erin said. "And your daughter is as beautiful as she is lively."

"I thank you very much for that, Erin, but I can't take much credit. She's always been a good girl. Haven't you, Maggie?"

"Most of the time," Maggie said.

"Ha ha," Sarah said. "Yes, most of the time. But even when you're not, Mama loves you."

"Now, Miss, your trunks will be up very shortly, and the staff will collect your linens and anything else, twice a day. Your mail will be placed on the tray by the main door, but no one will enter your suite without your permission or unless you tell us you are not in residence. Electric lights—of course—will work round the clock, but should you wish for candle- or lamplight, you are well supplied in your pantry."

"I can't thank you enough, Erin. I don't even know what questions to ask."

"The only thing you need to do now is to settle in, Miss. Dinner is served at seven, if you care to take it downstairs with Mr. Kendall and Miss Christine. If you do, our cook's assistant will feed your little lady in the kitchen."

"Oh, most certainly! I'd love to."

"Then I will ring you a half hour before dinner, to give you time to freshen up," Erin said. "Until then, Miss, please be at home."

"Thank you, Erin. You're most kind."

"Not at all," she said, and left Sarah and Maggie alone in the vast suite.

"Mama, it's like a fairy tale!" Maggie said.

"I know! It's so grand. Now you know that we're here only for a time, and then back to our little house on Norwood Street, don't you?"

"Yes, Mama, I know. While you are at work here."

"That's right, dear. Mama will be at work in the daytime, same as always, but you'll have people looking after you here, just as Ruth looks after you back home."

Maggie smiled. "May I look through the telescope?" she said, and Sarah smiled back and told her yes.

A buzzer went off, and for a moment, Sarah wasn't sure what it signified. Then she realized it was a doorbell for the door of her suite. She walked over and opened the door, and there stood Christine, leaning against the jamb with a broad smile on her face and one hand behind her back.

"Welcome home!" she cried, and produced a bottle of wine from behind her back. She wiggled it by the neck. "Look what I brought to celebrate your arrival!"

"I can't start drinking that before dinner," Sarah said. "I'd make a spectacle out of myself."

"Then you can watch me," Christine said. "Everyone already expects me to make a spectacle out of myself."

Private Spheres

Later that evening

"Well hello, Sarah!" Alicia said cheerfully into the telephone. She was sitting naked at her dressing table, waiting for Bert. "I hope you don't mind my calling you so soon at your brand-new home."

"Good evening, Allie," Sarah said, forcing a smile. She'd read recently in a magazine that the party on the other end of the telephone could "hear" a smile. "No bother at all. I'm only sitting in my rooms, writing a few letters. Settling in."

"*Rooms?*" Allie said. "As in more than one room?"

"Yes, more than one. You and yours are all well, I trust?"

"Same as always," she said. "The girls and my mother are a constant pain in my ass, as always. My girls aren't at all like your little angel."

"Your girls are wonderful," Sarah said.

"Any time you'd like to trade, let me know," Allie said. "Tell me, though—how are you finding the famous Kendall House? And your *rooms?*"

"Allie, it's been one day."

"I know, but an exciting one."

"It's a big adjustment, as you'll understand."

"I should think that adjusting to life in that castle couldn't be *that* difficult."

"The house is grand," Sarah said, "but most of my life has been in Buffalo. I don't know anyone here."

"You know *Charles Kendall*," Alicia said with a small but audible leer. "Who else matters?"

"I'm getting to know him. He's a very busy man, of course, so I won't have too much time with him."

There was a prolonged silence on the line. "What a pity," Alicia said. "He's *very* handsome, if the newspaper photos are to be believed."

"Yes, he is quite good-looking."

"And fabulously rich, of course."

"He's certainly been successful," Sarah said.

"And what's the rest of the package like?"

"Beg pardon?"

"You know. How is he in bed?"

"Oh, for heaven's sake, Alicia. I've not been to bed with him!"

"Why on earth not? You really are a china doll sometimes, Sarah."

"I just don't share some of your ideas," Sarah said. "I think that sort of thing is best kept within marriage."

"Now don't go all gooey on me. People say that all the time, but how would they know unless they'd had it both ways? And I hope it's not pressing on a bruise and all that, but surely you must have had *physical* yearnings for my husband." She paused. "What an *unusual* thing to say, come to think of it. But there it is."

Sarah frowned. "I didn't see Ed in that way."

"Well, then, we have that in common, too," Alicia said. "Because I didn't either."

Sarah tried to ignore the comment, tapping her foot under her letter desk, but failed. "Please. You had three children with him."

"Over fifteen years! The number of times at bat was not high, Sarah."

"You couldn't have been married so long without being intimate more than three times."

Alicia smiled. "I engaged in many years of extravagant solitary vice, my dear," she whispered into the mouthpiece. "Which was, frankly, far better than the real thing."

"Why in the world are we talking about this?" Sarah said. "What exactly was it that you wanted? You must have a reason you called."

"No need to get touchy, dear. I merely called to see how you are doing."

"And then promptly started down one of your rabbit holes."

"Fine," Alicia said, examining her chin in the mirror. Was that a *hair*? "If you don't want to talk like sisters, or go down rabbit holes, then we won't. I'll leave it all up to you, Sarah. Since I have you on the line, though, I did want to ask you about your dreamy Mr. Kendall."

"What about him?"

"I would like to meet him."

"Meet him? What for? I hope you're not getting any ideas."

"My, that's not very nice at all," Alicia said. "What kind of woman would go and steal another woman's man? Oh—wait, I'm sorry—I do forget myself sometimes."

"That's not very nice, either. And it's not true."

"It was a little joke, that's all. You need to laugh more, Sarah. But I have no designs on your Mr. Kendall, except insofar as his company's envelopes are concerned. I want to meet with him to tell him about my company. And why I think Kendall Electrolytic Abrasives ought to consider buying envelopes from me."

"You're really taking this business seriously," Sarah said.

"You inspired me. You're taking yours seriously, and you know I don't like to be put in the shade. All I ask is a short conference, and everyone knows that the only way to see Charles Kendall in the, er, *flesh*, is to be introduced to him by someone he knows and trusts. Which would be *you*."

Sarah held the earpiece away from her ear and stared at it for a few seconds. "I understand. And why would I do that?"

"How very direct!" Alicia said. "You know how I value honesty. All you would need to say—some evening over the walnuts—is that you have an old friend who owns an envelope company, and she'd like to meet with you. Although please do note, when you say 'old,' you clarify that you are not referring to my age. What could be the harm?"

"Alicia," Sarah said carefully, "I've found that, perhaps against my better judgment, I rather like you. But I also feel that maintaining a certain distance is prudent. I'm not so sure that allowing you entry into my new private sphere is—well, wise."

Allie's eyes opened dark and wide as she pulled at a little wrinkle on her face. "Now I'll have to give you top marks for bluntness on that one. But I think it's a little less than I deserve. What have I ever done to injure you? I might well say you've done more damage in my private *sphere* than I will ever do in yours. You were a bull—a very beautiful bull, mind you—in my personal china shop, and yet have never once apologized. I've apologized to you for doing far less."

Sarah leaned her forehead into her palm. "Good God, you're either the most honest person I've ever met, or the least."

"I think the more you get to know me, the more honest I will seem," Allie said. "You have to give me a chance, that's all. Will you do that?"

"Yes, Alicia, I will," Sarah said wearily, after a heartbeat or two. "I will mention you to Mr. Kendall. I can't guarantee he'll meet with you, but I'll mention you. Perhaps the best thing is to write a letter to him requesting a meeting, and send it to me. I'll give it to him and ask him to consider it."

"You are a *princess*," Allie said, triumphant. "And I won't even ask for any more apologies. I promise."

"I only hope you won't make me regret this. If you don't, then I promise you, I will apologize for having mistaken your intentions."

"You haven't a thing to worry about, dear. I'm nothing more than a little envelope saleswoman these days, and that's all I aspire to be."

13

KENDALL ELECTROLYTIC ABRASIVES

January 12, 1903
Monday

SARAH ARRIVED AT KENDALL ELECTROLYTIC ABRASIVES wearing A slightly somber grey flannel suit and a plain white shirtwaist. Her modest hat boasted only a single ostrich plume, though one as long as the tail of a comet—the one concession to fashion she was unable to forgo. At first, she had powdered her face, to make it look white and wan, but that only served to highlight her violet eyes and strawberry hair, so out came the cold cream and off came the powder. She opted instead to let her freckles show, which made her look more girlish.

"Mr. MacCormick, a pleasure," she said, sitting down in the chair across from the superintendent's desk.

"I understand you're to be my new secretary," he said. "Though not really, of course."

"Quite the contrary. I have to be your real secretary, and I will be. I've completed the whole secretarial course at Bryant & Stratton. I can take shorthand, dictation, do typing, everything."

"My, I didn't know that," he said. "That will certainly lend a certain air of authenticity."

"Yes, it will. And I enjoy the work."

"Well, all to the good, then. Now Mr. Kendall said that we might better give you an alias. Otherwise certain people might have heard o' you. From before."

"Hardly the kind of fame I'd once hoped for in life," Sarah said. "But yes, that is probably prudent."

"Do you have a name in mind you might favor?"

Sarah couldn't think of anything, and then blurted out, "How about Sarah Price?"

"Seems as likely as anything. Sarah Price it shall be, then."

"Good. Now how do we get started?"

"Twice daily, I walk the floor of the factory," he said, "making notes. How things are going."

"Makes sense."

"Normally I make marks in a wee notebook, but people know I've been looking for someone to tag along and do it for me, so I can be more attentive. That can be you. You'll observe everyone who works here, on every shift, and the men will get used to seeing you."

"Perfect," she said.

"Now, Miss—Price—I'd better get used to saying that myself—any number of the men will probably want to show you some—personal attention, if you don't mind my being so coarse."

"Nothing coarse about it, sir," Sarah said. "That's part of the plan. I assure you I can be appropriately flirtatious, if it will help us get to the bottom of this."

MacCormick laughed. "I'll gratefully leave that to your good offices. Now, if you are so inclined, I can take you on a little tour of the factory, and let people see you."

"That's right. I'm ready when you are."

FROM THE SUPERINTENDENT'S OFFICE, MacCormick and Sarah—now Miss Price—walked down the long office corridor and exited through a door leading out onto a grimy strip of packed earth. Across this yard was a towering building of brick and corrugated steel, with streaks of rust running down from the numberless rivets that held it together, making it look like the building was weeping from a thousand eyes at once. MacCormick and Sarah stepped up a metal staircase, their shoes ringing against the treads.

"It's a wee bit loud inside," MacCormick said. The metal cladding of the factory seemed to quiver with the noise coming from within. "Here," he said, reaching into his coat pocket and producing a wooly wad of pristine white cotton. "Put some o' this in your ears, or they'll be ringin' like cathedral bells for the rest o' the day." He tore off a hunk for himself and screwed a piece into each ear, then handed the rest to Sarah, who followed his example.

"All right," the superintendent said. "You ready?"

"Ready!" Sarah said, trying not to flinch as something heavy smacked into the inside wall of the building and made it vibrate like a drumhead.

"Then we're off!" MacCormick shouted, opening the door and stepping over the metal threshold.

It took a second or two for Sarah's eyes to adjust. They were standing on a raised metal platform perhaps fifteen feet above the factory floor. At least another thirty feet above, a dense cloud of smoke swirled under the peaked roof, snaking out of a row of grimy windows set under the eaves. Through this dark, roiling mass, huge skylights cast the manufacturing floor in a bilious twilight.

Thick electrical cables snaked across the floor, spooling over insulators and terminating in knife switches mounted on wooden poles next to what looked like large glowing beehives. Only when Sarah saw the waves of heat coming off the furnaces did she realize that she was already sweating profusely. MacCormick seemed unfazed by any of it.

"Electric arc furnaces," he shouted, pointing down at the beehives.

Men were walking to and fro, observing gauges, shoveling, and rolling barrels on iron-wheeled carts, which seemed to move along the concrete floor without the slightest noise.

"Let's go down," MacCormick said, gesturing to his feet. They climbed down the staircase onto the factory floor. A little mining car half-full of what looked like silver cinders sat on a set of polished rails, and a man was busily shoveling them into a wheelbarrow. The shovel, the hands holding the shovel, and the man to which the hands were attached were all covered with silver dust.

"That's coke," he said. "Made from coal. We use it to charge the furnaces. That's what this man is about to do. If we follow him, you can observe the process." The man shoveling paused and nodded, giving Sarah an especially long look.

"Doesn't speak a syllable of English," MacCormick shouted into Sarah's ear. "Good that way, too. I hire just enough Polish and Hungarian lads so that there aren't enough of any one kind to start a union. Like building the Tower of Babel."

After watching the man fill his wheelbarrow, the pair followed him to one of the glowing electric beehives, where the Scotsman stopped. The man began shoveling his load of coke into the oven.

"We put the raw materials into the oven, apply the electric current, and let it cook," MacCormick said. He looked around and spied a barrel filled with greenish sand. "Look," he said. He plunged his hand into the barrel, letting the sand run through his fingers. "The finished product— silicon carbide," he said with a gleam in his eye.

"Mr. Kendall tells me it's like diamonds."

"That's right. Only we make it by the trainload."

"Fascinating," Sarah said, her ears ringing from the noise despite the wads of cotton she pushed ever deeper into her ear canals.

They strolled around the factory floor for another ten minutes— long enough for Sarah to feel like she'd been caught in a sudden downpour—and then MacCormick signaled for them to go up the iron staircase again.

It was mercifully cooler in the corridor leading back to his office, and for the first time, Sarah was happy she hadn't spent much time on her hair.

"Ye're fitting in magnificently!" MacCormick said with evident glee when they got back to his office. He deposited his used cotton wool in a wastepaper basket, and held it out for her to follow suit. "And I'm here to tell you, every man in the factory got a good gander, too."

"That was our goal," she said, ears still ringing, even without the cotton.

"Now we'll do that twice a day, and you'll take notes. Soon enough, you'll have a man say hello, and then say more to you. And when there's a pretty lass involved, if you don't mind my saying, it's shocking how much English it turns out some of these foreign lads know."

"This promises to be a very interesting assignment, Mr. MacCormick," she said. If I don't go deaf in the process, she thought.

14

JEREMY

HER FIRST CONVERSATION WITH ANYONE OTHER THAN MacCormick didn't come until Friday. She'd noticed that one of the floor foremen, whom the Scotsman was interrogating about some operational detail, seemed to be showing more interest in her than he was in his boss's questions.

As they were completing their rounds, Sarah noticed that the foreman was still glancing her way. She pulled MacCormick to the side, in the lee of one of the beehive ovens.

"I think that man wants to talk with me," she said, inclining her head.

"Horn?" he said. "He's a decent lad. Production foreman."

"Perhaps you could tell him that you have to return to your office, and instruct him to show me some part of the works I haven't seen with you."

"Aye, good idea," he said, and they walked over to the young man, who acted as if he'd never noticed Sarah before.

"Horn," MacCormick said, "I have to return to my office. Be a good lad and show Miss Price the warehouse. She's new here, and hasn't seen it yet."

"Yes, sir," Horn said and smiled at Sarah. He motioned for her to follow him across the thundering factory floor. At the far end was a set of large doors hanging on an iron track. Horn rolled one of them to the side, and they stepped through. He shut the door behind them.

It was mercifully cooler in the cavernous warehouse, which faced out onto the railroad tracks fronting the Kendall works. Several of the big rolling doors—duplicates of the one they'd just walked through—were slid fully open, allowing cold winter air and natural sunlight to flood the space. The foreman pulled the cotton out of his ears, making a wry face of exaggerated relief.

"You won't need that in here," he said to Sarah. She obliged and removed her cotton plugs, and found that the warehouse—while still thudding and vibrating from the pandemonium on the other side of the brick wall—was tolerably quiet, and peaceable enough to talk in a normal voice. In every direction, hundreds upon hundreds of barrels—presumably full of silicon carbide—were stacked, each with a shipping manifest tacked to it. A few men were rolling barrels here and there.

"Very pleased to make your acquaintance," the young man said. "I'm Jeremy Horn."

"The pleasure is mine, Mr. Horn," she said, extending her hand. "Sarah Price. I've only recently started as Mr. MacCormick's secretary."

"I'm delighted," he said. "You are certainly a welcome breath of fresh air around here."

"I'm sure it's more the cold air from outside than anything to do with me. I've never been so grateful for winter weather."

Jeremy Horn was tall and lean, almost but not quite lanky, and while good-looking, almost but not quite handsome. His attire was that of an ambitious young man wanting to make a good impression: gleaming shoes and a neat tropical-weight wool suit—decidedly out of season, but anything heavier would have been intolerable in the heat of the production floor. His light brown hair, pale skin, and thin, carefully trimmed mustache made him look younger than he likely was—but mainly made him look very unlike the other foremen, who all seemed stocky, swarthy, and grizzled. His most striking feature was a pair of large lively hazel eyes.

"Nor I. But at least we can play hooky for a few minutes while I explain our distribution operation," Horn said. "It probably goes without saying that this is where we store and sort our finished goods, until they're taken away by rail. Which happens at least four or five times a day."

Jeremy's hands fluttered a bit while he spoke, the long fingers keeping cadence like a conductor's baton. He spoke in a somewhat tentative voice, which went up at the end of his sentences, making him sound as though he was posing a question, or seeking agreement.

"It's vast," she said, looking at the endless rows of barrels. "How many of these barrels ship out each day?"

He smiled. "I'll have to let Mr. MacCormick answer that. Mr. Kendall is very secretive about production volumes."

"I didn't mean to pry."

He smiled and leaned closer. "I'd tell you if I knew, but I don't," he whispered.

She laughed. "It's fine. I was merely trying to show interest. In fact, I don't yet understand very much about what goes on here."

"It's not only new people like yourself who don't understand it all," Horn said. "It's an explicit strategy that no one—other than Kendall and MacCormick, I suppose—can know the whole process. They are probably rightly concerned that someone will steal the secret."

"But you're a foreman. Don't you have to understand how it's made?"

"Yes, I'm a foreman, but I'm only in charge of what we call 'the cook.' That's the period of days when the material is kept at a very high temperature and the chemical change occurs that turns the raw materials into silicon carbide. I know how to cook it, and when it's done. But I don't know what the recipe is—how much of each ingredient, in what grades, and so on. And if I went nosing around in some other area of the factory than the one within my purview, I'd be severely reprimanded. Or discharged."

"That seems harsh," Sarah said.

He shrugged. "It serves a purpose. But I would say that after a few months, if you pay attention, in your position you'll probably know more than I do about how this stuff"—his hands fluttered around, indicating the countless barrels—"is made. Start to finish."

"I doubt very much I'd understand it."

"And I doubt very much you wouldn't. It's obvious that you are a very intelligent person."

"You mean a very intelligent *woman*," she said.

He shook his head. "No, I didn't mean that at all. Miss Price, I don't accept that women are any less intelligent than men. Now, I won't deny that a woman's intelligence may be *different* from a man's, in some respects. Like, say, a cat's intelligence is different from a dog's. But is a cat more or less intelligent, in absolute terms, than a dog? Of course not. They are formed for different purposes and put their minds to different uses. And thank God for it."

"You seem to have made a close study of my sex," Sarah said.

"I've never understood why so many men claim that it's difficult—impossible, even—to understand women," he said. "What seems glaringly obvious to me is that every man is half woman. Think about that for a moment! Why ought a man only be able to view the world through one side of his nature? He has no excuse—unlike our hypothetical cat, for example, which is most emphatically not half dog, and thus has every right to find dogs impenetrable."

"If your theory holds—which it seems it must, biologically speaking—naturally it would work in reverse. That women have an ability, even an obligation, one might say, to be able to see the world through men's eyes."

"Precisely! Miss Price, it's going to be delightful having you here. You have no idea how few and far between are the people in this city with whom one can have anything like a satisfying conversation." He leaned close to her. "People in Niagara Falls are generally as dull as a ham sandwich."

She laughed. "It can't be as bad as all that. And I do enjoy a good ham sandwich from time to time."

"As do I, but I don't have any desire to converse with one."

"You have a sharp wit, Mr. Horn."

"If only I had the wisdom to go along with it."

"Surely you must have a pearl or two you might share with someone new."

He stroked his chin with his long fingers in mock contemplation. "Let's see . . . I suppose . . . try to find a friend. That makes everything easier. Someone like, say, myself."

"How do you know that I have any openings for new friends?"

"*Miss Price!*" he said in mock horror. "That is a perfectly obscene thing to say."

She blushed. "My God, Mr. Horn, that comment should get you slapped."

He angled his cheek toward her. "You're right, I deserve it. Go ahead."

"I rather think somehow that might be giving you the reaction you wanted."

"Then I will apologize instead. Sometimes things pop into my head—and they seem so funny to me, that I blurt them out. I mean no harm."

"It's perfectly fine, Mr. Horn. I can tell you're harmless."

"Now, that's a little disappointing," he said.

"Then you are an unregenerate rake. Is that more to your liking?"

"Much."

"Well, as much as I'd like to converse with such a confirmed reprobate," Sarah said, "it's probably time for me to be getting back to the office."

"So soon," he mused. "I'm not sure I'm ready to let you go quite yet."

"Short of taking me hostage, I am not sure what to suggest."

"Don't give me any ideas. What say we walk back to the office along the railroad tracks, and keep the cotton wool out of our ears for a few more minutes?"

"An excellent idea," she said, and the two of them walked out a man door adjacent to one of the shipping bays and crunched down onto the rough gravel heaped against the steel rails. They had gone only two dozen yards when, in the distance, a steam locomotive pulled off its siding and began chuffing determinedly toward them, bound for the loading dock.

"Perhaps this wasn't such a good idea," Sarah said.

The locomotive engineer spied the pair wobbling unevenly toward him on the track bed, stuck a hand out of his window to wave them off, and angrily pulled the whistle cord with the other.

"I must confess I didn't count on this," Jeremy said.

"Maybe we should run back the way we came?"

"We won't get there in time," he said, looking around for another escape route.

The gravel sloped sharply downhill on both sides of the tracks. At the bottom was a shallow ditch full of half-frozen slush and fly ash.

"We'd better jump!" Sarah shouted over the shriek of the whistle.

"You'll forgive me later for this," Jeremy said, bending and sweeping Sarah up in his arms. Holding her, he jumped off the narrow path and down into the ditch. At the bottom, his feet cracked through the crust of frozen slush and sank into the soft muck beneath. The locomotive passed above them, the engineer still raging out his window and pulling on his whistle.

Jeremy struggled back up the gravel bank to the tracks and set Sarah down again.

"Beg your pardon for—that," he said, breathing hard.

"That was entirely unnecessary, Mr. Horn. I could have very well jumped on my own, you cad."

"*Cad*?" he said, recovering some of his sense of humor. "And here I thought you'd say, 'oh, my knight in shining armor!'"

"Well, your armor may be shining, Mr. Horn, but your shoes are another matter."

He looked sheepishly down at his feet. Shoes, socks, and trousers were slick with black mud.

"This will be difficult to explain. But better me than you. You have to go back to a nice clean office."

"Yes, and if I don't get there soon," she said, "Mr. MacCormick is going to wonder what's become of me. I can walk the rest of the way on my own."

"Are you sure?"

"I rather think I'll be safer that way."

"That is a very, very mean thing to say," he said with a wink. "But it was a pleasure to meet you, all the same."

"Likewise, Mr. Horn. Thank you for the most enjoyable tour. Even if you were perfectly vile during portions of it."

"What a compliment!" he said as she began walking away at double time.

"Oh, Miss Price!" he shouted behind her.

She turned and saw him standing by the side of the tracks, bespattered with mud and ash. He was calling to her through cupped hands.

"What now?" she shouted back.

"If MacCormick asks what you've been up to—tell him that you took a great leap today in your understanding of our business."

She smiled at him, turned, and resumed her trudge back to the office. What a scamp that one is, she thought.

FRESH COMPLICATIONS

"THAT'S A TERRIBLE COLD SORE YOU HAVE," ANNIE SAID TO HER sister, over their morning oatmeal. "It must sting something fierce."

"It doesn't hurt at all," Ruth said.

"It looks odd, though. You should ask Dr. Massey about it."

"It'll go away, I'm sure. Nothing to worry about."

"Maybe so. But you've never been one to get cold sores, and that one's a monster."

When they had finished, Annie stood and held out her hand. "Let me do the dishes today. I don't have to be in the office first thing, and you're forever doing all the washing up."

Ruth grabbed her bowl and spoon and put them onto her lap. "I'll wash mine," she said.

Annie flexed her fingers at her sister. "Don't be contrary. Give me your bowl."

"No!" Ruth said. "I said, I'll wash it myself."

"What has gotten into you?" Annie said, frowning.

"I can very well clean my own bowl and spoon myself, thank you."

"Then be my guest." Annie went over to the sink and began washing out her own bowl, muttering to herself something about her strange sister.

"I'm sorry, Annie," Ruth said after a moment. "You have a right to know."

Annie turned, her hands dripping soapy water. "A right to know what? That you're cantankerous? I already know that."

"Yes, I suppose. But also—the reason I don't want you to touch my bowl."

"This is bound to be good," Annie said.

"This isn't a cold sore," her sister said, pointing at her lip.

"What is it, then?"

"It's something worse."

"What's worse than a cold sore?"

"Annie—I kissed Harry."

Annie stared at Ruth in horror. "You did *what*?"

"I kissed him, and so this thing is—"

"Ruth, if this is your idea of a joke—"

"It's not a joke. I wish it were, because at least you'd forgive me for that."

"Did he force himself on you?" Annie said, her face flushing.

"Nothing of the sort. We were talking about him leaving for Niagara Falls, and then going off to die in the woods—and I got angry. So I kissed him. Against his will."

"What in God's name possessed you to do such a thing?"

"I wanted to share everything with Harry, and he wouldn't hear of it. I kissed him to contract his disease."

Annie slumped into her chair and put her head into her soapy hands. "You do realize you've gone mad, don't you?"

"It seemed to make sense at the time," Ruth said.

"*God*!" Annie said, stamping her feet in frustration. "I *knew* I should have nipped this infatuation of yours in the bud. Why did I ever *tolerate* such a thing?"

"Please don't be angry, Sister," Ruth said. "I know I did something stupid. But I can't go back and undo it. I've been reading about this— *thing*—and I don't know . . ."

"You don't know what?"

"I don't know if I'm brave enough to face what's ahead," she said quite calmly. "Without Harry, I don't much care about going ahead anyway, and if this disease is going to finish me eventually, I may as well get on with it. I thought perhaps you could take me to some lonesome spot, and I could drink carbolic acid."

"Aah, you're so frustrating!" Annie said. "Don't talk like that. Don't you even think about harming a hair on your head, or I swear I'll spit on your grave, and I mean it. There are doctors who treat this. There's that Dr. Porter's clinic on Main Street. He's famous. He has a big sign painted on the wall that he can cure—this kind of blood disorder."

"There's no cure," Ruth said, shaking her head. "No matter what Dr. Porter may claim."

"You don't know what you're talking about. He's famous for a reason."

"Lots of people are famous for no reason at all," Ruth said.

"What in the *world* will I tell Mother and Father?" Annie said, slumping over the table. "When I brought you here to Buffalo, I promised them I'd look after you, and help you find a nice husband. And now *this*? This will kill them, Ruth. You know they love you best of all."

"There's no reason to worry them yet. It can take a long time to develop. If—things progress faster than expected, then we can decide what to do."

"I just don't *understand*!" Annie said, pounding hard on the tabletop and making the glasses rattle. "Your whole life ahead of you—and you went and did *this*?"

"I thought I was doing something that would prove to Harry that I love him. And get him to stay here. But Annie—now I'm *scared*."

Annie looked at Ruth, her heart aching. "Of course you're scared. I'm scared, too."

"Maybe we can look into Dr. Porter's clinic," Ruth said.

"Yes. That's exactly what we will do. Getting busy—that's the best recipe for worry. I'll write to his office today and inquire about an appointment."

LATER THAT MORNING, ALICIA was in her office, riffling through the early mail—nothing of any interest, as usual—and was almost ready to throw the stack onto her desk in disgust when at the bottom she found a lovely linen envelope with an engraving of a large factory belching smoke, with bold cursive letters streaming beneath it that read:

Kendall Electrolytic Abrasives & Company
High Bank
Niagara Falls, New York

Well, now, she thought, good thing I didn't give up. She slit the envelope open with her silver letter opener and withdrew a single sheet of paper, which had a larger version of the engraving centered at the top of the page. The neatly typewritten letter read:

A. H. Miller, Director
Miller Envelope Company
Cashton Building
Buffalo City

Dear Mr. Miller:

In reference to your request of last week. Our President, Mr. Charles Kendall, will be pleased to receive you in his office, Administration Building, at the letterhead address, on Friday at 2:30 in the afternoon. If this is convenient for you, please confirm by return post or telephone Bell 3888, Niagara Falls City.

Yours very sincerely,
E. A. Marron
Private Secretary to Charles Kendall.

Alicia picked up the telephone and asked for the number. The call was answered by Miss Emily Marron, Kendall's pleasant young secretary, who was nonplussed to learn that Mr. A. H. Miller, Director of Miller Envelope Company, was in fact a Mrs., and named Alicia. She immediately asked Alicia to call her Emily, and the two chatted amiably for a minute or two.

"Mr. Kendall is very punctual," Emily told her. "So many people arrive here late, because we're not easy to find if you've not been here before. All the factories look alike, and people get lost. But tardiness is something Mr. Kendall doesn't like, so between us, best to get here in plenty of time." Alicia thanked her, and Emily said that she'd tack up a little piece of ribbon on the board fence around the Administration Building, so that Alicia would locate them more easily.

On Friday, Alicia hopped a morning trolley to Niagara Falls, and took a little sweet roll with her in a wax paper sack, so that she could have something to eat before meeting with Mr. Kendall. She'd planned to eat her snack in the pretty park surrounding the Falls, but there was a half foot of snow on the ground, and the wind was whistling daggers through the city streets. Instead, she ate as she walked over to the International Hotel to use the washroom and thaw out a bit before hoofing it over to the High Bank.

At the International, she checked her teeth in the washroom mirror and adjusted what hair had blown free of her hat. She liked what the cold wind had done for her color, rosying her cheeks in a very appealing and youthful way. For the occasion, she'd selected a new winter dress of soft close-fitting wool flannel, which followed her form. Under the flannel was a whisper-thin silk shirtwaist and an underbust corset to accentuate her breasts, and to allow the frigid air to perk things up there, too. Even through the fabric one could make out the points of her nipples, which was exactly the effect she'd desired. I need to get out in the cold more often, she thought.

Today she had dispensed with her usual high collar, too, and let her ouroboros torc blaze in all its glory around her muscled neck. She took a final turn in the mirror, feeling rather satisfied about the whole. Alicia was known as one of the best ballroom dancers in Buffalo—with the petite, firm, and curvaceous body to go with it—and at forty-two, she still could easily pass for thirty-five, although her almond-shaped coal-black eyes gave her face the air of confidence and command of a woman twice that.

Wouldn't little Edward just shit his pants if he could see me now, she thought. Almost ready to sit down with one of the most powerful businessmen in the country, perhaps the world, to talk about *envelopes*!

From the International, it was a ten-minute uphill walk to the High Bank. The air grew thick and tasted of sulfur as she neared the white board fence that Emily had mentioned. True to her word, the girl had thumbtacked a small piece of lavender ribbon to the picket gate.

Alicia was breathing heavily and regretted not having taken a coach, so she stood there and huffed the foul air through her handkerchief until she'd stopped wheezing. Then she pushed the gate open and stepped into the gravelly yard behind the Administration Building. Next to the door, there was an electric box with a pushbutton at the bottom, like a doorbell. Alicia pushed it, and was surprised to hear Emily's voice crackle out.

"Mrs. Miller?"

"Yes. Emily?"

"I'll be right there," the secretary said, and the box fell silent again.

The door opened less than a minute later, and a pretty brunette in a blazingly white shirtwaist invited her in.

"I'm Emily. It's so nice to meet you, Mrs. Miller. Hurry, come in, before you catch your death."

"Please, do call me Alicia," she replied. Emily smiled, pleased that a director of a Buffalo manufacturing concern would allow her to address her by her Christian name.

"If you don't mind my saying," Emily whispered as she escorted Alicia into the Administration Building, "I think it's simply amazing that a *lady* is a director of a corporation. It's wonderful. I'd love to hear how you worked your way into your position."

Alicia rested her hand on the young lady's arm. "A stroke of fate, you might say. It wasn't getting the position that was difficult—it's keeping it that takes work."

"That's so refreshingly humble," Emily said. "I'm sure you can imagine how rare that quality is among the men who hold such a title as yours."

"Oh yes, men do *love* being men, and especially"—she dropped her voice to a murmur—"reminding women of it. I find it's best to let them be who they are. What they don't expect is that we will be who we are, right back. And I'll take even odds against the best of them."

Emily smiled. "Thank you for that," she said, as they approached Kendall's outer office door. Emily showed her in and motioned to a polished wooden bench in the empty waiting area. "Here we are. Please make yourself comfortable. I'll tell Mr. Kendall you're here."

Emily sat down at her desk and activated another little electrical box. "Mr. Kendall," she said into it, "Mrs. Miller has arrived."

"Right on time. You may show her in."

Emily got up from her desk. Alicia stood up, too, and when Emily turned her back to open Kendall's inner door, Allie gave her nipples a good hard pinch to make them stand up again. Then Emily faced her again and smiled, sweeping the door open. Allie smiled back, and stepped into Kendall's paneled office.

He came around his desk to meet her and gave a little bow. She held out her hand and he shook it gently. The hand of a brawler, or someone who had been, once, she thought. God, he *is* handsome. About my age, too. What in the *world* is Sarah waiting for?

"Mrs. Miller, thank you for coming all this way," he said, pulling out a chair at a round table in the far corner of his office. "And for being so punctual."

"It's not far at all," she said. He held her chair as she took her time settling in, pretending to look out the window and arrange her handbag on her lap, to allow Kendall an opportunity to get a good look at her dancer's curves. If he likes that sort of thing, she thought, I might as well let him spy a little. She could tell he was looking at her torc—men seemed fascinated by the thing. She turned toward him at last. "It's an easy trolley ride."

Kendall sat down at the table. "You know, you're right. It is easy, and yet I rarely make it to Buffalo. It seems far away, somehow. I'm not sure why that is."

She smiled. "I'm guessing most people gladly come to *you*, Mr. Kendall."

"I suppose that's so," he said. "Though it oughtn't to be. I'm not so very grand."

"Grand enough." Sarah, *Sarah*, she thought. Six feet of rich, handsome man, with a mellow voice and big strong hands. My God. Best not to start down that slope, she thought with a start.

"I'm very grateful for your time today," Alicia said. "I know you're very busy."

"Never too busy to see someone Miss Payne recommends I see. And your letter was unusually engaging. You are a fine writer, Mrs. Miller."

"And you're far too kind," she said. "It was good of Sarah to mention my name. She and I have been great friends for a very long time."

"Oh?" Kendall replied, looking slightly bewildered.

"I'm sure she told you all about it."

Kendall paused. "She said only that it was *complicated*."

Allie smiled broadly. "And what friendship worthy of the name isn't? Between women, especially. Women are complicated creatures, Mr. Kendall, as I'm sure you've observed. It's in our nature."

"If my daughter is any example, I know that all too well," he said with a smile.

"Christine, I believe it is? How old is she?"

"Yes, Christine. She's nineteen now, and close to ungovernable."

"No girl can be governed at that age. Not the way they grow up nowadays. I have three girls myself—sixteen, fourteen, and nine—and my eldest is already asking to start seeing boys."

"The times we live in," Kendall sighed. "And I suppose you're right. I could be a little easier with her. But it's difficult. It's been just me and my daughter for years, since my wife died. I suppose I'm afraid I'll lose her, too, one day."

"You won't," Alicia said. "Remember, 'A son is a son till he takes a wife, but a daughter's a daughter all of her life.' And it's true. My mother lives with us, and it feels like the most natural thing in the world. Or it would, if she weren't my mother." She laughed, to Kendall's puzzlement.

"Well, thank you for your excellent advice, Mrs. Miller," he said, recovering. "I know it's heartfelt, and coming from a fellow parent of girls, especially pertinent."

"And like yourself, I'm going it alone. You probably know I lost my husband—who founded our family enterprise—a little over a year ago."

Kendall cleared his throat. "Yes, I had—heard about that, and you have my most sincere condolences."

"Everyone from Buffalo to Berlin heard about it, I think," she said.

"The press treated you and everyone involved most unfairly."

"And were particularly beastly to our dear Sarah. You know they tried to pin my husband's murder on her? Imagine."

He shook his head. "I cannot. I wish better days for you, madam."

"Thank you," she said, demurely looking down. "Now then—we ought to talk a little about envelopes, oughtn't we? My second-favorite thing on earth," she said in a husky voice, suddenly looking up at him with her dark, dreamy eyes.

Kendall looked slightly askance at her, afraid to pursue.

"After my girls, of course," Alicia added with a laugh. "I simply *love* envelopes. And as I said, we're a family business, started by my late husband. After he died, everyone told me to sell, but I said, 'Nothing doing!'

and so I took over recently. One day perhaps my girls will follow in my footsteps."

"Good for you," he said. "I started this concern from nothing, and now we have tens of thousands of customers, wholesale and retail, all over the world."

"You must go through quite a few envelopes, then," Allie said.

"Naturally. Now, to be entirely honest with you, madam—in all candor we've been very satisfied with our current envelope supplier. I haven't been looking to replace him."

"And I understood as much from Sarah. But if I may. How many pieces of mail do you send each month?"

"I'd have to get the precise figure from my office manager, but I won't be far off if I say ten thousand or so per month—"

Ten thousand envelopes a month, Allie thought, trying to keep her jaw off Kendall's table. A hundred and twenty thousand a year! That would be the biggest order in our history, after the Pan-American Exposition promotions in 1900, but that was a one-off, and more for image than for profit. Ed always made it seem like he built his company, when it was the Pan that—

"—most of which are sent to small retail customers, who often don't buy enough to pay for the stationery and the postage. In fact, my office manager has recently been urging me to reduce the mailings to make that part of the business more profitable."

"And that would be the *worst* thing you could do, Mr. Kendall," Alicia said, raising an index finger. "The single *worst*. On the contrary, you should *double* your mailings each month, if not triple them."

Kendall looked at her with a mix of astonishment and irritation. "Beg your pardon, Mrs. Miller? We're losing money on ten thousand a month. Imagine what would happen to my bottom line if we doubled— let alone tripled—that figure!"

"May I ask what you send out each month?"

"A standard envelope—I think it's called a Number 10—with a single page inside. Our price list."

"And *there's* your problem," she said, leaning forward and putting her palms flat on Kendall's table, giving him another good view of her décolletage.

"Where's my problem?"

"May I tell you a little story? I recognize your time is very valuable, but it's the best way to make my point. It's a kind of parable."

"You have my attention," he said.

"A few years ago, my late husband developed quite a taste for Force cereal. Breakfast cereal. Do you know it?"

"Of course. Made in your city of Buffalo. Sunny Jim is their droll little mascot."

"Exactly! Not that it made my husband any sunnier, but that was their claim."

Kendall chuckled a bit nervously.

"In any case," Alicia went on, "he did love his Force cereal, and he might go through a box a month. But then I started noticing three or sometimes four boxes in our pantry. Now, my Edward wasn't a large man, so he couldn't possibly have been putting away that much cereal all by himself. So I asked our hired girl, Annie, why we had so much of it on hand all of a sudden."

Kendall leaned forward, obviously intrigued. "That is a mystery. What did she say?"

"She showed me a little stack of letters that had come to us from Force cereal. She'd sent in a coupon or something, and twice a month— *twice per month*, Mr. Kendall!—Force cereal sent her—and all their other countless customers—a *two-page* letter, full of recipes and ideas for how to use their product. And a coupon she could take to our grocer for a little bit off the price. It turned out that Annie had taken all this to heart, and was putting Force cereal into meatloaf, bread, pancakes—on and on. And if they hadn't sent those ideas, we would have been buying our single box every month, and certainly not three or four. Now can you *imagine* how profitable those letters were for Force cereal?"

He frowned and sat back in his chair. "Yes, of course I can understand that, Mrs. Miller. But breakfast cereal and abrasives are rather different things, don't you think?"

"Of course they're different. But good ideas are good ideas, no matter what the product. You can probably sit here and in five minutes tell me a hundred uses for your abrasive that people don't ordinarily think of, and that you wish they would."

"Indeed I can," he said warmly. "For working men, for example. Mix in a little of my abrasive with some soft soap, and it'll take off all the oil and grime a man gets on his hands every day. One can use my finer grades of abrasive to clean pots and pans. To bring up the shine on silverware. Why—"

"I'd think one could spread it by the ton on all the ice on the sidewalks and streets," Allie interjected. "Or put it into golf club handles for a better grip."

"Precisely!" he said, almost coming out of his chair. "It drives me crazy that people can't seem to think of these things."

"They *can*, but they *won't*—unless you plant the seed of the idea in their heads, Mr. Kendall. Just like Force cereal did in ours. So instead of sending along your stodgy old price list—if you'll forgive me for saying so—why not send a folksy two-page letter from yourself, suggesting ten new ideas twice a month and giving a little discount for customers who buy, say, twice what they did the previous month. How about that?"

He shook his head slowly, looking down at the table and making a little figure eight with his forefingers. "That really is genius, Mrs. Miller. I wish my office manager had come up with it. Or that I had, for that matter."

"Mr. Kendall," she said. He looked up. "I want you to hear this from me very directly." She looked straight into his eyes. "I believe that any decent company can supply envelopes."

"You do?" he said, staring.

"I do. But you have a better-than-decent business, and you need a better-than-decent supplier. The hallmark of Miller Envelope Company—*my* company—is that we supply *ideas* along with our envelopes. That's what makes us better than decent. And if you favor me with your business, Mr. Kendall, you won't have to dream these things up on your own. Nor will your office manager. You can do what you do best, and leave the rest to me. And why should you believe me? Because the more of *your* product I help you sell, the more of *my* product you will purchase."

"Capitalism," he murmured. "In its purest form."

"And thank God for it. So I would like to ask you, Mr. Kendall, if you will transfer your current envelope business—all of it—to Miller

Envelope. I'll match your current price, whatever it is, and the ideas I'll provide will be provided at no additional charge. And I predict that you'll find that the ideas are worth as much as you pay us—which will mean that the envelopes themselves are *free*."

Kendall abruptly stood, and Allie stood with him. "I'll go one better, Mrs. Miller. I will bring all my current business to you, and double my current order, if you will agree personally to write our advertising letters. If your letters are as good as the one Miss Payne gave me, they'll sell." He held out his hand.

She took his hand and shook it firmly. "You have a deal, Mr. Kendall. Twenty thousand Number 10 envelopes per month, based on a year's commitment."

"A whole year?"

"I would normally ask for two, especially with the letter writing included, but you are a friend of Sarah's, and a friend of Sarah's is a friend of mine."

"Agreed, then," he said, smiling. "I'm overjoyed that Sarah—Miss Payne—introduced us, Mrs. Miller. She clearly wanted me to form my own opinion about your business skills, and not give anything away prematurely. I'm very pleased that she took that tack."

"As am I, Mr. Kendall. But that's our Sarah—she's complicated."

Kendall smiled. "I'll tell her you said so."

ALICIA CHATTED WITH EMILY for a few minutes, and then walked to the trolley stop on Prospect Street, not even noticing the rotten-egg atmosphere of the High Bank. Twenty thousand envelopes a *month*! For a *year*! Wait until smug old Howie Gaines hears about this one. He'll shit a cobblestone.

For the first time in at least a hundred trips on the Yellow Car Trolley Line between Niagara Falls and Buffalo—the girls had always enjoyed picnics by the Falls—Alicia noticed the scenery. Bustling tourist heaven gave way quickly to tightly packed worker housing, mostly cheap clapboard foursquares, street after identical street. Then the outskirts, and the enormous golden-brick Shredded Wheat factory and its towering tubular silos, before the grey industrial wasteland began, miles of power lines snaking from the Falls to Buffalo and beyond, volcanic plumes of smoke and soot vomited into the sky from scores of look-alike red-brick chimneys. It was amazing, how dispiriting it all became so quickly after leaving the beautiful, wondrous Falls.

She thought about Arthur, how much he'd enjoyed sneaking off to the Falls with her, even at the very end, before their escape to New York City and then . . . Ed's murder, Arthur's death, and again back to Buffalo, everything in her life gone from rosy to ashen in a matter of two weeks. Sunny Jim! First time I've thought of him in ages, she mused as the burned-over landscape trundled past. Hardly sunny, these past couple years—more like one damned thunderstorm after another, and I'm running from tree to tree, trying not to get hit.

But how strange and wonderful it all is—that after all that, I should be sitting with *Charles Kendall* himself, and not just sitting and talking about the idiotic things that women are supposed to talk about—the theatre and the new piano tune they're simply dying to play for him— but about business. And *winning* his business in *his* world. She smiled to herself.

Maybe all that shit was the price I had to pay for this moment.

16

ONE OF THE BOYS

AN HOUR AND A HALF LATER, THE YELLOW CAR DROPPED HER off on Main and Court, a few blocks from the Miller Envelope factory. Alicia checked her pendant watch. Five thirty. *Gaines should still be at the office, but perhaps I ought to tell him on Monday. No,* she decided, *I'll simply bust if I have to wait two more days to see the look on his face.*

She burst into their suite to find Abby sitting in the outer office, as usual, with a bored expression on her face, as usual. The young woman recovered as quickly as she could, but too late. "Hello, Abby," Alicia said. "Surprised to see me?"

"Not at all, Mrs. Miller," the secretary said.

"Is Gaines still in?"

"Yes, ma'am."

"Good, thanks."

Allie breezed into their office. Gaines was sitting at his desk, frowning at the *Racing Form*. He looked up with some surprise.

"Didn't expect to see you today," he said.

"You do remember I work here, don't you?" she replied.

"How could I forget?"

"Very funny." She sat down in her office chair and swiveled around to look over at him.

"What have you been doing?" she said.

"The usual."

"That sounds exciting," Alicia said.

"It's the usual. The usual is good."

He looked back to his *Racing Form*. It irritated her that Howie moved his lips as he read.

"Aren't you going to ask me what I did today?" she said after a full minute of watching his mouth forming silent words.

He put the paper down and looked over. "I figured you were shopping or something."

"Something that women might do, is that it?"

"I don't know about that," he said. "What did you do today?"

"I went on a sales call."

"A sales call?"

"Yes. You know, when you go to a business and try to sell them some of these envelopes we're making all the time."

"I know what a sales call is. I didn't know you were going on one, that's all."

"Well, I did. It's one I've been working to set up for a little while."

"Now doesn't that just beat all?" Howie said. "You probably should have had me along, though. Even if it was only for a lark."

"It was indeed quite a lark."

"Well, good. Local company?"

"No, Niagara Falls."

"You went all the way to Niagara Falls for a sales call? What business was it?"

"Kendall Electrolytic Abrasives. Do you know it?"

Gaines stiffened. "Of course I know it. Everyone knows it. The fellow who owns it lives in a damn castle."

"Charles Kendall."

"Right, exactly. Who did you meet with there?"

"Charles Kendall."

"You didn't! No one sees *him*. He's mysterious."

"Well, I did. He and I talked for quite a while, about this and that."

"I'd like to know how you managed to get in front of him. Even J. P. Morgan can't."

"Never you mind," Allie said. "All you should care about is whether he'll buy envelopes from us."

"We can certainly make up some samples for him. But I'm sure his current supplier bends over backwards for him—and I doubt he'd drop them so easily."

"Ah, Gaines, ye of little faith," she said, leaning back in her chair and putting her hands behind her head. "And yet he did. He placed quite a sizable order with yours truly."

Gaines's chair squeaked as he turned to face her full-on. "He didn't! What kind of order?"

"Twenty thousand Number 10s."

"Holy hell!" Gaines said, forgetting himself. "Twenty *thousand*! That's incredible."

"You think so?"

"I know so. Twenty thousand envelopes! That's astonishing."

"Thanks," she said, "but there's one more thing."

"What's that?"

"It's per month."

"Excuse me?"

"You heard me. Twenty thousand envelopes *per month*, for a year. That's the deal. Done." She dusted off her hands with a loud smack. "So *that's* what I was doing today."

"You're not joking?"

"Not even a little."

"How in the world did you do it?"

"Intelligence and charm, Gaines."

"Well, that's nothing short of amazing," Gaines said, shaking his head. "That's by far the biggest order we've ever had, other than the Pan. I must say, you landed that one like an old hand."

"And I must say, you have something else in common with Ed."

"What's that?"

"You both underestimate me."

"I didn't underestimate you. You're new to the business and it's a huge contract, that's all."

"Uh-huh. As you wish. In any case, it's done."

"You've certainly earned the weekend off," he said.

"Howard Gaines, is that a compliment?"

He leaned back in his chair. "Credit where credit's due."

Alicia smacked the top of her desk. "I don't know about you, Gaines, but I for one am not quite ready to go home after all today's excitement. I'd think that at least a toast would be in order before calling it a day."

Gaines smiled. "That's a swell idea. Ed and I keep—kept—some rye whiskey around for such occasions." He got up and opened the bottom drawer of a file cabinet sitting against the far wall, and took from it a pint bottle of brown liquor and a couple of glasses. He brought them over and set them on Alicia's desk, pulled the cork out with a hollow whump, and poured a couple fingers of whiskey into each. He pulled up a chair next to her desk.

"To Miller Envelope Company," she said, raising her glass.

He picked up his glass, but didn't extend it. "You know it's going to be *Gaines* Envelope Company," he said.

"I thought that was only an idea," she said, setting the glass down again. "Miller Envelope has a lot of history. Name recognition. Why change it? What's the point?"

Gaines cleared his throat and gazed into his glass before looking up at her. "Because I'm the majority owner now."

"Which you make abundantly clear every time you have an opportunity. But as majority owner, don't you want to build on the company's strengths? And one such strength is a known and trusted name. Surely you wouldn't disagree."

"I don't disagree, no, but—"

"Then we don't need to decide right now," she interrupted. "And anyway, no less a light than Charles Kendall bought almost a quarter of a million envelopes from the *Miller* Envelope Company today, so we can't change it for a while."

Gaines didn't respond. She picked up her glass again. "To partners," she said this time. Howie forced a tepid smile and clinked his glass against hers.

"Good night, this stuff is strong," she said, swallowing.

"It's been in there a long time. Can liquor spoil?"

She ignored him and took another murderous swallow of the rye. "What do you like to do on the weekend, Gaines?" she said after a minute or two of silence, trying to revive the conversation and steer it away from the company's name.

"Not a whole lot. Maybe take a walk. I like horse racing, in the season."

"Are you a gambling man?" She nodded toward the *Racing Form*.

"Penny-ante stuff. I don't like to lose money. It's too hard to make it."

She laughed. "I don't think it's that hard, not so far."

"Maybe it's beginner's luck." He took a drink and topped up their glasses.

"Very funny, Gaines. What about golf? Do you like golf?"

"I do, but I'm not very good. Ed had me out to the Red Jacket club a few times."

"Did he tell you that I golf?"

"Not that I can recall," Gaines said, shaking his head.

"Figures," Alicia said, tilting her glass. "Probably because I regularly beat him like a drum. From the men's tee, too. Drove him nearly crazy."

"You don't say?"

"I do say. You know, I've been thinking that we ought to take some of our bigger clients out golfing. I'm still a member of the Red Jacket. Though they have to rebuild their clubhouse after the recent fire. But it'll be ready in time for the season. What do you say?"

Gaines frowned. "I don't know how people might take that—a man and a woman who aren't married hosting them. They might think something's not quite right."

"Jesus, I'm your business partner," she said.

"Yes, I know. But you're not exactly one of the *boys*."

Alicia finished her whiskey and put the glass down on her desk. "And just what would I have to do—to be 'one of the boys,' I wonder? To get a chance to compete with you and the other *boys*? Fair and square."

Howie laughed. "I hardly think that would be fair."

Alicia scowled. "Fair?"

"Yes, fair. Like the dictionary says, equitable. Putting a woman up against a man isn't fair."

"Because you're afraid I'll beat you, like I did Ed?"

"I didn't make the rules, Mrs.—Alicia. You know the way the world works. Men are men, and women are women. They're not the same and never will be."

Alicia leaned back in her chair and suddenly put her dainty feet up on the desktop. She picked up her glass and held it up.

"Now with a little more liquor in my glass and a cigar, wouldn't I look like one of the boys?"

Gaines laughed and looked away. "You certainly don't look very modest," he said, finishing his second whiskey.

"Modesty is just another word for shame," she said. "The way I look at it, Gaines, you're a lucky man to have me as your partner, and not only because I can land the big deals. No, the more I think about it, you are a *very* lucky man to have me around."

"Why do you say that?"

Oh, what the hell, she thought. I've been good for too long, Bert is *hors de combat*, and my scintillating conversation's sure not winning Gaines over. And I have something he doesn't.

She swung forward in her chair, smacked her tiny boots onto the wooden floor with a noise like a firecracker, and swayed over to Gaines's desk.

"Look, it's quitting time on Friday," she said, looming over him, "and we've had a big week. One for the record books. So"—she picked up the bottle of rye from his desk and waved it—"how's about we take the rest of this over to your house and *finish it off*?" She chuckled.

He looked shocked. "I don't know if that's such a good idea."

"Whyever not?"

"Isn't it obvious?"

"Not to me. Why don't you tell me?" She put her hands on her hips, challenging.

"We're in business together," he said.

"And so we shall be, forever and amen, Gaines. I don't see how having a few drinks is going to change that."

"Well, I don't have a house, either, exactly. I live in an apartment on Swan Street. It's not very private."

"Does it have a door?"

"Of course it has a door."

"With a lock on it?"

"Yes, with a lock."

"Then how much more private do we need?"

Howie didn't respond.

"You hear that?" she said, cupping a hand behind her ear.

"Hear what? I don't hear anything."

"It's our lives ticking away, second by second. Can we please stop talking and see what this apartment of yours is like?"

"Oh fine," he said, getting up.

"God, you'd think you were going to the gallows. Cheer up, Gaines. It's your lucky day."

She tucked the bottle of rye into her satchel, and they pulled on their overcoats and walked down the stairs to the street. From the front door of the factory it was only two short blocks to Howie's building, a narrow red-brick townhouse with a shoe store at street level. He unlocked a door next to the plateglass shop windows and opened it into a dark corridor leading to a set of stairs in the rear. "I'm upstairs," he said.

"I certainly hope so," she said, letting him lead the way up the dingy staircase. At the top, he unlocked a second door and let them into his apartment.

Howie's lodgings were more a large single room than an apartment worthy of the name. There was a small oak table near the door, two ladder-back chairs, a washstand and basin, and a sideboard with a folding mirror and some glassware sitting on it, and that was all.

Except, of course, for a bed, set under one of the two windows overlooking Swan Street, and which looked as though it had never been made. Howie scampered over to it and pulled up the creased coverlet to make it look slightly less meager.

They sat at the table and Alicia half filled two smeary glasses from the sideboard with the whiskey they'd brought. She slid one over to Gaines. They clinked glasses and she took a big swig, feeling the liquor burn its way down into her stomach.

Gaines took his glass and sipped. "You know, I am thinking about moving out of this apartment soon."

"Why is that? It seems so convenient to the factory."

He gestured around. "Yes, it is, but it's not much to look at."

"You're a bachelor. You can't be expected to bring a woman's touch to your lodging."

"That's true, I suppose," he said, taking another sip.

"If I remember correctly, Ed told me that you aren't terribly interested in women."

Gaines flushed red. "I don't know that I'd put it *that* way. I think it's that the married people I know have all seemed so miserable." His voice trailed off at the end of his pronouncement. "I mean, present company excepted, of course. Not that Ed ever said—"

She lifted her glass and examined the brown liquid like a scientist with a test tube. "Oh, I'm sure Ed had plenty to say," she said. "Which is fine. I could say a lot about him, too. But yes, we were both most assuredly quite miserable."

"I'm sorry. I didn't mean to bring up a sore subject."

"It's in the past. I'm much happier now—and he's—well, I don't know if he's happier, but what do we really know about the afterlife? If there *is* an afterlife."

"I'd like to think there is."

"Seems like a colossal bore, if you ask me," Alicia said. "I thought that even as a little girl in Sunday school. The teachers would say that we'd all spend eternity playing harps and praising God. Nothing else to do. Doesn't sound like much fun."

"I don't suppose I ever thought of it that way, but you do have a point."

Alicia finished her glass of whiskey in one swallow and jerked her head over her shoulder at the bed. "Speaking of fun, how about we have some? I don't know about you, but this whiskey's got me feeling pretty well lubricated. So—bottoms up. In a manner of speaking."

He drank the rest of his liquor while she leaned over, unbuttoned her boots, and then stood up to shed her little flannel jacket and shirtwaist underneath. She unbuttoned her skirt, stepped out of it, and piled the clothing in a little heap on top of the sideboard. Then she tiptoed across the cold floor and sat down on the threadbare coverlet.

"Your turn," she said softly.

Gaines walked over and took off his collar, cuffs, and shirt, and then—more reluctantly—his undershirt. Stripped to the waist, he stood uncomfortably at the side of the bed, his thin arms dangling alongside a pale, reedy-looking chest. His full ruddy face and neck looked as though they should belong to some larger, redder man and had been inadvertently switched. He stuffed his hands into his trouser pockets and bounced a little on his toes as Allie looked up at him, unable to conceal her lack of enthusiasm for his physique.

"I need to take up a sport," he said, looking down at the little haloes of dark hair around his nipples.

"Maybe Indian clubs," Alicia said. "Build up your shoulders a bit. I find that it doesn't much matter what the rest looks like, once you get going, but a girl has to look at a man's shoulders the whole time, so they should look good and strong."

"I've been so busy at work, I've let myself go," he said. "I guess I could find time for a gymnasium, though."

"You can buy a set and do them right here, in your apartment. I've seen them at Walbridge's, in the sporting goods department."

Howie nodded. "I'll go over there tomorrow," he said.

She smiled and patted the mattress. "But we're not going to worry about that now, are we? How about you get the rest of that off and we'll make do with what we have."

Gaines unbuttoned his trousers and slid them off over his legs, and then sat down on the edge of the bed and started working at the clasps of his sock garters, his hands shaking a little. Allie lay back, watching him. The pillow smelled like stale hair oil.

At last Howie succeeded in stripping off his socks and stood up again in his undershorts. "These too?" he said, gingerly touching the fabric of his drawers.

"Not going to get very far with them on. Take them off. Let's have a good look."

He dropped his drawers around his ankles and stood there, unsure of what to do next. The room seemed too bright for such a public display. His cock looked as uncertain as he did, half-hard and drooping slightly. Alicia crooked a finger at him.

"Oh—wait a second, let me get out of these first," she said, hooking her thumbs into the waistband of her bloomers. Gaines turned toward the far wall as she lifted her hips to wriggle out of her underwear.

"I'm a little cold," she said to the back of his head. "So if it's all the same to you, I'd like to leave my camisole on."

"Yes, of course," Gaines replied, still looking at the wall. "I'm sorry about that. I must've told the superintendent a dozen times about fixing the heat."

"You can turn around now."

He turned around and tentatively looked at Alicia. His eyes went wide, ogling her smooth body. "Holy—"

"What's wrong?"

"Nothing's wrong," he stammered. "I just can't believe—how you look."

"Why thank you, you charmer." She patted the mattress, sending up a plume of dust.

Howie climbed onto the bed, which emitted a little squeak.

"Now don't be timid. We're well past that." She reached over and gave his tool a firm squeeze. "Very impressive, Gaines. Let's go."

He climbed on top of her, breathing hard. After missing his aim a couple times, Allie took charge and helped him enter her with a low moan. He thrust somewhat tentatively a few times, each time with less conviction. Alicia raised her hips to drive him deeper, but unexpectedly met no resistance, only empty air. He flopped down next to her, panting.

"What are you *doing*?" she said.

"What do you mean?"

"What do you *think* I mean? I mean, we're supposed to be fucking, not lying here examining the ceiling."

"But I—I already—"

"Are you *serious*?"

"Well, yes," Howie muttered. "It didn't take as long as I thought it might."

"You're joking."

"I'm not," he said sheepishly.

"Have you ever done this before?" Allie said, frowning.

"Of course I have. What kind of question is that?"

"More than once?"

"Is something wrong?" he said.

"I've had sneezes that lasted longer than that."

Gaines blushed. "I am sorry about that. You're so beautiful that—"

"Don't go and make it my fault," Allie said.

"Next time it'll be different," he mumbled.

"If there *is* a next time."

"Now, that's not fair."

"Fair? Remember what you said about the dictionary. 'Fair' means 'equitable,' right?"

"All right, I understand. I'm sorry."

"It's fine."

"Is there something I can do?"

"Oh, for fuck's sake," she muttered, pulling up her bloomers. "I'll handle it myself when I get home. You know, I ought to just do it now, while I'm undressed."

Gaines seemed puzzled by this comment and was about to question her. "Never mind," she said before he could get the words out.

They lay side by side for an awkward minute, Howie wishing desperately he could think of something clever to say, and Alicia desperately hoping he wouldn't.

"You know, this has been *loads* of fun," she said after a respectable time had passed, "but I should be getting home. Mother and the girls will be wondering why I'm working late on a Friday."

"Can't you stay a little bit longer? Maybe we could have dinner together?"

"Another time, Gaines."

"All right. Another time. I really am sorry—"

"Enough with the apologies," she said. "Opening night jitters. Don't worry about it."

AFTER A HALF HOUR rocking home on the streetcar, lost in thought, Alicia quietly stepped into the front foyer and carefully hung up her coat.

"Alicia? Is that you?" Mrs. Hall's voice called from the parlor.

"Yes, Mother." Alicia poked her head around the corner to see Mrs. Hall sitting by the fire with a book open on her lap.

"I was beginning to worry," her mother said.

"Nothing to worry about. Long day, that's all." She walked into the parlor and sat down heavily on the couch next to her mother's chair.

"Was it a hard day? You look a little disheveled."

"In a manner of speaking, I suppose. After work, I went over to Gaines's place to get into his good graces. You know."

"Not again, Alicia."

"*Again*? You make it sound as though I've had legions of lovers," she said. "When, in fact, it's been less than a half dozen. I'm hardly Catherine the Great."

"I don't want to see you cast Bert away. He's a good man."

"I have no plans to throw Bert over for Gaines. Especially not after today's little interlude." She rolled her eyes.

Her mother looked confused. "I'm not following you."

"Gaines is a two-pump chump," Allie said.

"Oh, for the love of God. Alicia, sometimes you can be as rough as wet burlap."

"Why waste words, Mother? Words are precious. We have only so many of them we get to speak in a lifetime, then all is silence."

"Half a dozen lovers are too many, and you know it as well as I do. You know it ought to be one, and one only. That's what the Bible teaches us."

"We're *Unitarians*, Mother. Since when do we care about the Bible?"

"You're impossible sometimes."

"Improbable, Mother. Not impossible. Now then, I want to go and change out of these clothes, and take a soak in the tub before dinner."

In her room, she stepped out of her new winter suit. When she stripped off her bloomers, she saw what was left of Howie Gaines, a spreading patch of wet cold. She studied the soiled garment. My favorite pair, too, she thought. I'll have to soak them. Oh, fuck it, she thought in the next instant, and tossed them onto the glowing bed of coals in the hearth, where they sizzled for a few moments, and were consumed.

Porter's Pelvic Disease Clinic

When Annie returned home from the Avenging Angels' office, she found Ruth sitting at the kitchen table, minding the oven and frowning over a thick booklet in front of her. She looked up when her sister walked in and managed a half-smile.

"Look what the postman brought today," Ruth said, holding out the booklet so that Annie could read the title on the front cover in large black type beneath an engraving of a distinguished-looking middle-aged man, slightly balding and with a luxuriant mustache.

Man's Main Maladies Mastered
By E. D. Porter, MD

"So he sent it, after all," Annie said. "Good. What does it say?"

Ruth closed the booklet and smoothed it flat. "It's gruesome stuff. It seems to be directed more at men, if the engravings are any indication," she said.

"But he treats women, doesn't he?"

"Yes, it seems so. He says he has a Ladies' Entrance to his clinic."

"Oh good," Annie said. "Does he say anything about a cure?"

"He says here"—Ruth opened the booklet again to a page she had dog-eared—"'My treatment pushes every particle of blood poison out of the body, leaving the patient completely free of impurity.'"

"That sounds encouraging," Annie said. "Let's book a consultation."

"He has evening hours from seven to eight on weekdays," Ruth said.

"After I read this the first time, I called and booked one for this evening, at seven thirty."

"Now that's the spirit—you're getting your moxie back! We'll go together."

"You don't need to go with me, Sister," Ruth said.

"I do, and I shall. Let's have a quick bite to eat and be on our way."

THE PAINTED SIGN AT 333 Main Street, mounted on the spalling brick next to a discreet wooden door, read:

Porter's Pelvic Disease Clinic
2nd Floor
Ladies' Entrance to Rear

"This is the place," Annie said, and she and Ruth walked to the rear of the building, where they found another neatly marked door. They went in and climbed two flights of narrow stairs to the Ladies' Entrance. Inside, a pleasant-looking young woman—albeit with an unusually large and somehow incongruous nose—was sitting behind an imposing desk, reading a magazine.

"You must be Miss Murray," she said, looking up over her spectacles, which seemed tiny by comparison with the nose keeping them aloft. "We've been expecting you."

"Yes," Ruth said. "I booked a consultation with Dr. Porter earlier today. When I received his booklet in the mail, I—"

"No need to be nervous, dear," the woman said, smiling. "Please, have a seat and make yourselves comfortable. The doctor will be with you shortly." She pulled off her spectacles, and curiously, her bulbous nose seemed to lift slightly.

Ruth and Annie sat side by side on a wooden settle in the small and silent waiting room, both thankful that they were alone, save for the young woman with the mysterious nose. It wouldn't do to bump into anyone, not in Buffalo. Though the nation's eighth-largest and fastest-growing city, Buffalo was still very much a small town, and word traveled fast—especially, they surmised, about pelvic disease.

The walls of the waiting room were adorned with oversized versions of the engraving from the cover of *Man's Main Maladies Mastered*—the sober, middle-aged, mustachioed face of Dr. Porter mounted atop a high, stiff collar and, under it, a list of ghastly, presumably pelvic, diseases: stricture, varicocele, blood poison. A few copies of the doctor's booklet were scattered about. Annie and Ruth were staring idly at the doctor's poster-sized face, and he was staring back, when a door opposite them rattled and opened. In the doorway stood a clean-shaven, trim young man with a copious head of wavy black hair.

"The Misses Murray?" he said, smiling affably.

Annie and Ruth stood. "Is Dr. Porter ready for us?" Annie asked.

"I'm Dr. Porter," the young man said, standing aside. "Do come in."

The two ladies walked into Dr. Porter's office, which was also decorated with more poster-sized versions of the cover of his booklet. Annie and Ruth sat in two oak chairs facing the doctor's desk. There was a painted plaster model of a diseased man's lower torso on the corner of the desk, the tortured penis aimed at Ruth's eye level. Dr. Porter's hand darted out and spun the model around to face him, leaving Ruth to stare at a pair of plaster buttocks.

"My sister received your booklet today," Annie said.

"The demand for our little book has been nothing short of astonishing," Dr. Porter said. "And Miss Ruth—if I may call you Ruth—I'm delighted that my words encouraged you to visit."

"*You're* Dr. Porter?" Ruth blurted.

"Yes, of course," he said. "Who else would I be?"

Annie put her hand on Ruth's arm, but it was too late.

"It's only that—well, you don't look anything like your portrait," she said, pointing to the huge poster hanging behind the doctor's desk.

"Artistic license," he said. "Have you ever seen a photograph of the real Lydia Pinkham?"

"No," Ruth said.

"Well, I can tell you she looks nothing like her image on her Vegetable Compound bottle," Dr. Porter said, a little indignantly. "And when it comes to pelvic disease, people expect to see an older face."

"Yes, we understand," Annie said. "Ruth was only being nosy, after being in your waiting room and so on."

Dr. Porter returned a stern stare. "Is that an attempt at a joke, Miss Murray?"

Annie blushed a deep red. "A joke? Of course not. Why would it be a joke?"

"My mistake," Dr. Porter said, relaxing. "I thought momentarily you were referring to"—he pointed quietly toward the door they'd entered—"*my nurse*," he whispered, one hand cupped around his mouth.

"I'm terribly sorry, Doctor," Annie said, "but I'm still not following."

"You said *nosy*," he whispered again. "My nurse. She came to me after the disease claimed her nose. She wears a prosthesis now. I thought you were poking fun."

"God, I would never dream of such a thing," Annie said.

"I'm probably a bit too sensitive about it," Dr. Porter said, in an impossibly low voice, "because some people think it happened—the *loss*, that is—on my watch. But she was *like that* when I met her. I was able to arrest the disease, at least, before it did further damage."

"Are you telling us she's wearing a fake nose?" Ruth said.

"Please, Miss Ruth," the doctor said, alarmed. "Keep your voice down. You can perhaps imagine how self-conscious she is about it."

"Holy mother," Ruth breathed, crossing herself. "Is my nose going to fall off?"

"Not if we act quickly," Dr. Porter said. "Nor does it always happen, in any case. My nurse has had the disease from birth—contracted it from her mother, as is not infrequently the circumstance—so she was well along when I met her. Ravaged."

"*Ravaged*?" Annie said.

"Syphilis is a progressive disease," Dr. Porter said. "It waxes and it wanes, as the years pass, though it most always worsens. For some reason, it likes to attack the nose. But we don't need to worry about that just yet. Now, then, Miss Ruth—will you tell me how you contracted your condition? I don't need details, only the avenue through which you acquired the disease."

Ruth told him the story of her argument with Harry Price.

Dr. Porter shook his head mournfully. "That was exceedingly unwise," he said.

"She realizes that now," Annie said. "It was a moment's impulse."

"Unfortunately, one that can have lifelong consequences. But," he said, perking up, "you've come to the right place. It's not too late. I believe I can help you."

"We've been told that mercury preparations are hazardous," Annie said.

"I'm afraid they can be—yet I don't think we can avoid using mercury entirely," Dr. Porter said. "There is some very promising research going on in Germany now, but the results are not yet available to the medical community. In France, radium water—regular water infused with the amazing new substance recently isolated by the Doctors Curie—is also said to be showing good results. But again, not yet available to practitioners."

"I see," Annie said. "Your booklet says that your treatment forces out the poison in the blood, though."

"It does indeed."

"How does it work?"

Dr. Porter opened a file folder that was sitting on his spotless desk, and took out a single crisp sheet of paper. He placed a pen atop it and slid it over in front of the two ladies.

"As I'm sure you understand, my methods are proprietary to myself, and as such can be shared only with patients who have engaged my counsel on a paid basis. You see before you my simple contract. Five sessions, along with any required adjunct medications, for one modest fee."

"*Two hundred dollars?*" Ruth said, goggling at the contract. "I don't have two hundred dollars."

"You may pay on time, if that's easier for you. Five installments, payable at the time of each of the five sessions."

"I have the money," Annie said. "I'll sign it."

"Don't you dare!" Ruth said. "You can't afford two hundred dollars, either."

"If you refer another patient to my practice, I can extend a ten percent reduction," Dr. Porter said.

Annie thought a moment. "We know only one other syphilitic," she said. "As far as we know, that is. But he'd never agree—"

"This is stupid," Ruth said, starting out of her chair. "Let's go. We

PORTER'S PELVIC DISEASE CLINIC

can't pay you two hundred dollars, let alone find someone else with blood poison or varico-whatever-it-is—"

"Varicocele," the doctor said calmly. "Although that's a male problem."

Annie tugged Ruth gently back into her chair, and then picked up the pen and signed the contract. "There," she said, sliding it back to Dr. Porter, "I can pay. Five installments, please. Now just fix my sister." A single sob burbled out of her throat. "I can't lose her, Doctor."

"Your sister will be well again, Miss Annie," he said, "and thanks to your generosity, at that."

"My God, Annie," Ruth said. She looked at Dr. Porter. "Now will you tell us how it works?"

"Of course. I practice what is known as pyrotherapy," the doctor said. "You might think of it as inducing an artificial fever."

"Aren't fevers bad?" Annie asked.

"It's a common misconception, but an understandable one. Often fevers can—and do—get out of hand. But there's a good reason that the body creates a fever, it's now believed—and that is to raise the internal temperature sufficiently to destroy whatever foreign organism has taken up residence. If a fever is temporary, and kept below a certain temperature, it will do no lasting harm."

"How do you induce this artificial fever?" Annie asked.

"I have a special chamber in the adjacent room. The patient removes her clothes and sits comfortably in it, the head protruding from the top through a rubber gasket. I then introduce live steam to raise the temperature of the chamber until the body temperature—which I monitor with a thermometer held in the patient's mouth—reaches 105 degrees or so. We then hold it there for an hour, unless the patient can't tolerate the treatment."

"Tolerate it?" Ruth said.

"Meaning," he said, "that the patient suffers convulsions or slips into delirium. In such rare cases, I suspend treatment at once."

"This isn't worth your life savings," Ruth said out of the corner of her mouth. "It sounds medieval."

"I concur that it's not pleasant, Miss Ruth," the doctor said, seeming stung, "but it's hardly medieval. As to whether it's worth the fee, there

I must disagree with you. The alternative is far more hideous. I'm sure you've seen photographs of syphilitic persons left untreated."

"He's right, Ruth," Annie said. "We have to do *something.*"

"Oh fine," Ruth said. "I'll try it, since you've already gone and signed your life away."

"A wise decision," young Dr. Porter said. "My nose—my *nurse,* I mean—can arrange a suitable time and date for your first session." He stood and gave a little bow. "Thank you for entrusting me with your case."

"Thank you, Dr. Porter," Annie said. "I feel a little hopeful for the first time in weeks."

On the streetcar back to Norwood Street, Ruth continued to grouse about the money.

"You do realize that it took you five whole years to save up that money," she said.

"You're all I have in the world, Sister," Annie replied. "I don't care about the money. I never knew what I was going to do with it, anyway."

"It doesn't matter. You certainly didn't think you'd throw it all away on a doctor who doesn't even resemble himself. He's probably a quack."

"I can't imagine he's been so successful if he's a quack. Let's try to be hopeful. And forget about the money. What's done is done, and I haven't the least regret about it."

Ruth put her head on Annie's shoulder and gave her arm a little squeeze. "I'm sorry," she said. "I've been terribly foolish. And now I've gone and cost your life savings."

Annie looked out the trolley window, blinking back tears. "Life savings," she said, almost to herself. "If they can save yours, that will be the best thing I could have ever used them for."

LONELINESS

THE QUIET ECHOES IN THE LONG CORRIDORS OF KENDALL HOUSE took some getting used to, compared to the bustling little house on Norwood Street. In Ashwood, four talkative women occupied a fraction of the space that Sarah and Maggie had for just the two of them. Christine could be noisy enough, once she got going, but much of the time she was off by herself, doing whatever she liked to do. Sarah wasn't entirely certain what that might be—for all of Christine's forthrightness, there was at the same time a deep secrecy about her. And Kendall was Kendall—a polite, personable, if somewhat reserved, gentleman, who spent most of his time at the factory and the rest of it working noiselessly in his private office.

Moreover, neither Christine nor Charles Kendall—not to mention the house staff—could be her *friends*. They were her employers, in the former case, and in the latter, her servants. On one occasion, Sarah had tried to strike up a conversation with Erin, but after a few staccato exchanges, the girl was plainly uncomfortable and eager to go about her work. On another, Sarah had decided to seek out Christine in her lair—another large wing on the opposite side of the house, and one floor down from Sarah. She had tentatively rapped on the outer door, to no answer. She had already turned to go when the door flew open, and Christine appeared, looking flushed and somewhat disheveled.

"This is unexpected," she said, in an unexpectedly hard voice. The voice of the boss's daughter, Sarah thought briefly.

"I'm terribly sorry. I've disturbed you," Sarah said, backing away.

"No, no—come in. You surprised me, that's all."

Once in Christine's sitting room, Sarah could detect nothing out of the ordinary, nothing amiss. Yet Christine had remained distant—polite, of course, but inscrutable, as though Sarah had walked in on something.

After only a few minutes, Sarah was squirming in her chair. She was about to excuse herself when she thought she heard someone cough, back in the far recesses of Christine's suite, where the bedrooms must be. She pretended not to notice, though Christine stiffened and her eyes narrowed. Sarah stood, gave the girl a hug, and left.

She had gone directly back to her own suite after that, resolved never to try that stunt again and to remember her place in this household—as a temporary, paid guest, nothing more. She walked over to the giant windows overlooking the snowy back lawn and the mighty gorge, and was gazing out vacantly when, down below, she saw a man come out of the back entrance of the house, moving fast in long strides toward the carriage house. It was Stefan, smoothing down his coat and trousers as he disappeared around the far end of the mansion.

There was something about it that made her ache. It was too great a coincidence—Christine's discomfiture and then, so soon after, Stefan's hasty retreat across the back lawn. Everyone has *someone*, she thought, while I'm stranded here all by myself. She looked at the clock. Maggie would be downstairs in the little schoolroom for another hour, at least. Sarah walked into her bedroom, closed the door, and drew the curtains. She leaned back against the headboard of her bed, lifted her skirt, and wasted no time getting some consolation. Yet even her climax—which was so sharp it made her cry out, despite biting down on her lip hard enough to taste blood—felt more like punishment than pleasure, and left her no less profoundly alone.

ON MONDAY, SARAH KEPT an eye out for dirty-minded Jeremy Horn, but he was nowhere to be seen on either of her walk-throughs. The other men continued to stare at her, but even if she flashed them her most stellar smile, not one of them took the bait, as though they sensed something dangerous about her. Perhaps my proximity to the boss, she thought. Two days passed, and then on Thursday, Jeremy was back, his pale face bobbing toward her through the thin smoke of the factory floor. She glanced at MacCormick, and he went up the iron stairs without her.

Horn strolled over to her. "Why hello again, Miss Price!" he shouted.

"Where have you been all week?" she said into his ear.

"Were you looking for me?"

"I thought you might have a few days off."

"And you'd be right. I was moving into new quarters. Would you like to talk in the warehouse? It will be easier." He motioned for her to follow him through the giant rolling doors. "Let's sit on those barrels and watch while we chat."

When they reached the large barrels, he brushed the tops off with his handkerchief. Sarah wasn't quite sure how to climb up with appropriate discretion.

"May I assist?" he said.

"You may. And well done—you asked before picking me up this time."

"Oh my," he said with mock horror. "I may be in danger of becoming a gentleman."

"I wouldn't be too worried about it."

Jeremy told her to put the small of her back against the curve of the big barrel staves, and then he delicately slipped his long hands between her arms and body, lifting her gently to sit on the barrelhead. He was surprisingly strong, and gentle, she thought. No funny business, either, trying to feel something he oughtn't.

He then hopped up easily on the barrel next to hers. "There. Isn't that better?"

"Yes, it is, and thank you for the help. They should put stirrups on these things."

"Do you ride?"

"No more than anyone else does," she said. "I wouldn't say that I'm an equestrienne, but I'm competent. Yourself?"

"I grew up riding. I played polo in preparatory school. I'm good enough, I suppose. Not like a cavalry captain or a Plains Indian, but adequate."

"Preparatory school? Polo?" she said. "You didn't grow up in England, did you?"

"Oh no. Canada. Near Toronto."

"That explains your peculiar accent."

"I don't have an accent."

"We'll agree to disagree on that."

He smiled. "As you wish. And I don't like to disagree with such a lovely woman, anyway."

"Are you trying to be charming today?"

"Not a bit of it. Simply honest. You see, in reflecting on our first conversation, it struck me that I neglected to tell you that you are, without the slightest doubt, the most beautiful woman I have ever seen."

She waved her hand. "Be careful. I'm likely to start believing you. You are all moved into your new lodgings, then?"

"Yes, for the most part. Where do you live, Miss Price?"

"The north—east—part of the city."

"Northeast? That's the part of town I lived in until this week. What street?"

Sarah tried to think of the few street names she could recall from her trolley journey to and from Kendall House. "Cedar," she said. "Cedar Avenue."

"Oh, then you're probably not far from Oakwood Cemetery."

She had seen signs for Oakwood Cemetery from the trolley, but didn't want to be too precise. "Well, a little bit east of that, but yes."

"That's curious," he said. "I didn't think Cedar continued east of the cemetery."

"Of course! What was I thinking? West. I meant west. My sense of direction is terrible."

"In life or just in geography?"

"Sometimes one, sometimes the other," she said. "Now what about you? Where are your new lodgings?"

"Downtown, in the tourist district."

"How exciting that must be!"

"Not in the winter," Horn said. "Most everything's shuttered up for the season. Only a few hardy souls are out and about. Probably Eskimos on holiday."

"I predict we'll be happy for the cold when summer comes. Now, at least, with these big doors open, the factory's tolerable. I can only imagine what it must be like in August."

"Like one of the inner circles of Hell, I'm sure," he said. "But I wouldn't complain too loudly about it. Kendall and MacCormick don't tolerate whiners."

"They don't care about the working conditions?"

"Look at the men who work here. Almost every last one of them new to this country, so they don't know any better yet. Now Kendall does pay better than most other factories, but the bargain is this—do the work and keep your mouth shut. And for God's sake, don't ever mention the word 'union.' That'll get you sacked on the spot. The unions will do anything to get in here, and Kendall and MacCormick will do anything to keep them out."

"Why don't they want a union?"

"Why do you think?"

"Because they would have to pay more?"

He shook his head. "Union men don't typically make more than nonunion men. If anything, they make less, after their union dues are deducted. The reason people join unions is because, otherwise, management has all the power. And the reason management doesn't want unions around is because—they want all the power."

"And all the money, I'd suppose."

He whistled through his teeth. "Indeed. Look at Kendall. The man makes King Midas look like a pauper." Jeremy gestured around the warehouse. "This company is his own private gold mine."

"He's a millionaire, I understand."

He laughed. "*Millionaire*? His house alone cost *five* million. Have you ever seen it?"

"I've seen photographs of it in the newspapers."

"Well, if you like, we can take the trolley up toward Lewiston and walk past the place. It's a palace."

"I think I might feel awkward gawking at the man's residence. What if he saw us?"

"It's right along the main road, or at least one side of it is," Jeremy said. "People are coming and going all the time. He wouldn't have built it there, if he hadn't wanted people to gawk."

"We need those barrels you're sitting on," a burly fellow interrupted. "They go on this car."

"Beg pardon," Jeremy said, and hopped down. He reached out to help Sarah, and this time his hand brushed along the front and side of her breast. She gave him a look.

"Terribly sorry," he blurted.

"Is that a question?" she said, smiling. She declined his offer to walk her back to the office along the tracks, letting him return to the factory while she picked her way along the gravel pathway, deep in the cold shadow of the waiting freight cars. Her mind wandered back to his errant hand, its gentle brush against her nipple, and she found herself wanting to feel it again.

EACH AFTERNOON AFTER THAT, she and Jeremy found excuses to spend time together in the loading dock, talking about everything and nothing at all. He was an engaging fellow, well-educated, well-spoken, and—except for an occasional naughty crack that he didn't try to suppress, or couldn't bear to—well-behaved. He asked more questions of her than she asked of him, which was a first. Most men could barely wait to steer the conversation back around to their own exploits. Not Jeremy, who seemed reluctant to talk about himself very much at all, as though he didn't find himself very interesting.

That alone was liberating. Without any discussion of his past, she had no obligation—no opportunity, even—to talk about hers. And for the first time since before she'd married Seth, she felt, too, as though the past had no hold over her. Not her parents, not Buffalo, not all the drugs and drink that Seth had put away, not even Ed's murder. There were moments during their chatty conversations that she forgot entirely that there had ever been a Sarah Payne, so easily did she fit into her new skin as Sarah Price.

And as the days went by, she also forgot—all too often—the reason she was supposed to be talking with Jeremy Horn in the first place: to get to the bottom of Kendall's production problem, and find his missing water. On too many afternoons, she returned to the office with the guilty knowledge that she'd advanced the case not a step. And more and more she felt as though she was stealing from Mr. Kendall, accepting her fee for entertaining herself with her new and rakish young friend. And each afternoon, she'd resolve that the next day, it would be down to brass tacks.

Captains of Infantry

On Saturday, Mr. Kendall asked Sarah to join him in his private office at Kendall House. They sat at a round table in the corner of the large office, in a cozy nook where the floor-to-ceiling bookshelves came together. Along the adjacent wall was another huge fireplace, flanked with leather armchairs and Tiffany floor lamps in a pattern that struck her as vaguely Moorish.

"Miss Payne," he said, spreading his hands out on the table, "I thought it might be time to check in with you. Have you picked up any productive leads yet?"

"A few. Most of the men steer clear of me, but one of your foremen—Mr. Horn—seems to be taking me under his wing. He's been more forthcoming."

"Horn. I don't know that much about him—he's been with us only a few months. He seems promising, and still young enough to make something of himself."

"He can't be more than thirty," Sarah said. "That would seem to allow plenty of time to become a captain of industry."

"Captains of industry have to begin as captains of *infantry*. That's what foreman are. They lead reluctant men into battle every day, and fight on the front lines along with them. It's hard work. Demanding. Exacting. And it ages a man quickly, so if a man hasn't made his mark by forty, he's probably not going to."

"I see. Well, Mr. Horn seems like an especially nice young fellow."

Kendall seemed surprised. "That's interesting."

"How so?"

"As I said, I don't know him too well, but Mac says—and

often—that he's the hardest man we have in the foreman position. Which, as I said, is the hardest job of all."

"That's surprising," Sarah said. "He seems to feel a certain solidarity with working people."

"God help us if he does. Sympathy is the single worst quality a foreman can have."

"Why on earth would you say that?"

"Because if a foreman doesn't rule with an iron fist, he's finished. To follow a man into battle requires absolute, unquestioning obedience. If the laborers don't feel that, they'll eat him alive."

"But how, if I may ask? The laborers don't have any authority."

"Miss Payne, you must understand something. You may have heard the saying 'When a man has a hard master, he dreams of having an easier one, but when he has an easy master, he dreams of being his *own* master.' And that I cannot have. That is anarchy. It is up to my foremen to enforce discipline, and get the job done."

"I understand," Sarah said, a little disappointed by his harshness. "One doesn't have to spend much time in the factory to know that it's a very strenuous occupation for all concerned. I mean no offense."

"None taken. Though I'm perhaps a bit too sensitive. I was a working man myself, but I never hated my bosses the way men do today. And the newspapers whip it all up, too. One can't open one of the damn things without reading some blowhard pontificating about how evil we so-called robber barons are. No wonder people want to hurt me."

"Tell me, Mr. Kendall, who would want to hurt you? Your competitors?"

He shook his head. "They surely want to better me, but they're not dishonorable people. It's the unions who will stoop to anything. They'd kill me if they could. That's why I have Stefan."

"I got that impression from Mr. Horn. About the unions, that is."

"What did he say?"

"He said they're desperate to get into your factory. And desperate people resort to desperate things. Even murder."

"Do you think someone in my factory could be culpable?"

"While it's possible," she said, "your strategy of divide and conquer—making it so that no one knows the whole secret of your operation—makes it seem unlikely."

"Mr. Horn has indeed been forthcoming, I see," he said.

"And I think he has more he wants to share, but it will take time. You and Mr. MacCormick certainly have put the fear of God into your employees."

"Surely I'm not quite such a tyrant."

"And surely you didn't get to your station in life by being weak. I make no judgments, sir. I am your employee, too, and you have been especially kind to me."

His eyes softened. "It's that I find you . . . to be a fine detective, Miss Payne. I hope I can make your assignment as pleasant as I can."

"And I am grateful for that. Now I do think it's time for me to turn some of my attention to the unions. Which ones ought I to begin investigating?"

"It's really only *one* union in my line of work," Kendall said. "The ABW—the Abrasive Workers Union. They're headquartered here in Niagara Falls. And they are a ruthless bunch, entirely capable of devising a scheme to steal my water. But I must say—how they could accomplish a technical feat of this magnitude is a mystery to me. Why, even my most experienced men refuse to enter those underground tunnels—which is where someone would have to go to divert my water. If it's not happening in the factory, that is."

"The only way to get to the bottom of it, sir, is for me to meet with the ABW, if I can. Do you know who their top man is?"

Kendall rolled his eyes. "Yes, unfortunately. A perfect scoundrel by the name of Aaron Brass. When he succeeded in unionizing Carborundum, he was the talk of the town."

"I'll see if I can find a way to meet him."

He inhaled sharply. "I'd advise caution about that, Miss Payne. Brass isn't above hurting a woman. Indeed, I don't feel right about putting you in that kind of danger."

"Mr. Kendall, it's what you hired me to do. I have to be a captain of infantry, too."

He paused for a moment, looking away. "You're right, of course.

I wear my heart on my sleeve too much, and I oughtn't to, but you see . . . I . . . Miss Payne—"

"No need to explain," she said with a slight smile. "I'm very much the same way."

"And yet you've chosen to be a detective. It would seem secrecy would come easily to you."

Sarah didn't know quite how to respond. "Perhaps a little too easily."

"Beg pardon?"

"I don't know what I meant," she said with a light laugh. "Forgive me. I was thinking about Aaron Brass."

"I could telephone him tomorrow and arrange a conference with him, of course. He'd welcome it."

"But that would instantly tip our hand," she said. "But I think I may have another idea. One that will make me irresistible to him."

"A talent of yours, Miss Payne."

She looked at him quizzically.

"I mean to say—you do have a certain magnetism. Look at Mrs. Miller—she's nobody's fool, and is quite taken with you."

"She is?"

"Without the slightest doubt." He chuckled. "And she's quite a character, in addition."

"That would be putting it mildly. Your meeting with her was productive, then?"

"Very. I'm giving her all of my envelope business."

"I'm sure she's delighted. That said—I hope you didn't—because—"

"Oh no," he said with a wave of the hand. "I wouldn't do that. She won the account, fair and square. It's just that it's not often that I take such satisfaction in a business conversation."

"Well, good. I am happy to hear it." She flashed Kendall a dazzling smile, and left his office before it could die away.

20

The International Café

THE FACTORY WHISTLE HAD SOUNDED TEN MINUTES BEFORE, and Sarah was already waiting at the trolley stop when she heard a voice from behind.

"Sarah!"

She turned to see Jeremy jogging toward her.

"I've been calling after you for two blocks," he said when he caught her up. "I was waiting for you outside the factory, but you walked right past me."

"I must have been lost in my own thoughts. Or my ears were still ringing."

"Understandable. Well, then—what do you say about having some ice cream with me? Before you go home."

"I'm not sure it would be prudent for people to see us together outside of work."

"Eating ice cream? How much more prudent can it get?"

"I'm not sure," she said. "I really ought to be on my way."

"And why the trolley?" he asked. "Don't you live on Cedar Avenue? That's two hundred yards from here, at most."

She hadn't considered this. "Oh yes. I was going to visit my—mother. She lives in Lewiston."

"Lewiston? And yet you've never seen Kendall's place?"

She felt her heart miss a beat. "Oh, why not? What could be improper about an ice cream?"

"Wonderful! Then I can walk you up toward Cedar. There's a soda fountain that's probably not two blocks from where you live."

"You know, I'd love a change of scenery. Would you care to walk downtown, instead? I've not really seen much of the tourist part of the city."

"Even better!" he said, his hands fluttering. "We'll go to the International Hotel. They have a beautiful café with a big fireplace. We don't have to have ice cream, either. Anything you like."

"All right. But I can't stay very long. It'll be dark soon."

"Then we'll have to hurry," Jeremy said.

The International Hotel sat on a low rise above the turbulent rapids, a few hundred yards above the brink of the Falls. In the summer, the hotel's broad verandahs were full of guests and tourists, all raptly watching the water tumble and race toward the edge. In January, though, no one was brave enough to sit outdoors. Because of the cold, naturally, but also because the freezing spray whipped up by the flowing water—and the dense mist rising from the Falls themselves—coated everything in a layer of crystalline ice. Every tree branch, railing, and bench was encased in ice, and on a sunny day, the effect was magical—a world made of sparkling crystal. Today, with the sun declining, the red glow of sunset turned the landscape into one of frozen fire.

Sarah and Jeremy took a seat in the hotel's cozy café, in an inglenook near the big fireplace. The café served both men and women, so nothing seemed amiss about the two chatting over the same small table. Yet even with the fireplace roaring, and a steam radiator hissing and spitting like an angry cat in front of each of the tall windows facing the rapids, the room struggled to stay warm. The host had taken from them their outerwear, and after a few minutes Sarah was shivering. Without a word, Jeremy quite chivalrously went to the hotel sundry shop and purchased a souvenir shawl for Sarah, which she gratefully draped over her shoulders.

"I'm so happy you decided to spend time with me instead of with your mother," he said. "Is that selfish of me?"

"It's incredibly selfish. But it's honest. I'll give you that much."

"What ice creams do you have today?" Jeremy said when the waiter came by.

"It's much too cold for ice cream, Mr. Horn," the man said.

"We're two feet away from an inferno. What's wrong? You don't have any?"

"We have it, but I can see that your lady friend already has a chill. I wouldn't advise it."

"I'll have a cup of tea," Sarah interrupted. "And a little piece of cake, if you have some."

"We do indeed. A better choice," the waiter said.

"Make it two, then," Jeremy said.

"They certainly don't scruple about service," Jeremy grumbled when the waiter had departed.

"The waiter had our interests at heart, I suppose. Say, how did he know you by name?"

He smiled. "I live here now." He pointed at the ceiling. "My new lodgings are on the top floor."

"That's unexpected."

"You're surprised I'd want to live in a hotel?"

"No—I mean—just that, well, it's probably rude of me—"

"You wonder how I can afford to live in a place like this on the pittance that Kendall pays," Jeremy said, nodding.

"Yes, I suppose that's it."

He leaned forward across the table. "I'll tell you a secret, if you promise not to let on to anyone at work."

"I promise," Sarah said.

"I live on ill-gotten gains," he said in a low voice.

"Be serious."

He chuckled, with the air of a man comfortable with himself. "It's true. My fiancée's father paid me to leave Toronto."

Sarah sat bolt upright in her chair. "Oh my—you're *engaged*? How did I not know that?"

"No, no," he said, holding out his hands. "I'm *dis*engaged." He laughed.

She crossed her arms. "I fail to see the humor. Unless you want me to get up and leave right now, you owe me an explanation."

"You're right, and I'm sorry. It was nervous laughter, I suppose. I was engaged to a young woman in Toronto, a very wealthy one. Her parents decided that another fellow would be a more advantageous match, so they forced her to break off the engagement. But my father is a barrister—a lawyer—and he threatened to sue them for breach of marriage promise. My fiancée was to receive a very substantial dowry, which of course would have been ours. Eventually, they settled a sum of money on me and—here I am."

"But why leave Toronto? Surely they couldn't banish you."

"The city held too many bad memories," Jeremy said. "Everywhere I went, all I could think about, all I could see, was—*her.*"

I can understand that, Sarah thought, watching the flames dancing in the fireplace.

"I'm very sorry, Jeremy," she said.

"Water under the bridge. Or, better—over the Falls. Life goes on."

"Yes, it does. But that doesn't make a loss like that any easier."

He lowered his voice again. "I have a feeling that you've suffered similar losses."

"Why would you say that?"

"I see it in your face, Sarah. It's part of what drew me to you."

"I must not be very mysterious."

"Mysterious," he repeated slowly, looking past her. He shook his head. "No, I wouldn't say that you're mysterious."

"Then I might at least try to be less transparent."

"But you're not transparent, either. I can't see *through* you—but I do think I can see *into* you."

"Now that's a provocative statement," she said. "And what do you see in there?"

"Hmm," he said. "Do you really want to know, I wonder?"

"I do. I think I do, at any rate."

"Well then," he said, interlacing his fingers, "I see someone who's been hurt, who has been disappointed, and who needs to keep people—including me—at a safe distance."

Sarah sat back in her chair.

"Am I right?" he said with a thin smile.

"More so than I'd like to admit. Perhaps you are clairvoyant?"

"I'm a good detective, that's all," he said, and she looked down.

"How do you mean, 'detective'?"

"I observe things, Sarah. And I've been observing you, from the start. I've developed a mental outline, in fact, of who you are."

"And what are your conclusions?"

"You're in your late twenties, I would guess."

"Twenty-eight, yes."

"And at age twenty-eight, most young women have children and are at home. But you don't wear a wedding ring, and you're clearly not at home, since you are beginning a new situation as a secretary in a manufacturing concern. That suggests to me that you've either never been married, or are a young widow. In either case, a very difficult and disappointing state for a woman of your age. And your cheerfulness sometimes seems to me a bit forced, so I reason that you are concealing some deep injury, or simply putting up a shield that most people will not dare challenge—mainly because of your beauty. And as to that, I also don't mind mentioning that a woman of your beauty would not lack for suitors. If you aren't married, it must be because you are not allowing men to court you."

"You're a veritable Sherlock Holmes. I am indeed a widow. My husband passed away about a year ago."

"My condolences. Was it unexpected?"

"I wouldn't say that. He was a dipsomaniac. His body finally gave up."

"I am sorry. Drink is the cause of untold evil."

"A lot of people say that. But I tend to think that alcohol is like any other weapon—how dangerous it is has mostly to do with the hand holding it."

"Well said."

"So much for all that," she said. "As you said, water under the bridge."

"See how that went?" he said. "You opened your door a tiny crack, and then slammed it shut in my face before I could peer in."

"Not everyone enjoys being spied on, Jeremy."

"Then if we leave the past where it belongs—what about the future? What plans do you have for it?"

"I'm making it up as I go. You?"

"Who knows?" he said with a shrug. "Like you, I'm a bit at sea."

"Do you like your position with Kendall?"

"No, not particularly. It makes me angry."

"How so?"

"I get angry about the same things that probably bother you about it. The heat. The noise—especially the noise. The fact that you live near a cemetery, while Mr. Kendall lives in a palace."

"Does that make you a socialist?" Sarah said.

"No, it makes me jealous."

She laughed.

"In all candor, however unfair the world may be," he said, "I could never be a socialist. Socialists are idealists, and I detest idealism."

"I used to be an idealist. But like you, I was quickly disillusioned."

"And good for both of us, that we were. The best thing that can happen to one in life is to become disillusioned. Or disenchanted. Or both. And as early as possible."

"You're a curious fellow, Jeremy Horn," she said.

"Not really. I've never understood why those words—'disillusionment' and 'disenchantment'—are taken as negatives. It seems to me that letting the scales drop from one's eyes and living in reality, rather than fantasy, is a very positive development."

She'd never thought of it that way, and studied Jeremy's face—not quite handsome, perhaps, but kind and intelligent—wondering how to respond.

"Most people aren't like us, Sarah," Jeremy said. "They think the normal state of life is—or ought to be—happiness, and when they don't have it, they feel they've been cheated. But they have it backwards."

They chatted for another half hour, until the tea was cold and there wasn't a crumb left on the plate.

"You know," she said, glancing up at the clock, "I've enjoyed our conversation so, that I've let time get away from me. I really do need to be getting home."

"Will there be another time, then? To continue our conversation?"

She smiled. "Yes, I'd like that."

"Wonderful. That makes my week. May I walk you to your lodgings?"

"Oh no. I'll be perfectly fine. It's not far."

"All the way to Cedar Avenue? In the dark?"

"Really, it's nothing. I'll get a coach." She hastily gathered her handbag and stood. "Perhaps you can still return the shawl and get your money back," she said, sliding it off her shoulders.

"Nothing doing. That's yours. Think of it as a little gift to commemorate our first *real* conversation. It *is* a souvenir shawl, after all."

"Then I will gladly keep it," she said. "And I will see you on Monday."

"In the noise and the heat."

She gestured around the room. "At least you have a good spot for rest and relaxation, in the meantime."

"I hope your lodgings are at least as comfortable."

She thought of Kendall House. "Yes, I'm very comfortable, thank you."

"Would you like to see my new lodgings before you go?"

"Jeremy!" she said. "What kind of a question is that?"

"I didn't mean anything by it."

"If you didn't, you're either a masher or—stupid as a ham sandwich."

"Touché," he said. "I'm probably a little of both."

ONCE THE TROLLEY WAS safely out of the city, Harry Price moved up from the rear of the car and sat down in the seat behind Sarah.

"Who was *that*?" he said, over her shoulder, making her jump.

"You startled me," Sarah said.

"Didn't mean to. So who was the guy?"

"His name is Jeremy Horn. He's a foreman at the factory. I'm trying to find out what's going on. I've been chatting with him at work, but today he invited me for an ice cream."

"I see. Did you learn anything?"

"Not really, and I doubt I will. He's not the type."

Harry looked straight ahead and didn't reply.

"What is it, Harry?"

"What is what?"

"Don't think you can fool me. I know you're thinking something about him."

"You seemed to enjoy his company, that's all."

"I did. He's well-spoken and he seems unusually perceptive."

"And good-looking."

"Yes, he's handsome. But that's not what I enjoy. I enjoy hearing his ideas."

"I see."

"Is there something wrong with that, Harry?"

"Just be careful. There was something about him I didn't like."

"I swear, Harry, you are the most suspicious man I've ever known."

"I've seen a lot of men who ain't the 'type' they make out to be."

"Well, so have I."

"I know his *look*."

She sighed and looked up at the ceiling of the trolley. "And what exactly is this *look*?"

"Too trustworthy to be trustworthy."

"What is that supposed to mean?"

"He has the eyes of a confidence man," Harry said.

"A *con man*? Really? Are you perhaps being a touch overprotective, Harry?"

"Don't think so, no."

"Well, I think you might be."

They rode along without speaking again until they got down from the trolley at Riverdale Cemetery. Isadore was waiting there, as usual, just inside the iron gate. They began walking toward the coach when Harry put his hand on Sarah's forearm. His hand was so strong that she stopped and turned toward him.

"What is it now?"

"Look, I hope you're right about him. But I'm telling you flat out—keep your guard up. Something's *off*."

"I do keep my guard up," she said sharply. "Now come on. Isadore's going to wonder what's wrong."

They walked into the craggy, leafless forest of Riverdale Cemetery, and Isadore helped Sarah into the cab. Then it was back to Kendall House.

21

PYROTHERAPY

RUTH AND ANNIE SLOWLY CLIMBED THE STAIRCASE OF THE Ladies' Entrance in the rear of Porter's Pelvic Disease Clinic.

"Ought I to feel so nervous, I wonder?" Ruth said at the top of the landing.

"Anything new will make one feel nervous," Annie said. "It's natural. I'm nervous, too, but so very hopeful."

"Will you be able to stay with me? In the treatment room?"

"I certainly should think so, but we'll ask right away."

They stepped into the waiting room, and were again greeted by the nurse, whose prosthetic nose seemed somehow different this time. Smaller.

"I'm here for my first pyrotechnic session," Ruth announced.

"Pyrotherapy, dear," the nurse said. "Yes, we're all ready for you. The doctor will be with you shortly."

Annie and Ruth sat in the familiar waiting room, hearts beating hard in the quiet, holding hands. Soon the younger version of Dr. Porter emerged from his office, smiled, and beckoned them in. They sat in front of his desk again.

"Tonight, ladies," he said, "we take our first step toward recovery. Are you ready?"

Annie smiled and squeezed Ruth's hand. "I'm so happy, Doctor. We did have one question, though—will I be able to accompany my sister into the treatment room?"

"Naturally," Dr. Porter said. "There's a comfortable chair in there for family. And also my"—he seemed to take a moment to navigate to the right word—"*nurse* will be with you the entire time, to monitor Miss Ruth's temperature. I'll see you both after the treatment, briefly, as well."

"I suppose we'd best get on with it, then," Ruth said. "This waiting is the worst part."

"You will find the treatment quite pleasant, at first," Dr. Porter said. "But after your body temperature reaches a certain level, you will feel uncomfortable, as you would if you had the grippe or other febrile condition."

"Febrile?" Ruth said.

"Feverish. Sometimes we medical men forget ourselves when speaking with the lay public. Now then," Dr. Porter said, "you may both go into the room to our right, through that door. My—the young lady will meet you inside. Good luck, and I will see you in an hour or two."

Annie and Ruth stepped into the treatment room. In the middle of the space was a large tentlike enclosure made of what looked like rubberized cloth stretched over a frame. The nurse was standing nearby, smiling cheerfully.

"It looks like a big raincoat," Ruth said.

"That's what it is, dear," the nurse said. "This rubber cloth keeps the heat and moisture in."

"What do I do?"

"First, disrobe—"

"Right here?"

"Yes, this room is private, and we're all ladies. Then I'll get you situated inside the pyrotherapy chamber, and start warming you. I'll take your temperature every ten minutes or so. When it reaches the correct level, we'll keep it there for an hour. Then I'll let you cool down, give you towels to dry off with and a big tumbler of water. You'll dress, see the doctor briefly, and go right home. That's all there is to it."

"So you should undress," Annie said.

"All right," Ruth said, and began stripping down. Annie took her garments, one by one, and carefully folded them on a table adjacent to the chamber. Soon Ruth was naked, and Annie almost burst into tears at the sight of her sister's young, lithe body—so lovely and perfect on the outside but hiding, inside, a deadly contagion.

The nurse pulled open a laced flap in the rubber cloth. "Duck in here and sit on the chair. Put your head up through the hole in the top," she said.

Ruth did as she was instructed, and soon her pale, frightened face popped out of the top of the rubber tent. The nurse pulled a cord on the flap and the laces tightened, sealing it tightly together. She put a thermometer in Ruth's mouth and waited a minute, then removed it.

"Perfectly normal," she said. "Ninety-eight-point-six degrees, on the nose."

Ruth nearly burst out laughing, but quickly turned her smile into a grimace. "I feel cold, though," she said.

"You're probably a little nervous. And, of course, you're undressed. That's quite typical. As soon as I start the heat, you'll feel better." She turned a handwheel mounted near one of the bottom corners of the rubber chamber. "Do you feel that?" she asked Ruth. "It's nice hot steam."

"Yes, I do. Very nice. I'm much warmer already."

"Then you have nothing further to do but to relax. I'll take your temperature again in a little while."

Ruth's face grew a little redder as the minutes passed, and small beads of sweat began to appear on her forehead.

"Are you feeling warmer?" the nurse asked.

"Yes, I'm quite warm now," Ruth said. "Not bad, though."

"You're doing wonderfully," Annie said, smiling at her.

"I feel like one of your steamed dumplings," Ruth said.

"Mine are nothing compared to yours. Yours are scrumptious."

"I'll make some for Sunday dinner, if you like."

The nurse took Ruth's temperature again. "You're at 102 now." She opened the steam valve a little more.

"I'm glad I'm sitting down, at least," Ruth said. "I'm feeling rather dizzy."

"Can we give her a glass of water?" Annie said.

"I'm sorry, but no. That would cool her down inside and make this take all the longer."

"I feel sick to my stomach," Ruth announced after her temperature was gauged at 103 degrees. She was sweating profusely now.

"That's normal," the nurse said. "Only a little more to go."

"This is rather distressing," Annie said quietly to the nurse.

After another ten minutes, Ruth mumbled something.

"What did you say, dear?" Annie said.

"I'm . . . cold," she said.

"Has the steam stopped working?" Annie asked the nurse.

"Quite the opposite," she said. "When the body gets very warm, patients often have chills. Let me take her temperature again."

"One hundred five," she said, looking at the thermometer and nodding, which made her nose wobble strangely. "That's where we want you. Now we keep you there for an hour."

"I don't know if I'll last an hour," Ruth stammered, her head lolling. "I feel awful."

"Stay with it, Sister," Annie said. "You can do it." Ruth nodded weakly.

Fifteen minutes passed, with Ruth's temperature holding at 105. She was silent now, and seemed to be drifting in and out of consciousness.

"Is this normal?" Annie inquired of the nurse.

"Completely, yes."

Ten minutes later, Ruth's eyelids fluttered open. "I think—" she gurgled, and then vomited profusely on top of the rubber chamber.

"Good heavens!" Annie said, jumping up. "What—"

"Did she eat supper?" the nurse asked with some irritation.

"Yes, some," Annie said.

"She wasn't supposed to eat before this. Didn't you read the instructions?"

"We didn't get any instructions! We were told to come here tonight at the appointed hour, and that's what we did."

"Then that was an oversight. I had best ask Dr. Porter if we ought better to stop the treatment." She knocked on the doctor's door, went in quickly, and was back in a moment. She bent over and turned off the steam.

"We'll have to suspend tonight's treatment," she said. "The doctor feels it will be too great a strain to continue if she's vomiting. Next time, nothing to eat after lunch, please."

"I understand," Annie said. "I'm terribly sorry. We didn't know."

Ruth's head rolled backward and she started to heave again. The nurse reached over the top of the rubber shroud and pulled Ruth's head upright, just as Ruth again vomited copiously.

"I have to steady her head," the nurse said to Annie. "Unfasten the flap, will you?"

Annie unlaced the flap. "Now switch with me, and hold her head upright," the nurse said. "We can't let her vomit go down her throat, or she'll suffocate. I'm going to get her out."

She ducked under the flap and pulled Ruth out of the chair. The young woman's head disappeared through the hole in the rubber, and at least a quart of vomit poured down into the vacant opening, as though a sink stopper had been removed. "Help me!" the nurse called. "Help me pull her out."

Annie went under the flap and helped the nurse pull on Ruth's legs, until her limp, naked form was lying prone next to the pyrotherapy chamber. Ruth was slick with vomit, as was Annie, and when the nurse struggled out of the rubber tent, her nose had been knocked askew and was now positioned over one cheek. Annie tried not to, but she reflexively looked away from the sight of the holes in the center of the young nurse's face, where a nose ought to have been.

"How mortifying," the nurse said quietly, hurriedly adjusting her prosthesis. "This is something one never grows accustomed to."

"I'm so sorry," Annie said.

"We all have our crosses to bear. Attend to your sister while I fix this thing."

Annie patted Ruth's cheeks, but her sister was out cold, breathing shallowly. Once the nurse's nose was back in good order, she quickly retrieved a couple blankets from a cabinet against the wall and laid them over Ruth's body.

"She'll cool down quickly now," the nurse said. "Best to let her lie here for a little while. I'll clean her up."

Between the tile floor and the cool cloth the nurse used to wipe the vomit off her skin, Ruth's eyes soon fluttered open.

"What happened?" she said to Annie, who was hovering over her.

"You got sick, that's all. We didn't know you weren't supposed to eat supper."

"Is that what that smell is?"

"I'm afraid so."

"You mean I puked in the chamber?"

"More *on* the chamber than anything, but when we took you out, a lot went down inside."

"I'm so sorry," Ruth groaned.

"I'll clean it up," the nurse said. "Don't concern yourself. It's part of the job." She turned to Sarah. "Now that your sister's come around again, let's get her dressed."

When the two finally managed to get Ruth dried and dressed, the young woman sat weakly on Annie's guest chair. The room reeked of damp rubber and vomit.

"I think I'm going to be sick myself, if I don't get out of here soon," Annie said. "Does the doctor want to see us before we go?"

"No, he said to come back next week at the same time, and we'll resume treatment. And remember—"

"I know. No supper," Annie said.

The bedraggled nurse nodded, her nose only slightly out of beat.

The Gluck Building

THE HEADQUARTERS OF THE ABRASIVE WORKERS UNION WAS located on the fifth floor of the Gluck Building, a brutal rose-brick structure fronting Falls Street in downtown Niagara Falls. The Gluck, like every building along the main drag of the tourist district, was built atop ground-floor shops with elaborate window displays. Also like every one of its neighbors, the Gluck's aesthetic appeal stopped at the ground floor.

Above the shop windows were four stories of flat, unadorned masonry. The center section of the building was set back, recessed behind and flanked by massive oblong blocks of yet more identical brick, each topped by a pyramidal grey slate roof, unrelieved with dormer windows. To complete the collection of architectural oddments, there was an unlikely-looking Roman-style marble arch set to one side of the central section of the building, throwing the whole thing out of balance. The effect of the entire Gluck Building was that of an edifice built by a committee of architects, none of whom could agree on a single theme and who had instead contented themselves with contributing one idea each, and probably their worst.

Sarah entered through the marble arch, reasoning correctly that it must lead into the recessed section of the building, which connected the twin pyramid-topped towers. Inside, she consulted an office directory on the wall and located two elevators that squared off against each other in a cold, shadowy lobby. The elevators, too, were an incongruity in such an uninspiring building—each a new automatic Otis, brass polished to a mirror sheen, and yet almost entirely hidden from view.

An office on the fifth floor of the Gluck wouldn't have been too bad, though, had it overlooked bustling Falls Street, from which perch one could have watched the tourist trolleys crawling by below like scarabs. But the offices of the ABW were situated along one side of the building, with no better view than the rooftop of a soot-stained, yellow-brick building next door. She rapped gently on the glass, and soon a figure wavily appeared behind the pane, and the door opened.

"Well, hello," a man in a bold pinstripe suit said, looking Sarah up and down without the slightest attempt to conceal his interest. "And how may I help *you*?"

"I'm Sarah Price. From the *Buffalo Guardian*. I've arranged a conference with Mr. Brass."

The door swung open wide and the man stepped to one side. "I'm Aaron Brass," he said. "And very pleased to meet your acquaintance. I have to say I didn't expect *you*."

"Have I mistaken the time?" she said, looking at her pendant watch. "I thought sure we'd said ten o'clock—"

"Oh no," he said, gesturing her toward a shabby table in the middle of the equally shabby office. He heaved a pile of what looked to be handbills off the table and set them down on the board floor, scaring up a little bloom of dust. "You have the time right. You just don't look like a union lady."

"How's that?" Sarah said, sitting and taking out her notebook.

"No one's ever told you that you're a hell of a lot easier on the eyes than most of the hags in the labor movement?"

"That's not much of a compliment. But no, I don't suppose anyone has."

"You seen Emma Goldman? Jesus Christ, homely as a mud fence."

"None of us has any say in our looks," she said. "Purely an accident of birth."

"Then I hope I crash into more like you along," Brass said, still ogling her. "Get it? Accident."

She ignored his question and opened her notebook. "Shall we make a beginning, Mr. Brass?"

"Sure thing," he said, taking a gold cigarette case and a match safe from his vest pocket. He flipped open the case with a well-practiced flick of the thumb, and held it out.

"Would you like a cigarette?" he said.

"No, thank you. I don't smoke."

"Lot of women are taking it up these days," Brass said, selecting one for himself. "In fact, so many of 'em that you got to ask, or some of 'em will get offended if you don't. I never know what to do with ladies anymore." He struck a match and flamed his smoke, inhaling deeply and looking appreciatively at the ash.

Aaron Brass was still a young man, lean, midthirties perhaps, but with the dark leathery skin of an old book binding. He had a full head of curly black hair, cropped close to his skull, and intense hazel eyes, set deep in their sockets. His distinguishing feature, though, was the penetrating acrid smell of stale cigarette smoke. Tobacco—acres of it—had stained his fingernails and teeth the color of old ivory. In general, he possessed a slightly desiccated air that made him look as though he had been hung up in a smokehouse.

"I don't suppose you mind if I smoke?" he said. "I probably should have asked that, too."

"Not at all," she said, although wishing he might smoke slightly less aggressively. He seemed to produce enough fumes for a whole roomful of smokers, and in three long draws, he had already smoked the current cigarette so far down that it looked as though he was pinching a glowing ember between his fingers. Yet he unflinchingly held on to the tiny spark as he took a last puff, squinting as he stubbed out what little was left in an overflowing ashtray.

"Must say that I don't know your newspaper," he said, exhaling reluctantly. "Though when you called, I figured it was worth taking a flyer. We can use all the publicity we can get."

"It's new. Our focus is on labor matters. The *Guardian* is a working man's paper."

"Did you bring a copy?"

Sarah hadn't thought of this. "I'm terribly sorry. I came up to Niagara Falls last evening, and I didn't think to bring one with me."

"I'll find one at the newsstand. But what's a woman doing at a working man's paper?"

"Working women have it worse than working men, Mr. Brass."

He took out another cigarette from the open case, tapped it on the table, and lit it. He pulled on it hard and laughed, huffing out smoke.

"Can't say I disagree. So what can I do for you today"—he glanced expertly at her ring finger—"*Miss* Price?"

"As I mentioned on the telephone, we'd like to do an article about you and your union."

"And like I said, I appreciate your interest," he said, picking a shred of tobacco from the end of a purplish tongue that looked like a small eggplant. "What can I tell you?"

"First, let me make sure I have your name correct," Sarah said. She poised her pencil. "First name spelled with two *A*'s?"

"That's right."

"And the last name is 'Brass,' like the metal?"

"Yup, that's what I go by nowadays."

"Is that not your name?"

"Get this part down—it'll be good for your article. When my parents brought me here from the old country as a kid, guess what? My name was Urinov Brazhnik. But who wants a handle like that in America, right? I mean, *Urinov*. Can you imagine?"

Sarah's pencil traced over her notepad.

"You take shorthand," he stated, craning his neck to see. The tiny movement caused a fresh ripple of stale smoke to wash over her.

"It comes in very handy in my line of work."

"I'll bet it does. You ever think about giving up this line of work?"

"I like my job."

He smiled his yellow smile. "Too bad," he said. "I'm looking for a secretary—but haven't found the right girl. I'd pay you well."

"That's very kind, but I enjoy writing for the paper. Now then, Mr. Brass—"

"I wish you'd call me Aaron."

"Thank you. Now then. How did young Urinov Brazhnik become Aaron Brass?"

He looked at her, puzzled. "Um, I picked the name out myself. Made it up."

"No, I'm sorry—I meant in a larger sense. What made you decide to go into the union field?"

He stubbed out his cigarette, looked at the case thoughtfully, and immediately lit a third. He waved the match to extinguish it, and Sarah could taste the warm sting of sulfur. "It was a cop who steered me into it," he chuckled, squinting and hissing out smoke.

"You don't say?"

"Yeah, it's true. I was a troublemaker as a kid. Always raising hell. One time, a friend of mine and I lifted a few things from a store, and damned if there wasn't a cop standing right outside. Saw the whole thing! He grabbed me by the collar and told me that the next time I got into trouble, I'd go to jail. I figured I'd better find something else to do."

"You still like to raise hell?"

"You write for a labor paper, Miss Price. What do you think?"

"I don't like to write my own opinions," she said.

"I could tell you a lot more of the story over supper."

"Mr. Brass." She gave him a pretty pout. "Do you really think that would be appropriate?"

Brass tittered. "Please, it's Aaron. I'm serious. Come out with me. I'll bet you've never seen the *real* Niagara Falls."

"If I'm not mistaken, you're wearing a wedding ring, Mr. Brass."

"And you're not. So long as one of us isn't, everything's copacetic. Why aren't you married, anyway?"

"I used to be," Sarah said.

"What happened?"

"He died."

"Hell of a shame," Brass said.

"For him, or for me?"

"You're snappy. I like you."

"You like my looks," Sarah said.

"So? What's wrong with that? If I looked in the mirror every morning and saw what you do, I'd be pretty pleased with myself."

"I'll try to remember that next time I dress," Sarah said. "Now then, why did you choose to lead the Abrasive Workers Union? And not some other one? A bigger one?"

"You're all business, that's for sure," Brass said wistfully. "Fine. You know how hard it is to get anywhere in the big unions? The Wobblies, the Teamsters? Forget it. Guys are lined up ten deep trying to be the next fellow to run the place."

He took a last, deep drag on his cigarette, so hard that Sarah could hear the tobacco crackle. "The ABW was small when I got my foot in the door. Still is on the small side, but we're going places." He moved a pile of cigarette remains out of the way to mash out the current one, and Sarah could have sworn he was hoping he hadn't abandoned anything usable.

"The whole abrasives industry has exploded," he said. "Because of electricity. And where is there more electricity than in Niagara Falls?"

"Are you finding it easy to expand the ABW, then?"

"Sometimes easy, sometimes not. The coal miners' strike didn't do the unions' reputation any good, but then you had other actions where strikebreakers came in and cracked heads and so on, so that balanced it out. Sympathywise. For us, the big break came when we harpooned the whale last year—Carborundum—and now it's just cleaning up the rest, one by one. The holdouts."

"Can you give me an example?" Sarah said. "Of a holdout?"

"The biggest one left is Kendall Abrasives." Brass motioned over his shoulder with a thumb. "On the High Bank. If we get them, the rest will fall. But business is good, so it's been tough to organize there."

"Why would that be?"

"Hey, when things are good, who complains?" Brass said, shrugging. "Kendall pays his men top wages and treats them like human beings. When we send our organizers in there, we have no luck at all. But give it time. We'll get our chance."

"What will it take to get that chance, Mr. Brass?"

He squinted at her, studying her face. "When Kendall stumbles, as he will eventually."

"Understood, I think," Sarah said, scribbling in her notebook. "When you say 'stumbles'—"

Brass frowned and stuck a fresh cigarette in his mouth. He lit it and blew a billow of blue smoke toward the ceiling. Sarah was relieved, until in blowing out the match he emptied the other lung in her direction.

"You're asking some pretty specific questions," he said.

"I'm merely trying to understand your strategy."

Aaron Brass winked at her again, a horrid little convulsive wink. "Some things don't belong in the newspaper." He sucked on his smoke. "But I like to get the word out when I can, so I'll make you a deal."

"What kind of deal?"

"You agree to take supper with me, and I'll tell you more about my strategy."

"As I said, I don't think that would be appropriate."

"I'll give you a good story."

"I'm sure you would," she said.

"Then how about next Friday?"

Sarah put away her notebook. "If that's what it will take, Mr. Brass."

"That's what it will take," he said. "How about seven o'clock at The Oaks Restaurant? You know it?"

"I'm sure I can find it."

"You can't miss it. It's right on Falls Street. When you get there, ask for me. I keep a little private table in the back of the place."

"PHEW," CHRISTINE SAID WHEN Sarah walked into the parlor. "I could smell you from the doorway. Were you caught in a house fire?"

"Is it that bad?" Sarah said, sniffing her sleeve. "I think I must have gotten used to it."

"Trust me, it's bad. I don't think I've ever smelled anything quite like it."

"You've made your point. I'm going to get changed."

"You'll have to wash your hair, too."

Sarah rolled her eyes and left. On her way to the staircase, she spied Kendall studying the tape spewing out of his stock ticker, just inside his office. He looked up and motioned to her. At the office door, he greeted her with a slightly strange look, but didn't say anything more.

"I know I stink," she said.

"I didn't say that."

"No. But you didn't have to. I had my meeting with Aaron Brass, and the man smokes cigarettes like a chimney."

"Well, that explains it," Kendall said. "I thought you might have taken up the habit."

"Very funny. But it was time well spent."

"What did he have to say for himself?"

"He most definitely sees your company as his next target."

"He said that?"

"Not in so many words, but that was the gist of it."

"Anything about my water?"

"No. He's too cagey for that. But I'll find out more soon enough."

"How?" he said.

"Brass wants me to go out with him. To supper."

"To *supper*?"

"That's what I believe I just said, yes," she said, laughing.

"I don't think that's such a good idea."

"It's all in a day, Mr. Kendall. It's very fortunate that he's willing to talk. Who knows what I might find out."

"And you might get more than you bargained for. Aaron Brass is no gentleman."

"Oh, he made that abundantly clear."

"Well, then? Perhaps you can find out some other way?"

"If it will put your mind at ease, sir, Mr. Price will be shadowing me."

"Perhaps I ought to send Stefan, too."

"Mr. Kendall, please—let me do what you are paying me to do, and don't worry."

He blushed. "I'm not *worried*."

"Good," she said. "Because I'm determined to get Aaron Brass to tell me where your water's going. And I'll do whatever it takes to do it."

The Way to a Woman's Heart

ALMOST OVERNIGHT, THE KENDALL CONTRACT HAD TURNED black the sea of red ink that had threatened to overwhelm Miller Envelope. And Alicia's copywriting skills hadn't been oversold—in the days after the very first batch of letters had gone out, new orders had tripled. There could be no mistake: Alicia Miller promised to be the best salesman that Kendall Abrasives had ever had.

Yet good fortune hadn't led to good moods for the owners of Miller Envelope. Bert had been gone for more than a month now, and Alicia was missing the old fart, and it was making her a little blue. Howie, too, while generally happier than he'd been in a year—keeping his machines humming along steadily and with purpose—seemed to be strangely out of sorts. It was Alicia's phone that was ringing, Alicia who was cementing the existing client relationships, and—above all—Alicia's surname that was still painted on the top ten courses of brick along the top of the Cashton Building. The more business she brought in, the more it seemed like it would always be *Miller* Envelope Company, even though he owned two-thirds of it.

When Friday came around at last, though, no one could deny that it had been an unusually productive week. Plenty of new orders, steady production again, and workers who were too busy to stand around and complain. Around six o'clock, Allie and Howie were sitting in their office, weary after another long day. Abby had gone home a quarter hour earlier, and even she had seemed positively cheerful.

Alicia reckoned that if she didn't broach the topic, no one would. She leaned back in her chair and put her boots up on her desk, which always made Gaines take note.

"Why the long face, Gaines? After only a month or so, it seems we may just pull this thing out of the fire, after all. And yet you seem—well, a wee bit glum."

"I'm not glum," he said, rather glumly.

"I know glum when I see it."

"I'm not, really."

"You are, really. Come on. Tell me what's bothering you."

He rubbed his temples and looked out the window as he spoke. "I—I think I'm a little disappointed that I didn't—I couldn't do more, and things got to where they got. And then you come waltzing in here, and saved our bacon."

"And what possibly could be wrong with that? You and I agreed that I'd try my hand at sales, and I never questioned for an instant your ability in the factory. Seems to me that things are working out rather well. And especially since neither of us probably thought they would."

"I know," he said. "It makes no sense. I should be on top of the world."

"Then we need to do something to lift your spirits. Cheer you up. Let's talk about something you plan to enjoy doing this weekend."

"I'll probably stay home and read. There are some adjustments to the glue feeder that I'll come in here and make, so that come Monday, we can be up and running at full steam."

"Now that's just *sad*," she said. "Reading? All weekend? And adjusting a machine. Really, Gaines, you need to get out more."

"Well, what are you going to do, if you know so much?"

"Bert's still away in Hamburg. So I suppose I'm in no position to criticize you for being boring. I'll likely be even more bored than you."

He craned his head around to make sure Abby was gone. "There is one other thing that keeps—bothering me," he said quietly.

"Then you'd better tell me, partner. Don't keep it bottled up."

"It's a little difficult to talk about."

"Come on, Gaines, quit stalling," she said. "Out with it."

"All right. Well, you remember that time that—we . . ." He trailed off. "*You know.*"

"Fucked?" she said.

"In a manner of speaking," Gaines replied, "yes. I must admit that since then, I've been rather down in the dumps over my—I don't know how to put it—my *performance*. I humiliated myself."

"Oh, Howie, it was nothing. Like I said, just jitters. And it had probably been quite some time since you had any."

"That's certainly true," he said, looking away again. "But—I don't have—well, I'm a little embarrassed to admit that I don't have a *lot* of experience."

"You said you'd done it before."

He leaned forward. "I had—I mean, of course I have. Loads of times. But not with anyone like *you*. I never had occasion to learn much about what's good and what's not."

"I understand." She was quiet for a few seconds. "Then I have a suggestion."

"What's that?" he said, now feeling mortified by his admission.

"You do your reading and your glue adjusting in the forenoon on Saturday. I'll come over to your apartment around midday, and we'll pick up where we left off. I'll show you a few little things. I *was* married for almost twenty years, after all. What do you say?"

Gaines stared at her, uncomprehending. "Are you serious? You'd *do* that? For *me*?"

She looked at him steadily. "Don't sell it back, Howie."

ON SATURDAY, ALICIA DECIDED to take advantage of a beautiful day—cold and clear—and walk from Ashwood Street to Howie Gaines's apartment downtown. Buffalo was blessed with a rare blue sky, and the wind had shifted, blowing all the factory smoke out over the lake, toward Cleveland.

Bert's not going to be happy about this, she thought as she strolled. But I'd be a fool not to press my advantage, when I can. And besides, a girl's entitled to a little fun.

When Howie answered her knock, he was in trousers, shirtsleeves, and stocking feet, and his face looked redder than usual. "Do come in," he said, as grandly as he could, and stepped aside.

"Do you typically entertain ladies in such modest attire?"

"No," he replied. "I mean, I don't really entertain ladies here much."

"Well, if you are going to be schooled, then the first lesson is that you must dress appropriately, whether you're expecting a call or not. Now go and put on a proper tie, vest, jacket, and shoes. Chop-chop."

He hustled over to his wardrobe and began getting himself dressed. He seemed to have gone to considerable effort to tidy the place up, at least. From Alicia's vantage point, it looked as though the bed had been made, with a clean coverlet placed on top. The floors had been scrubbed and mopped, and even the previously stale air smelled faintly of cologne.

When Howie was done dressing, he strode over to her and held out his arms at his sides. "There. Is that better?"

"Much," Allie said. "You look very handsome. And tell me the truth—now don't you feel more like a man who's likely to impress a woman enough to coax her into your bed?"

"I confess I do."

"You learn quickly, Howie Gaines. That's encouraging. Now are you going to take my wraps, and invite me to sit?"

"Oh, of course," he stammered. "Sorry about that. May I?" He took her things and showed her to an overstuffed chair.

"A lady doesn't sit in this kind of chair, my dear."

"Why not?"

"Corset," she said. "We ladies have to sit upright. If I lean back into that plush, I'll never get out again without assistance, which is undignified. A straight-backed chair is always the appropriate choice for a lady visitor."

He pulled one of his dining chairs from under the table and arranged it for her. She sat down gracefully.

"Next, you offer me something to drink," she said. "Lemonade is always favored."

"Um, I don't have lemonade."

"What do you have?"

"I could make some coffee," he said.

"Coffee is not the thing to drink if you want to be close to a woman's face."

"Then I am afraid I don't have anything."

"Wine? Liquor?"

"I have some whiskey."

"Well, fetch it," she said. "But only because I know you. Do *not* offer spirits to any other lady. Understand?"

"Yes, I do," he said, getting a couple fairly clean glasses and a bottle of whiskey. He poured quite a bit into her glass, handed it to her, and sat down facing her in another chair from the table.

"Thank you, Gaines. And again, this is fine for me, but this would be three times the amount of whiskey you ought to offer to a lady. If you did at all, that is."

They sipped the whiskey, and Allie was surprised to discover that it was of rather decent quality.

"You've done a very nice job of tidying up," she said.

"Thank you. I spent most of last night and part of this morning doing it."

"Good. Now then, do you like my outfit? You should always compliment a lady on her attire."

"You look beautiful," he said, and meant it.

"You know what's special about my dress today?"

"No."

"Look," she said. She lifted her skirts slowly, to reveal nothing underneath.

"Oh no," he said, squirming. "May we get going?"

"Now, that's hardly a graceful way to entice me, and besides, I haven't even finished my glass of whiskey. But I *will* give you your next lesson, while I do."

"What's that?"

"Come over here and kneel between my knees."

He complied, looking up at her with a beet red face.

"Stick out your tongue," she said.

"My tongue?"

"This will be a lot easier if you don't question everything."

"Fine," he said, and stuck out his tongue.

"Very nice," she said, examining it. "Now here's what you do. I want you to take that handsome tongue of yours and run it between my legs."

"Between your *legs*?" he said, astonished.

"Howie, really. You're not that dense."

"Are you serious?"

"Do I look like I'm joking?" she said, opening her legs wider. "Now get your head under my skirt and do what I say. And follow my instructions while you do."

He bent forward cautiously, and Allie felt his tongue brush against her, gingerly.

"Harder," she said. "You have to be more decisive."

He popped out from under her skirt with a frightened look. "Are you sure this is even *legal*?"

"Gaines. I've told you what you need to do. I'm showing you the way to a woman's heart. Pay attention and do what I say."

"All right," he said, and descended again.

"Good, that's better. Much better." She sat back and closed her eyes. "You're not half-bad at this," she murmured. "Now keep doing it, just like that."

"For how long?" his muffled voice inquired.

"It depends." She gulped down the rest of her glass of whiskey and threw her head back, looking at the ceiling and focusing on the dance of Gaines's tongue. He really is pretty goddamn good at this, she thought.

He emerged a few minutes later, massaging his jaw. "How much longer should I keep at it?"

She wanted to smack him on the top of the head. "What's with all the questions? For God's sake. I'm getting close."

"Close to what?"

"Will you shut up and get back at it?" she almost yelled. He disappeared under her skirt again.

"Here we go, Gaines," she said in another minute. "Do not stop. Do not even *think* of stopping. I don't care if your damn jaw falls clean off."

He made some muffled grunt and kept going steadily. Amazing, she thought. Really.

"Here it is," she hissed. "Oh, fuck, fuck, fuck, this is good." She grabbed the back of his head and thrust her pussy forward into his face. "Come on, that's it. Yes. I'm almost—"

Then everything went blank in her head, and she very nearly toppled backward in the chair. "You can stop now," she gasped.

He reemerged, tie askew.

"Was that all right?" he said.

She blinked slowly a couple of times, trying to focus.

"Is that *really* the first time you've done that?" she said hoarsely.

"Yes. I don't even know what you call—whatever that is."

"I'd call it either beginner's luck or raw talent. You'll have ladies lining up outside your door, if word gets out."

"Really?"

"Gaines," she said, evening out her breathing, "not one in a hundred men—a thousand—could have managed that. Well done. Credit where credit's due, as someone once said to me."

Howie beamed. "That's terrific. Now, um—" His eyes strayed toward the bed.

"Yes, it's your turn. Get out of those duds, and we'll get on with the next lesson."

"Oh good!" he said, and began stripping.

Alicia unbuttoned her skirt and put it on the chair, then took off her shirtwaist, corset, and camisole. When she turned around again, he was already naked, standing at full attention.

"You poor, poor man," she said, cupping his balls.

"What is that around your neck?"

"It's an ouroboros," she said, touching it. "A snake eating its own tail."

"What does it signify?"

"Gaines, would you prefer to talk about jewelry, or get busy?"

"Get busy."

"I thought so."

AFTERWARD, THEY LAY THERE for a while, looking at the ceiling.

"Was that—was I better this time?" he asked.

"Much. Solid progress, Gaines. Very credible effort."

"Alicia?" he said, after another long pause.

"Um hmm," she said drowsily.

"May I ask you a question?"

"Go right ahead."

"Should I have told you I love you?"

"Why in the world would you do that?" she said, laughing softly. "You don't love me, Howie. I'm not even sure you *like* me."

"It seems like something that one ought to say, that's all."

"Oh, Howie. That's fairy-tale stuff. But I will say that it gives you a certain charm that you think that way."

ON HER WAY HOME from Howie's apartment, Alicia was looking forward to a long, hot soak. She felt pleasantly spent. After a few more whiskeys, they'd done it a second time, and he'd proven himself a good student. She had made her excuses and slipped away after that, leaving him relaxing on top of the tangled bedclothes.

He's not much to look at, she thought, but then again, neither was Bert. But that wasn't the point. Howie had learned to take her direction, found he could trust her—after a fashion. But if a man had anything fragile about him, she thought, it was his sexual pride. And Gaines had gladly surrendered that to her, and she'd taken good care of it. That was not something he would forget. We both did just fine today, she thought with some satisfaction. This may work out, after all.

NEGOTIATIONS

On Monday, Alicia arrived at the office precisely at 7:30, yet Gaines had already beaten her there. He looked up from his desk and smiled warmly.

"Hello there," he said with unusually good cheer.

"Hello yourself. I trust you had a pleasant Sunday?"

He continued to smile, and sat up high in his chair to look over her and make sure Abby wasn't outside. "Not nearly so pleasant as Saturday was," he said. "If you take my meaning."

All Sunday she'd feared that Gaines would pull some sentimental horseshit—there was a look in his eye when she'd said goodbye on Saturday that she recognized all too well. It was the look of all men: momentarily grateful for having been fucked, but already scheming the next one. She wanted to slap the smirk off his face, but instead managed a bland smile.

"Howie, I hope you're not planning to bring that up every five minutes."

His smile disappeared. "It's just that I kept thinking about—*you*, all the rest of the weekend. And this morning, too."

She sat down behind her desk and picked up her copy of the *Buffalo Commercial*. "You do understand that we mustn't talk about this while we're at work," she said, opening it to the editorial page, which she always found amusing. "It's not the place."

"Alicia, if you don't mind—"

"What is it, Gaines? I'd like to spend ten minutes reading the paper, and then I have a lot of work to do today. I'm off to Niagara Falls tomorrow, to see Kendall again."

"It's only this," he said. "I keep thinking about what you said—about how I don't love you."

"So? It's the truth."

"I'm not so sure." He leaned toward her, his chair creaking.

"Come on, Gaines, what's on your mind? This is excruciating. And I'm a little hungover, too, so I'm officially not in the mood for suspense. Spit it out."

"Simply put," he said, wringing his hands, "I believe I may have fallen in love with you. There it is!"

She looked at the ceiling and exhaled hard. "Oh, for fuck's sake, Howie. You haven't fallen in love with me. You and I—"

"If that's so, then why can't I stop thinking about you?"

"Because you shot your *load* in me, you idiot—Abby, is that you out there?" she said as they heard the sound of a phony throat clearing.

"Yes, ma'am," Abby said, easing her very red face around the door-jamb. "I'm sorry I'm a few minutes late."

"No problem at all, dear. Perhaps you could fetch us some coffee?"

"Happy to, ma'am," Abby said. "Um, shall I close this door in the meantime?"

Alicia looked at Gaines and rolled her eyes. "No, you may leave it open."

When Abby had left to go downstairs to the kitchen, china cups clinking in distant haste, Alicia glared over at Gaines.

"Why do you have to be such a moron?" she said. "See what I mean? We're chatting away about your load, and—God—*falling in love*, of all things, while the goddamn secretary's listening at the keyhole. Jesus!"

"Well, how was I supposed to know she was out there? She must have been wearing gum-soled shoes when she came in. I was telling you something important. That I love you."

"Gaines," she said, still glaring, "if you keep on like this, there will be positively no more fucking. I am not about to have you go all gooey on me just because we had a little fun. Trust me on this—you don't love me, and I most assuredly do not love you. Naturally, everyone feels a bit sentimental after doing it, but it's not *love*. Do we understand each other?"

"If you say so. But I don't know how you can tell me what I feel is wrong."

She put her head into her hands. "God, why me?" she mumbled. She looked up at him. "Look, Gaines—"

"You have newsprint on your cheeks now. It's cute!" He took out his handkerchief and half stood. "Here, let me get that off for you."

"Will you sit down!" she growled. "Don't you dare come over here and start wiping my goddamn face. If you want something to wipe, wipe that shit-eating grin off yours, and we'll be getting somewhere. Have you completely lost your marbles?"

"Coffee's here," said Abby's tremulous voice from the doorway.

"Just put it on the bookcase," Alicia said.

"Sorry I brought it up," Howie muttered, getting up to retrieve their coffee. "I thought you'd be happy."

"Imagine for an instant how I feel," she said through gritted teeth, as he set her cup down on her desk. "As if my reputation in this city—such as it is—wasn't sufficiently in tatters, you have to get me in more trouble. This hole is getting so deep that I'll never see the sun again."

"I said I was sorry. You said I ought to be honest."

"Don't be so thick," she said. "Thank heavens I have to go to the Falls tomorrow. You'll have all day to spoon all by yourself."

"Why do you have to see Kendall again so soon?"

"He has introduced me to two more prospects, whom I'll meet tomorrow as well. With any luck, you'll be running those machines of yours two shifts a day soon."

"You'll charm them, I'm sure." He dropped his voice. "You look stunning, if I may say."

"Will you *stop*?" she said.

THE NEXT DAY, ALICIA was getting ready to leave the office for the Yellow Car trolley to Niagara Falls when a telegram arrived with the news that Bert would be coming home on Thursday. The old fart's finally had his fill of country living, she thought. She left the telegram open on her desk, hoping that Howie might get curious and read it.

The benches in her Yellow Car were shiny with fresh varnish, and with the windows sealed shut, the concentrated reek of curing varnish was strong enough to make her feel a little dizzy—though it might as well have been her lingering hangover from the night before.

After turning out the lights at ten o'clock, she'd lain in bed for another hour, staring at the ceiling while sleep eluded her. Giving up, she'd tiptoed downstairs, past Ed's den—it still seemed unreal that he'd been *murdered* in there—and into the pantry, where, after some cursing and clattering around, she'd scrounged up a half bottle of cheap brandy that Melissa used for cooking. There hadn't been a clean glass in sight, so she'd taken a coffee cup upstairs with her bottle, and then sat at her dressing table, drinking and looking at herself in the mirror by the sifted glow of the streetlamps outside. This tastes like pure, unadulterated shit, she thought, but it'll do the job, and after three coffee cups brimful of the stuff, her head was spinning like a top, and she had grown more than a little morose.

It was at such times that Arthur's memory gnawed most at her, and his brutal, stupid, pointless death. Had he been thinking of her when the end came, when the Empire State Express had turned him into lifeless pulp? She'd never know, and that was not the only certainty that had died with him and left her adrift in mystery. Work, and sex, and booze were useful distractions, but how long would they serve? Not so very long ago, two stiff drinks had brought welcome oblivion—now it took three or four. Where does it end, she thought—eight? Ten?

There had been a time, one orange sunset beneath the rafters of their favorite trysting place on Whitney Place, when she and Arthur had promised each other that when the noose tightened around them, they would take morphine and drift off peacefully to sleep together. And on his final day, when there had been no escape from the trap he had set for himself, he had been as good as his word. He had come calling. Yet she had turned away, and let him go on alone. It wasn't the first pledge she'd broken, to be sure, nor probably the last—but it was the only one that mattered.

Now, while Arthur slept his eternal sleep, she was punished with wakefulness, whether alone in her bed above Ed's cursed den or in a rattling, reeking, crowded trolley on the way to Niagara Falls, her relentless thoughts churning about what, precisely, had been the point of it all. For today, at least, the object had to be selling more envelopes, so she once again said goodbye to Arthur as the Yellow Car neared its Niagara Falls terminus. But she knew he would return.

"MRS. MILLER, HOW DELIGHTFUL to see you again!" Kendall said, coming around his desk to shake Alicia's hand.

"The pleasure is all mine, Mr. Kendall," she said.

"Please, sit. I have some good news for you. I wanted to tell you in person."

"I can't wait to hear. Everyone well at home, I trust? Your darling daughter?"

"Oh yes, Christine's her usual self. Full of—oh, I'm sorry, I'm forgetting myself."

"Piss and vinegar?"

Kendall laughed. "I'm terribly sorry, Mrs. Miller. I was raised in the poor Irish part of New London, and I suppose I've not been able to leave it entirely behind."

"Well, I was raised a stone's throw from the ditch they call the Erie Canal, and I don't mind telling you, those boatmen are pretty salty types. I'm not easily shocked."

"I can imagine. That's still a rough part of Buffalo."

"I think it's worse now than it was when I was a girl. Fewer canal types, but the ones who have hung on are the mean ones."

"What a fascinating life you've had, Mrs. Miller, and for such a young woman, too. Your success in business does you enormous credit."

"High praise indeed, sir, but it can't compare to your own."

"I've been lucky more than anything," he said. "Right place, right time. Now then—are you ready for my good news? May I share it with you?"

Men, she thought. It's like Gaines asking me if he could come yet. Am I really going to say no? And would it matter if I did?

"Of course you may. Please do!"

"Your second letter campaign was even more successful than the first. So much so, I would like to do an additional mailing each month— this time in a different form, though. Perhaps a larger envelope, almost magazine size?"

She tapped a finger on his table. "An excellent idea. Magazine size will make it look like nothing else in the market. We include photographs of your works, and perhaps some testimonials from clients."

"Perfect," he said.

"I'll work up a quote for you."

He shifted in his chair. "On that score, I've been thinking—about proposing a different kind of relationship between us."

"Have you run it by Sarah?" she said with a little smirk.

He seemed confused. "Do you think she'd want to join in?"

Oh Christ, the man has no sense of humor, she thought, and now I'm in over my head.

"I suppose I am just so grateful she introduced us," she said. "I'm not sure what I was thinking. But in any case, do go on. I'm intrigued."

"Oh good. Then I'd like to suggest that we share in the risk and reward of this new experiment," he said. "You supply the envelopes and the copy. I will pay all the printing and postage. And you and I share in the revenues generated by the mailing."

"It's an excellent idea," she said. "How would you propose we split it?"

"I'm not entirely sure. My product, of course, costs much more than an envelope, so I was thinking perhaps your company would receive, say, fifteen percent of the take?"

"Fifty percent?" she said. "Yes, that sounds about right."

"Oh my, no," he said, his eyes opening wide. "I said fif*teen* percent. Not fifty."

"Mr. Kendall, if our companies were of similar size and equally well capitalized, fifteen might well be the right number. But a small company like mine will have to invest a disproportionate share of the initial capital. Money for new machinery that can produce a magazine-sized format. Cash upfront for new personnel to handle it all, if we're going to take it seriously. Which I know we'd both want to do."

"You do make a very fair point," he said. "What would you propose instead? I very much doubt my business manager would accept a fifty-fifty split."

"And I wouldn't dream of expecting it in perpetuity," she said. "But I might propose it for the first year. While I believe—deeply—that your idea will be profitable, you and I both know it'll take at least a year to find out. But whether our efforts succeed or fail, I will have fronted all that money. Hence I would suggest a fifty-fifty split for the first year, to allow me to make the necessary capital investments, after which my share would gradually decline to fifteen percent."

"Mrs. Miller, you are a genuine pleasure to work with. No nonsense about you. You have a deal. How soon can we get started?"

"I'll talk with my partner later today, or tomorrow at the latest. He's what he calls a machine-man."

"A machine-man?"

"Not like half man and half machine," Alicia said. "I think he means he has a feel for his machinery." She almost laughed out loud at this. "Anyhow, I don't meddle in his area, and he doesn't meddle in mine."

"Works out best that way."

"It does. I'll telephone you tomorrow and give you a firm schedule. And one other thing, Mr. Kendall, if I may?"

"Yes, Mrs. Miller?"

"I want to be able to focus entirely on delivering you the very best copy and envelopes that you've entrusted me to supply. We currently have a one-year arrangement for your regular supply, and hard as it may be to believe, we're already a month into that. Since we've had such considerable success together, I don't have to spend a minute of my time worrying about contracts instead of being focused on your business. So I'd like to extend our regular arrangement to run concurrently with the new, more speculative one. Four years."

He laughed. "Mrs. Miller—how can I refuse you?"

"I don't know. Can you?"

"No. Four years it is. Now tell me—do you have time for luncheon today? Something simple—to celebrate."

"I would love that, but—thanks to you—I have two new prospects elsewhere in Niagara Falls I must visit with today."

"Revenue comes first, last, and always, Mrs. Miller. I completely understand. You'll take a rain check, though, I hope?"

"I'll be looking forward to the rain for once, Mr. Kendall," she said.

PANDORA'S BOX

THERE WAS A SUDDEN, EARSPLITTING BURST OF STATIC ON the line.

"I can barely hear you, Sarah," Allie said. "This connection is terrible. It's like talking to someone at the North Pole, instead of Niagara Falls."

"I can hear you perfectly!" Sarah said at the top of her lungs.

"I called to thank you once again for the introduction to the handsome Mr. Kendall. It's really working out."

"You're very welcome!" Sarah yelled. "He told me he's buying lots of envelopes from you!"

"You don't have to shout. I can hear you now. The static's gone."

"Thank God. I don't know what I'd do without the telephone, but often I'd like to chuck the thing right out the window."

"Do you know who hated talking on the telephone?"

Don't say Edward, please, Sarah thought. Let's not get into that. "I don't. Who?"

"Arthur. Arthur Pendle."

"That's peculiar. He was such a well-spoken, even eloquent, man."

"In person, yes, but you should have heard him on the phone sometimes. It was pathetic. He'd say something foolish, and then get more and more nervous about his blunder, and more and more foolishness would come pouring out. He was much better at letter writing. As you know all too well, having read all of the ones he wrote to me."

"I said I was sorry I did that. I didn't know what else to do."

"I understand, dear. The only consolation I have is telling myself that a few of them must have made your hair stand on end."

"Allie—"

"Nothing more than curiosity about how another woman views certain things. I know what's in them, and I'll tell you it's *all true*. Can you believe it?"

"Speaking frankly, some of them *were* quite incredible. Oh, for heaven's sake—why are we talking about this?"

"Well, I do beg your pardon, Sarah. Isn't a girl allowed a little nostalgia every now and then? I need to tell *someone*. Look at what I've had since poor Arthur met his Maker. Bert. And now *Gaines*."

"*Howie* Gaines?" Sarah said.

"Yes, *that* Gaines. Though I may have let the genie out of the bottle with him."

"I don't know what to say to that."

"No, dear, how could you? Suffice it to say that old Gaines has caught the bug."

"Oh Lord."

Alicia laughed. "Did you know Bert calls my pussy 'Pandora's Box'? Isn't that funny?"

"It is rather droll," Sarah said.

"I'm glad you think so. By the way, how are things going up there?"

"Going along fine, I think."

"What about with Charlie? What's going on there?"

"You mean Mr. Kendall?"

"Of course I mean Mr. Kendall, silly. When I saw him recently, I swear I detected a slight gleam in his eye when I mentioned your name."

"Nothing's 'going on' with Mr. Kendall," Sarah said. "There's no *gleam*."

"You ought to have become a nun," Alicia said. "I sincerely don't know how you manage it. I find your self-restraint either admirable or deplorable, depending entirely on my mood."

"I didn't say there wasn't any man in my life."

"So he *has* fallen for you, after all! Well done, dear. If I do say so through gritted teeth."

"Mr. Kendall is my *client*, Allie. He's entirely off-limits."

"That's an artificial barrier, if there ever was one. Who is it, then? Your new beau?"

"He's a foreman in Mr. Kendall's factory. A man of very good background, too."

Silence.

"Allie? Are you there?"

Alicia's voice crackled back over the wire. "Well, it proves that beauty and brains don't go together, after all. Allow me to savor this for a moment. You've passed over *Charles Kendall*—handsome, rich Charlie Kendall—in favor of one of his *factory foremen*? I must say, you are truly a wonder."

"Money and power aren't everything, you know," Sarah said indignantly.

"Who says? I'll tell you this, if I were in your shoes, living in that dreamy man's house, seeing him every day, brushing against him—why, inside of a week I'd be sitting on his *face*."

"Fortunately for us all, you're not in my shoes, Alicia."

"If you don't want him, then, I trust you won't mind if I show him a little attention?"

"I do mind, very much. We've had this conversation."

"True, but that was before you fell in love with"—she gave a throaty laugh—"a *factory foreman*. Sarah, it's going to be all I can do not to tell the other Ashwood ladies."

"Tell them what you like. I don't care. And I don't think you'd just throw Bert over. You're not so heartless as you like to make yourself out to be."

"Now, that is about the sweetest thing you've ever said to me, dear. And no, I wouldn't just throw him over. I would tell him, quite calmly, that I have a chance to snare *the* Charles Kendall. Bert's not stupid. He'd understand. He'd probably ask to become the man's attorney."

"Do as you wish, then, but just don't do it while I'm here. I don't need you pecking around while I'm trying to do my job."

"That's a very reasonable request," Allie said. "Anyhow, I have more than enough on my plate already without plopping yet another man on it."

"I can only dimly understand, I'm sure," Sarah said.

"Say, before I let you go. One of these evenings, when you come back to Buffalo—I want to have you over to the house."

"Whatever for?"

"My, how abrupt you can be! Because I like you, first off, and I want to thank you in person for introducing me to Charlie. But second, I want to see if I can get you good and drunk and get you talking about some of *your* secrets, for a change. You know so many of mine. But what do I really know about what makes Sarah Payne's heart throb?"

"I'm sure it wouldn't be nearly so fascinating as you imagine," Sarah said. "I don't have too many secrets anymore, and I'm happy that way."

"Better you than me. I think people without secrets are boring. Dull as dishwater. So in that spirit, may I share one other little secret with you?"

"I don't know, Allie. Is this something I need to hear?"

"I think you might. It's about you."

"All right, if I'm an interested party, let fly."

"When we get good and drunk, I'd like to see you naked."

"Oh, for God's sake, Alicia. Not this again."

"I'm quite serious. What I can see of you is so lovely, I can only imagine what the rest of the package is like. I wouldn't *do* anything, mind you, if you didn't want—just to *look* at you would be plenty."

"I'm hanging up now," Sarah said.

"It's a compliment," Allie said. "You really are that fetching."

"And I thank you for saying so. But mostly, I'm glad I could help you with the introduction to Mr. Kendall."

"A particularly deft valediction. Talk soon, dear. And do tell poor, neglected Charlie that Alicia blew him a kiss."

TEMPTATIONS

ALICIA QUIETLY HUNG UP THE EARPIECE AFTER HER TALK WITH Sarah. Pandora's Box, she thought, with a flat little smile. Never thought I'd miss that old fart so much. At the end of a day like today—a big expansion of the Kendall deal, two new prospects signing on—it would be nice to see him.

"Where's Mr. Gaines, Abby?" Alicia called out to the outer office.

"Still down in the factory, I think," the secretary said. "He told me something was malfunctioning."

"I'm going to go and find him," Allie said, getting up and walking past the secretary's desk. "I need to talk with him."

Abby nodded, wearing what seemed like a slightly snide grin. She's probably told everyone she knows about Gaines's *load*, Allie thought, walking down the corridor to the staircase. And probably thinks I'm hunting him down because I'm ready for another go. Which I am, if I'm being honest.

In the factory, Alicia found Gaines wearing a stained leather apron and leaning into the guts of one of his mechanical crustaceans.

"Hi there," he said when she walked up. "One of the poor girls threw a rod."

Alicia was tempted to make a joke, but again it seemed too soon. "Can you fix—her?"

"Oh yes. It's a little complicated, but that's all."

"Glad you're on the task, Howie."

"How did your day turn out?"

She filled him in.

"I dare say you're better at this than Ed was," he said. "Better at a *lot* of things," he said in a stage whisper.

"What did I tell you?"

"Sorry, it slipped out."

"And if you ever want to slip it back in, you'd better cease and desist."

"Yes, yes, I know. That's great news, though. Well done."

"Thanks. I did have a question, though. Do we have to buy a new machine to make envelopes the size of a magazine?"

"What kind of magazine? Six by nine, ten by twelve, ten by thirteen?"

"For fuck's sake, Howie, I don't know. A *magazine*."

"There are lots of different sizes," he faltered.

"I'll ask it a different way. Do we have a machine that will make the biggest of the envelopes you just rattled off?"

"Ten by thirteen. Absolutely. All these machines"—he waved his arm at the neat line of clattering mechanical choreography—"can make large or small. We simply change the settings and the steel-rule die that cuts and creases the paper."

"You don't have to buy a bigger machine?"

"Oh no. They're designed so that we can adjust them any way we like."

Fifty percent of the revenue, and no new investment, for a year, Allie thought. I'm going to start writing tonight.

WHEN ABBY LEFT FOR the day, Alicia was still at her desk with her hair down, finishing up a few quotations. She was pondering Kendall's new campaigns when Gaines returned from the factory, shirtsleeves still rolled up.

"Everything working again?" she asked.

"You look good with your hair mussed like that," he said. "It reminds me of Saturday."

She sighed and rolled her eyes, but felt a little shiver inside that gave her a start. She knew she was perilously close to caving in. For God's sake, Gaines, don't be so nice.

"Thank you. You've become quite the gentleman almost overnight."

"I have a good teacher."

"Hmm. So is everything fixed up?"

"Yes, I got the old girl running strong again."

That you seem to have done, she thought. Alicia put her feet up on her desk, half hoping that Gaines would look up her skirt and suggest another go. Instead, he glanced away demurely.

"That's good news," she said, unconvincingly. "And just in time, too. I'm going to call Kendall about the big envelopes. I'd like to tell him we can start producing soon."

"We could start this week," he said.

"There's one small problem with that. I told him we had to buy a new machine."

"Alicia, I told you—that's not so."

"I didn't know that at the time. I had to think on my feet."

"So tell him that we don't need one and can get started right away. He'll be happier."

"It's not so simple. I got him to agree to split the revenue fifty-fifty for the first year because we had to invest."

"Then there's only one solution," he said.

"Which is?"

"We buy a new machine that makes *only* large sizes. I've wanted one for years, but never had call for one. Now we do. Kendall will pay for the new machine, and you can then sell the bigger sizes to all the clients. As creative as you are, you can come up with ways they can use them."

"I like it," she said. "How long will it take to get a new machine ready to go?"

"If I place an order tomorrow, three or four weeks. Five, tops."

"Go ahead and do it. He's not going to back out now. I'll tell him we can start in six weeks."

They sat there in their office, watching dust motes floating through the slanting evening sunlight.

"I suppose I should be getting home," she said.

"Do you have to?"

She took a deep breath. "I have three children and a mother, Howie."

"And Bert will be back on Thursday, right?"

So he has read the telegram, she thought.

"I think so, yes."

"I probably won't see very much of you after that," Gaines moped.

"You'll see me every day in the office."

"No, I mean outside of that."

"Howie."

"I accept it, I do," he said. "But you had a wonderful day today, and I had a good day, too. And Bert's not back yet. Don't you think we deserve to celebrate a little bit?"

"I don't think it's a good idea. It'll only mix things up in ways that we don't want."

"I promise not to go gooey on you. You'll see. I can control myself." He smiled that odd little smirk again.

"Let's be content for now."

He's really not *that* bad-looking, she thought.

"What if we went to my apartment before you go home, and I could do that—thing—with my tongue, again? It would make you feel good, like you did before."

Alicia could feel something very dangerous stirring down below, and her resolve wavered. Maybe just this once? It would feel *so* good, and it *has* been a long day . . .

"Another time, Gaines," she said abruptly and stood, smoothing her skirt. "I need to be getting home now."

"Then maybe tomorrow? We'll have one more day."

She nodded. "Maybe tomorrow. We'll see."

"I won't touch myself tonight."

"Howie, please don't carry on so."

Alicia wished him a good night and hurried out of the office. Out on Division Street, she had gone only a half block toward the trolley station when, unaccountably, she burst into tears.

She bit her lip. What the *fuck*? I didn't cry at Edward's funeral, for Pete's sake, or by Arthur's grave. What the hell is wrong with me? Her skin crawled with the need to be touched, and none too gently, either. But by *Gaines*, of all people?

I must be losing my marbles, she thought, quickly brushing away the tears. This is stupid. She walked past the Division Street trolley stop, and on to Bernhardt's liquor store, where she purchased a pint bottle of Catherwood's whiskey, the good stuff.

SHE TUCKED THE PINT of Catherwood's into the bottom of a drawer in her wardrobe and cleaned up for dinner, which was unremarkable. Some nondescript stew, the chattering of the girls—how can they always be so cheerful, she wondered—and the background drone of her mother's endless gossip about the ladies of the Unitarian Church. Alicia smiled from time to time when one of the girls said something that was supposed to be funny, and parried her mother's jabs about what the other ladies had to say about women who had to *work*.

It was all very tedious, but it petered out eventually, as it did every evening. "Girls," she said as she was rising from the table, "is your homework all done?" desperately hoping that it was so. Fortunately, the homework had indeed been done, Mrs. Hall was tired—her creaky old bones, and so forth—and Allie was free to escape to her bedroom again. As usual, she stripped down, got out her writing notebook and a few pencils, and sat naked on the bed, writing in her diary. When it was quite dark, she drew the curtains, lit the gas, and got out the Catherwood's.

The Hotel Napoléon

AFTER MORE THAN A MONTH AWAY, BERT RETURNED FROM GLEN Creek Farm. He came through the front door of 101 Ashwood Street with a broad smile.

"Alicia!" he called. "I'm back!"

She trotted downstairs in a stunning dusty-rose velvet jacket and dark grey skirt. "Well, howdy, stranger. I was beginning to wonder if you'd ever return." She embraced him.

"You look beautiful. Are you happy to see me?"

"Of course I am. Can't you tell? I missed your stuffy old lawyerly self. Did you miss me?"

"More than you can know," he said.

"I'll bet you had to play with yourself a lot."

"That wasn't what I missed, Alicia. Well, not only that."

"Everyone's different, Bert," she said, hanging up his hat. "I know I nearly gave myself blisters. But that's me."

He laughed. "I have a proposition for you."

"The girls are upstairs doing homework, you rotten old man."

"Not that. If Melissa will make dinner for the girls and your mother, I want to take you out for dinner. Downtown. Maybe we can go to the theatre. And you can tell me all about your new job."

"That sounds delightful." She twirled around. "Am I dressed appropriately?"

"You'll be the tastiest dish on the menu."

BERT AND ALLIE GOT out of their carriage at the Hotel Napoléon, on Main Street.

"When was the last time you were here, Bert?"

"It's been a very long while. But I remember that the food was excellent then, so I thought we might give it a try."

"You know there was a man shot here two weeks ago," Alicia said. "An Italian, at that. This place has gone a bit to seed."

"It has?" he said. "That comes as a surprise. Ought we to find another spot?"

"No, it'll be an adventure. The food might still be good, however unsavory the clientele. And they have added an accent over the *e* in 'Napoleon.' That classes the place up a bit."

They went in and were seated at a corner table, in the back of the room. It was a cozy enough space, wood paneling and candlelight, though it did seem that most of the patrons were speaking Italian.

"I'm keeping my back to the wall, in case someone comes in firing," she said. "If I tell you to run for it, run for it."

"We don't have to stay, Alicia, if it's all that bad."

"I'm having fun with you, Bertie boy. We'll survive."

Their waiter walked up and nodded, but said nothing.

"Do you have a wine list?" Bert asked.

"We have Italian wine," the man said. "Chianti."

"Do you have Rhine wine?"

"No."

"Chautauqua?"

"*Italian.* Chianti."

"Then we'll have a bottle of the Chianti," Bert said cheerfully, and the waiter disappeared.

"You really charmed him," Alicia said. "And you speak excellent Italian, at that."

"Stop, will you? Are you going to poke fun at me all evening?"

"I haven't made up my mind yet. You have to admit, it is a bit funny. After your long absence, taking me out to a fancy dinner at a Mafia restaurant."

"Keep your voice down," he said. "They may not understand much English, but they know *that* word."

"They ought to—it's an Italian word. Now then. Did anything unusual happen in Hamburg?"

"Not a thing. It was very quiet, but I'm getting the old place into shape again. The roof needed replacing, and lots of other things I've been neglecting. We'll go there this summer, I hope."

"I can go on the weekends," she said. "My schedule is not my own anymore."

"Golly, I slipped. Of course."

"It's all new, Bert. It'll take some getting used to."

"How did your first month go? Are you and Gaines getting along?"

She pondered this for a second, and decided to wait until after some Chianti.

"Up and down," she said at last. "The first few days were a bit rocky. I had a look over the records, and the company is in considerable trouble." She explained to Bert the slowing flow of cash, the lack of new customers, the lax management. Meanwhile, the Chianti arrived— which really wasn't so bad—and Bert ordered an osso buco for the two of them.

"I confess I'm a bit stunned," he said, sipping his wine. "Gaines seems like such a solid character. But as you say, he's not a salesman. Ed could sell ice to the Eskimos."

"Maybe so, but I haven't told you the best part."

"Which is?"

"I have become the company's top salesman."

"Go on!"

"It's true. I got the bright idea to ask Sarah Payne to introduce me to her new beau, Charles Kendall. You know, *the* Charles Kendall. And not only did I have a conference with him, but I also landed the biggest deal in Miller Envelope history. And he's already introduced me to several of his rich friends. And they've signed on, too."

"Well done, my dear," Bert said, raising his glass.

"Thank you, counselor," she said, clinking his glass with hers. "I must admit—I'm not sure what felt better, closing the deal or seeing Gaines's face when I told him about it."

"I can only imagine."

"But it's only a first step, Bert. I'm going to help Kendall grow that business of his, and when I do, he'll introduce me to all the big buyers in Niagara Falls. Pretty soon Howie Gaines will find me indispensable. And then I won't be satisfied with my measly thirty percent."

"You do know it's thirty-three and a third."

"I suppose. To my mind, it's seventy–thirty, and that bugs me."

"I'm very proud of you, Alicia," Bert said. "There's only one of you."

"Don't fall over kowtowing to me just yet. I have a big fight ahead to get my fair share."

They attacked their osso buco, and ordered a second bottle of Chianti. As the dishes were cleared away and the place began to empty out, she leaned over the table toward him.

"There is one other thing I do want you to know," Allie said, taking a gulp of the fresh Chianti. "About Gaines, et cetera."

"What's that?"

"I hope you won't mind too much."

"I can't begin to imagine," he said, more than a little tipsy. "Lately you've been going from strength to strength. What is it?"

"I fucked him a couple times."

"You *what?*"

"I don't know how much plainer I can make that particular admission," Alicia said.

"Jesus Christ!" Bert almost shouted, and then lowered his voice when a few Italians across the room looked their way. "I go away for a few lousy weeks, and you can't even hold out until I get back? And with *Gaines*, of all people?"

"Will you listen?" she said. "I'm not interested in Gaines. Not in the way you think. The way I see it, he may own a majority of the company's shares, but I have a monopoly on the company's pussy. That counts for something, Bert."

Bert put his head into his hands. "And here I thought I *meant* something to you," he said quietly.

She reached across the table and gripped his forearm. "Bert. Shut up. You do mean something to me. In fact, you mean more to me than I ever thought possible. When we're together, it's not for any reason other than I want to be with you. But with Gaines, it's part of a game. And in any game, you play the cards in your hand. I'm not making a habit of sleeping with him. I had an ace up my sleeve, or rather"—she couldn't resist a chuckle—"up my skirt, and I played it."

"I fully understand the poker reference, but now you've given him a *taste*!" Bert said, straining to keep his voice down. "He'll be like a stray dog now, sniffing around. I know what it's like to be with you. Once he's had *that*, he's ruined. Like me. *Ruined*."

"And that'll be his problem, not yours. And I don't mind saying, he's terrible in bed."

"Well, I have that as cold comfort," Bert murmured. "I should hate you, you know."

"Why? I'm exactly the same person I was when you left for Hamburg. And I couldn't very well telephone you and ask for permission. Imagine!" She adopted a stuffy old businessman's voice. "Say, Bert, old boy, old chum, just rang you up because I need to let old Gaines have a poke, if we're going to get control of Miller Envelope one of these fine days."

"I would have preferred that, actually."

"Bert," she said, "now you are becoming a trifle irritating. This"— she pointed down at her crotch—"does in fact belong to *me*, not to *you*. You're welcome to borrow it as often as you like, and I like it when you do. But beyond that, it's a weapon of war. I don't send it into battle very often, but when I do, you'll have to trust that it was for a good reason. Are we clear?"

"Yes, Alicia," he said, a smile creeping across his face despite his best efforts to suppress it. "It's difficult for me sometimes, though. How *different* you are."

"I'm not so different, Bert. Perhaps I'm a little blunter, or even more honest than most people, but time's always racing by and there's no time for pussyfooting around. If you'll pardon the expression."

"I will admit that is part of your appeal," he said.

"Then don't you worry. I'm not throwing you over for Gaines, or anyone."

"He really was terrible? In bed?"

She reached under the table and put her hand on his knee. "Oh, you don't know the half of it, Bert. Perfectly awful, two left feet. And such a teeny little cock, compared to yours."

"Shhh," Bert said. "I'm not that big. Am I?"

"Big enough."

"May I at least ask how many times you—"

"Twice," she replied. "Once after the big Kendall deal, and once a few days later, mostly because I felt sorry for him."

"That was it?"

"What do you mean? Twice, I said. I don't lie."

"No, I mean—you won't—anymore, will you?"

"Now, Bert, what did we just discuss? I am not sporting and cavorting with our friend Howie Gaines. But if in my good judgment I feel it helpful to our cause to let him part the Red Sea again, then I will. How many times, I don't know. Maybe none. Maybe more."

"I wonder how you'd feel if I did the same? With some woman I might be trying to win as a client?"

"First of all, you did exactly that with *me*, so you may get down from your high horse. Second, you're a man, and men don't fuck for any *strategic* reason. They want release, pleasure—victory, maybe—and that's the extent of it. If I were taking my pleasure with Gaines, you'd have every right to cut my head off. And if I find out you're taking yours with anyone else, you'll also have a little bit removed."

Bert sighed. "All right then. I understand, and I'm not angry with you. I wish it weren't so, of course, but there's no doubt you live by your own rules. And I will admit they have a queer sort of logic to them."

"Thank you, dear. Part of what I love about you—and there, I said it, and don't ask me to repeat it—is that you understand me, and don't seem to mind. Don't ever lose that, Bertie."

"I won't. Now how about some dessert?"

"Let me guess—Italian ice?"

"That's probably about right," he said, signaling for the waiter, who was mainly waiting to go home.

"Or," she said, "if you can't tell, I'm more than a little bit drunk. Maybe we skip dessert and go home, and I'll let you take horrible advantage of me? Whatever you fancy."

"I'll have the check," he said when the waiter got to the table.

"DID BERT GET BACK from Hamburg yesterday?" Gaines asked the following morning, trying to sound nonchalant.

"He did," Allie said, putting down her newspaper. He's going to be a dog with a bone on this, she thought.

Gaines was quiet for a minute, looking out the window over Division Street. "I'll bet you were glad to have him back," he said, studying a trolley car creeping by in the shadow of their building.

"He'd been away quite a while," she said into the silence.

"Probably quite a happy reunion, I'd expect."

"Gaines, what are you scratching at?"

He intensified his scrutiny of the goings-on down below on Division Street. "Not a thing," he said in a voice even reedier than usual. "Passing the time of day with you, that's all."

"Then I'm grateful for your cordial interest. Always appreciated." She picked up the paper again and put her feet up on the desk. Gaines turned away from the window and began staring at the far corner of the room, where wall and ceiling came together.

He's not done, Allie thought.

"I do wonder about one thing," Howie said.

Allie's paper went down again and she looked over at his red face. His collar seemed particularly tight today. Was he gaining weight, or did the laundryman boil it too long? she wondered.

"I'm on tenterhooks over here," she said.

He swiveled toward her. "Did you tell him about—*us*?"

"Us?"

"Yes, us. About what we've gotten up to while he was away."

"Why would I tell him about that?"

"To be honest, I suppose. It's a pretty important thing to keep from him."

Alicia tapped her fingertips on her newspaper, scratching the nails against the chalky newsprint. She leaned over to make sure Abby wasn't in.

"Do you think I ought to tell Bert what I ate every day while he was gone?"

"Of course not. What does that have to do with anything?"

"Then why should I feel any more obligated to tell him who I fucked?"

"You know it's completely different," Howie said.

"Appetites have to be satisfied, Gaines. I'm allowed to satisfy mine, and I don't need Bert's permission to do it. Or yours, for that matter."

Howie picked up a pencil and began doodling on a tablet on his desk. "Well, I'll bet you both got good and satisfied last night," he muttered.

"Wouldn't you like to know."

Gaines seethed in silence for a bit. "Maybe the right thing to do is to tell Bert myself. Talk it over with him, man-to-man."

"I wouldn't do that if I were you. It might not end well for you."

"Ha. I'm not afraid of him," he scoffed.

"I'm not talking about *Bert*. It's *me* you ought to be afraid of. I'll wring your neck personally if you breathe a word about anything we did. To anyone."

"You wouldn't."

"Oh, but I would. Why can't you leave well enough alone? In the past month, the business has started looking up again, and you got laid in the bargain. Twice. We can make a lot of money together, and if you're nice to me, I'll most likely want to fuck you from time to time. It's as simple as that. Don't spoil a good thing."

"And what if I want more? More than you're willing to give?"

"Then you'll have to get it from someone else."

"I'm not giving up so easily," he said. "You'll see. You think I'm nothing but a dopey envelope maker. Well, I'm every bit the man Bert Hartshorn is, even if I don't have a fancy law degree."

"You may be every bit the man he is, but right about now you sound like a lovelorn boy. And it doesn't do you any credit."

Howie returned to staring out the window at the streetcars creeping along Division Street, but didn't reply.

Maid of the Mist

It seemed inevitable that Sarah and Jeremy's conversations would have to continue mainly outside of work. After their first tête-à-tête at the International, sitting on barrels in the warehouse seemed illicit, as though anyone with eyes to see could tell that they weren't working but flirting.

For the next two weeks, the pair engaged in a minuet of nods and glances, a private code that would arrange another private chat at the café. One Friday, as they were finishing an ice cream float—the waiter had at last agreed to serve them something cold—it was clear that neither of them was eager to say goodbye for the weekend.

It was Jeremy who came up with the solution. "Since you're still new in town," he said, "why don't you let me take you on a little tour of the city tomorrow? Unless you have something else on the boil. Or another fellow who wants to squire you around."

"No other secret swains, at present," Sarah replied. "But mightn't it be a little too cold for a walking tour?"

"On foot, sure. But I'll engage a coach. They'll have plenty of blankets."

She considered a moment. "Yes, then I'd like that."

"Shall I pick you up at your lodgings at, say, ten? What number is it, on Cedar?"

"Oh no," she said. "I live with—two other women, and I don't want them gossiping."

"Are you afraid one of them might steal me away?"

"If you want to be stolen, there's not a thing I can do to stop it."

"So you say. Where should we meet instead?"

"Prospect Street trolley station? Where you first shanghaied me?"

"Perfect. I'll be out front at ten."

THE NEXT DAY, SARAH was fifteen minutes early to the trolley stop, but Jeremy was already waiting in the hired coach. When he saw her, he threw off what must have been five heavy blankets and jumped down before the hackman could assist. "I've got it," he said to the driver, and handed Sarah up. He arranged the blankets over her and slid the coal foot warmer under her feet. Then he climbed up next to her and wriggled under the covers. She could feel his hip pressing against hers.

The weather report, for once, had been correct. The sky was painfully blue, unmarked with even a wisp of cloud, and since quite a few factories were shuttered for the weekend, there were only a few stray plumes of smoke rising above the Mill District—which normally looked as though it was roofed by a permanent lowering thundercloud. The coach turned around in the middle of Prospect Street and drove south, until they came to a statue of a Civil War soldier. Jeremy asked the coachman to stop.

"This is the foot of Falls Street," he told Sarah, gesturing. "It runs due east from here, all the way to the edge of the city. The first ten blocks are the tourist district, which you and I will stroll in the season."

"That would be fun," Sarah said. "And what comes after the tourist district?"

"Rough territory. I'd advise not going beyond Tenth Street."

"Have you been?"

"A couple times, and I was thankful each time to escape with my life."

They turned into the snowy parkland along the crest of the gorge, along the icy carriageway that led to the Falls themselves.

"I must admit, it's a little colder than I expected," he said. "Perhaps we can see the Falls and then come back and warm up over coffee downtown, at our little café?"

"That sounds perfect. Even with all these blankets, the cold does seep in, doesn't it?"

"You can get a little closer to me, if you'd like. If you think it proper."

"Warm beats proper on a day like this," she said, pressing up against him.

At a walking pace, the carriage took them upstream alongside the raging rapids, and then turned right over a wide bridge, the angry water roaring and tearing at its stone supports.

"This is Goat Island Bridge," Jeremy said. "It goes over to—guess what?—Goat Island, and that's where we'll see the Falls."

"That's a peculiar name for an island," she said.

The coachman overheard. "I can tell you that story," he said. "Many years ago, there was an old farmer who lived on the island. Before this bridge was built, there was only a flimsy wooden one and no one could cross in the winter. One springtime, the old farmer didn't come into town as usual, so people went to check on him. Turns out he'd died during the winter, and all of his animals had, too, except for one—a goat, who was as hale and hearty as a goat could be."

"How did the goat survive?" Jeremy asked.

"Let's put it this way," the driver said. "Goats will eat anything."

"Oh God," Sarah said, laughing. "What a gruesome story."

"Can you take us to Luna Island?" Jeremy asked the coachman. "We'd like to walk over and see the Falls."

"Sure thing. Just be careful—the walkway is going to be very slippery. I don't want either of you going over."

"Bad for business," Jeremy said.

When the coach came to a halt, Jeremy hopped down and helped Sarah find her footing on the slick pavement. They navigated down a steep flight of stairs and across an icy causeway extended over a narrow portion of the rapids, which were shooting by at top speed just beneath their feet. The causeway was heavy with ice, and the leaping water reaching for them was dizzying.

Luna Island wasn't so much an island as it was a tiny rocky outcrop rising only a few feet above the raging water of the broad American Falls. To their right was an uninterrupted view along the sweeping crest line of the Falls and, half a mile away, Kendall Electrolytic Abrasives and the rest of the Mill District. To their left was the turgid Luna Falls, so named for its famous "moonbow" that its rising mist created on nights of the full moon.

Today, the mist was so cold that it was heavy and sticky, eager to congeal on anything that didn't keep moving. The already perilous walking path, the tourist telescope, and the iron railings were all hung with stalactites of ice—like rows of organ pipes, fusing the handrails to the bedrock of Luna Island. Sarah and Jeremy carefully approached the iron railing overlooking the big plunge, and stared in silence at the bottle-green water sliding by, hurrying along with it blocks of ice as large as the coach they had just left behind. The ground beneath their feet rumbled and shook with the angry force of countless tons of Great Lakes water pummeling the boulders at the base of the Falls.

"It's awe-inspiring, isn't it?" Sarah said.

"I find it beautiful, but frightening," Jeremy said. "And somehow strangely alluring. I wouldn't want to be here by myself. Not that I want to be anywhere without you anymore."

She felt his arm encircle her waist, and she thought to pull away, but didn't. He drew her closer.

Sarah looked up at him with her bright violet eyes. "We'll be ice sculptures soon," she said, laughing, as the cold mist swirled around them.

"I wouldn't mind at all, if it meant that I could look into those eyes of yours forever."

"But there's so much spray," she said, squinting, "that I can barely keep them open."

"Then close them," he said, and she did, without thinking why.

He kissed her eyelids first, and then her lips, his mouth warm and tender against hers. She clasped her arms tightly around him and kissed him back, urgently, in the way she'd wanted to kiss Edward, and yet had done only once—on the night he was murdered. It had been their first kiss, and their last.

"You've suffered so much, Sarah," he said quietly. "What I don't know is how you've managed to stay so strong."

She almost said, "For Maggie's sake," but bit her tongue in time. "We both have," she said.

He whispered something into her ear, so softly she couldn't make it out over the rush of the water.

"What did you say, Jeremy?" she asked, opening her eyes.

"I said that I love you, Sarah."

"Jeremy, that's very strong talk," she said, stunned.

"I don't care. Life is so short, and when I'm with you—I find I have no room for loneliness anymore."

"I understand," she murmured. "But love? We hardly—"

"You'll take a chill," he said abruptly. "We'd best get you warmed up."

"I'm fine. But I am feeling a bit soaked."

"I could say something very naughty now, you realize."

"Good God, Jeremy, you truly are—"

He leaned down and kissed her again, a long, deep kiss, and she gave herself up to it, the penetrating cold and the slick, drifting mist, and everything, lost in the rush of her blood and the booming of the Falls.

"We'd best get back before our coachman gives up on us entirely," he said, after they'd parted and there was nothing else to say.

They started back across the narrow causeway, carefully mounting the stairs to the coach. Once in and under the blankets, he dispensed with ceremony and put his arm around her again, and buried his nose in her hair. She rested her hand lightly on his thigh, which she knew was far too bold, but then again, what did it matter when life was flowing past so quickly?

"To our café, then, for something warm?" he said.

She smiled and nodded, and in half an hour, they were thawing out over mugs of hot chocolate.

"May I try your chocolate?" Jeremy said.

"You have the same thing, silly. There's nothing different about mine."

"But there is. Your lips have been on yours."

She smiled and handed him her mug. "Jeremy, you do know we have to keep ourselves from getting carried away."

He took a sip of her hot chocolate, looking into her eyes. "Why? Why not get carried away?"

"For one, it hasn't worked out so well for me in the past."

"The past is gone, Sarah. You needn't continue reliving it."

She sipped her chocolate, considering. "Jeremy, twice in my life I've allowed myself to stop thinking, and twice it caused me no end of heartache."

"Will you tell me? You can trust me completely. Whatever passes between us is *sacred*."

"You know, I think you may really mean that," she said softly.

"And I do. Tell me, then. I want to know everything that makes you happy—and the things that have made you sad."

"All right. The first time was when I was only seventeen—marrying my husband. We had our reasons, but I'm not sure we ever loved each other, and for almost ten years, we were very unhappy. And you already know how that ended."

"I do," Jeremy said. "And I'm terribly sorry. What was the second time?"

"It's awkward."

"You're safe with me, Sarah."

She looked into her hot chocolate. "I know. My husband was still alive when I became attached to a man—a very dear friend—who was also unhappily married. And I let myself get so carried away that he and I took the fool notion to run away together, to California, and escape from both of our old lives. Whatever that means."

"Who could blame you?" Jeremy said. "Why didn't you?"

"Things changed, and it wasn't a possibility anymore. Then, not long after, I learned that this man I got carried away with—that I wasn't the only other lady in his life. He hadn't been completely honest with me."

"That would be difficult to bear."

"I think since then I have been reluctant to trust anyone."

"You can trust me, Sarah," he said, grasping her hand. "I meant what I said by the Falls."

"Jeremy, you barely know me."

"I know I haven't known you for very long, but I don't need to. You're the most honest and decent person I've ever met."

She looked into the fireplace, blinking back tears. *The man thinks I'm* honest, she thought. *Decent. He says he loves me, but what he loves* is a pack of lies. I don't live on Cedar Street, nor have a mother in Lewiston. Even my name is fabricated. And then there's Maggie . . .

"I should be getting home," she said suddenly, overcome by a sudden desire to flee.

He looked surprised. "So soon? I thought we could perhaps have a nice luncheon and—"

"Not today, Jeremy. Let's leave some things unsaid. We've had a truly wonderful morning. Let's try to be content with that, for now."

BY THE TIME SHE walked into the great foyer of Kendall House, lunch was long over, the plates cleared away and cleaned, and Christine was off taking a nap. She could hear Charles's baritone laughter echoing from his office, far down the corridor. He was probably talking to someone from back home in New London, she thought. That's always when he laughs. For all his money, the grand house, the legions of admirers—he seemed happiest talking to the regular fellows back in The Fort, men who knew him before he had become what he had become, and who always would. No accumulation of time or money could change that, and with them, he could be Charlie Kendall—just himself.

It's good he has that still, she thought, as she slowly climbed the grand staircase. I wish I did. With Maggie I must be Mama, with Ruth and Annie and Harry I am the boss, and with the Kendalls, an employee and a guest. And now, with Jeremy—to reveal *myself* would be unforgiveable.

Sarah Payne could have dropped her disguise, and revealed herself—but Sarah *Price* could never. She had sworn herself to a life as a detective, and in detective work, the mask can never be discarded. Her seduction of Jeremy had had its decisive moment, its fork in the road between truth and lies.

That moment had now passed. She had chosen.

CORRUPTION

RUTH'S SECOND TREATMENT—THIS TIME ON AN EMPTY stomach—went considerably more smoothly than the first. She passed out again, which worried Annie, but the nurse reassured her that it was probably better to be unconscious than to suffer through such a high fever for an hour.

As had been the case after her first, truncated session, though, it required two full days for Ruth to recover her strength. She remained prostrated most of the time, sleeping on and off, unable to cook and clean for Annie. She was none too happy about her debility, and it was all Annie could do to keep her from staggering downstairs to "get a few things done."

On the third day after Ruth's second treatment, Annie was luxuriating in bed for a final few minutes as the sun crept through her bedroom windows. The house was quiet, and no comings and goings had yet begun on Norwood Street. The distant ticking of the grandfather clock in the hallway had almost lulled her back into sleep when she was jolted by a shriek from the adjacent bedroom.

Annie shot out of bed and into the hallway, yelling her sister's name, and was a foot away from Ruth's door when it was slammed shut, hard, from inside. Annie rattled the knob.

"Ruth? What's the matter? Are you unwell?"

"Go away!" Ruth's voice said through the door.

"What's wrong?" Annie said, trying the knob again. "I heard a scream."

"I can't come out now."

"Please, Sister," Annie pleaded. "Open the door. I know something's not right."

There was silence on the other side, and then the lockwork clicked and the door swung open. Ruth was standing behind it, out of sight.

"What is all the mystery about?" Annie said, frustrated.

Ruth stepped out from behind her door and into a ray of sunlight.

"Oh my," Annie said.

"Something's gone terribly wrong," Ruth said, bursting into tears. "I—I don't know what to do."

Ruth's face, neck, and forearms—everything not concealed by her nightgown—were covered with angry red pustules—some tiny, some as large as a dime. A few had burst, and thin, watery fluid was weeping over her skin.

"They're all over my body!" Ruth wailed, pulling her nightdress out and looking down into the neckline. "They're everywhere! I don't know what to do, Annie!"

"Sit down on the bed," Annie said, guiding her sister gently onto the mattress. "It must be some sort of reaction to your treatment, that's all. It's probably entirely normal."

"This is not *normal*! I'm covered head to toe with these things."

"Let me take a closer look," Annie said, reaching for her sister's chin.

"Don't touch them," Ruth said, pulling away. "They're full of corruption. Don't touch my skin!"

"Yes, dear. You're going to be fine. We have to stay calm."

"How will I even leave the house this way? I can't be seen like this. I'm disfigured."

"I'm sure it's temporary, Ruth," Annie said. "For now, you get back into bed, and I'll call Dr. Porter's office as soon as it opens. We'll take you in and see what he has to say."

"I can't go until after nightfall," Ruth said. "I can't very well walk around with a pillowcase over my head."

"We'll hire a coach and you can wear a veil."

"We can't afford a coach. You've already spent all your money on that—fucking Dr. Porter."

"Try to rest and don't worry about all that," Annie said. "I'll go downstairs and make some eggs, the way you like them. We'll eat them together, here in your room, and by the time we've finished, Dr. Porter's office will have opened up."

Ruth started to cry again. "Oh, please, Annie, bring me something I can take—to end this. It's misery for me, and it's misery for you. I brought this on myself and it's—"

"Stop that nonsense. I'll kill you myself if you keep talking like that. I have to be able to trust that you won't hurt yourself."

"Oh fine," the sobbing girl said. "I'll suffer. It's what I deserve, anyway. And I don't want eggs. I'm not hungry. I don't ever want to eat again."

"You need to keep your strength up. And you like the way I make your eggs, don't you? Scrambled with a little bit of milk?"

"Annie, please don't be good to me. You ought to turn me out of the house. I've gone and done something so stupid, and I've cost you every-thing, and now"—she held out her afflicted arms—"*this*!"

"And we're going to get you all fixed up. I'm sure Dr. Porter will tell us that this is simply a reaction to your treatment. Now we must try to stay calm until we find out more. Can you do that for me?"

Ruth sniffed. "Yes."

"You promise?"

"Yes, I promise."

"Good girl. Now I'll go downstairs and make our eggs, and even if you can have a single mouthful, that'll be good for you. And then I'll call Dr. Porter."

"All right," Ruth said. When Annie looked back in at her from the hallway, her sister was sitting quietly on the edge of her bed, staring down at her arms in what seemed like a kind of trance.

MAGNIFYING GLASS IN HAND, Dr. Porter examined Ruth's arms, face, and neck.

"They're everywhere," Ruth said. "Under my clothes, too."

"So it seems," the doctor said, peering through his glass. "It's what we call a generalized pustular syphilitic outbreak." He straightened up again, smiled at Ruth, and walked back around his desk. He set his magnifying glass down carefully on the blotter and looked at it thoughtfully.

"You've seen this before, at least," Annie said.

"No, I can't say I've seen it myself, until now," he said quietly. "I've read about it, of course. But it's quite rare."

"Well, what do you know?" Ruth said. "I'm a rarity."

"What is it, then, Doctor?" Annie said. "Surely you know how to correct it? Perhaps the next treatment—"

"We won't be able to continue with the pyrotherapy, I'm afraid," he said. "That's what's caused this—generalized outbreak."

"You see?" Annie said to Ruth. "I told you that it was only a reaction." She turned back to Dr. Porter. "But why wouldn't you continue with the therapy? Once this calms down, that is."

The doctor sighed deeply. "For reasons we don't yet understand, very, very occasionally, the treatment—the high heat in the body—fails to eradicate the organism," he said. "In fact, quite the opposite happens. The heat seems to encourage it to—to bloom."

"*Bloom*?" Ruth said in horror.

"Yes," the doctor said. "Think of, say, chicken eggs. You put them in an incubator, and warm them, and they hatch more quickly than at room temperature. This must be some strain of the syphilis germ that is encouraged by heat, contrary to the usual response."

"Oh my God," Annie breathed. "So what is it? I mean, what are *they*?"

"They're eruptions of the disease," Dr. Porter said. "And you must not pick at them, or get the fluid onto anything or anyone, as it will be highly contagious. The good news is—from what I have read about such cases—this outbreak is temporary. Then it will go away again."

"Thank heavens for that," Annie said.

"Yes, but what is not known—but is suspected—is that this bloom may have inadvertently accelerated the course of the disease."

"What does that mean?" Ruth asked.

"Well, it means that the progression of the disease may have been sped up. Accelerated."

"How much sped up?"

"We don't know. But possibly the development of tertiary syphilis may now take only months, instead of years."

"So I'll wake up one morning without a nose?" Ruth said.

"Please, Miss Ruth, keep your voice down," Dr. Porter said, looking nervously at the door. "I can't predict what course your disease will take. I certainly didn't predict *this*."

"But if my sister can't have any more treatments, whatever will we do?" Annie said.

"I'll administer the more traditional medicines," he said. "That will be the best we can do, in a case like this."

"Mercury?" Ruth said. "It was to avoid mercury that we came here in the first place."

"I'm afraid that is the best alternative now. The only alternative."

"If I understand, then," Ruth said, "you charged my sister two hundred dollars to kill me quicker."

Dr. Porter wheeled back in his chair, directly under his poster, so that it looked as if an older man's head was sprouting from the crown of the younger one's. "That was certainly not our intention, Miss Ruth," he said. "And as I'm sure you noticed in my booklet, I do have a money-back guarantee. No cure, no charge. I'll be mailing your sister a bank draft for a full refund."

"No cure," Annie said softly.

"No charge," Ruth said.

"I'm afraid even medical science has its limitations," Dr. Porter said. "There's a great deal about the human body and its afflictions that we do not fully fathom."

"We understand," Annie said. "It's not your fault."

"It may come as little consolation, but I will describe your case in the *Journal of Modern Pelvic Medicine*. Without using your name, of course. Your experience will expand our knowledge, and potentially help others."

"Oh joy," Ruth said. She pulled her veil down over her ravaged face. "Let's go, Annie. The longer we stay here, the sicker I get."

"I wish you both the best of luck," Dr. Porter said, rising. "And although I would have preferred a better result from the pyrotherapy,

I do stand ready to provide a supply of medicines and, if necessary, prosthetic devices."

Annie and Ruth left his office, and smiled at the nurse sitting tidily at her large desk, but she was engrossed in her magazine, or seemed to be, and didn't look up.

"AT LEAST YOU ARE getting your money back," Ruth said to Annie in the coach back to Norwood Street.

"That's the least of my worries. I would have paid ten times what he charged if he'd only fixed you up."

"I know you would have. You're the only thing that keeps me going."

"And I'm never giving up, either. You'll see. There's hope out there somewhere. We have only to find it."

Ruth looked out the window of the coach. "It is possible to hold on to hope for too long, you know. It can be deceptive."

"None of that, now. There's always something else we can try."

"What's that?"

"I can talk to Sarah about it," Annie said.

"You said only last week you didn't care if you ever spoke with her again. You said some pretty rotten things about her."

Annie rubbed her eyes. "I was angry. That she'd gone off and left us here—and now with this, on top of everything else. I didn't mean it."

"You certainly sounded sincere."

"Maybe I was. I don't know anymore. But what I do know is that Sarah is the smartest person I know, and she loves you. She'll have some idea of what we can do."

Ruth sighed. "But she'll go and tell Harry. No thanks."

"She won't if I ask her not to."

Ruth sighed. "It's all so awful. But if you think talking with her is the right thing to do, then you have my permission."

Annie nodded. "I wasn't looking for permission, but I'm happy to have it all the same."

30

The Dose Makes the Poison

The next afternoon, Sarah greeted Annie at the giant Gothic door of Kendall House.

"Annie!" she said, embracing her friend. "I've missed you so. You're looking very well."

"You are, too. I'd almost forgotten how beautiful you are."

"Please. I'm not feeling so beautiful lately."

The two looked at each other, not quite knowing what to say.

"Well, why don't we sit, and you can tell me what's on your mind," Sarah said, breaking the silence. "I must say your call made me more than a little concerned—and that you wanted to come all the way here to talk."

The pair sat in the grand parlor. "This house is astonishing," Annie said, looking around.

"I still haven't quite gotten used to it. Sometimes I get turned around, and I find myself completely lost."

"I can understand that. You must love it here, though?"

"I do like it here, but it's not my home. I'm looking forward to getting back to Norwood Street."

"I still can't believe Mr. Kendall will let you go."

"He doesn't have a choice, dear. Now may I offer you some lemonade and something to nibble on?" Sarah said.

"No, I can't stay long. I must be getting back. That divorce case again."

"Then we'd best get on with it. What's troubling you? Ought I to be worried about something?"

"I didn't want to tell you this at all, but it can't be avoided anymore," Annie said.

"That's an odd comment."

"It's about Ruth. She's gotten herself into trouble."

"Into *trouble*?" Sarah said, astonished. "Ruth's not that kind!"

"Not *that* kind of trouble. A different kind. Worse."

"What in God's name could be worse?"

Annie recounted the whole of it to Sarah.

"I honestly don't know what to say," Sarah said when she had finished. "I hoped for a moment there that the doctor's treatment would fix things. What's left, I wonder?"

"I'm at my wits' end," Annie said. "I try not to show Ruth, but I'm beginning to feel despondent. But now—with the disease picking up speed, I'm afraid she might not have very long."

"Did the doctor have any thoughts about that? How long?"

"Not really. He's not seen this before. If it keeps going as fast as it is, perhaps only months. But it could go into hiding again. We just don't know."

"You've done all the right things, Annie. And now we must resist the urge to give up. We will find a solution somehow. How much does Harry know?"

"He must know that Ruth is infected, but that's all. They haven't spoken since you left, so he wouldn't know any of this. And Ruth was emphatic that you not tell him."

"That's our Ruth," Sarah said. "Stubborn as a mule."

"You don't know the half of it."

"We can table the matter of Harry for now. First, we need to fix Ruth."

"I'm open to anything," Annie said. "I don't care what it costs, or where I have to take her. All the way to China, if I have to. And I won't blame you if you dismiss me from the agency if I cannot be depended upon."

"Don't you worry about the agency. We'll be fine, and if you need time off, I'll continue to pay you and you can come back when you like. The only important thing now is Ruth."

"You mustn't be kind to me," Annie said, tearing up. "I can't stand it."

"Whyever not?"

The young woman began crying softly. "Because the truth is—I've been so angry with you since you left. I've been terribly jealous. And hateful."

"You stop that, right now," Sarah said. "That's nonsense. I left abruptly, and then *this* happened to you and Ruth, and you had no one to lean on. You have every right to be angry."

"You don't think I'm horrible?"

"No, I don't think you're horrible."

"I've gone to confession three times a week since you left," Annie sniffled. "And it doesn't help. I feel as though God is punishing me and Ruth for the—thoughts I've had about you. My dearest friend."

"Annie, I can't claim to understand God. But if he's really so cruel as that, then we're all barking up the wrong tree."

"But can you forgive me?"

"Can you forgive yourself?"

"I don't know."

"I believe you can, and must. And in any case, we must think only of Ruth now."

"All right," Annie said. "Yes, Ruth is the most important thing now."

"Then if you will allow me, I would like to take Mr. Kendall into our confidence. He has connections all over the world. If someone somewhere is working on a new treatment, he'll be able to find out. May I speak with him?"

"Of course you may," Annie said. "And if it's of any help, Dr. Porter told us that there's research going on in Germany."

"If anyone can find out, it's Mr. Kendall."

"You know," Annie said, looking into her lap, "I rather dreaded coming here today, but now I feel a glimmer of hope again."

"You dreaded telling me about Ruth?"

"Mostly I dreaded seeing you."

"You certainly haven't lost your forthrightness."

"I don't mean it badly. I was afraid we'd drifted apart."

"Have a little faith, Annie."

"Lately that's been hard to find."

"And that I can understand. But try to keep your spirits up, even if it feels forced. You and I can cry on each other's shoulders, but we can't let Ruth see that we are frightened."

"THANK YOU FOR TAKING dinner with me privately tonight," Sarah said that evening.

"Of course," Kendall said. "Though Christine seemed unusually happy to be let off the hook. I did wonder a bit about that."

"I arranged for her to have dinner with some of her friends in the big dining room."

"That's a relief. Under our roof, at least, she'll be able to drink as much of my Margaux as she likes, and there's no risk she'll wind up in bed with a seminary student."

"For heaven's sake, Mr. Kendall!"

"You are right to object, Miss Payne. It was unkind of me to speak of my daughter's misstep."

"It was indeed. And haven't you ever done anything a little naughty, Mr. Kendall?"

"I'm sure I have, but really—a *seminary student*?"

"Seminary students are terribly repressed. If anything, Christine was performing an act of charity."

"Now you sound like your friend Mrs. Miller," he said.

"You could have talked all evening and not said that."

"I take it back."

"A little too late, but I'll let it go by—because I have a situation that I hope you can help with."

"About your dinner with Brass tomorrow night?"

"No, not Brass. This is something entirely different."

"Go ahead," he said. "I'm listening."

"How very distressing," he said, after she'd finished telling Ruth's story. "The poor young thing. And I wasn't aware that Mr. Price was similarly afflicted."

"You're our last resort," Sarah said. "I've been hoping against hope that you may have heard of some other kind of treatment."

Kendall thought for a few moments, carefully arranging his silverware in precise order.

"I certainly don't want to raise hopes unduly, but I do know a man who may have an answer for us."

"Even a glimmer of hope would be welcome," she said.

"There's a fellow in Germany, Professor Ehrlich, who is the world's expert in arsenic."

"Rat poison?"

"Well, yes, but arsenic is a naturally occurring element—just like, oh, sulfur, for example. And about a year ago, a shipment of one of my raw materials was found to have a very high level of arsenic—so high that if I didn't purify it, it could endanger my workers. The risk was low, but it was one I couldn't take. Ethically speaking."

"I see," Sarah said. "I wish Aaron Brass knew about this. I'm sure most factory owners wouldn't take such deliberate care about the welfare of their men."

"It wouldn't change his mind," Kendall said, with a casual wave of his hand. "To him, I'm the Devil, and always will be. But that's life. Yet—it was that which led me to Dr. Ehrlich. The man knows *everything* about arsenic."

"Why is he so interested in arsenic?"

He tapped the table with his finger. "That's where it gets interesting. He is finding all sorts of unexpected uses for it—even in medicine."

"But it's a poison," Sarah said.

"True, but anything can be a poison." He gestured to the saltcellar in front of his plate. "Take salt as an example. A little bit sprinkled on one's food is delicious—but half a pound of it would kill you almost instantly.

"And most medicines are poisons, too—it's the dose that makes the difference. Morphine is a good example. The point here is that among Ehrlich's other discoveries—which he related to me over dinner one evening in Bad Homburg—is that certain compounds of arsenic show great promise as an agent against syphilis."

"Do you think he might know of something that Ruth and Harry could try?"

"If he does, he'll tell me. I very freely shared with him everything I learned about removing arsenical impurities, and I know he's used some of that knowledge to develop treatments for arsenic poisoning. He owes me a favor or two."

Sarah put her hand on Kendall's forearm. "Could you speak with him soon? Annie fears that Ruth may not have much time."

Kendall patted her hand gently and slid his chair away from the table.

"Then as pleasant as it is to spend time with you, Miss Payne—why, simply looking at you—I had better alert my telegrapher and get a wire off to Bad Homburg."

31

The Oaks Restaurant

It was a short walk from the trolley stop to The Oaks Restaurant, but not even the layers of Sarah's furs and fabrics could have thwarted the bitter wind and freezing mist roaring off the Falls. She pulled her coat close around her as she started east on the deserted main drag, with only snow whirling along the empty sidewalks.

Niagara Falls, like most summer resorts, was lonely and desolate in the dead of winter. The streetlights along Falls Street still glowed, and shopkeepers still stood dutifully in their windows. But no one was posing for snapshots under the cold iron lampposts, no one buying honeymoon souvenirs, and no one riding the trolleys except the motormen.

She wondered where Harry was. She had told him that dinner with Aaron Brass was set for that evening at The Oaks, and that was all. He had nodded and given her that odd, slow blink he had when he was digesting some new fact.

After two more freezing blocks, she arrived at a hanging overhead sign that read:

Oaks Restaurant.
Fine Food and Drink.
Ladies & Gentleman Welcome.

Gentle*men*, they must mean, she thought. The Oaks looked, to all appearances, like every other one of the shopfronts along Falls Street, with large windows weeping condensation down inside and a central doorway crouched beneath an overhanging brick brow. Someone had forgotten to crank in the tattered red-and-white-striped awning over the front—or, more likely, it was frozen in place—and its canvas snapped and trembled like a sail in a hurricane. She ducked under the rattling frame—her hat added almost a full foot to her stature—and stepped across the threshold and into the restaurant.

From the penetrating cold outside to the stifling heat inside was the difference between the Arctic and Equator. Inside The Oaks, an iron stove and its red-hot metal chimney superheated the smoky atmosphere. Even the patrons sitting by the front door were dripping sweat, and seemed grateful for the frigid draft created by Sarah's entrance. In the very rear of the joint were a few individual partitions of heavy brocade, looking like beachfront dressing booths.

A host in a shiny tuxedo greeted her. "Welcome," he said, and took her coat, scarf, gloves, and fur muff.

"Thank you," she said. "I'm here to meet Mr. Brass."

"Right this way," the host said.

He led her to the rear of the room, the temperature rising with every step. "Here we are," he said, parting the curtains of the rearmost table. Immediately a cloud of cigarette smoke and a wave of moist heat burped out of the opening. Inside sat Aaron Brass, drinking a glass of wine and smoking. He stubbed out his cigarette and stood.

"Miss Price," he said. "That's some smart getup."

"Thank you, Mr. Brass," she said.

The host squeezed sideways into the little curtained space and, with some effort, pulled out Sarah's chair, knocking it forcefully into another patron seated just on the other side of the drapery. There was a muffled yelp of protest, which the host ignored.

"I know I'm not supposed to smoke in here, on account of the curtains," Brass said to the host. Sarah felt a wave of pure joy wash over her.

"Mr. Brass," the host said, "for you, the usual rules *do not apply*." He squeezed out of the booth and left them alone.

Brass held up a half-empty bottle of wine. "I'm two glasses ahead of you," he said with a wink. "You'll have to catch up."

"I'll join you in a small glass," she said.

He poured her glass almost brimful. "Whoops. Maybe just bend down and sip a little."

"My feathers will get wet," she said, pointing to her elaborate hat.

"All right, then, here." He picked up her overfilled glass and dumped some into his glass. "Problem solved. Now for a toast. To the most beautiful woman I've ever seen," he said, raising his glass.

"And to the labor movement," she said, raising hers.

"That too."

Sarah took out her steno pad and pencil from her handbag. "Shall we pick up where we left off?"

"Come *on*," he said, snatching the pencil out of her hand and tucking it into his jacket. "Let's have a couple drinks first and get better acquainted."

"One drink, then. Although this one is still the size of three normal ones."

He chuckled and adjusted his collar. "Why don't you tell me where you hail from?"

"I'm from a little town north of Buffalo."

"Family?"

"My father was a Presbyterian minister, but he recently retired. My mother's at home."

"A minister's daughter, then?" he said with a thin yellow leer. "Ministers' daughters are always the naughtiest ones."

"Not always, Mr. Brass."

"What about children?"

"No, my late husband and I didn't have any. And you?"

"I have a son," he said.

"How old?"

"Ten."

"A charming age for a little boy."

"He's a hellion," Brass said.

"Oh," Sarah said, and sipped her wine. "And your wife? Is she from the old country as well?"

Brass heaved a deep, smoky sigh. "Can't we just forget about all of that for a little while? I could just sit here and get lost in those eyes of yours. What color would you say they are? They're deeper than the usual blue eyes."

"They're a very dark blue. Sometimes they look violet. They came along with the hair." She touched a lock of strawberry blonde hair straying down the side of her face.

"God," he said, shaking his head, "I'm trying to be polite, but—what would it take to get you to come with me to a cozy room someplace?"

"Other than putting knockout drops in my wine?"

"Now that's nothing but pure meanness. I'm paying you a compliment."

"Would your wife like it if you paid me that kind of compliment?"

"Her again," Brass said, opening his cigarette case.

"Would you mind—" she began, and then was cut off when the brocade curtains parted and a waiter entered, carrying a silver platter on which a large steak was sizzling.

"This place is famous around the world for this steak," Brass said. He leaned out of the curtains and called for another bottle of wine.

The steak was indeed delicious, and while they ate, Brass carefully steered her away from anything more serious than baseball. When the dishes were cleared away, though, Sarah was determined to get back to her topic.

"When we left off in your office," she said, "you were telling me about Kendall Abrasives. And how you'd like to unionize their works."

"Kendall again?"

"Yes, you promised me you'd tell me about your strategy to get into their factory."

He took a gulp of wine. "I also seem to remember that I said some things are not for the newspapers."

"You did."

"Yet you're *still* interested in Kendall, even if you can't print it. I find that interesting."

"Put it down to curiosity, then." She closed her notebook. "Besides, you took my pencil."

"You don't think much of me, do you?"

"Why on earth would you say something like that?"

He reached for a cigarette. "Because it's true. I know I smoke too much. I'm not very well educated. But I'm not stupid, Miss Price."

"I don't think any of those things. What is this all about?"

"Your paper," he said. "The *Buffalo Guardian*, wasn't it?"

"That's right."

"Maybe you should have picked a different name."

"What's wrong with the name?"

"What's wrong," he said, inhaling deeply, "is that there ain't no such paper."

"I beg to differ," she said, feeling a chill.

"See, this is why I think you think I'm stupid," Brass said, exhaling. "How difficult do you think it is for me to check up on some *reporter*—who drops in one day, asking questions about my strategies? A *reporter* who doesn't look like any reporter I've ever seen?"

"What are you getting at?"

"Sweetie, I know *everyone*. In Niagara Falls—and in Buffalo, too. It took me only two calls to get to the bottom of your little stunt." He sat back and took another drag.

"Mr. Brass, I haven't any idea—"

"That's all you call me. Mr. Brass. I asked you to call me Aaron. I even told you that my real name is Urinov Brazhnik. But after all that, I'm still 'Mr. Brass' to you."

"I'm merely being polite," she said.

"Naw, honey, let's stop kidding around. That's not why you do it. You do it to keep things straight. You know that if you call me Mr. Brass, and not Aaron, or Mr. Brazhnik—I'll have to call you Miss Price. And not Sarah. Or Miss *Payne*. Or the Avenging Angel."

Sarah felt all the blood leave her face, and the hot brocade booth become strangely cold.

"If you know who I am," she said quietly, "why did you agree to meet me tonight?"

"Why do you think?"

"I'll caution you, Mr. Brass, if I don't return home—"

"Please. I'm not going to do away with you, honey. You know why?"

"I can't wait to hear," she said, as bravely as she could manage.

"Because you're going to be useful to me."

"And why would I want to be useful to you, sir?"

"Does the name 'Maggie' mean anything to you?"

"You wouldn't *dare*."

"But you don't *know* that, now do you? So here's what you're going to do for me."

"What?"

"You're going to deliver a message for me. To Charles Kendall."

"Charles Kendall?" she said. "And how would I know Charles Kendall?"

"See? There you go again, pretending I'm stupid. I know your daughter's *name*, Miss Payne. Oh, and that she's nine years old, was born in Tonawanda, and her father's name was Seth. I know where you live. I know the names of your friends."

Sarah wasn't sure whether to scream, throw her wine in his face and run, or continue to sit paralyzed in the brocade booth.

"What is the message, then?"

"The message," Brass said, leaning over the table, "is that he needs to quit stalling and meet with me, face-to-face and man-to-man. No more hiding behind lawyers and"—he smiled broadly—"*detectives*. Tell him he has to carry his own *water*, for a change. Tell him that, in those words exactly."

She managed a slow nod.

"Good. Now that's out of the way, maybe we can just be—Sarah and Aaron, without all the phony stuff."

"I think it would be better if I delivered your message without delay. May I leave?"

"*May* you? Of course you may, dear," he said. "Though it seems a shame to leave before dessert. They have terrific ice cream here. And a little birdie tells me you *love* ice cream."

"Another time," she said. She shoved her chair back and stood, again smacking into the poor diner next door, who again yelped piteously.

"You forgot something," Brass said. He took her pencil out of his jacket pocket and ran it under his nose, scenting it as if it were a fine cigar. He smiled and tucked it away again.

"On second thought, I think I'll keep it," he said, smiling. "A little souvenir of Niagara Falls."

SARAH HURRIEDLY RETRIEVED HER coat and weather gear, imagining Brass's eyes on her, burning through the heavy brocade. She hurried out into the cold and ducked under the awning, which was still beating itself to death in the whipping wind. She turned west toward the

Falls and, after only two blocks, was shivering fiercely—from fear, the freezing wind, or both.

When the yellow lights of the trolley emerged from the whirling snow, she boarded quickly and huddled in her seat, watching the front entrance and hoping that Brass wouldn't hop on at the last minute. When the trolley pulled away, Sarah nearly sobbed with relief. Then she jumped when she heard a soft voice from the seat behind her.

"I'm here," he said. She turned around to see Harry Price, the brim of his derby an inch deep in snow.

"Harry," she breathed, "you're a sight for sore eyes. I didn't see you board."

"I came up the back steps. I followed you from the restaurant."

"I was so worried you wouldn't be able to see me in there. When he told me a private table, I hadn't imagined he meant behind heavy curtains."

Harry gave her a ragged smile. "I saw Brass arrive and get into his private booth, so I took the table in the booth next to his."

"You were the poor devil I was knocking into with my chair?"

"None other," Harry said. "At least I heard every word."

She shook her head. "I took him for a fool, Harry. I ought to have planned more carefully."

Harry gave a little snort. "His world is not your world, Sarah. You don't want to be like him."

"What will I tell Mr. Kendall?"

"Tell him that you got him a meeting with Aaron Brass," Harry said. "It's the truth."

"HOW DID IT GO last evening with Brass?" Kendall asked her the next morning, over their French toast. "Stefan told me you got home safely. I was quite relieved."

"Harry was with me," she said. "I was fine. But Brass was a step ahead of me."

"How so?"

"He knows that I'm working for you. And he knows a lot about me. He threatened my daughter if I didn't agree to give you a message."

"That scoundrel!" Kendall said, smacking his fist down. "He's a paper tiger. He'll not harm a hair on your head, or hers, while I'm alive."

"That's what concerns me. I fear I may have led him to you."

"Don't you worry about me. I can take care of myself, and I have Stefan if needed. What was his message?"

"He said that it's time to meet with him, man-to-man, and that you need to carry your own water for a change. Without the help of lawyers and—detectives."

Kendall set his napkin down. "*Carry my own water.* So he is behind the theft, after all."

"It would seem so."

"You know, this whole situation makes me furious," he said abruptly.

"Naturally, sir. You placed your trust in me, and I was outwitted. You have every right to be furious with me."

"Not with *you*—with myself. All this time, I've allowed you to put yourself and, now, your daughter in harm's way, when I could have simply picked up the telephone and arranged a conference with the man myself. And I'm angry because he's right. I have been hiding from him. Behind a woman and a child. It's disgraceful."

"That's preposterous," she said. "It was my decision to get into the detective business, not yours. If anyone has put me and Maggie in harm's way, it has been I."

"I don't see it that way, Miss Payne."

"Then we will politely disagree. Now then, if you decide to meet with him, I want to go with you."

He frowned. "We'll see about that, Miss Payne. Let's see how he responds first."

"Very well. But I will insist on going, all the same."

"You're a very determined woman. I value that more than you can know."

He sipped his coffee. "But let's set this matter aside for a moment—for a much more encouraging one. Just this morning, I received a telegram from Dr. Ehrlich. He's devised an antisyphilitic compound called arsphenamine, which is showing considerable promise. He's dispatched a supply by train and fast steamer—enough for Ruth and Harry. It ought to be here in two weeks."

"That is simply wonderful news! Thank you ever so much, Mr. Kendall. I was certain you could help us. And just in time. Annie told me yesterday that Ruth seems to be failing."

"Tell her to stay as strong as she can for a couple weeks. Ehrlich also wired me the instructions for the drug's administration, which I'll give to Dr. Hindman, my private physician. The treatment does not sound very pleasant, however."

"How so?"

"Not to be indelicate, but it requires an injection into the posterior with a very large needle. The substance itself is apparently thick and viscous, and therefore hurts like the devil going in. And then—since it is a form of arsenic, after all—the initial reaction is one of muscular pain and contractions. Possible convulsions."

"But it will kill the thing?"

"He believes it will. But he cautioned me that the syphilis bacterium—in dying under the action of the arsenic—in its death throes gives off a toxin that itself can be lethal."

"God, the thing is determined to kill, isn't it?"

"It's a scourge. How people can live an entire lifetime with that Sword of Damocles hanging over them, I do not know. It's no wonder so many lose their minds long before the end comes."

"How will we know whether it works?"

"Ehrlich said that if the patient has a rash—and Ruth certainly does, from what you tell me—if the drug is effective, the rash will disappear in a matter of days. Whatever is going on deeper in the body will change more slowly, but if the rash goes, the disease is dead. Or dying."

Hidden in Plain Sight

"Do you think we ought to find a different spot to meet?" Sarah said the next afternoon, rubbing her palms in front of the fire at the International's café.

"What's wrong with our little café?" Jeremy asked.

"Nothing, but—I'm afraid eventually someone from the factory is going to show up here."

"Sarah, I rather doubt it. We're hiding in plain sight."

"Perhaps, but it's the 'plain sight' part that's bothering me."

"Well, it's far too cold to go out looking for another place just now," he said. "But I have an idea, if you're amenable."

"What is it?"

"Come up to my lodgings."

"I'm not sure that would be appropriate, Jeremy."

"Why not? You can trust me to be a gentleman."

She felt a cold pang of guilt. "I know."

"Then why not?"

"I'm not sure I trust myself to be a lady."

Sarah stayed two hours in Jeremy's suite, which overlooked the foaming rapids. The view was better than the furnishings, however—for a wealthy young man, even if one not yet come into his inheritance, the few sticks of furniture seemed too cheap, and the bed sagged and creaked.

When nothing remained but to say goodbye, she told him she could find her way out on her own, but he demurred. "I don't think that's a good idea," he said.

"Whyever not? I can't very well get lost on the way to the front door."

"It's not that. It's—er, we met in the café, and came up here together, and now if you leave alone—someone might . . ." He trailed off.

She blushed, her violet eyes opening wide. "Of course. They'll think I'm a whore."

"I wouldn't put it that way—"

"There's no reason not to. I hadn't considered that. I'm not in the habit of visiting men's lodgings."

"And I'm not in the habit of having ladies to mine, either," he said. "I merely want to protect you—that's all. I feel that we are very close now."

"I do too," she said, but without conviction. For all that had passed between them—the awkward endearments, the aching comfort of skin on skin, and then the plunge—there was now only a hollow echo, like the deep, unplaceable boom of the distant Falls. Shame? she wondered. The prick of conscience? No, it was something else, something that had nagged at her from the moment he'd left her body. Perhaps it had only been imagination, but Jeremy had seemed less tender, and more triumphant, afterward.

"Then we shall go downstairs together," she said.

He put his clothes, cuffs, collar, and tie back on, and quickly smoothed his fine brown hair in the mirror—again with what Sarah imagined seemed a touch of swagger. "Now for a proper escort," he said, when he was ready. She took his arm, and they left his suite, ignored the look of the elevator operator—who seemed to know exactly what they'd been up to—and in the lobby of the International, said a chaste goodbye.

It was Alicia who occupied Sarah's mind on her long trolley ride back to Kendall House—specifically, what she would think of her encounter with Jeremy. Probably laugh, call it a lark, an experiment perhaps, and attach no more significance to it than eating a sandwich at a railway lunch counter.

Alicia was hard in the places Sarah was soft, and Sarah envied her for it. There had been one time, after a dinner party that the Millers had hosted—with Seth and Sarah, Arthur and Cassie Pendle, the Warrens, and two other couples lost to memory—that Allie had pulled Sarah aside and whispered that she, Sarah, was the only woman there who hadn't fucked at least two of the men around the table, and that she should get on with it.

Her head was in a hopeless muddle by the time she stepped down from the trolley at Riverdale—having kept long-suffering Isadore waiting for two hours in the cold. When the coachman handed her down from the brougham at Kendall House, she thanked him quietly and went upstairs to her suite. There, she kissed Maggie hello and told the little girl that Mama needed a nap. Alone in her bedroom, she stripped off her guilty undergarments, threw herself on the bed, and sobbed herself to sleep.

HARRY HAD WATCHED SARAH'S trolley pull out of Prospect Street Station and start back toward the safety of Kendall House. For two hours, he'd lurked in the lobby of the International, fuming at her for disappearing where he could not follow. And fuming especially about the young man she'd chosen to disappear with. Everything about Jeremy Horn rubbed him wrong—the way he walked, his college-boy smirk, and now his unaccountable hold over Sarah, who had always held herself at a prudent distance from most everyone. He didn't like this young Svengali. And that suited him just fine. He'd found it much easier not to like people that one day he might have to kill.

33

A Delicate Matter

THE MOON WAS WELL UP WHEN HARRY WAS BUZZED THROUGH the electric gates of Kendall House. No carriage was sitting in the circular drive, so Isadore must have put the horses up for the night. That meant everyone was in—Kendall, Christine, Erin, Sarah, and Maggie. And Stefan, of course, who'd most likely been the one to open the gates.

Isadore had his faults, but he seemed like a decent-enough sort. Harry wasn't so sure about the big man, possibly because Stefan seemed to avoid speaking directly to him. At first, Harry thought it might be a lack of English, but he'd heard Stefan chattering away with Kendall and Christine and Sarah enough by now to know otherwise. It had to be some personal aversion the Cossack had taken to him. Harry had filed this curiosity away in his mind.

But tonight he would have to talk with the big bodyguard, like it or not. On his long walk up from Riverdale Cemetery, he had steeled himself to confront Sarah about her two hours with Jeremy Horn. He knew it was a delicate business, and he knew well enough that he wasn't usually the man for delicacy, but he'd have to try. He couldn't protect Sarah if Sarah wouldn't let herself be watched.

Harry climbed the three shallow steps to the front porch, under the *porte cochère*. Stefan was standing in front of the door, blocking it. "Evening," Harry said. "I need to see Miss Sarah."

"She has retired," Stefan said.

Harry was in no mood to argue, but as a guest, a degree of diplomacy was required. "Good to know. I need to see her."

"I heard you the first time," Stefan said. "Perhaps you did not hear *me*?"

"It's important. Either let me in, or go and get Erin."

Stefan looked at him, his craggy face hard and implacable. "Once the house is shut for the night, no one comes in. You know the rules."

Harry was beginning to go into a slow burn, but it wouldn't do to get into a scuffle on the doorstep of Kendall House. Besides, the Cossack was on home turf and, unless Harry could get the drop on him, would be a formidable opponent. Harry shrugged and gave him a little smile. "Suit yourself," he said, and turned on his heel. He could hear Stefan exhale with satisfaction—or relief, that he didn't know. Asshole, Harry thought on the way to the carriage house.

He didn't need to go *through* Stefan, though—if that had been the only way in, he would likely have taken the gamble, and let the chips fall where they may. But the Kendall House staff had long since connected the private telephone line between Harry's quarters and Sarah's suite, so he'd ring her up from his room.

In his room, he picked up the earpiece and jiggled the hook.

"Harry?" Sarah said, when she picked up. "Is everything all right?"

"I just got back. I told the nutsack I wanted to see you, but he turned me away."

"You mean Stefan?"

"Yeah, him."

"It's Cossack, you know. Not nutsack."

Who gives a shit, Harry thought. "Oh, well, then, the Cossack turned me away."

"Is it something you can tell me on the phone, or do you need to talk in person?"

"In person," he said. "I'll come back to the front door."

"I'll throw something on. Give me five minutes."

Harry thanked her, hung up, and strolled across the pavers to the front door. As he stepped onto the porch, he saw Stefan peering out of the sidelight. The door opened and the big man stepped out again. He closed the door behind him and stood with his arms folded.

"You again," he said in a low voice.

"Yeah, me again. I'm here to see Miss Sarah."

"I told you twice already. If you know what is good for you, you won't ask a third time."

"Third time's the charm, they say," Harry said, his hands in his pockets. His right hand rested on his razor.

Stefan took a step forward. "I can be *very* charming," he snarled.

Sarah stepped past the Cossack and into the glowing doorway. "Stefan! Please. Harry is always welcome to see me."

Stefan stood aside and bowed, looking down. "Yes, Miss."

"Please don't turn him away again," she said. "And certainly not in the threatening way you did just now. Or I'll speak with Mr. Kendall about it."

"I understand, Miss," Stefan mumbled, plainly furious. "That will not be necessary."

"'Scuse me, coming on through," Harry said in a singsong, taunting tone of voice. He made a show of stepping very gingerly over the threshold, looking down as if he'd dropped something.

"Did you lose something?" Sarah said.

"Oh no. I just didn't want to step on Stefan's balls, which you just cut off," Harry said, smiling. "I thought they might be rolling around here in the dark."

Stefan was silent, every muscle tensed.

"Will you look? The cigar store Indian wants to say something!" Harry said, pointing with his thumb. "Is there such a thing as a cigar store Polak, I wonder?"

"That'll be plenty, Harry," she said. "You're both ill-behaved louts, as far as I'm concerned. Now stop feuding and come in so we can talk about whatever it is you want to talk about."

Harry nodded and stepped into the great foyer and, with Sarah, walked toward the grand parlor. He could feel Stefan's eyes boring into their backs.

"Why do you have to antagonize him?" she asked, when they were seated together on the big leather couch. "I know you don't like him, but we're guests here. And Mr. Kendall trusts him with his life."

"His poor judgment, not mine," Harry said.

"Will you *please*?" she said in exasperation. "It doesn't matter. You didn't call me to complain about Stefan, so what's on your mind?"

"It's a rather delicate matter," he said, having rehearsed his opening.

Sarah rolled her eyes. "Harry, I know you far too well to expect delicacy."

"Well, it's sort of my business, and sort of not my business."

"Harry. Quit stalling."

He nodded and swallowed hard. "All right. After work today, I followed you, as usual."

"You did," she said. It wasn't a question. "And what, may I ask, would you like to report?"

"I saw you with your boyfriend at the International Hotel."

"Mr. Horn?"

"I suppose that's his name, yes."

"He's not my *boyfriend*," she said.

"I don't know what else to call a man you spend two hours with—privately."

She reddened from the neck of her gown to the roots of her hair.

"Boyfriend, then," she said.

"You have to believe me about him, Sarah. I have a bad feeling—"

"You've made your views amply clear," she snapped. "Though I can't for the life of me imagine what you have against him. Other than he's been showing me some attention."

He laughed, a smoky little snort. "I'm not jealous, if that's what you mean."

"Good. Don't be."

"Sarah, I can't protect you if I can't keep eyes on you."

"It's not like The Oaks Restaurant, Harry. You can't be in the man's room with us."

Harry's craggy face darkened. "You shouldn't be in the man's room, either."

"That'll be sufficient," she said, standing. "Effective now, we're going to have to have a new rule, you and I."

"Which is?"

"When I'm with Jeremy, you may not follow me."

"But Sarah—"

"It's not negotiable, Harry. Do we understand each other?"

He looked into the dying fire and nodded. "Yes, we do."

"Thank you, Harry."

"Don't mention it," he said, standing. He walked out of the grand parlor, passing by Stefan, who was still glaring at him.

The night had turned bitter cold, and the air smelled of snow as Harry ambled back to the carriage house, half expecting Stefan to jump him. Harry sat down in the shadow of the side door to Kendall House, and slowly rolled himself a cigarette.

There's an exception to every rule, he thought.

34

TALES OUT OF SCHOOL

AFTER ANOTHER LONG TRYST WITH JEREMY ON MONDAY, SARAH visited the factory floor four times on Tuesday, looking for him but, to her disappointment, failing each time. It seemed that some of the men were looking at her oddly, but she dismissed it as imagination.

Near quitting time, she was packing up her things when MacCormick called out to her.

"Miss Price," he said, "would you have a minute?"

"Of course," she said, and sat down across from his desk.

"There's been a wee *situation* arise," the superintendent said.

"A situation?"

He put his fingers together in a little steeple. "Mr. Kendall tells me you're looking into the union now. I'm reassured that you don't think the problem's here in the works."

"I'm not certain, but it does seem the union is involved."

"Aye, there's nothing certain in this life," he said. "But in view of developments, I was thinking that perhaps in this phase of your investigation you might base yourself at Kendall House. Which will be much more comfortable for you than this bowfin place."

Sarah looked puzzled. "I'm not sure I understand."

"Bowfin. It means smelly."

"Not that," she said. "Why I ought to work at Kendall House."

"Well—if what you need isn't here at the factory, then you might as well be elsewhere."

"I wish you'd tell me directly what's on your mind," Sarah said.

He swallowed hard. "It concerns Mr. Horn."

Sarah's stomach flipped over. "What about him?"

"Do understand, now, I find Mr. Horn a good lad. I like him."

"I do too," she said.

"Aye, well, you see, that's the problem."

"The *problem*?"

"Miss Price—the past few days, there's been a lot of talk among the men."

Sarah thought she was going to be sick, but calmed herself.

"I can't imagine what about," she said.

MacCormick flushed. "Well . . . to hit it square . . . Mr. Horn's been vaunting a bit. With the other men."

"*Vaunting*?"

"Bragging."

"Bragging? About what?"

He looked down at his desk. "Well, about *you*, Miss. You and him."

Sarah again felt that she might vomit. "May I—may I ask what he's been saying?"

"It's a tricky matter."

"He hasn't—"

"He's claiming that you and he have been intimate."

"My God," Sarah said.

"Now, mind you, it's not something I care to know about, your personal business, but it's becoming a disruption on the floor. So I think it might be better if you stayed up at Kendall House."

"But, sir—"

He ignored her. "And since Mr. Kendall's bound to hear about it soon enough, he'll need to hear it from me first. I didn't want you to be surprised, Miss Price, because we all have the highest respect—"

"Well, you oughtn't to," she blurted out. "If I've behaved in such a way that you have to banish me—"

"Ach, banishment's a strong word, lass."

"You do understand that Mr. Kendall will dismiss me," she said quietly.

"Well, now, that'll be up to Mr. Kendall," the superintendent said. "But as I have the say in this factory, I'm afraid I can't have you back."

"I understand," she said, feeling as though she were floating above her body. "I don't know what to say, Mr. MacCormick, other than I'm sorry. You've been good to me. I'll speak with Mr. Kendall tonight."

IT WASN'T UNTIL AFTER dinner that her stay of execution was over. Christine had single-handedly kept the conversation going over the meal, while Sarah ate little and Kendall smiled indulgently at his voluble daughter.

"You'll want to speak with me, I assume?" Sarah said quietly to Kendall, after the dishes were cleared away and Christine had gone off to her rooms.

He nodded gravely. "Would my office be acceptable?"

"Of course," she said, and walked down the long corridor to the paneled office, Kendall following behind. She sat down in the chair in front of the big desk and folded her hands in her lap.

"Please, let's sit at the table," he said. "There's no need for any formality between us."

She got up and relocated to the table. He sat down across from her.

He swallowed hard. "I understand that you spoke with Mr. MacCormick today."

"Yes, and I'm fully aware of the problem I've caused."

"But *is* it a problem? I said to Mac—we may have it all wrong—that your, er, *cultivation* of Horn may be a detective's stratagem. In which case, then we owe you an apology."

"No, sir," she said. "I wish I could say it was a detective's trick. It was, if anything, a trick I played on myself. I liked—like—Mr. Horn, and events overtook my better judgment. It's very kind of you to allow me to save face, but to accept such an indulgence would be heaping dishonesty atop poor judgment."

He tapped on the table with his finger, considering. "You know, Miss Payne, between the danger I've put you in, and now this, I've come to the conclusion that your assignment here—"

"No need," she said. "Please rest assured that I'll be ready to leave by the morning. I only hope that you will speak kindly of me to Christine. She's a very special young woman." She bit her lip, hard, and put her hands flat on the table to push her chair back.

Kendall sat back, looking bewildered. "What in the *world* are you talking about?"

"I presume that I am to be dismissed. Which is precisely what I deserve."

"*Deserve*," he said. "God forbid that any of us should get what we deserve. No, that's not what I was going to say."

"Then I am at a loss, sir."

"I've not been honest with you, Miss Payne. Not much in my factory escapes my notice, and I knew from very early on that you—had *feelings* for Mr. Horn."

"I don't understand."

"I know what it's like to be lonely," Kendall said. "And I can recognize it in others. I knew you were lonely, too, from the very first time we met. But did I say anything? No. Did I offer you any real kindness? No, I did not. Instead, I stood by and watched as you fell in love with Jeremy Horn."

"It's not your responsibility to save me from myself," Sarah said.

"No, it's not that. It's that—it's that as it was happening, I kept thinking—why not *me*?"

There was a long silence.

"Oh my," she said. "I don't know what to say."

"There's nothing to say. I would fight to the death to beat out a competitor in business—but I didn't fight for you. I let another man win the greatest prize of all—your love."

"But I don't love Jeremy," she blurted. "I don't know quite what I feel, but it's not *love*. It was mostly—*life*. To wake up from this cold deadness I feel. Jeremy revived me, and I felt indebted to him for that. And then only to learn that I was just a feather in his cap."

"Try not to be so hard on him," Kendall said. "He may have been boasting a bit, but that doesn't mean his feelings are not genuine. It may have been only youthful exuberance on his part."

"You must be the most magnanimous man I have ever met," she said softly.

"No," he said, shaking his head. "I have many faults, Miss Payne. But I do have compassion, and I wouldn't want Mr. Horn—or any person— to feel the way I do now."

"How do you feel?"

"Like a man who threw away the biggest opportunity of his life."

She groaned and put her head in her hands. "You're not the only one," she said to the table. "You're my employer, sir—and I thought it unworthy to—to even admit the possibility . . ."

"Then there's only one solution to our shared dilemma, Miss Payne. Only one way out."

"And what is that? Because God knows I need a way out right about now."

"And I have one for you," he said. "You're fired."

"I'm *fired*?"

"Allow me to repeat myself. You are fired. Effective immediately."

"But I thought you weren't going to dismiss me!"

"I wasn't. But now I know something I didn't know then. If I'm not your employer—then I no longer have to be 'Mr. Kendall,' nor you 'Miss Payne.' We can be Charles and Sarah—if you'll allow it, that is."

"You dear, dear man," she said, grasping his hand in both of hers. "But may I still try to solve this mystery of your missing water?"

"I know better than to try to deny you," he said. "So yes, you may, if you so desire. But only on one condition."

"Which is?"

"That you and Maggie continue to live with us here, where you'll be safe—until Brass is behind bars, where he belongs."

"Agreed, and gratefully, Charles."

"Good. Actually, there's one more condition . . ." His words dissolved into a smile.

"Yes?"

"Which is—if, in time, you discover that you don't have lasting feelings for Mr. Horn—you'll let me try to bring you a little happiness."

Sarah stood, came around the table, and threw her arms around his neck. He gently put his arms around her, feeling her warmth.

"Sarah," he whispered into her hair. "Sarah. How many times I've whispered that name, to myself. A beautiful name for a beautiful soul."

"Charles—I've been so—"

"Well, *finally*," said a voice from Kendall's office door. Sarah sprang away from Charles, and they both snapped around. Christine was leaning against the doorjamb, wearing a sly expression.

"Christine!" Kendall said. "I thought you'd gone up to your rooms."

"Sorry to disappoint, lovebirds."

"Your father and I were—"

Christine held up her hand. "Please, spare me. You can't know how long I've waited for this very moment. The only question in my mind now is—"

"Christine, stop yourself," her father said.

"—how quickly I can get back upstairs so the two of you can consummate this thing."

"Christine!" Kendall said. "You know better!"

"Uh-huh," she said. "I'll be going now." She disappeared down the corridor.

"Now we've both been embarrassed today," Sarah said.

He smiled. "It has been quite a day."

"You know, Charles," she said, "an hour ago I thought my whole world was coming to an end."

"And now?"

"I feel that it may be just beginning."

CHRISTINE WAS WAITING FOR her at the top of the stairs. "Well, well, well," she said.

"Your father is a wonderful man," Sarah said, wiping her eyes.

"I told you that you'd love him, didn't I?"

"Now, let's not get ahead of ourselves."

"Why not? I don't want you to leave, and neither does he."

"I thought I'd be leaving first thing tomorrow, after the stunt I pulled."

"You? A stunt?"

"It's a bit of a sore subject," Sarah said.

"Oh, come on!" Christine said. "It's just *us*. Look at all the things I've told you about my antics. You have to balance the scale a little."

"Let's say I became a little too involved with one of the foremen at the factory."

"*Involved?*" Christine said, wide-eyed. "As in—*involved* involved?"

"As in," Sarah said. "And I relied upon his discretion, but he—tattled—to some of the men at the factory. It didn't take long for the news to reach your father."

"That *scoundrel*! Isn't that just like some men, beating their chests about their conquests. Someone should cut that masher's balls off. You ought to tell Harry about him. He'd fix him."

"God, I'd never tell Harry, because that's exactly what he'd do."

"HARRY, DARLING," CHRISTINE SAID later that night, from the shadow of the overhanging carriage house roof.

"Miss Christine," Harry said, sauntering up the cobbled drive. He tipped his hat. "What are you doing out in the cold?"

"I saw you come through the gate, and wondered if I might have a word."

Harry motioned for her to follow him into the carriage house. They leaned against the brougham, which Isadore had neatly put up for the night.

"Mind if I smoke?" Harry said, taking out a package of tobacco and a rolling paper.

"Not at all," she said.

"Thanks. Now what's on your mind?"

"Sarah. She told me about her little—situation—with the foreman at the factory."

"Not sure I'm following you."

"Harry," Christine said, "you know what I'm talking about."

"I'm not sure that I do."

"I don't know the fellow's name, but he's done something very wrong."

Harry finished rolling his cigarette, stuck it in the corner of his mouth, and lit it. "What?"

"Sarah told me that he's told some of the other men at the factory about his private doings with her. Word got back to my father."

Harry breathed out smoke. "The man's rancid."

"I'm sure she'll talk with him about it, but if you want my opinion, that's letting him off too easy. And Sarah wasn't about to tell you this little detail—"

Harry laughed. "I can guess why."

"She doesn't want anything to happen to him," Christine said. "That's the way she is. Now, I'm not that way, and I think something ought to happen to him. Something *bad*."

"I'll have a talk with him," Harry said.

"She'll be angry with me if she finds out I told you."

"You did the right thing, Miss Christine."

"Thank you, Harry," she said.

He nodded. "The pleasure's all mine."

The Old Girls

THE FLOOD OF NEW BUSINESS INTO MILLER ENVELOPE QUICKLY revealed that, under Edward's leadership, the company had not been built with expansion in mind. Gaines's vaunted machines—The Old Girls—were quickly overwhelmed, and Howie seemed always to be running down to the factory to revive one or another of them.

"I never thought I'd say it," Howie said to Alicia one day after returning from the factory floor. "You are bringing in more orders than we can fulfill."

She looked at him with a skeptical pout. "Something of a high-class problem, don't you think?"

"It's still a problem."

"Why can't you make them run faster? You said it yourself, you're the best machine-man in the business."

"You wouldn't understand. It's like asking my grandmother to run as fast as I can. Suffice it to say, we're working The Old Girls to death."

"Well, we've got customers now who need their envelopes on time, or they can't do their mailings," she said. "I can't very well tell them, 'Sorry, but we've got a bunch of shitty old machines, and you'll have to wait while they take their time about fulfilling your orders.'"

"You're going to have to tell Donohue & Hill that very thing," he said. "Leaving out the shitty part. Number Three is down completely, and it's going to take me hours to put her right again. It's five o'clock now, so that means I can't get started on it until tomorrow."

"Their order is due in their factory the day after tomorrow, full stop," she said. "They've already called me twice this week to see that it's arriving on time. We have to make the deadline."

"I'm sorry, but it's not going to happen. There isn't enough time."

"Then work tonight. All night long, if that's what it takes. I don't care. Get the damn thing running and get their order fulfilled. I'd do it myself, if I knew one end of a wrench from the other."

"I can't do it tonight," he said, shaking his head. "I'm supposed to watch my sister's children tonight."

"You detest children, Gaines."

"I know, but I don't have a choice. I agreed to do it."

"Then call her and tell her you have something more important to do. Or changed your mind. Or the truth, that you hate children, I don't care. As I said, if I knew how to fix it myself—"

"But you don't, do you?" he said, with a little smile that infuriated her.

"I don't think you're taking this seriously enough, Mr. Majority Owner. This is a big new customer. If we fuck this up, we'll lose all credibility. Word will get around."

Gaines tossed a pencil onto his desk. "Fine. I'll disappoint my sister, and stay here and pull an all-nighter to get your order out."

"It's not *my* order, you moron. It's *our* order."

"I am well aware of that, but there were many times when Edward and I had to let a deadline slip because of mechanical problems. It happens."

"I won't even comment on what the two of you did. I do know what the books looked like when I got here, which gave me a pretty good idea."

"That's a very nasty comment, you know," he said.

"And no less than you deserve for trying to welch out on getting a big order done. Now will you get your lazy ass down to the factory and get to work?"

"Yes, Your Royal Highness," he said in a mock-English accent, which sounded like a man from Buffalo imitating a man from England. "Your wish is my command."

"I'll remember that," Allie said.

THE NEXT MORNING, HOWIE was sitting at his desk when Alicia arrived at a quarter to seven.

"You're in early," he said.

"I couldn't sleep a wink," she replied. "Worrying about your old Number Three machine and the Donohue & Hill order. *Please* tell me you got that thing running."

"That *thing*, as you call her, is indeed running—and like a top. It took me most of the night, but not only is she in fine fettle again, I ran your order myself. It's ready to be boxed and shipped."

"Howie!" she said, smiling broadly. "You're a prince, and a mechanical genius. I'd kiss you if I thought you wouldn't get ideas."

"No one's here. You could kiss me, if you felt like it."

She smiled, walked over to his desk, leaned over, and gave him a long kiss.

"There," she said. "Don't say I never gave you anything."

"That wasn't much of a kiss," Gaines said.

"I knew you'd get ideas. And it was a good kiss. Better than any your former business partner got from your current one, I'll tell you that."

"So you say," he said, as she sat down and began writing out her list for the day, "but I think I deserve a little more than a peck, don't you?"

"Not *this* again?"

"I seem to recall that you told me not too long ago that if I made you happy, you'd make me happy."

"It sounds like something I might say."

"So—you're happy now, aren't you?"

"What do you want, Gaines? Just come out with it, and stop scratching like a chicken."

"I'd like the two of us to have a nice dinner together tonight, and then—can you guess the rest?"

"Oh, I believe I can. Subtlety is not among your gifts, Howie."

"Well, then, what do you say?"

"If I understand correctly, the price for your doing your goddamn job is I have to fuck you."

"That's a very coarse way of putting it."

"But not inaccurate."

"You'll get something out of it, too."

"You do know that Bert is back," she said.

Howie leaned back in his chair and examined his fingernails. "Last evening, after you directed me to, I telephoned my sister and told her that I had something to do at work that couldn't wait. You can easily call Bert and tell him the same thing."

"Of course. 'Hello, Bert, I'm not coming home tonight until late— Gaines fixed our machinery, so I have to fix him.' Yes, I think that's got the right ring to it."

"I've said from the start you ought to be honest with him, and then there'd be no need for lies. But since you won't be, you'll have to be creative. You can come up with something."

"If I agree, will you promise that you won't keep pulling this stunt? I don't want to have to spread my legs every time you turn a wrench."

"I promise. And I wish you wouldn't say it like that."

"Do you swear?"

"I swear."

"Fine, then," she said. "I'll tell Bert I'll be home late. But I'm not staying the night, so don't start on me afterward that you don't want me to leave."

"You're welcome to leave—"

"So long as you get some first."

"That's not nice. I love you, whether you want to hear it or not."

"Fuck's sake, Howie. Can you spare me the sentimental stuff, at least?"

FROM HER OFFICE WINDOW, Alicia watched as the wagon containing the last of the Donohue & Hill order crept slowly down Division Street toward the New York Central freight depot. It had taken all day to sort, box, and crate the order, but it would arrive by tomorrow morning, on time.

She picked up the earpiece of her telephone and asked to be connected to the Miller residence on Ashwood Street.

"Hello, dear," Bert's voice said when the line engaged. "I thought you'd be getting home by now. It's almost six thirty. Is everything all right?"

"More or less," Allie said. "I have a problem with a big order that has to go out today. A machine broke down, and we're trying to make up for lost time. I won't be home until late."

"I'm terribly sorry to hear that, dear. Is there anything I can do to help?"

"No, it's merely a matter of my supervising things until we get it done. Thanks all the same."

"Call me if you'd like me to escort you home."

"You're a dear," Allie said. "But I'll be fine. Don't trouble yourself."

She hung up the earpiece and looked over at Gaines, who was reading the *Racing Form*.

"I hope you're satisfied," she said in a monotone. "Now that I'm back to my lying ways, are you ready for your throw?"

"Where would you like to have dinner?"

Alicia sighed. "I'm not hungry."

"You don't want to have dinner?"

"Like I said, I'm not hungry."

"May I have a rain check?"

"Yes, you may have a rain check," she murmured, still looking at the telephone, which stared back at her, accusingly.

"Shall we then, dear?" he said.

ON ASHWOOD STREET, BERT replaced the earpiece with a soft click. Poor thing, he thought. She can take care of herself, but all the same, it's not very chivalrous to leave her all alone.

"Melissa!" he called toward the back of the house.

"Yes, Mr. Hartshorn?" the maid said, coming out of the kitchen, wiping her hands on her apron.

"Mrs. Miller has to work late tonight, and I'm going downtown to keep her company. Don't wait dinner for us. We'll have something cold when we get home."

"Very well, sir," Melissa said. "I'll tell Mrs. Hall and the girls."

"Thank you, Missy," he said, taking his derby down from the hat rack.

Bert crunched down the porch steps and thought about walking downtown, but the air was cold and heavy with coal smoke. So he hopped aboard the trolley at the Summer Street station and, after twenty minutes of clanging and rocking, stepped down at Division Street. He looked up at the stained brick hulk of the Cashton Building, to Alicia's office window on the fifth floor. Strange, he thought, there's no light going in there. She must be down in the factory. He walked a half block to the factory entrance, and pulled on the handle of the heavy metal door. It was locked. He put his ear against it, but there was none of the usual clattering from inside.

He walked around to the rear of the building, and again found nothing but a couple of men loitering outside Clinton's Saloon, holding mugs of beer and smoking. "You gents happen to work at the envelope company?" he said.

"Yep," the one man said, while the other one ignored Bert entirely. "Why?"

"I was looking for someone who works in the offices," Bert said, "but everything seems to be closed."

"It is," the man said. "We closed around six thirty. We had to finish shipping out a big order, and once that was done, they let us skate."

"It's all done, then? The big order?"

"Believe me, we wouldn't be here if it wasn't," the fellow said.

"Well, thank you, gentlemen," Bert said, tipping his hat.

He walked back to Division Street, rattled the door of the office building once more for good measure, and looked up at Alicia's window again. Still dark. Of all the luck, he thought, our paths must have crossed. She's probably already back home, or on her way.

As Bert was stepping aboard the northbound streetcar to return to Ashwood, Howie Gaines was positioning himself above Alicia, savoring the last delicious moment before entering her.

"Are you ready?" he whispered.

"Do I look ready?" she said with a flat smile.

Howie slipped inside her. "I love you, Alicia," he whispered.

Alicia said nothing, and was happy that Gaines seemed eager to get on with it.

WHEN ALICIA GOT HOME, she hung up her hat, kicked off her shoes, and padded down the hallway to the kitchen, where a light was burning.

Bert was sitting at the kitchen table, eating a cold roast beef sandwich.

"Well, hello there," he said. "Back at last."

"Yes, back at last. A bit early for a midnight snack, isn't it?"

"This is my dinner," he said, swallowing.

"You didn't eat with Mother and the girls?"

"No, I had to go out for a little while."

"Oh," she said, flopping down on one of the chairs around the table.

"You must be exhausted," Bert said.

"I am, to be honest," Allie said, brushing away an errant wisp of hair. "It's been a long day. Can you pour me a drink?"

"Poor dear," he said but didn't get up to get the whiskey.

"Not much choice in the matter. If these new customers don't get their orders on time, our reputation is going to be ruined."

"Your *reputation*," he said, with a little chuckle.

She frowned. "What's that supposed to mean?"

"You've been at the office all this time? Or was it the factory?"

She looked at him, her eyes half closing. "I told you. I had to work."

"I know that's what you said. I'm merely wondering what time you left."

The old fox has got me cornered now, Allie thought. Well, fuck it. I'm not going to lie twice. I didn't like the way it felt the first time. It was one thing to lie for Arthur Pendle, but it's quite another to lie for Howie Gaines.

"I left the office around six thirty."

"Oh, I know *that*," he said.

She folded her arms and looked at him without replying.

"I *know*," he said, "because after you called, I decided to go downtown and surprise you. You know, be a good sport and keep my lady company while she worked late. Now imagine my surprise when I arrived to find Miller Envelope Company locked up tight, and no sign of life. I did bump into a couple fellows who said that after the big order was done, everyone went home."

"For Christ's sake, Bert, you're *spying* on me now? You're taking a page from Edward's book."

"I was hardly spying. I intended to keep you company and then escort you home. As any gentleman would."

She looked down at the table, and tightened her arms around herself. "Yes," she said quietly. "That was very sweet of you, Bert."

"Thank you. Now would you be willing to tell me where you were between six thirty and"—he looked up at the clock on the wall—"almost ten?"

She put her hands flat on the table. "I was with Gaines."

"Well, now. How about that. Let me guess—dinner and a show?"

"You know very well it wasn't dinner and a show. Look, you've extracted your pound of flesh. May I go now?"

"Don't make this out to be my failing, Alicia. You told me you had to work late—and instead you went to bed with Howie Gaines. I think you owe me an explanation—especially since, if I hadn't gone downtown and found you missing, I might not have known at all. Since you *lied* about it."

She rapped her knuckles on the table. "Here's how it went. The machine that was assigned to my big order did, in fact, break down yesterday. Gaines was going to go home at the end of the day, and I read him the riot act. I told him he needed to work all night to get the goddamn thing running again, if that's what it would take. He had to cancel some bullshit favor he was doing for his sister. This morning, when he told me of the big sacrifice he'd made and that he'd gotten the order done, he said it was only fair that I do the same thing to you that he had to do to his sister. Call and say I'd be late, and spend a little time with him."

"Three hours? That's not a *little* time."

Alicia sighed. "He wanted to have dinner, and I told him I wasn't hungry. So we went to his apartment. We had a couple glasses of whiskey, and we fucked. Twice. And that's the whole sordid tale."

Bert pushed his half-finished roast beef sandwich away and shook his head. "And that's the right word for it. Sordid."

"Bert, trust me, I am twice as disgusted with myself as you are with me. But I'm in a tight spot with Gaines just now, and he's pressing his advantage."

"I'm sorry, dear. Thank you for being honest about it."

"Better late than never, I guess. But I do hate lying. To you, of course, but also to myself."

"Don't you worry about me," he said. "I understand the spot you were in. Let's go upstairs and get some sleep. Tomorrow will be a brand-new day."

"Maybe, but you don't have to face Gaines first thing. I have to figure out what to do, pronto, because I am not being put into this position again. Ever."

EIGHT O'CLOCK THE NEXT morning came and went, with Howie nowhere to be seen.

Where is that piece of shit? Alicia thought. He and I were supposed to discuss the manufacturing schedule first thing this morning.

"Abby?" Allie called out. "Have you heard anything from Mr. Gaines this morning?"

"No, ma'am," the secretary said, hustling in.

"Not like him to be late."

"No, ma'am."

"Well, no matter. Here," Alicia said, thrusting out a few sheets of typing paper covered with her neat handwriting. "Type these up, please. It's the next campaign for Kendall—"

"Good morning, ladies!" Howie said, hustling into the office, his face blazing redder than usual.

"Nice of you to show up," Allie said.

"Ha ha," he said, sitting down.

"Let's do this later, Abby," Alicia said, and the secretary turned to go. "I need to talk with Mr. Gaines. Close the door on your way out, if you would."

"Sorry I'm late," Howie said after the door clicked shut behind Abby. "Completely overslept this morning. Tuckered out, I guess." He chuckled softly to himself.

"Very funny. We do have work to do, you know."

"Can I help it that you are so amazing"—he lowered his voice to a whisper—"in *bed*?"

"Well, I'm glad you had fun. But soon enough, that's going to be a moot point."

"What's a moot point?"

"It means something that has or will soon become irrelevant and unworthy of further discussion."

"I know what a moot point is. I meant, what is going to become a moot point?"

"I had a long talk with Bert last night."

"About *us*?"

"You might say that."

"Did you tell him—that we've been together?"

"I did."

Gaines looked triumphant. "And what did he say *then*?"

"He asked me to marry him."

Howie went as bolt upright and rigid as a convict in the electric chair. "He *what*?"

"It ought to come as no surprise, Howie. Bert's been living in my home for almost a year. His divorce is final now, and he asked me to marry him. It was the honorable thing to do, and if anything, it was somewhat overdue."

Gaines's red face had gone white. "And what—what did you say?"

"Naturally I told him yes."

"You said *yes*?"

"Are you suddenly hard of hearing? Yes, I said yes. What else would I say?"

"I—I don't know what to say."

"'Best wishes' is customary for the bride-to-be, and 'congratulations' for the groom."

"I'm not talking about etiquette," he said. "You and I have been building something here."

"And so we are. A company."

"That's not at all what I mean. I've told you—how I feel. That I love you. And in time you'll come to love me, too. It's destiny that brought us together."

"You sound like a schoolgirl. *Destiny*. Really, Howie?"

"So that's how this"—he motioned between them with his finger—"ends? When and how you say it does?"

"That's generally how these things go, Gaines. It's not a voting matter. We're colleagues, not a couple. Whatever off-the-books fun we've had can't continue."

"I've got to look in on the factory," he said abruptly, standing.

"I thought we were going to discuss the manufacturing calendar for the Kendall contract?"

He turned and looked at her, his fists clenched at his sides. "Why don't you just tell me when you want them made, and I'll make them? You seem to be pretty good at making decisions all on your own and then telling me how it's going to be."

"Howie, be reasonable."

"No. You write down what you want, and I'll make sure it gets done. Let's not pretend that my opinion matters around here. Or my feelings, for that matter."

He jerked the door open and slammed it hard as he left, leaving Abby staring wide-eyed after him.

"IF TODAY WAS THAT brand-new day we talked about," Alicia said to Bert over a glass of whiskey before dinner, "I'd just as soon not wake up at all tomorrow." She held up her glass. "This won't be my last cocktail tonight, I can tell you that much."

"That bad?"

"Worse than you can imagine. But let's put it this way. You won't have to worry about him fucking me anymore."

Bert studied his whiskey. "I haven't made a peep about that since last night."

"And that's part of what makes you so delightful."

"Why, thank you," Bert said.

She took a sip of her drink. "You're welcome. And I did feel terrible about lying to you. But on top of that, I'm not about to be blackmailed. So I came up with a way to shut him down for good. And he didn't like it—not one bit. He got quite worked up."

"I told you this would happen. You've ruined him for other women."

"Flatterer."

"If you're willing to share, I am curious about what you said that shut off his water."

"I told him you'd asked me to marry you," she said.

"*What?*"

"Don't have a stroke of apoplexy, Bert. I know it's a fantasy, but that's what it took."

"I'm surprised even that would do the trick. You've got a certain kind of voodoo about you."

"I'm beginning to wonder about that myself. He didn't cool down all day."

"I can't say I feel too sorry for him," Bert said.

"And I have to say I did, a little. You didn't see his face. Crestfallen."

"This is a first—you, getting sentimental. Don't worry about him. In time, he'll settle down. What other choice does he have, after all?"

"None, but until he does, you might say that relations are going to be somewhat strained."

"More than somewhat, I'd think. But it won't be forever. Time will heal his wounds, as it does for every jilted lover."

Alicia finished off her whiskey. "I hope you're right," she said, jingling the ice in her empty glass. "Another one of these would help to heal mine, if you wouldn't mind."

GAINES'S COLD SILENCE LASTED another day, and then another, until Alicia grew tired of walking on eggshells.

"I do wish you'd pull yourself out of your funk, Gaines," she said to him as they descended in the creaking freight elevator to the factory floor. "It's becoming rather tedious."

"I'm not in a funk," he said.

"I know a funk when I see one."

"I don't think you do. I don't have anything particular to say, that's all."

"Suffering in silence doesn't help anyone, Howie."

The elevator hit bottom with a jarring thud, and Gaines opened the cage to let Allie step out. "Mrs. Miller," he said grandly, gesturing like a bellhop.

Alicia rolled her eyes and stepped out onto the whirring, clacking factory floor. She looked down the line of machines, each with a young lady sitting nearby, inspecting the final product and neatly putting them one by one into boxes.

"I'll bet you never thought we'd be this busy," she said.

"Yes, yes, I know. You saved the company. I'll have a sign painted up shortly."

"I didn't say it to give myself a pat on the back. It's something we can both take pride in. You keep this place running like a top."

"It's not easy," he said.

"No, I'm sure it's not. A year of this, though, and we'll be able to afford to buy you some nice new machines that aren't breaking down all the time."

Howie gave a small bitter chuckle. "My consolation prize."

"Will you stop? Why can't you tell yourself that we had three little interludes that no one can ever take away?"

"You know the old saying: 'Three times a bridesmaid, never a bride.' I guess there's more truth in it than I knew."

No-Man's Land

On Friday afternoon, Sarah was finishing up her week over one of Christine's shockingly strong special cocktails, laughing at another of the younger woman's crazy stories.

Meanwhile, Harry Price was loafing out of sight near the Kendall works, watching. He was still stamping his feet at a quarter to six, and beginning to wonder what was keeping Jeremy Horn, when the young man at last emerged from the white board fence surrounding the Kendall operation. Horn was walking purposefully in the direction of downtown, as though he had someplace to go.

Harry tailed Jeremy down Main, and then made a sharp left up Falls Street. Horn didn't slacken his pace until he was out of the tourist district and well into no-man's-land, two dozen long blocks of Niagara Falls where only the poor or disreputable—or both—went about freely. Odd place for a young swell to be walking, Harry thought. Lots of dandies went slumming in Harry's old haunts in The Hooks, Buffalo's red-light district, and presumably they did in the slums of Niagara Falls as well. But rarely, if ever, alone.

It seemed to Harry, though, that Jeremy Horn was at his ease in no-man's-land. The way he moved, how he walked, carrying himself with a purposeful, slightly rolling gait, was something a man learned only one place—in prison. Harry had seen that walk many times before, both in the joint and out, and it was a sure sign that a man had seen the elephant, as the saying went.

Just past Thirteenth Street, Harry's quarry finally turned into the doorway of Pusatier's Saloon. Pusatier's was a standard-issue blind pig, a narrow storefront containing only a long bar without stools and a few old tables occupied by men and a couple of battered gas chandeliers. At the bar, a small kerosene cigar lighter was always kept burning. Cigars and booze made up the dive's entire menu, not counting a few ancient pickled eggs sunken like stones in a solution murky with dirt from the hands daring or desperate enough to plunge in and fish one out. Most people—especially the habitués of a place like Pusatier's—tended to look at the pickled-egg jar as a kind of prop, not as something edible. Everyone knew that, to be licensed, saloons were required to serve food—and almost everyone knew just as well not to touch it.

Harry killed time in the cold for a few minutes, and then went in.

Jeremy Horn was standing at the bar, holding a glass of whiskey. Harry took his place a few feet down, toward the entrance. He ordered himself one, and when it came, he noticed that Horn's drink seemed considerably darker than his. A regular, then, he thought—not getting the watered-down stuff. Horn tossed the liquor back, while Harry let his sit untouched. In a place like this, a stranger was likely to get not only diluted whiskey but also possibly a jolt of chloral hydrate—knockout drops—along with it.

Jeremy bought a cigar, a five-center, and leaned toward a device mounted to the bar, a heavy cast-iron arch with a long curving handle, like a pump handle over a well. One lifted the handle, and a wicked-looking steel guillotine blade, designed to cut off lengths of densely packed plug tobacco—and for the much lighter task of clipping the ends off cigars—rose inside the arch, which resembled a huge upside-down horseshoe. Harry watched as Jeremy placed his stogie under the blade, carefully lowered the handle, and neatly sliced off the tip. The bartender held out a match—Horn was definitely a regular—and Jeremy puffed out a big cloud of blue smoke.

By this point, Harry's rapt attention had not gone unnoticed, neither by the bartender—who caught Horn's eye and then gave a sidelong glance toward Harry—nor by Jeremy himself.

"Do we know each other, friend?" Horn said, not turning to look at Harry, instead studying his cigar ash.

"Don't think so," Harry said, extending his hand. "I'm Harry."

Horn turned and shook his hand. "Pleased to make your acquaintance, Harry. I'm Jeremy. Jeremy Ahearn."

"Didn't get that," Harry said, tapping his ear. "Bad ears from working in a sawmill. Did you say Jeremy A. Hearn or Jeremy Ahearn?"

"Ahearn," he said. "One word."

"You don't sound Irish."

"I'm Canadian."

"No offense intended, Mr. Ahearn."

"None taken," Horn-or-Ahearn said, tapping his empty glass for a refill. "I haven't seen you here before, Harry. You new in town?"

"Yeah, moved here only a month or so ago. Trying to get the lay of the land."

"Takes a while. Are you looking for work?"

"I'm always looking for work," Harry said. "You know of any?"

"Depends what kind of work you're looking for," Jeremy said.

"I was a logger in Pennsylvania. Any kind of labor, I guess."

"You seem too smart to be a common laborer."

"Have to start someplace. You look like you've done pretty well for yourself," Harry said, nodding at the man's suit.

"I'm a foreman in one of the big factories here."

"Good for you. It must pay well."

"It does, but I don't do it for the salary. Am I right?" he said to the bartender, who nodded.

"Why else would you do it?"

"Girls. Girls like a man who's got a good job. The old meal ticket, you know."

"You have a girl, then, too?" Harry asked.

Jeremy stuck the cigar in the corner of his mouth and reached into his jacket pocket. "Have a look. Pusatier, you've seen her already, so don't start drooling."

The bartender laughed as Jeremy pulled out a cabinet card photograph, with the logo of the International Hotel in fine, flowing script along the bottom. It was a portrait of Sarah, dressed for their weekend tour of the Falls. He held it out to Harry. "That's my girl," he said, tapping the photograph with a finger.

Harry took a long look at the photograph. "Is this real?"

Jeremy tucked the photo into his coat again. He puffed with some satisfaction on his stogie. "Yes, it is. She's beautiful, is she not?"

"Yep. Looks like a sweet kid, too."

"She is. Though she's a little saucier than you might think."

"How do you mean?"

"Don't get him started," Pusatier said. "He's told this story to every-body who'll listen."

"Hey, now," said Jeremy. "Not *everybody*."

"What's the story?" Harry said.

"If I told you the whole thing, it'd give you a hard-on that you'd have to cut off to get rid of. So I'll give you the abridged version. I'd been seeing her for a few weeks, and she was giving me the look—you know—the *look*."

"Oh yes, I believe I know the look," Harry said.

"I could tell she was good to go," Ahearn continued. "So I came right out and asked her—'How about we go up to my lodgings?' And she doesn't bat an eye, and we go up together."

"I don't think this part is any of my business," Harry said, wav-ing a hand.

"But this is the good part," Jeremy said. "So we're up in my room, and I swear before God and all the saints"—he crossed himself—"we weren't there for five minutes before she starts stripping off her clothes. And if you think she looks good with the clothes on, you cannot begin to *imagine* how good she looks without them."

"No, that I can't," Harry said, fidgeting with his razor in his trou-ser pocket.

"Now here's the best part," Jeremy said, puffing furiously on his cigar. "The poor girl is positively starved for affection. She's a widow, and her late husband was a drunk, so God only knows how long it'd been since she'd had any. She pulled me into bed with her, and in no time flat, we're having the time of our lives, you know—and believe me, I'm doing everything I can to make it last, thinking of my grandmother naked and so on—and then—"

"*This* is the good part," Pusatier said, hastily drying a glass on a bar towel.

"Right. So all of a sudden she makes this funny sound—I can't begin to describe it—and damned if her pussy doesn't clamp down on me like a vise." He made a tight fist. "I couldn't even move the thing in or out.

And her whole body goes stiff as a board. I thought for a second I'd killed her. But then in the next instant she goes completely limp, and everything relaxes again."

"Good God," Pusatier said. "I've never heard of such a thing."

"Nor have I," Harry added.

"Well, it would have been perfect, but of course I went and fucked it up—temporarily anyway. I told a fellow at work about it—you can't keep a thing like that to yourself—"

"Try as you might," Harry said.

"—and word got back to her that I'd spilled the beans. The factory *fired* her, no less. Boy oh boy, was she steamed. But next time I see her, I'll straighten things out. She's not the type to hold a grudge."

"No, she's not," Harry said quietly.

Jeremy looked at him quizzically. "Well, even if she does—hold a grudge," Ahearn went on, "I'll never forget that scene."

"Nor will I," Harry mused, looking deep into his watered-down drink. "I suppose I ought to thank you for that." Harry raised his glass in a toast but put it down without taking a drink.

Jeremy's long fingers fiddled with his empty glass, sliding it back and forth like a shuttlecock, while the bartender tried to follow it around with the bottle of whiskey.

"You don't like the whiskey?" Jeremy asked as the bartender finally found the bullseye and refilled his glass.

"Can't afford more than one, so I have to take it slow."

"Then finish that one, and let me buy you another. As my welcome to Niagara Falls."

"I couldn't let you do that, Mr. Ahearn."

"My money's not good enough for you?"

"All right, what the hell," Harry said. "But if I can be choosy—since you're buying—I wouldn't mind one of those cigars, instead of a whiskey. It smells awful good."

"Best nickel cigar going. Another Counsellor for my friend," Jeremy said to the bartender, who handed one over the bar. Harry sniffed it appreciatively. "Very kind of you, Mr. Ahearn."

"You're most welcome, Harry. By the way, I didn't get your last name."

"No, you didn't," Harry said, still studying his cigar.

Jeremy seemed irritated. "Well, what is it, then? Your surname."

"Price," Harry said.

"Price? Why, that's my lady friend's last name, too. But that was her husband's name, though."

"Naw," Harry said. "Price is her maiden name. After her husband died, she took her name back. I guess she felt let down by men. Imagine."

"Who gave you that idea?"

"My sister. Sarah Price."

"Sarah is your *sister*?" Jeremy said, going paler than usual.

"Uh-huh. My kid sister. We came to Niagara Falls together."

Horn and Pusatier both goggled at Harry, unsure of what to say or do.

"I wouldn't have—told that story," Jeremy said. "You saw her photograph. You could have said something."

"What for?" Harry said. "I wanted to see what kind of fellow broke my sister's heart." He shrugged. "And now I know."

Jeremy threw his whiskey back, pushed his glass forward, and took a half step back. "Getting near my bedtime. Nice meeting you, Mr. Price."

"But we're almost like family now," Harry protested. "Stay a little bit, why don't you? Have another whiskey, while I smoke your excellent cigar."

"Sorry, time flies," Jeremy said, eyeing the exit.

"Suit yourself. But before you go—would you mind clipping this beauty for me?" He inclined his head toward the long-handled cigar cutter in front of Jeremy. He held out the cigar.

Jeremy took it from him and nodded. "Sure," he said, lifting the cast-iron handle. The guillotine blade rose in its horseshoe frame, and he put the end of the cigar under the blade. "How much you want off?" Jeremy asked.

"That depends on you," Harry said and, quick as a cat, seized Horn's forearm and jammed the man's hand under the guillotine blade, peeling the skin on the back of his hand like the top of a sardine can. Pinioning Jeremy with a grip made ferociously strong by years of swinging an axe, with his free hand Harry grabbed the long handle of the cigar cutter and eased it down, until the heavy steel blade was pressing hard into the groove of the young man's wrist.

"What the *hell*?" Jeremy screeched, as the bartender made a move to reach under the bar.

"Move a muscle, and your friend loses his hand," Harry said. "Don't try me."

"For fuck's sake, do what he says!" Jeremy howled. "Let me out of this thing, will you?"

"Couple things before I do. First, my sister. After today, you don't bother her again. You don't talk to her. You don't even *look* at her."

"Fine, fine. She's the one who played the flirt with me!"

Harry pressed the handle down a bit more. "Careful, now, unless you want my full weight on this handle. I've seen men lose a hand in the sawmills—they don't always make it. The ones who did wish they hadn't. You're already cut pretty bad, as it is."

"I can see that," Jeremy said, ghastly pale, looking at the pool of blood spreading under the cigar cutter. "Now let up, will you?"

"And no more dirty stories about her. To anyone. Do you understand that, too?"

Jeremy winced and nodded. "Yes, I do. I've already apologized about that."

"Your apology ain't worth shit."

"I never meant to hurt anyone. I'm sorry, Mr. Price. I really am. Just let me out of this."

"I will."

"You swear to God?"

"I swear to God."

"I love your sister, if you want to know," Jeremy said. "You can ask her."

"Funny way to talk about someone you love," Harry said.

"I was just blowing off steam. It doesn't mean anything."

"And *there's* the problem. It doesn't mean anything."

"Will you *please* let me out of this?" Jeremy whined. "My hand is starting to go numb. You swore to God you'd let me go free."

"And I keep my promises. Just one last question, since God's in our deal."

"What?"

"You know your Bible?"

"What the hell does that matter?"

"Do you know Matthew 5:30?"

"Not offhand, no, damn you," Jeremy said.

"Let me refresh your memory, then," Harry said in a monotone. "Because—although you've committed some very serious sins—you have a chance to redeem yourself."

"Oh, what the fuck now?"

Harry put his free hand over his heart and quoted, "And Jesus said, 'If thy right hand offends thee, cut it off. For it is profitable that one of thy members should perish, than that thy whole body be cast into Hell.'"

Jeremy's eyes opened wide.

"So in keeping with the Good Book, you do have to pay for your sins. But today I'm giving you a choice. Your hand, or your whole body? One of them is going to Hell today."

"You're insane," Jeremy hissed.

"If I am, at least I came by it honestly," Harry said. "Now which is it going to be? Choose, or I'll choose for you."

Sweat beads were puddling on Horn's forehead. He nodded in the direction of the guillotine blade, and Harry made a little hop into the air, bringing his entire weight down on the handle. There was a loud gristly crunch, like the cracking of knuckles, and a soft thud as Jeremy's severed hand hit the floor at Pusatier's feet. Pusatier crumpled over and started puking as Jeremy lurched backward away from the bar, howling, his blunt wrist spurting blood.

"Told you, my word is my bond," Harry said. "You're free to go now. But you'd best have that seen to fairly soon."

Jeremy had grabbed Pusatier's filthy bar towel and was wrapping it frantically around his stump, his face chalk white. He opened his mouth to say something to Harry.

"Shhh," Harry said, holding his finger to his lips. "Another word, and I'll forget myself. You have Sarah to thank that you're still breathing—if it was up to me, you'd be face down in your own blood."

Harry began backing toward the door, and then reversed course, sending a fresh ripple of fear across Jeremy's ashen face. "Oops, forgot my cigar," he said, picking up the forgotten stogie from the pool of Jeremy's blood on the bar.

Harry stepped out onto Falls Street and darted down Thirteenth, deeper into no-man's-land. He'd made it almost across and out of the blighted district when he noticed that tears were running down his cheeks. Going soft in my old age, he marveled, wiping them away with a sleeve. He'd seen a lot of men get what they deserved, had himself doled out punishments far worse than what Jeremy had received. And he'd never lost a second of sleep over any of it, nor would he now.

But poor, dear Sarah, who would never hurt a fly—*that* was hard to take. Very hard. He tried not to think about it, but couldn't banish the image from his mind, the image of his dear Sarah letting that piece of shit have his way with her. Twice, he almost turned back toward Pusatier's, to finish Jeremy off properly, and make it so hard on him that he would beg for permission to die. But he knew that his way was not Sarah's, and so he reluctantly boarded a trolley near St. Mary of the Cataract, a lovely downtown church on the border of no-man's-land.

On the trolley, he realized he was still clutching the cigar that Jeremy had given him, one side drying black. He sniffed it carefully, with his eyes closed, but not for the tobacco—too good for the likes of him anyway. Only to savor the metallic, rusty scent of Ahearn's blood. He opened his eyes again, tossed the evil thing out the trolley window, and settled in for the long ride back to Lewiston.

37

A Wounded Animal

Sarah was sitting in the grand parlor of Kendall House when she heard the front gate creak open. She got up and looked out the front window, past the *porte cochère*, to see Harry coming up the circular drive, heading for the carriage house. He was walking fast, as usual, trailing smoke from one of his foul Five Brothers cigarettes, as usual. She picked up a lap blanket that was hanging on the back of a couch and slung it over her shoulders, like a shawl, and went out the front door.

He was almost at the carriage house door when she caught up with him. He heard her step and turned around. He lifted his derby in greeting and set it back down again.

"Where have you been?" she said.

"I had an errand to run."

"Is everything all right?"

"It is now," he said.

"What is that supposed to mean?"

"I don't think we'd best discuss it out in the open. And you'll catch your death out here." She'll find out eventually, he thought. Might as well get it over with.

"Come back to the house, then," Sarah said. "We can sit by the fire."

He nodded and they walked silently back to the mansion. The grand parlor was unoccupied—Christine had gone off to read in her room some time before, and Mr. Kendall was nowhere to be seen. Harry threw a few more pieces of firewood on the embers and sat down with Sarah on the couch in front of the hearth.

"There's something special about a fire, isn't there?" she said.

He nodded. "Yup. Back in the old days, no matter how hard the work had been, there was nothing like nights spent sitting around the campfire in the woods. I worked with one fellow who had the sweetest voice you ever did hear. He'd sing songs until he was the only one left awake."

"That's a lovely scene," Sarah said. "Are you still friends?"

"With him? Oh no. He got killed. A big hemlock fell on him."

"That's horrible."

Harry chuckled. "It sure was quieter around the campfire after that."

They watched the flames for a few minutes.

"Is something bothering you, Harry?"

"Don't think so, no."

"You haven't seemed yourself recently. Out of sorts."

"Can't imagine why that would be."

"Sometimes I wonder if you miss anyone back in Buffalo."

"I didn't know that many people there."

"You don't find yourself missing Ruth?"

He crossed his feet in front of the fire. "I miss her beef stew."

"Her beef stew?"

"Best beef stew I've ever had. I think it was better than most of the fancy stuff they cook here. Not that I'm not grateful for the food, mind you. But I know good stew when I taste it."

"Ruth is an excellent cook. Maybe she could come for a visit here, and teach the cook how to make that stew you like so well?"

He squinted into the fire. "I don't think that's such a good idea."

"Why not?"

Harry hesitated. "Ruth and I had words before I left. Probably best to let sleeping dogs lie."

"I see. I'm sorry to hear that, Harry. I know that she cares about you a great deal."

"Now that's just silly," he said.

"It's true," Sarah said. "We don't have to talk about it, if you don't want. But if you'd like her to visit, I'm sure she'd be glad to put behind her whatever little spat you had."

"I'll think about it." He got up and stoked the fire.

"Are you going to tell me about your mysterious errand, Harry?"

Sarah asked, when he sat down again. "I didn't like the sound of it, to be honest."

He watched the dancing flames for a few seconds. "I followed your fellow this evening," he said reluctantly.

"My fellow?"

"From the factory. Jeremy."

"Didn't I tell you about following him?"

"No, you told me not to follow the two of you. He was alone."

"God, you should have been a lawyer. Why'd you follow him? It's over between us, anyway."

Harry looked at her sidelong. "A little bird told me he'd been telling tales out of school."

"How do you know about that?"

Harry pointed to the ceiling. "Miss Christine told me."

"Why, that little tattletale! I'm going to wring her neck."

"It was long past time someone had a talk with him," Harry said.

Sarah rubbed her palms on her skirt. "Where did you follow him, then?"

"East on Falls Street, to a dive bar called Pusatier's. At Thirteenth, in the bad part of the city. Which, by the way, seems to be most of it."

"It does get rather questionable as soon as you leave the tourist district," she said.

"Funny place to become the honeymoon capital of the world."

"They say it's the electrical charge in the air created by the Falls. The falling water. It sparks romantic attraction."

"Hmm," Harry said. "I wouldn't give you fifty cents for the whole place. Phony."

"So—he went into the bad part of the city. What then?"

"I followed him in, and stood at the bar with him, and we got to talking."

"Why are you drawing this out?"

"Sorry. First off, his surname's not Horn. It's Ahearn. Jeremy Ahearn."

"Why would he use an alias?"

"Same reason you're using one, I guess. He doesn't want people at

Kendall to know who he is. Or was. I reckon he's got a past he wants to keep there."

"This is difficult to believe," she said, folding her arms across her chest and staring into the fire. "Are you quite certain it was the same man?"

"I've seen him at least a dozen times with you, Sarah."

"So what did he have to say?"

Harry didn't know how to bring it up, but took the plunge. "He said you were his girl."

She put her head down. "Please, not this again."

"He has your photograph. He showed it to me. And to the bartender."

Sarah reddened. "He had that photo made at the International."

"I know," Harry said. "I saw you."

"Of course you did. Did he say anything else?"

"I'd rather not go into it."

"You'd rather not go into it? He was talking about me, with you and some bartender, and you're not going to tell me what he had to say?"

"You don't want to know."

The blood drained from Sarah's face. "That asshole."

Harry nodded. "That he is."

She was silent for a moment. "You didn't—"

"No," Harry said, with evident pride. "I let him go. I knew you wouldn't like it—the other way."

"Thank you. You showed admirable restraint, Harry."

He shifted on the couch. "Now, to be square with you—I did hurt him a little."

"Hurt him *how*?"

Harry related the tale of the cigar guillotine.

"You're telling me you cut off the man's *hand*?" she said when he was done.

"That's pretty much it."

"What the hell, Harry? You can't go around chopping off people's hands."

"It was just the one," Harry protested.

"Good Lord," she breathed. "What am I going to say to him?"

"It doesn't need to be awkward. You weren't the one who lopped off his hand."

"Harry, I can't have you around if you maim everyone who offends me."

"How come? That's the only way some fellows learn. He certainly won't forget what he did, every time he looks at that stump." He chuckled.

"You'll never understand, Harry," Sarah said with a sigh. "What is poor Jeremy going to do now with only one hand?"

Harry gave her a broken smile. "Poor Jeremy's a wounded animal now, and wounded animals do one of only two things. They either run away and die, or turn and attack. I don't know which one he'll choose. But I do know I sure didn't like leaving him like that."

"Leaving him like what?"

"*Alive*," Harry said.

38

A World of Pain

IN THE MORNING, SARAH WAS PUZZLING OVER WHAT TO DO about Jeremy—ignoring him entirely didn't seem right, even after everything—when her telephone rang, and Erin put MacCormick through.

"Miss Price," the Scotsman said. "I don't suppose you've heard about young Mr. Horn?"

"What about him?"

"He's been involved in a hideous accident. He got his arm torn off or some such."

"It was his hand," she said, "but yes. Hideous all the same."

"Better than a whole arm, I suppose," he said. "I'm told he's laid up at Mercy Hospital, all wrapped up in miles o' gauze."

"How horrible."

"Ach, the lad's probably in a world of pain. But I thought you'd want to know, even considering the circumstances."

"You were right, Mr. MacCormick. I'll pay him a visit."

"I'm sure that'll cheer the lad a good bit."

SHE FINISHED DRESSING AND went looking for Isadore, breezing by Harry without a word as he was smoking in front of the carriage house, away from the combustible hay.

"Where you headed?" he called after her.

"Downtown," she said. She called for Isadore up the staircase in the back of the carriage house.

Harry flicked his cigarette away and walked into the big barn. "I do know how to drive, you know," he said, spitting out syllables of smoke, like a dragon. "And besides—"

"I'm still angry with you, Harry."

"What for?"

"What for?" She stamped her foot. "What do *you* think?" She made a chopping motion with her hand.

"Oh, that again."

She looked at him, exasperated. "MacCormick called. Jeremy's at Mercy Hospital, and I have to go and see him."

"You're still not done with him? After all his shenanigans?"

"It's the decent thing to do, that's all."

"Then I'm going with you," Harry said.

"Well, if you do, please let's not talk. I'm not in the mood."

BY THE TIME THEIR trolley arrived in the city, Sarah was half sick to her stomach at having to confront the now-maimed Jeremy Horn. Or Ahearn. Or whatever. When she and Harry stepped down from their car, she walked quickly along Riverway Avenue, skirting the tourist district.

He fell into a near jog next to her. "I was quiet the whole way here, like you asked. I just don't understand why you're so upset."

She stopped abruptly on the icy sidewalk, slipped, and almost fell on her ass before recovering her balance. "Can you imagine what it's going to be like to see him? Lying in a hospital bed, missing a hand?"

"I guess I can imagine it," Harry said, trying desperately to suppress a smile.

"Harry, sometimes you really do try my patience," she said, striding away again.

Harry trotted after her. "I was only trying to look out for you."

"I know, I know. But you have a queer way of doing it sometimes."

"May I come along with you?"

"Are you joking? He'll die of apoplexy if you walk in with me."

"It's not all that bad. I'll tell him that we're all square, and that'll be that."

"Are you from another planet? He's not going to forgive you, and I've not yet made up my own mind if I will," Sarah said.

"I'll wait outside, then. Be careful in there, though. He may have some tough friends around."

"Oh God, Harry, again with the suspicions. The man is a college boy with one hand."

"Don't make me smile, Miss Sarah," he said.

"Don't you dare smile," she said, jabbing her finger in his face. "And don't call me 'Miss Sarah.' You're just trying to get on my nerves."

AT THE MERCY HOSPITAL reception desk, Sarah inquired after Jeremy.

"Horn is the gentleman's name," she said.

The receptionist consulted a ledger on her desk. "I'm sorry, Miss, but we don't have a Mr. Horn registered."

"But you must. He had his hand cut off."

"Oh," the receptionist said. "The gentleman with the severed hand, yes. Mr. *Ahearn*."

"I'm sorry, of course it's Ahearn. I had a tooth extracted and I'm having some difficulty with words."

"Poor dear. You're too young and pretty to be losing your teeth," the receptionist said.

"It's just the one."

"Good. Well, Mr. Ahearn is in room 230, on the second floor."

"Thank you," Sarah said, and slowly climbed the stairs. The corridor was hard and echoing with voices, rolling carts, and the occasional groan from one of the wards.

Room 230 was a large space with twin parallel rows of beds. Sarah walked in and was intercepted by a nurse in a spotless white dress.

"Help you, Miss?" she said.

"I'm here to see Mr. Ho—Ahearn."

"Poor Mr. Ahearn," the nurse said. "He's in a great deal of pain. The doctors have given him morphine, of course, so he's sleeping a good bit, too."

"I'll be brief," Sarah said. "I'm just hoping to cheer him up a bit."

"And you will," the nurse said, smiling. "Right this way." She led Sarah between the rows of beds to the last one on the right.

Jeremy was asleep, his stump lying atop the covers, mummified in gauze.

"Thank you," Sarah whispered to the nurse, who nodded and went back to her station. Sarah sat down very quietly on a chair next to Jeremy's bed, hoping he'd keep sleeping.

She sat there, mooning off and looking around the ward. She turned around to look out the window behind her, and her chair creaked. Jeremy's eyes flew open, and his body stiffened.

"Holy hell!" he said, in a parched croak. "What are *you* doing here?"

"I heard about—your injury," she said, clearing her throat.

"I'll bet you did," he said, looking away. "Come to gloat, have you? Well, I hope you're satisfied, now that you had your brother extract your pound of flesh."

"My *brother*?"

"Yes," he said, his eyes flashing. "Your goddamn brother, Harry. I may not remember much of what happened, but I won't forget his name. Or that *face* of his."

Of course, she thought. Harry *Price*. Why in hell did I choose Price as an alias, I wonder?

"I know it won't help, but I'm very sorry he took matters into his own hands," she said, and immediately regretted her choice of words. "Oh my, I didn't mean—"

"No, go right ahead. Have a good laugh. You've earned it. Ha ha. Look at piece-of-shit Jeremy, lying there with the one hand. Ha ha. You know these pathetic assholes here tried to sew it back on? Pusatier brought me and—it—in, and the thing was purple and had God knows what else stuck to it from lying on the floor, and for a whole night, I had a dead hand attached to my wrist, until it fell off again. How do you think that feels?"

"I can't begin to imagine," Sarah said, shaking her head slowly. "I'm truly sorry."

"And well you might be, but sorry's not worth a plugged nickel. They threw my hand into a wastebasket! My *hand*!"

"I don't know what to say," she murmured.

"How about 'goodbye'? I don't ever want to see you again."

"Jeremy, I do need to ask you—why didn't you tell me your name is Ahearn?"

"God," he said, rolling his eyes. "My name's Horn. Whenever I did a little slumming, I didn't want people in those parts of town to know my real name. When Pusatier dumped me on the front steps here—with my hand in a sack next to me—that's the name he knew to give them. Chrissake, Sarah."

"I'm at a loss, Jeremy."

"And I'm at a loss, too," he said, holding up his stump. "Thanks to you, I'm crippled for life. Now please go and leave me alone. This thing hurts like hell, and I can only hope they'll give me another jab of morphine before I start climbing the curtains. Oh, and I'll probably leave here addicted to the stuff, too." He turned his head away.

"All right, I'll go," she said, rising. "All I can say in my own defense is that I never meant—"

He raised his stump and waved it, presumably forgetting it no longer terminated in a hand.

"Please, spare me. It'd be easier for me if you'd just go."

"Did you see him?" Harry asked quietly, creeping up behind her on the homebound trolley.

"Harry, I don't want to talk with you about it."

"I'm trying to show some concern."

She whipped her head around. "Yes, I saw him. He's a cripple."

"I know *that*."

She glared. "The doctors tried to reattach his hand."

"Did it take?"

"No, it didn't. It fell off again."

"Lord," Harry said, putting his head down behind her seat. "Don't say it that way."

"Go ahead, laugh your head off," she said. "I'm not going to stop you."

He struggled to wipe the smirk off his face. "I'm not laughing," he said with some effort. "It was just the way you said it, that's all." Harry cleared his throat, which set off a deep, racking spasm of coughing.

"Are you coming down with something? That doesn't sound good."

He shook his head, trying to catch his breath. After a while he swallowed hard and said, "Just from being out in the cold, I guess. Seems like winter gets harder every year. Anything else about Jeremy what's-his-name?"

"He was very angry," Sarah said. "And he never wants to see me again. Oh, and by the way, 'Ahearn' was just so that if he went slumming, people there wouldn't know his real name."

"He seemed pretty darn comfortable in that blind pig," Harry said.

"Well, it's a moot point now. That's the last we'll see of Jeremy."

Harry was quiet. "I'm not so sure about that. Like I said, it could go one of two ways."

39

UPSTAGED

THE OLD GIRLS CONTINUED TO STRUGGLE, AND ORDER AFTER order was late, or botched. On a cold, rainy Wednesday, Alicia was sitting at her desk, staring at not one, not two, but *four* letters cancelling her recent contracts. Small ones, fortunately, but she feared they were the first freshets of a coming flood. When she complained to Howie, he would just shrug and say something like "Well, I guess you've been too good a salesman" or some such rot.

She was close to pulling her hair out when Howie trudged in from the factory, with grease up to his elbows.

"The Donohue & Hill order is going to be late again," Howie said.

"Come on, Gaines!" Alicia said. "We can't run a company this way. You were able to make it work last time."

"By the skin of my teeth. But this time, not only is the machine for D&H down, but also the one that's working on the Lorenz Paint job, too. There aren't enough hours in the day for me to fix both by the deadline."

"Shit. John Lorenz is a coldhearted bastard. He'll cancel us without batting an eye. Do you know I've received four cancellations only today? Pretty soon we'll be right back where we started from. But with a ruined reputation on top of it."

"Maybe you shouldn't set expectations we can't meet."

"Get your ass down there, Gaines," she said, "and do whatever diddling is required to get Lorenz done. I'll drop over to D&H and give them some song and dance. They won't be happy, but they're more reasonable people."

"Maybe it would be a good idea for me to come with you? To D&H?"

"Come with me? Why?"

"Because I could explain to them why their order is a difficult one, mechanically speaking. And not only difficult for us, so they wouldn't do any better taking their business elsewhere. Any manufacturer would have trouble with their order, because of the weight of the paper and the lining they have us insert. If I explain it that way, I might be able to buy us a little more leeway with them."

"That's actually not a bad idea, if you're willing to do it. They're mechanical people and you can speak that language better than I can. And at this point, I'm willing to try anything."

"Very well. I'll get the Lorenz order done somehow, though I'll have to pull another all-nighter to do it. You telephone to D&H and tell them the order will be a couple days late, but that we can explain it to them in person tomorrow."

"Good," she said. "Thank you, Gaines. This could end up working in our favor."

THE NEXT DAY, HOWIE and Alicia took an early afternoon trolley to Niagara Falls, where they were to meet with Mr. James Hart, Donohue & Hill's purchasing manager. The D&H factory was an enormous stone oblong with a bulbous raised roof, looking very much like a giant grey coffin. The company made pigments, concocted mainly from mercury, lead, arsenic, and other unspeakable substances, which, under the application of Niagara Falls' cheap hydroelectric current, were transformed into every brilliant hue of the spectrum.

D&H's catalogues—mailed every month, without fail, in Miller's best envelopes—featured on the cover a colorful engraving of a spotless factory manned by sturdy workers and showing dray horses pulling endless wagonloads of pigment out to coat the hinterlands, where not a soul had ever beheld so modern and tidy an enterprise as Donohue & Hill.

The reality was more than a little different. Eyes began watering and noses running a thousand yards from the works, and persisted for at least a day after a visit. The penetrating chemical stench made everything—food, drink, even one's own saliva—taste slimy and bitter. Every now and again, some reactive chemical process would get out of hand, and D&H would experience a euphemistically dubbed "fume release." An air horn would sound, to warn anyone in the vicinity to get upwind, and fast—just as one of the towering brick smokestacks would belch forth a lurid plume of crimson red or sinister bilious yellow-green. With luck, the wind would be at D&H's back, and the unholy ejecta would blow across the Niagara River to settle on the hapless Canadians. But that was not always so. Since the prevailing winds were more frequently coming out of the west, the poisonous cloud would drift over the city of Niagara Falls or—God forbid!—shift northward, to the tourist district itself. Then, as it cooled and congealed, the particolored fog would settle onto the heads of the good citizens, and the even-better tourists, of Niagara Falls, sending droves of them sputtering and coughing to the hospitals. It was also noticed that the acrid goo would stick to any painted surface in town, turning the cheerful white clapboards of tourist homes pale ocher streaked and weeping with red, as if afflicted with a bloody flux.

Thus the management of Donohue & Hill were rarely in the mood for other types of accidents, such as the late delivery of a supply of their envelopes. As Howie and Alicia approached Mr. Hart's office, escorted by a young woman who might have been pretty but for a pair of ghastly blue eyes, both sclera bright red and without a trace of white. Whether this was the result of some unfortunate accident of birth or heredity, or whether due to the constant exposure to the sour air, it was not possible to know. But it was more than a little disturbing. They were shown into Mr. Hart's office, where they found two men chatting.

"So this is the famous Mrs. Miller," said a tall, distinguished gentleman, who rose and walked over to greet them. "And Mr. Gaines. I'm Bill Donohue."

"Mr. Donohue," Alicia said, "this is an unexpected honor."

"Not at all, madam. When Hart told me you were visiting, I simply had to meet you in person."

"Now I hope you don't believe everything you have read about me," she said. "Half of it's untrue. That said, I'll leave you to guess which half."

Donohue roared with laughter. "You're even saucier than I expected."

They sat, and Donohue listened quietly as Hart broached the topic.

"I understand that our order may be somewhat delayed," Hart said. He was a smallish, bookish sort of fellow, and reminded Alicia more than a little of Edward.

"That's why we're here today," she said. "Mr. Gaines and I thought it wise to review with you certain—complexities—in the making of your—"

"You're both technical men, I understand?" Gaines interrupted.

"Oh yes," Donohue said. "Hart and I are both Rensselaer men. Engineering."

"A very fine school," Howie said. "I bring it up because I know you gentlemen will understand the technical aspects of our manufacture. In fact, it will be trivial by comparison with what you do here. Technically speaking."

"Not at all, Mr. Gaines," Hart said. "It's always pleasant to talk technical-man to technical-man. No offense intended, Mrs. Miller," he added quickly.

"None taken," she said. "Mr. Gaines is our—"

"Because of the weight and the additional lining of your envelopes," Gaines went on, "we have to run our machines at half-speed, in order to get the quality you're looking for. And ours are some of the best machines made in the world. Since your envelopes are of exceedingly high quality, they require more precision than speed in their making."

"Makes perfect sense to me," Donohue said. "We certainly don't want you to rush. Our last supplier shipped on time, but often a quarter of the envelopes were useless. They ought never to have been passed out of their factory and on to us."

"And because I'm a machine-man," Gaines said, "I can't in good conscience make my ladies—that's what I call our machines—run faster than they can manage. It wouldn't be right."

"You have a real feeling for your equipment, Mr. Gaines," Hart said. "That's as it should be. Mrs. Miller, where on earth have you been hiding this fellow? He's quite the find."

"Mr. Gaines and I have—"

"Mr. Gaines, if you ever grow tired of making envelopes, we have a home for you here," Donohue interjected. "Your love for machinery is what makes the difference between middle-class production and top-class production." He winked at Alicia. "Don't worry, Mrs. Miller, we won't poach him—not right away, anyway."

Donohue, Hart, and Gaines all laughed, and Allie tried to hide a grimace. I'm going to poach him myself, she thought, as soon as we get out of here.

"Would it help if we gave you a little more lead time on our orders?" Hart asked. "That is, if Mr. Donohue would find it acceptable."

"Why, of course, Hart," Donohue said. "Quality and perfection. That's what I want in all areas of my business. No compromises."

"Thank you," Gaines said. "That will allow me to have my ladies turn out perfect, quality product, every time."

"That's all I need to hear," Donohue said, standing and sticking out his hand to Gaines. "Hart, I'm satisfied that this little delay is nothing more than Gaines, here, trying to get it right the first time. Let's make sure that we give them more time. However much they need."

"Yes, sir," Hart said, standing too. "Mrs. Miller, thank you for bringing Mr. Gaines today. Sometimes it's best to get right down to brass tacks, and cut through all the sales talk."

"We're happy to do anything we can to earn—" Alicia began.

"Gaines," Donohue said, "Come back sometime, and we'll give you the nickel tour. I'd love to get your opinions on some of our machinery. We have our fair share of production woes, too."

"I'd be delighted," Gaines said. "Ought I contact your secretary?"

Donohue fished out a card case from his vest and handed over a calling card. "No need. Call me directly. We'll talk man-to-man. It'll be a good time."

Gaines and Donohue chatted amiably as the four of them walked to the front door, and then Alicia and Howie hailed a coach to take them to the Yellow Car trolley. The coach was pulling away from Donohue & Hill when Allie and Gaines were startled by the shuddering blast of a horn. Alicia turned and gasped. From the stack of the D&H factory, a roiling, viscous column of deep iris-purple was rising into the air, fast, tumbling over itself in its haste to escape. The eruption was both beautiful—a lavender brushstroke against the blue sky and puffy white clouds—and horrifying.

Alicia and Howie didn't talk much on the way back to Buffalo, but Gaines's little smirk said everything she needed to know. I'd like to knock his fucking teeth down his throat, she thought, but instead she smiled blandly at him whenever she caught him looking her way.

"I COULD EASILY HAVE slaughtered them all," Allie said.

"That's nice, dear," Bert murmured over his evening paper.

"I hope that's a particularly interesting article you're reading. It's obviously more so than what I'm trying to tell you. You haven't heard a word I've said."

He put the paper down quickly. "Not at all, dear. I've been paying close attention."

"What was it I told you? Go ahead, repeat what I said. From the beginning."

Bert was trapped. "You said something about—your customers."

"No, what came before that, and after? Come on—since you were paying such rapt attention, you ought to be able to quote me word for word. Let's hear it."

"My mind may have strayed here and there, but I got the gist of it," he said feebly.

"To such a degree you can't recreate a syllable of it."

"Would you go over it again? With my apologies?"

"Yes, Bert, I'll happily repeat myself. I have nothing better to do. But this time—you'd better fucking *listen*."

"I promise," he said.

"Gaines went with me to Donohue & Hill today. He'd suggested that he explain why their orders are always threatening to be late. And from the first whiff of his cologne, the two other men—Donohue himself and his purchasing man—were following him around like a couple of orphaned puppies. And the whole time I'm sitting there like a bump on a log, unable to get a word in edgewise."

"I don't know how to account for that, Alicia. You were the one who landed that account. They'd never met Gaines before."

"Oh well," she said, waving her arms, "it's all his 'I'm a *machine-man*' and 'my machines are my *ladies*' horseshit, and that gave the other two machine-men massive hard-ons. I could have been sitting there stark naked and they wouldn't have noticed."

"They would have noticed," he said. "I promise you that."

"Maybe, but damned if I'm not sick of having to screw people to get their attention."

"You're done with all that."

"Apparently at the cost of having Gaines horn in on my part of the business," Alicia said. "I'm not sure it was worth the trade. He's going to push me out, if this continues. Mark my words."

"You won't let that happen, dear," Bert said, patting her on the arm. She jerked it away.

"Will you stop trying to mollify me, you asshole? I want your suggestions, or believe me I wouldn't have gone through my whole script *twice*."

Bert was silent for a full minute.

"Have you fallen asleep?" Allie said.

"Good Lord, Alicia, I'm trying to *think*. I do do that occasionally. Give me a minute."

"Fine. I'm going to get myself a whiskey while you do. Would you like one?" He nodded.

When she returned, she handed the glass to Bert. He was still sitting quietly.

"I'm not saying anything," she said. "Just sitting here quietly, watching the great Buddha."

He sipped his whiskey, licked his lips, and set the glass down carefully on the side table. "Something did occur to me while you were away just now."

"What is it?"

"I'm sure you know that when Edward was my client, I was a frequent visitor to the factory."

"I didn't know that, but it doesn't surprise me. He never told me shit about what he was doing all day."

Bert ignored her. "And I wonder—since you started as star salesman, how much more business do you have—no, that's not the way I want to say it—how many more envelopes per day are you making, than when Ed was there?"

"That's easy. Hold on." She got up and trotted out of the parlor. He heard her footsteps go up the stairs, above his head to her bedroom, and then head back down again. She returned to the parlor holding a ledger.

"Weekly production records for the past two years," she said, flipping it open in her lap. "All right, let's see. Two years ago . . . and now. It appears that we are making about, roughly, ten percent more envelopes now than when Ed was there. It was more, but we've had some cancellations recently because of the fucking machines."

"Only ten percent?"

"What's that supposed to mean? The business was in the crapper when I came, so I've built it back to where it was when Ed shuffled off this mortal coil, and then some."

"I didn't mean that. I meant only that today you are making only modestly more than in the heyday of the business."

"Yes, that's fair. So what?"

"Now *you're* the one who isn't listening," he muttered into his whiskey.

"Shut up, Bert. I can't help it if you're obscure."

"What I'm driving at is this," he said. "I was at your factory at least once a week back in the days before the business eroded. It was Edward, and Gaines, and the same old machines then. In fact, as I understand it, you bought a brand spanking new one only recently."

"That's right, for the larger sizes. It's a monster."

"Right. Here's my point. I never, ever heard Ed—or Gaines, for that matter—complaining about breakdowns and late orders. None of that—and I would have heard, because I knew all the details of the contracts. I knew the equipment was old, but they were running just fine. Now, less than two years later, you are making only modestly more envelopes, *and* have added an additional machine—"

"And yet we're forever breaking down, and late."

"Right. So what's going on, I wonder?" he said. "Something's rotten in Denmark."

"Where Ed had the advantage on me," Alicia said, "is that he understood those machines. He ran that business for ten years before Machine-Man Gaines showed up."

"And since you don't know about what makes them go—"

"I can easily be lied to."

"That's what I'm wondering," Bert said.

"Hartshorn, sometimes you truly are a goddamn genius," Allie said, getting up and kissing him full on the lips. "An old-fart genius, I say."

"Now that's a nice surprise."

"There's a *lot* more where that came from, for that brainstorm," she said, smiling. "But the question is—we need proof that Gaines is hoodwinking me."

Bert took a long sip of his drink, thinking deeply about his upcoming reward for his brilliance. "I've figured that out, too."

"You've already impressed me enough, but do enlighten me, Great One."

"Sarah Payne. She's a detective, and a good one."

"She is, but she's in Niagara Falls now. And she can't very well be snooping around the factory. Gaines would recognize her immediately. He knew her, even before Ed started—doing whatever Ed was doing with her."

"Anyone would recognize Sarah," he said.

"Down, boy. You know what I mean."

"Annie Murray is the better choice anyway. She's plainer, she's still in Buffalo, and she's a mechanical whiz. You remember that contraption she came up with that we used with Penrose."

"How could I forget? That was quite an evening."

"It was, Alicia. We've had some real adventures, haven't we?"

"We have indeed, Bertie boy. And now this."

"We'll get through it," he said. "Sarah and Annie will know better than I what to do. But since neither Gaines nor anyone at the factory would recognize Annie, get her into the factory somehow, and have her observe. She'll figure out those machines in no time, and will be able to form an opinion about why they are not performing as they should."

"Bert, you're a prince," Allie said. "I knew that once you decided I was worth listening to, you'd be helpful."

"Faint praise, Alicia," he said, sipping his whiskey. "But I'll take it."

40

ON THE CASE

"DEAR SARAH!" ALICIA SAID INTO THE MOUTHPIECE. "HOWEVER are you keeping these days?"

"I'm well," Sarah replied cautiously. "I trust you are, too?"

"Oh yes, never been better."

There was a long silence on the line.

"To what do I owe the pleasure of your call this morning, Allie?"

"You do get right to the point, don't you?"

"You know as well as I do that you don't call me unless you want something."

"Now that's simply uncharitable. And untrue."

"Last time I heard from you, I introduced you to Charles. Now you're all he talks about."

"Oh, so he's 'Charles' now, is he? Have you and he—"

"Don't start, Allie."

"You can't blame me for being curious," Alicia said. "And I am grateful that you helped my business along. I will forever be in your debt."

"Happy to help. Now, then, what's on your mind?"

"I'm calling because I want to help *your* business along this time."

"And how do you propose to do that?"

"I need Annie's help," Allie said. "I have a little problem on my hands."

"GOOD EVENING, MRS. MILLER," Annie said. "I hope this is still a convenient time?"

"Of course, Annie," Alicia said, swinging open the front door of 101 Ashwood.

Annie followed her into the parlor, where Bert was standing. "Mr. Hartshorn, it's good to see you."

"Likewise, Annie," he said. "You're looking well."

"Thank you, sir."

"Mrs. Miller," Annie began, taking out her notebook, "Miss Payne said you were having a problem at your company."

"Yes, though I didn't tell her much over the Bell line," Alicia said. "In short, I believe my business partner—Howie Gaines—is up to something. It seems that our machinery conveniently breaks down whenever doing so might embarrass me. *That* I could stand, mind you—I've had more than my fair share of that—but more and more orders are delayed, or incorrect, and it's beginning to lose business for us. I need to get to the bottom of it before we don't have any business at all."

"I see," Annie said, looking up from her tablet. "You believe he's intentionally causing them to fail?"

"I do," Alicia said. "He does what he calls an 'all-nighter' to fix one of them, but then another one will fail. And he has to swoop in again."

"He certainly would be in a position to do that," Annie said. "Though one thing does puzzle me, if I may. One big thing."

"Anything, dear."

"As I understand it, Mr. Gaines is the majority owner of Miller Envelope."

"Something he reminds me of most days, yes."

"Then what I can't understand is this. Embarrassing you is one thing, but to injure his own business? Why would he do such a thing?"

Alicia looked at Bert and cleared her throat. "Jealousy, I'd imagine. I stepped in when the business was in very bad condition, and I brought in a lot of accounts."

Annie chewed on the end of her pencil. "I'm sure that's so. But what business owner would be so jealous about someone helping to make him—well, rich?"

Alicia and Bert exchanged another glance, and Allie shrugged. "Oh, what the hell? Annie's all grown up now."

Annie looked quizzically at her. "Ma'am?"

"Here's what happened, dear," Alicia said. "When I first showed up, Gaines was all down in the dumps because the fortunes of the place had suffered so much on his watch. I thought it might be helpful to—cheer him up a bit, you know—"

Bert gave a little sigh of resignation.

"That seems very kind of you," Annie said. "Whatever could be wrong with that?"

"There's no roundabout way to say it, Annie," Alicia said. "I cheered him up, all right. By letting him—" She made a circle with her thumb and forefinger and dramatically thrust the other forefinger in and out of it. Bert looked up at the ceiling.

"Oh my," Annie murmured. "I see."

"I'm not saying it was the best decision I've made, but it did cheer him up."

"Did it ever," Bert said in a stage whisper.

"Yes, I may have laid it on a bit too thick. Mr. Gaines took the queer notion that he loves me—"

"*Loves* you?" Annie breathed.

Allie fixed her with a stare. "People do love me, Annie, as hard as that may be to believe."

Annie reddened. "I didn't mean—"

"No matter," Alicia said. "Mr. Gaines believed it, and as a result he came to look forward to being—cheered up—whenever I needed him to fix an ailing machine."

"Now that's just blackmail," Annie said.

"That's certainly the way it felt to me," Alicia replied. "And I got a little weary of it, so I cut him off. I told him that Mr. Hartshorn here had asked me to marry him."

"My!" Annie said. "I'm so sorry—I had no idea! Best wishes, Mrs. Miller. And congratulations to you, Mr. Hartshorn."

"Annie," Alicia said flatly, "it was a ruse. Old Bert here's not going to buy the cow if he can have the milk for free. I said it to get Gaines off my back." She laughed. "Not that it was my *back* he was on, to be precise."

There was a long silence before Alicia spoke again.

"So—you see, now old Gaines is furious with me because he claims that my little cheering-up sessions caused him to fall in love with me.

And now I think he wants to settle a score, embarrass me, and eventually push me out of the business. If he can successfully insert himself into the relations with the new customers I brought in—or so he tells himself, even though he has all the charm of a toad—he won't need me anymore, and I'll be forced to leave. You can bet that he's already been telling the trustees how I'm pushing the business so hard that it's breaking under the strain. Then of course once I'm gone, everything will smooth out again, and he'll be the Messiah."

"That's a devilish thing to do," Annie said. "All you have done is helped him along."

Alicia's face rippled into a wry smile.

"Don't say it, Alicia," Bert said. "I know what you're thinking."

"Isn't Bert just the oldest stick-in-the-mud prude you've ever met?" Alicia said to Annie. "One can't even make a decent joke around him without him getting his underwear in a twist. It's like living with a Puritan, Annie, I swear it is."

"Ma'am, I'd love to take on this case, if you'll have us," Annie said, ignoring Allie's comment. "I can start when you like. I'd suggest you tell Mr. Gaines you've found a cleaning lady, and let me start a week or so before you think he might pull one of these all-nighters. I can easily observe him then."

"That sounds grand," Bert said.

"Very well then," Annie said, closing her notebook. "I'll review all this with Miss Sarah, and she'll go over our fees with you."

"Will you have to review *everything* with Sarah?" Alicia asked.

"Well, yes, ma'am, as you know Miss Sarah owns the agency—and she'll want to help me formulate my plan."

"What about—um—Gaines's *motive*? I suppose you have to tell her about that?"

"You mean the cheering up?"

"Yes, that's what I mean."

"I'm afraid so, ma'am. But you may count on our discretion."

Alicia shook her head slowly. "Sarah's going to have a field day with this one."

"CHEERED HIM UP, DID you?" Sarah said over the line the next day.

"I didn't suppose Annie would leave that part out," Alicia said wryly into the mouthpiece. "But yes, I cheered him up. Good and proper, too."

"I have no doubt."

"You're eating this up, aren't you?"

"Not in the slightest."

"You might have a little sympathy, you know, for a fellow businesswoman who had to resort to the Old Ways to make things go her direction."

"I do have sympathy, Alicia. You seem to like to joke with me, and so I was throwing one back your way."

"Turnabout is fair play," Allie said. "I will tell you a little secret that I didn't share with Annie. Not even with Bert."

"What's that?"

"I did most of the cheering, to be sure, but there was one time that old Gaines cheered me up as much as I think it's humanly possible to be. I swear to God, I thought the top of my head was going to blow off."

"That's saying something," Sarah said. "There's a part of me that almost wants to know exactly how that transpired, but another part that wishes I'd never heard about it."

"Exactly how these things are, dear. Fascinating and repulsive, depending on how personally one is involved in them."

"Nicely said."

"I would tell you, you know," Allie said. "Sometimes I do find myself thinking about it."

"That's probably best kept for another time, I should think. Are you agreed to our fees, then, and we'll get started?"

"Yes, I am. Let's see if we can catch the old bastard in the act."

"We'll do our best, Allie. Thank you for choosing us. Annie is very excited about your case."

41

THE ALL-NIGHTER

IT TOOK ANNIE LESS THAN A WEEK TO FIGURE OUT WHAT WAS going on. One evening, she walked from Norwood Street to the Miller residence on Ashwood and sat down with Bert and Alicia.

"So you know what he's been up to?" Alicia asked, sipping her drink.

"It's pretty simple, as it turns out," Annie said. "On his all-nighter, fixing the ailing machine took him only about a half hour. Then he went up to the office and slept for the rest of the night."

"He *slept*?" Alicia said. "This is the famous all-nighter?"

"Yes. I went in to clean the outer office and awakened him. He was stretched out on the visitor's couch. He didn't seem bothered in the least, and asked me to clean your office while I was at it."

"He did, did he?"

"He did. I said to him, 'My, Mr. Gaines, you're here so late!' and he said that he had to do some work in the factory."

"So what has he been up to?" Bert asked.

Annie smiled. "It's very clever, and unless you know those machines, you'd never even notice. You see, each machine has a speed-control device, which allows one to run them faster or slower. A large dial with a knob."

"That much I know," Allie said. "I've seen the operators adjust them."

"Right, they're on the front of the machines. And because you are so busy now, the dials are all set to 'maximum,' which to the casual observer makes it seem that they're running at full capacity. But they're *not*. The dials show full capacity, but the machines aren't running as fast as they are able. Not if Mr. Gaines doesn't want them to."

Bert frowned. "They're not? How is that possible?"

"The speed control simply slips a leather belt up and down on a conical pulley. The higher the belt rides on the pulley—the fattest part— the higher the gear ratio is with the driven wheel, and the faster the machine goes."

"I'll take your word for it," Alicia said.

"It works the same way your bicycle does," Annie said. "When you have a bigger gear on the front, and a smaller one on the back, you go faster."

"That much I understand."

"This is nothing more than a variable version of that. The pulley looks a bit like a fez—a blunt cone, wider at the bottom than the top, so the belt can slide up or down and make the machine go faster or slower. When the speed control is set to maximum, the drive belt rides at the very fattest part of the pulley. It can't go any faster—unless you change the pulley itself out for one that's fatter. And change the belt, of course."

"Of course."

"What Mr. Gaines is doing is simple—once you understand how it works," Annie said. "He removes the drive belt and then the conical pulley, and replaces the pulley with a bigger one. Now, without changing the speed control knob at all, the machine automatically runs faster when production resumes in the morning. You make more envelopes, and the machine can catch up to your order. I expect that when he wants to cause you trouble, he does the reverse—replaces the big pulley for a smaller one. Then the machine can't run as fast, but no one is the wiser because the speed control is still set to its maximum. It's simple physics."

"That little turd," Alicia said. "Now that you know what he's doing, how do we prove it to the trustees? They won't believe me—or you—just because you say so."

"Proof is in hand," Annie said.

"You really are something, Annie," Bert said.

"These days, it's easy, with all the magical new devices we have. I've taken my little Kodak into the factory each night. I conceal it in my cleaning cart. I took photographs of each machine at the beginning of the night—and then again at the end—each time with a little ruler sitting next to the conical pulley. To show that the size has been changed, if it has been."

"Gaines could still claim someone else made the modification," Bert said.

"Not likely. The machines are equipped with counters and time clocks, so that they can't be started without someone clocking in first. That's for safety, but it's also how you pay people who are paid on piece-work. You need to know when they clock in and clock out, and how many envelopes were made while they were working, so each operator has his own code. Gaines can't make the machine run—as a test to ensure the pulley is installed successfully—unless he clocks in with his master code. And then clocks out when he's done. Any machine he's tinkered with will show a half hour of operation in the middle of the night—but without any envelopes being produced—under his master code. That, along with my before-and-after photographs, is all you need to prove that only Mr. Gaines could be the culprit."

"Your mind is a thing of beauty, Annie," Alicia said. "And to think I thought you were only a hired girl."

"Thank you, I suppose," Annie said.

"I THINK IT'S TIME I had a chat with the trustees about Mr. Gaines," Bert said, after Annie had gone home.

"You mean *we* had a chat, don't you?" Alicia said.

"They . . . er . . . don't care for you too much."

"You may tell them for me, then, that I don't much care for them, either. Couple of overstuffed lard-asses."

"I think I'll keep that to myself. I'll ask Annie and Sarah to go with me. They can go over the evidence."

"When will you meet with them?" Alicia asked.

"Depends when they're available. If I tell them it's about a problem with *you*, they'll be eager to meet."

"It's so reassuring that I still have such clout," Alicia said. "But give me a week or so, would you? There's something I need to straighten out before you sit down with them."

"Why wait?" Bert said.

"Trust me, you old fart."

42

ARSPHENAMINE

"You did it, Annie," Sarah said on the telephone the following day. "I just now got off the phone with Alicia. She's happy as a clam."

"Mr. Gaines made it too easy," Annie said. "I almost felt sorry for him, he took so little care to cover his tracks."

"Well, I wouldn't want to be in his shoes now."

"I'm sure Mrs. Miller will have her revenge."

"You can take that to the bank. And she'll take her time about it, too."

"I could tell you stories," Annie said.

"I've no doubt. But today I'm calling not *only* to congratulate you—though congratulations are in order—but to tell you that the experimental drug from Dr. Ehrlich is due to arrive in New York City tomorrow. It should be here the day after that, so you need to get Ruth here."

"If she'll agree to it. She's weak, but as stubborn as ever. If she thinks Harry will get wind of it, she'll refuse."

"You can tell her for me that if she gives you any guff, I'll come to Buffalo myself and drag her here by the roots of her hair."

"Now that might motivate her. I'll do my best."

"Bring her tomorrow. Don't take no for an answer."

"How is Harry?"

"Harry always seems about the same, but it's impossible to know with him. He insists on living in the stable, still, but I think the disease is taking a toll that he simply refuses to show."

"Does he ever ask about Ruth? Or talk about her?"

"He mentioned once that he missed her stew."

"Sounds like him," Annie said.

W*HEN* A*NNIE AND* R*UTH* arrived at Kendall House, Ruth was weak, still covered in countless pustules, and seemed more and more confused about what was happening around her.

Dr. Hindman turned one of the many bedrooms of Kendall House into an operating theatre. The doctor had been informed that neither Ruth nor Harry knew of the other's participation in the experiment, but he shook his head severely when asked to administer the injections separately. "Impossible," he said. "I must prepare everything under as controlled a set of conditions as I can, and going from room to room, risking the contamination of a very rare commodity, simply to spare someone's *feelings* is not something I'm willing to do."

The procedure was set for four o'clock in the afternoon, and as luck would have it, that morning, snow began howling down. It took Isadore almost four hours, round trip, to fetch Dr. Hindman from the city and haul him up the slippery Lewiston Road to Kendall House. Meanwhile, Sarah was given the task of telling Harry that he was going to be treated.

"I'm not too keen about becoming some doctor's laboratory rat," he said.

"I figured you'd say something like that."

"I've lived my life," he said.

"Don't be so dramatic, Harry. Just take the fucking medicine and don't give me a hard time."

"Good night, you've got sand. Well, fact is, if you told me to jump over the Falls, I'd do it without a second thought."

"Thank you," she said. "But there's no call for that just yet, even after—"

"Don't say it," Harry said.

"All right. Now stay put. The doctor will be here soon." She turned to leave.

"Sarah?" he said.

"Yes?"

"There is something I need to tell you."

"Whatever you like."

"It's about Ruth."

"Our Ruth?"

"Yes. Our Ruth. I don't know quite how to tell you this—but we—I—Ruth and I had *feelings* for each other."

"I think I may have suspected something of the sort."

"Yes, I expect you might. Well, we didn't do anything—you know—improper. But she didn't want me to come here with you, and before I left, she did something very foolish—and—"

"Harry, stop," Sarah said, laying her hand on his arm. "Annie's told me about this. I know."

"You do?"

"Yes, I do."

"I was so angry, I wouldn't speak to her. But since then she's all I can think of."

"About Ruth—"

"Wait," he said. "Here's what I want to ask of you. And I'll never ask you for another thing."

"Anything within my power."

"This medicine. Send it to Ruth. Give it to her, instead of to me."

"Harry, you leave that in my hands."

"Why do you have to keep bringing up hands?" he said with a crooked grin.

"RUTH," ANNIE SAID GENTLY, after helping her sister into a loose cotton gown, "we're going to get you to the treatment room now. Do you understand?"

"Yes," Ruth said weakly. Her face was terribly distorted with pustules—pustules upon pustules, in some places. "I hope it works, Sister," she mumbled. "Or if it doesn't, that I don't linger much longer."

"You're going to be well again. I promise you."

"We both know what your medical promises are worth," Ruth said.

"There's an invalid chair here. Can you sit in it for me? I'll roll you to the treatment room."

Ruth stood and eased herself into the wheeled chair. "I wonder if this is how someone feels in the electric chair," she said.

"Only difference is that you'll be well again when you get out of this one."

Annie wheeled her sister down the hall to the treatment room. There was a bed near the door, and a movable cloth partition next to it, dividing the bed from the rest of the room. Annie helped her sister onto the bed. Ruth sat with her legs dangling over the end of the flat mattress.

"You'll feel better soon, dear," Annie said.

"Thank you for everything, Sister," Ruth said. "However it goes, I never deserved you. There's only one other thing I'd like you to do for me, though."

"What's that?"

"If—this doesn't work—tell Harry that I'm sorry. And that I will always love him."

A muffled sound came from the other side of the movable partition, and a hand reached around the frame and slid it aside.

RUTH WAS TOO WEAK to look up. "Watch out—the wall is moving," she said.

"Ruth?" Harry walked around to the end of Ruth's bed and knelt in front of her. "*Ruth*? Dear Lord, what's happened to you?"

Ruth's puffy eyelids opened a bit. "Harry? Well, speak of the devil. Are you real?"

"Yes, you silly girl, I'm real, and—" He threw his arms around Ruth's wasted frame and began covering her face with kisses, heedless of the pustules.

"You're not supposed to touch these things," she said wanly. "You could catch something."

"Please save her," Harry said to Dr. Hindman.

"If you'll let me get on with it, Mr. Price, I shall do my best," the doctor said. "The sooner you stop talking and lie down, the sooner I can get this medicine into both of you. So if you please, sir, return to your bed, lie on your stomach, and pull your pants down below your buttocks."

"Her first," Harry growled, wiping his eyes hurriedly.

"I won't hear of it. You're far the stronger, and I need a trial if I am to find the right spot with my needle. We have just enough for both of you, but if you want the best chance for Miss Ruth, I can't make any misstep in injecting her."

"All right, then," Harry said. "Under that condition." Harry went back to his side of the partition with Hindman close behind.

"On your stomach, then," Dr. Hindman said, holding up an out-sized syringe. "Trousers down. Miss Payne, perhaps you can help steady Mr. Price."

"Sarah, maybe you'd better leave," Harry said.

"I was married for nine years, Harry," Sarah said.

Harry blushed but complied. "Let's get going, doc," he said, when he was situated.

"Here we go, then," the doctor said. "This is likely to hurt." He stuck the needle into Harry's buttocks, and went in at least a couple inches.

"It ain't so bad," Harry said.

"I haven't injected it yet."

"Holy shit!" Harry yelled as Dr. Hindman depressed the plunger. "Oh, for—it feels like my whole body's on fire."

The doctor stood back. "Good. Then I have hit the correct spot."

"Now her," Harry said, panting hard.

"Yes," Hindman said, stepping to the other side of the partition. After a few seconds, Harry and Sarah heard Ruth gasp, and then moan heavily as the fiery medicine flowed through her system.

"Bear *up*, Ruthie!" Harry called out. "You're tougher than I am, girl."

"I don't feel well, Harry," Ruth said feebly. "I think I'm dying."

Still on his stomach, buttocks in the air, Harry shoved the partition aside. "Don't you dare say that! I'm not losing you twice."

"That's quite enough mooning," Dr. Hindman said. "The worst is ahead. You've been injected with a compound of arsenic, and you need to rest now. Both of you."

"Look, doc—" Harry began.

"Mr. Price, if this works, you'll have plenty of time for gallantry. But for now, I'm not having you endanger yourself or her with your importunacy."

"My what?" Harry said to Sarah.

"He's telling you to shut up, Harry," she said. "And so am I."

THREE DAYS PASSED, AND both Harry and Ruth remained in pain, their muscles taut as ropes, pulling their bodies into strange and horrifying contortions. Dr. Hindman remained at Kendall House, checking in on his patients almost hourly.

Harry remained alert nearly the whole time. He had become too used to sleeping with one eye open, as he said, to let himself slip into anything but a doze. He had relented about sleeping in the drafty carriage house, though, and was housed in a huge bedroom down the hallway from Sarah's suite.

Ruth drifted in and out of consciousness, and Annie stayed by her bedside, refusing to leave and insisting on sleeping on a camp cot nearby.

On the fourth day, as the sun streamed into Ruth's bedroom through the leaded glass panes, Annie awoke and, as usual, looked immediately at her sister, and noticed something very strange.

The pustules were nearly gone.

"It worked!" she shouted, knocking over her cot. Ruth remained asleep, so Annie ran out of their room and down to the end of the hallway, to Sarah's suite. She pounded on the door as though she might batter it down. "Sarah! Sarah!" she shouted.

Sarah yanked the door open, her strawberry blonde hair in her eyes, still half-asleep. "Is something wrong, Annie?"

"No! Something is very right! Ruth's rash—it's going away!"

"She's saved!" Sarah yelled, and the two women embraced and danced in the hallway.

"She is!" Annie said, tears running down her cheeks. "Come and see!"

Still in her nightdress, Sarah followed Annie to her sister's bedroom, where Ruth was now sitting propped up, roused by all the commotion.

"Ruth!" Sarah said. "You're beautiful!"

"I think those days are behind me," she said.

"No, they're not," Annie said, giving Ruth a hand mirror from the dresser. Ruth looked into it and almost dropped it in her lap. She touched her face with her fingers.

"What about Harry?" Ruth said. "How is he?"

"We haven't looked in on him yet," Sarah said.

"Well, go on and don't worry about me," Ruth said. "Go see how he's doing."

"I'll check on him," Sarah said. "And I'll fetch Dr. Hindman."

She was back in ten minutes, the doctor in tow.

"Harry's feeling better this morning, too, Ruth," Sarah said. "It's a miracle."

"A miracle of *science*," the doctor said, squinting at Ruth. "Sit up, if you please, so I can look at your back." He peered down the back of her nightdress. "Significant improvement," he said. "This is very encouraging indeed."

"Is it dead, then?" Annie asked. "It worked?"

"From what I understand, it has very likely been killed off, yes," the doctor said. "What you are seeing is the body starting to heal itself, now that the contagion has been vanquished."

"May I see Harry?" Ruth asked.

"Young lady," the doctor replied, "let's not get ahead of ourselves. You need rest. In a few more days, if you continue to improve, you may see your friend."

"Just wait until I tell Charles," Sarah said.

"Knowing Mr. Kendall as I do, I should think Dr. Ehrlich's clinic will be receiving a significant donation," Hindman said. "I think it's fair to say that the man has very likely found a cure for one of the most dread diseases in history. Something that has destroyed millions of lives—itself destroyed with a single injection."

"That's quite a feat," Sarah said.

"He'll be immortal," Dr. Hindman said.

43

AN UNEXPECTED LETTER

WHEN KENDALL RETURNED HOME AFTER WORK THAT DAY, HE signaled for Sarah to join him in his office. Annie was fast asleep upstairs, with Ruth. Harry was still weak from the arsenic, but had grumbled so about the soft bed that he and Dr. Hindman had very nearly come to blows. Sarah had finally had to intercede and have Hindman agree that Harry could go back to the carriage house.

"I have only a few minutes," he said as they settled onto the big leather couch in his office. He glanced at the clock above the mantel. "But when I heard we had some very good news today, I wanted to celebrate a bit with you."

"The best news I can imagine. A happy ending," Sarah said. "Thanks to you and Dr. Ehrlich."

Kendall smiled. "Ehrlich gets all the credit. I'm just delighted I knew him well enough to ask for his help."

"Well, I'm grateful beyond words, Charles. It'll just take them a little time to recuperate now. The cure certainly isn't worse than the disease, but it's pretty bad."

"Very true," he said. "Speaking of recuperating—if it's not indelicate to bring it up—MacCormick told me about Mr. Horn's injury. I'm genuinely sorry."

"Thank you for saying so," she said.

"However did such a thing happen, I wonder? An accident of some kind is all Mac knew."

"It wasn't precisely an *accident*, as it turns out," Sarah said, trying not to blink.

Kendall looked confused.

She sighed. "Harry followed him to some dive bar, masquerading as my brother. Jeremy started in with his boasting about—well, you know what about. Harry didn't take too kindly to it."

"And?"

"He proceeded to cut off his hand. With a tobacco cutter."

"Good God," Kendall said, wincing. "The man takes no prisoners."

"That's fair to say. Anyhow, I went to see Jeremy—it seemed the only decent thing to do—and he and I are finished. Not that we ever really began."

"I'm sorry, Sarah."

"It's better this way. Now I can get back to finishing our case. Have you set a date with Aaron Brass?"

"I had Stefan hand deliver a letter to him, and I had his reply today."

"Then have we a date with him?"

"We do. We'll meet with him at his office tomorrow evening."

"His office? Why not meet at your factory, where you'd be safer?"

"Imagine the reaction from my men if Aaron Brass walked into my factory for a conference with me. It'd be nothing short of pandemonium."

"I wish Harry were strong enough to come with us," she said.

"My dear, that won't be necessary. We'll have Stefan. And furthermore, I don't expect any funny business."

"And while Stefan is formidable, Harry's a tiger."

"No doubt about that," he said. "But we'll be fine, and he needs his rest."

"I know. I just wish—"

Kendall glanced at the clock over the mantel. "Oh my. Why is it that when I'm with you, I completely lose track of time? I have a business affair downtown tonight, so I'd best go and get changed."

"Tonight? In this weather? It's blowing up a gale out there."

Kendall swiveled around and looked out his office window. The gorge was hidden behind a curtain of blowing, blinding white.

"Good heavens," he said. "That does look like a bad one. Well, nothing to be done about it. Business goes on in any kind of weather."

❧

AFTER KENDALL LEFT TO dress, Sarah walked slowly to the grand parlor. It had been such a happy day. Things are looking up at last, she thought.

As she was enjoying the fire, Stefan strode in, carrying a brimming cocktail glass.

"I'm sorry, Miss Sarah," he said. "I did not know you were here. I'll leave you to yourself."

"Not at all, Stefan. Come sit down with me."

"No, thank you," he said. "Mr. Kendall will be leaving shortly, and I'll be going with him."

"Is having a cocktail before you go out in the snow part of being a Cossack?" she said with a laugh, nodding at the glass in his hand.

Stefan blushed. "Oh no. Mr. Kendall likes a cocktail after work, and Erin was busy with supper, so I arranged it." He set the glass down on the table near the door and stood nearer to Sarah. They watched the fire for a few moments.

"What brought you to Niagara Falls, Stefan? If you don't mind my asking."

"So much work here. Opportunity."

"But why leave Russia?"

Stefan stroked his big mustache. "Russia is—complicated these days. My brother and I came here, and worked construction before Mr. Kendall hired me as his bodyguard."

"And he made an excellent choice," she said. "And your brother? Is he still doing construction?"

"No," Stefan said, shaking his head. "He died."

"Oh my. Please accept my condolences."

"Thank you. It was God's will."

"People say that, but I haven't found that it helps me much to think that way."

The big man shrugged. "It does not hurt."

"You know, Stefan—I'm sorry you and Harry don't see eye to eye."

Stefan's mustache concealed what may have been a tiny smile. "He has his job, and I have mine. That's all."

"I understand. I suppose it's—"

"*There* you are, Stefan," Kendall said, poking his head into the parlor. "I'm ready to go. Sarah, long time no see."

"Are you still going to brave the snow?" she asked.

"It's not all that bad," Kendall replied. "I'm in good hands with Stefan."

"Isadore's not driving you?"

"Isadore wanted the evening off," Stefan said. "And believe me, I know how to drive in the snow."

She laughed. "I have no doubt of it."

"Your cocktail is on the table, sir," the Cossack said to Kendall.

"You know, I was hoping that was mine and not yours, Sarah," Kendall said, picking up the glass and downing it. "Nothing like a little Dutch courage sometimes."

"I know the feeling," Sarah said. "You two be careful out there."

"We will. I'll see you at breakfast," Kendall said to Sarah.

"Perfect," she said.

"Good night, Miss Payne," Stefan said.

Sarah settled down into the couch again, watching the leaping flames. The case clock chimed six, and Sarah was soon dozing off.

"Pardon me, Miss Payne," Erin said, jolting her awake.

"Yes, Erin?"

"I have something for you from Mr. Kendall." She reached into her apron pocket and brought out a small envelope. "He asked me to give you this at six thirty."

"He did?"

"Yes, Miss."

"How queer," Sarah said, taking the envelope from Erin. She slit it open with a forefinger.

On a single sheet of Kendall's monogrammed stationery was a handwritten note.

Dearest Sarah:

Aaron Brass has agreed to meet with me tonight. I hope you won't be too upset with me for fibbing, but I felt strongly that it's best I go alone. Stefan will be close by, so I'll be safe.

You deserve all the credit for solving this mystery. Tonight will merely be negotiation.

I'll be home later, and if you are still awake, I'll give you all the details. If not, we'll see each other at breakfast. I'm overjoyed by today's good news about your friends. And by new beginnings.

Yours affectionately,
Charles.

Sarah refolded the note and stuffed it angrily into its envelope. She trotted up the stairs and rapped on Christine's door.

"Who is it?" Christine said from inside.

"It's Sarah. Open up!"

The door flew open a second later. Christine was standing there in a bathrobe. "I was dressing for dinner. What's wrong?"

"It's your father. He's done something very foolish."

Christine motioned for Sarah to come into her room, and shut the door behind them. "Whatever has he done?"

Sarah thrust the note out. "Read this."

Christine read the note, and looked up puzzled. "I'm not sure I understand what's—what's got you so upset. He's meeting with Brass. So what? He meets with people all the time."

"He was supposed to take me with him, and he's gone and slipped away. Brass is capable of anything, and I don't like that he's there alone."

"But isn't Stefan with him?" Christine said.

"Yes, but what does Stefan know about Brass? I've met the man, Christine! I know what he's up against."

"What do we do? Should we call the police?" Christine said, now looking very alarmed.

"Brass may have the cops in his pocket," Sarah said. "We can't trust them, except as a last resort."

"What then?"

"I'm going to find Isadore and follow them. I'm sure they're meeting in Brass's offices."

"What about Harry?"

"Harry's still not over that injection. He's supposed to have bed rest, and isn't in any shape to go out in *this*." She motioned to the snow-smeared window.

"So you're going alone?"

"I'll take Annie with me. You stay here in case I have to call."

"The hell you say. I'm going with you." Christine flung off her bathrobe and began racing around, stark naked, grabbing up clothing.

"Don't be silly," Sarah said.

The nude young woman came to a halt directly in front of Sarah. "Now see here," she said, jabbing her finger, "You're not the only one who loves my father. And I'm sure as hell not going to lose both of you, if you get yourself in over your head."

"And I'm certainly not going to argue with a naked lady. Pull something warm on, and meet me downstairs. I'll tell Erin to stand by the telephone in case we need help. I'll get Isadore. You go fetch Annie."

Christine nodded and darted back to her wardrobe.

"STEFAN AND MR. K. took the brougham," Isadore said when he reined in under the *porte cochère*. He was driving a massive carriage, behind a matched pair of equally massive black horses. "But we can make better time with this team. These big fellas can *pull*."

"Don't get down," Sarah called up, and she opened the carriage door to let Christine and Annie pile in. "Gluck Building, fast as you can."

"You ladies hold on tight," Isadore called down. "I'm going to make time down the hill."

He slapped the reins, and they shot forward, around the drive and out the iron gates. As they began the long descent down the Lewiston Road, the coach picked up speed, with Isadore shouting encouragement to his team.

"If I'd known he could drive like this, I'd ride with him more often," Christine said as they bounced along, swaying and sliding on the snowy hill. The two huge kerosene lamps mounted on the front of the rig struggled to cut through the squall.

"Why would Mr. Kendall go out in this?" Annie said, looking out the window.

"Because he's a pigheaded asshole," Christine said, "who thinks he's invincible."

"I think she meant other than that," Sarah said.

Riverdale Cemetery, Cataract College, the weird old ruins of the Suspension Bridge—long since collapsed into the rapids below—all swirled by as the carriage tumbled downhill, toward Niagara Falls. It took only twenty minutes until the three women felt Isadore reining in, gently applying his brakes, as the ground leveled out and the first haloed arc lights of the High Bank factories bloomed out of the driving snow.

"Almost there," Christine said, squeezing Sarah's hand. "He's going to be all right."

"I should be the one reassuring you," Sarah said, putting her hand over Christine's.

From the High Bank, it was only five minutes to Falls Street, where Isadore turned left toward the Gluck Building. When they were a couple blocks away, Sarah reached up and pulled the bell cord. The carriage came to a short stop, and Sarah climbed out.

"Wait here," Sarah shouted up to Isadore.

"I can livery the rig at Level's, down Prospect, if you want me to come along."

"No, we'll need you here if we have to make a quick getaway," she said. She waved for Christine and Annie to join her in the wailing wind.

The three began hurrying up Falls Street, their faces pelted by the snow. "I do have one question, if you don't mind," Christine shouted over the wind.

"What's that?"

"Harry's not here, and Isadore's with the carriage. We're three women walking into—well, I don't know what we're walking into. Don't you think we're a little overmatched?"

Sarah pulled her nickel-plated .32 Smith & Wesson halfway out of her coat pocket, letting it catch the streetlight. "This may even the odds."

"I should have known," Christine said.

"She's pretty good with it, too," Annie said.

They walked two more blocks up Falls Street, and then the twin pyramids of the Gluck Building rose up in front of them, wrapped in whirling snow and darkness.

"Brass's offices are around the side," Sarah said, and motioned for Christine and Annie to follow. They walked up the alley next to the east wall of the Gluck, and looked up into the falling snow. There was a yellow gleam oozing from Brass's windows.

"I think we've found them, ladies," Sarah said.

THE HEIRESS AND THE ANGELS

THE FRONT DOORS OF THE GLUCK BUILDING WERE UNLOCKED, but had sealed shut with ice and snow. They took turns yanking on the big brass doorknobs, hands slipping while the doors held fast.

"For heaven's sake," Annie said. "Maybe Isadore has a crowbar or something."

"No time," Sarah replied. "Wait here." She left the other two standing in the snowy doorway and ran back to the alleyway. When she returned, she was carrying a brick.

"What good is that—" Christine began, just as Sarah chucked it against the window in one of the twin doors. The brick bounced off, but cracked the glass. She picked up the brick and carefully broke out the window.

"Now we have leverage," she said, reaching into the hole and hooking her arm around the doorframe. She gave it a good pull and it snapped open.

"Good thinking, there," Annie said. "I wish I'd thought of that myself."

Sarah smiled and, crossing the dark lobby, they found the two Otis elevators. They rode them to the fifth floor and tiptoed to the door of the Abrasive Workers Union's offices.

Sarah rapped on the door, and after a few seconds, it cracked open.

"You've got the wrong place," a man with a scruffy beard said, peering out.

"We're looking for Aaron Brass," Sarah said. "Is he here?"

"Who wants to know?"

"Sarah Payne."

"Doesn't ring a bell," the fellow said, and slammed the door in her face.

Sarah and Christine exchanged looks. "What now?" Annie said.

Sarah banged on the door again until it rattled in its frame. A few seconds passed, and the scruffy man opened it.

"You again?" he said.

"I'll ask you one last time to tell Mr. Brass that Sarah Payne is here to see him."

"Let them in," came a voice from inside the office. The door swung inward, and the three women entered, scattering snow from their coats and hats.

Aaron Brass was sitting at a table in the main room with two other men. He waved.

"Miss Payne! What a pleasant surprise. Couldn't bear to be away from me?" He laughed. "No, don't answer that. And who might *these* two dishes be? You didn't tell me you had *sisters*."

"I'm Christine Kendall."

"As in Charles Kendall's daughter?"

"That's right."

Brass gave a low whistle through his stained teeth. "Boys," he said to the other two, "this may be the only time any of our kind meet an actual hair-esse. Take a good gander while you can."

"You don't say," one of them said, a swarthy man with pockmarked cheeks.

"I do say," Christine said.

"And who might *you* be?" Brass asked, turning toward Annie.

"Annie Murray. I'm Sarah's—friend."

"*Enchanted*," Brass said.

"Three of them, three of us. It's perfect," said the pockmarked man.

"Where are my manners?" Brass said. "Ladies, meet Ed Utting. And the quieter one is John Mars. Like the planet."

"It's short for Marszulek," John Mars said.

"Join us and thaw out a little?" Brass said, gesturing to a whiskey bottle in the center of the table. "Pull up some chairs for our guests, boys."

"No, thank you," Sarah said. "We're not here to socialize."

"Neither are we," Brass said. "Does this look like a social club to you?"

The ladies remained standing. Brass took a smoke from his cigarette case and flamed it off.

"It's much easier to drink sitting down," Brass said, blowing smoke.

"No, thank you," Christine said. "We don't plan to stay."

"Now I know you're better bred than that," he said. "So, one more time—*pretty please*?" It wasn't a request.

The three women sat down on the sticky chairs that the others had arranged.

"Now then," Brass said, pouring some whiskey into three more glasses, "isn't that so much better? Now we can all get acquainted more politely. The first question in my mind is what in God's name brings you lookers out, at night, in a snow squall, *here*?"

"We're looking for Mr. Kendall," Sarah said. "He's supposed to be with you."

Brass looked at Mars and Utting. "Boys, have you seen Charles Kendall around here? I sure haven't." The other two shook their heads over their whiskey.

"Don't lie to me, Mr. Brass," Sarah said.

Brass laughed, and showed his entire mouthful of yellow teeth. "*I'm* the liar, is that it? Wait—it was *you* who was doing all the lying. I didn't tell you so much as a fib, but you sure told me some whoppers."

"Then tell me where he is, and we'll leave you in peace."

"You'll leave *us* in peace?" Brass said. "Before you've even touched your whiskey? Drink up, and then I'll tell you whatever you like. You ought to know by now that I'm a man of my word."

Christine picked up her glass and slugged it back in one gulp.

"Damn, this one's a live wire," Mars said, looking at her hungrily.

"You haven't seen the half of it," Christine said.

Sarah took a tentative sip from the filthy glass. "How about it, then? Where is Mr. Kendall? He told me that he was coming to meet you tonight."

Brass took a huge, final drag on his cigarette. "You got your days mixed up. It's true that he and I are meeting, but not until tomorrow, about this time. So you gals are, let me see, a little shy of twenty-four hours early."

"What do we do now?" Christine whispered to Sarah, trying to ignore Mars's leer.

Brass heard her, leaned forward, and rapped gently on the table. "Well, my dear, all three of you are cordially invited to stay with us overnight, if you'd prefer to wait. We can find *some* way to pass the time, I'm sure." Brass and his men laughed uproariously.

"Very funny," Sarah said, grimacing. "You were to meet him *tomorrow*? Not tonight?"

"You want me to repeat the whole thing?"

"No, I do not," Sarah said. "Then you swear you don't know where he is?"

Brass shook his head. "Maybe he stood you up, darling. Though rumor has it he's gone a bit goo-goo on you."

Sarah drank down the rest of her whiskey. "He didn't stand me up, thank you."

"Touched a nerve there, did I?" Brass said.

"I don't know what you mean. Now, if we've no further business," she said, standing up.

Brass laughed again. "Be careful out there, Miss Payne. You never can tell who might be hiding behind a snowdrift."

"Thank you for the advice," Sarah said.

"Don't you *dare* threaten her," Annie said, leaning across the table and jabbing her finger under Brass's nose. He crossed his eyes to look at it and chuckled.

"Miss Payne," he said, "you do run with a rough crowd, don't you? Though if you don't mind my saying, sweetie," he said to Annie, eyeing her up and down, "you're much more my type than your friend here is. She's a stunner, no doubt about it, but she's cold. You've got a fire inside. I would *love* to get to know you better."

"Lucky me," Annie said.

"Time to go, ladies," Sarah said. "Good evening, Mr. Brass."

"And to you, too. And do come back tomorrow with Mr. K., won't you?"

"You're welcome anytime," Mars said to Christine, attempting a wink.

"For the love of God," she muttered.

The three women got up and walked out of the ABW office, took the stairs instead of the Otises, and hurried back to the carriage.

"I have a bad feeling about this," Sarah said. "I'd hoped against hope he'd be with Brass."

"Where could he be?" Christine said. "I thought sure we'd find him with them."

"Do you think that horrible man Brass was lying?" Annie asked.

"No, I don't. He's no liar. But he is indeed a horrible man."

"And yet the only one who's shown the least interest in me for two years," Annie said.

"Stop that," Sarah said. "There are lots of good men out there if you—"

"I really do hate to interrupt this girl talk," Christine said, "but can we think about where my father may have disappeared to?"

"Maybe he got confused himself about the day, and he and Stefan turned around and are on their way back home now," Annie suggested.

"Unlikely," Sarah said. "He's not the kind of man to make a mistake like that."

"What, then?" Christine said, exasperated.

"There's only one other place they can be," Sarah said as they came alongside the waiting carriage.

"Isadore," she called up, "do you know where the water intake is? For the Niagara Falls Electric tunnel?"

"I do," he said. "I took Mr. K. over there any number of times when it was under construction."

"Then that's where we need to go," she said. "In a hurry."

INTO THE LABYRINTH

As the carriage negotiated another downhill grade, Sarah tried to squint through the frosted window, but her breath fogged it as quickly as she could wipe it clear. She was thinking they must be nearly to the river, when Isadore rang the bell inside the carriage and brought the horses to a sliding halt. Sarah hopped out and looked up at him. "Look!" he shouted over the wind, pointing. Fifty yards or so ahead, Charles Kendall's horse and rig were tied to an iron railing next to a small squat blockhouse rising above the river's edge.

"Can you see anyone?" she yelled up, squinting into the snow.

He shook his head. Sarah nodded gravely and climbed back into the carriage.

"The brougham's just ahead," she said to Christine and Annie, "tied up next to the water intake. But there's no sign of either Stefan or Charles."

"You don't think—?" Christine said.

"If you're thinking what I'm thinking, I'm afraid so," Sarah said. "That bullheaded father of yours has decided to take matters into his own hands. Now that he knows the problem is in the tunnel, he's gone to figure it out himself before he meets with Brass."

"That *fucker*," Christine muttered. "He really has outdone himself this time."

"You mean to say that they've gone *underground*?" Annie asked.

"Unfortunately, that's the only logical explanation," Sarah said.

The slope grew steeper as Isadore eased the carriage forward toward the blockhouse. He carefully halted his team next to Kendall's rig and set the brake. Sarah threw open the door to step out, and was almost blown back into the carriage by a gust.

"Careful, Miss," Isadore said, helping her down.

"I swear I'm going to kill him for this," Christine said, as she and Annie followed Sarah out of the carriage and into the swirling snow.

"We need to get you ladies out of the wind," Isadore said, gesturing to the blockhouse. "They must be inside. Not even Stefan could stand this cold for long."

"And from the look of it, they've been here for some time," Sarah shouted, pointing to Kendall's horse. There were several inches of snow piled up on the blanket buckled over its back.

"Everyone join hands," Isadore said. "And follow me. The door's on this side, but watch your footing anyhow. It's as slick as a baby's bottom out here, and one false step—"

"I get the picture," Annie said, looking out at the cold water speeding by at the bottom of the sloping ground.

The blockhouse was perched on a steep plateau above the rushing river, where the normal gentle slope of the riverbank had been cut away to create a sheer wall of earth tall enough to enclose a giant masonry conduit at least ten feet in diameter. It was this intake that bled millions of gallons from the inexhaustible Niagara into the vast underground arteries that fed the throbbing turbines of the High Bank, more than a mile away.

In the hazy moonlight, an irregular, oblong boom of chains, extending fifty yards into the river and held in place by floating buoys, outlined what looked like an ice-free millpond in front of the cavernous intake.

"I want to take a look on the other side first," Sarah shouted over the blizzard when the four of them stood safely in the lee of the blockhouse, near its rusty iron door.

"What for?" Christine said. "It's just a cliff—" She stopped herself, horrified.

"Isadore, you wait here with them," Sarah said.

Sarah carefully followed the iron railing surrounding the structure to the river side. There, she leaned over the railing to peer down at the mouth of the intake, which jutted a few feet into the river. Mounted to the front of the conduit was a heavy iron portcullis, intended to prevent any stray ice or floating debris from entering the tunnel beyond. Curiously, there seemed to be almost no water flowing directly into the opening, only a deep, slow eddy of viscous black water sucking and slapping against the iron bars. Glancing out over the main body of the Niagara, though, she could see how fast the river moved. Bobbing chunks of ice, some larger than the big carriage, raced headlong toward the mist rising from the Falls only a half mile downstream.

Sarah's heart was beating hard as she studied the inlet, but there was thankfully no sign of Kendall or Stefan. Nothing was trapped against the iron grate, and the icy crust on either side of the conduit's inlet looked fresh and undisturbed.

"No sign of them," she said to her friends when she returned to the lee of the blockhouse.

"Thank God," Annie said, crossing herself.

"Let's go in, then," said Sarah. Isadore tugged the rusted door open on squealing hinges and poked his head in.

"It's black as night in there. I'll be right back." Isadore trudged back to the carriage and soon returned with two bullseye lanterns. He stepped into the shelter of the doorway and, after a few failed attempts, managed to keep a match going long enough to light one. "Come on. I'll get the other one lit inside."

"Nice job getting that going in a squall," Christine said. "You have only two of these?"

"I usually keep three of these in my pannier," he said. "But two ought to do it. I'll handle one and you ladies can take turns with the other."

Sarah shook her head. "No, you need to wait here. If they're in any trouble, we're going to need to get them home quickly. We can't have anything happen to you."

"I don't think that's a very good idea," Isadore said. "You can't— three ladies—"

"Quit while you're ahead," Christine said. "You heard her. Wait here for us."

"Well, then, for heaven's sake be careful," he said, handing his lantern to Sarah. "I'm going to blanket the horses, and then I'll check back here from time to time." He eased out of the door into the squall, and the three women were left alone.

Sarah played her lantern around the interior of the blockhouse, which was every bit as plain as the outside—nothing but four thick walls and a flat roof. The structure's sole function seemed to be to protect an iron staircase, its treads fanged with icicles, which went down into blackness. From below, they heard the hollow reverberation of moving water.

"It's like the entrance to a catacomb," Christine whispered. "But less cheerful."

"It is pretty grim," Annie said.

Sarah leaned over the slick railing and called down into the shaft. "Charles! Stefan!"

There was no answer, only the ceaseless drip of cold water from the ceiling, and a humming vibration transmitted up the iron staircase.

"I won't lie to you," Christine said. "I'd half hoped we'd find them both loafing in here, having a cigar. No such luck."

"No indeed," Sarah said. "We're going to have to go down and look for them."

"Seems like it," Annie said.

"How far down does it go?" Christine asked.

Sarah shrugged. "I couldn't say. It's not very deep here, but the tunnels go more than a mile, and deeper all the time. Hopefully we won't have to go—"

"A *mile*?" Christine said. "Underground?"

"Afraid so. But I doubt we'll have to go very far before finding them. They're probably on their way back here right now."

"Perhaps we ought to wait here, then?" Annie said.

"The problem is," Sarah replied, "if one of them is injured or stuck."

"This just gets better and better," Christine said.

Sarah gave her a thin smile. "Well, we might as well get on with it. I'll go first. Christine, you follow me, and Annie, you bring up the rear with the second lantern." Annie and Christine stared down into the dark staircase, unbelieving.

They were only a couple of clanking steps down when the sound of rushing water replaced the howling of the wind, and grew louder with each step. Annie kept her beam focused in front of Christine's feet, so she could be sure of her footing on the slick iron tread. Underneath the hem of Sarah's coat she could see that the base of the staircase stood perhaps fifteen feet below on a concrete pier rising a foot or two above a wide pool of swirling water.

At the bottom, the three stood quietly on the little concrete island, watching the black water dashing itself against their perch. In the beams of the bullseye lanterns, they could make out that the pier and staircase were centered in the mouth of an underground river. Behind them, toward the Niagara, was the portcullis, moonlight seeping between its bars, and a few idle, lost flakes of snow drifting in with it. Ahead was a broad canal, forming the base of an enormous masonry arch—a tunnel that sloped down and away from them into blackness, like a mineshaft flowing with ink.

For all the apparent indolence of the river in front of the intake, here the water seemed to make up its mind. After a few feet of hesitation, chasing its tail around the concrete pier, the dark water shot forward, coursing down the giant bore of the tunnel and diving away into the darkness. Against each wall of the tunnel was a narrow concrete walk-way, raised a half foot or so above the water level, presumably to allow access for inspection and repair.

Annie followed the water with the beam of her lamp, as it sped away under the dark masonry arch into nothing. "Good heavens," she whispered.

"You do realize we're fucked," Christine said.

"At least we're out of the wind," Sarah said quietly.

"Ever the optimist," Christine said. "But I swear it feels even colder down here." She hugged herself. "Why in God's name would my father venture down *here*?"

"Taking charge, as usual," Sarah replied. "He must have prevailed upon Stefan to bring him here, and he's down—*there*—seeing if he can find a way to restore his water."

Their breath hung in the damp, chilly underground space, but instead of slowly dissipating, the little clouds fell like the smoke of dry ice, down to the churning water, to be whisked away with it into the bedrock.

Sarah's beam played briefly across Christine's face, and she could see that the girl was plainly terrified. "Dear," she said, "why don't you go back up and wait with Isadore? Annie and I can take it from here. This is our job, not yours. We'll have a quick look around and be right back."

Christine's mouth took a harder set. "Nothing doing. Don't ask me again."

Sarah nodded slowly. "Well, then we three have to get from here over to the footpath."

"Which side, though?" Christine asked. "What if the tunnel splits and we have to be on the other side?"

"No way to know."

"Then let's take the left side," Annie said. "It looks a little drier."

"Left side it is," Sarah said. "We'll have to make a little jump. I'll go first, and Christine, you come to me. I'll catch you."

"I wonder how deep it is?" Christine whispered.

"Don't think about that. Just don't fall in."

"That is *such* good advice."

"Let's go, smart aleck."

Sarah gathered up her skirt and overcoat and hopped over the torrent. She set the lantern down and held out her arms.

"It's probably only three feet deep," Christine said. "I could probably wade."

"Don't try it. You'll get frostbite," Sarah said, opening her arms. What she didn't say was that a misstep would be certain death. No human strength could resist the pull of the weight of all that frigid water, shallow or deep, racing downhill under the city, all the way to the Mill District. If you weren't drowned or frozen to death by the time you reached the factories, you'd be ground to mincemeat in the turbines at the end of the Long Drop.

"I'll say it again," Sarah called over, as Christine continued to hesitate, "if you don't want to go, or can't go, there's no shame in it. You don't have a thing to prove."

Christine frowned, pulled up the skirt of her coat, and jumped. She cleared the distance easily, and Sarah steadied her on the footpath, pushing her closer to the wall.

"That's the worst of it," Sarah said. "Now it's straight ahead."

"Straight *down*, you mean."

"Come on, Annie, you're the best athlete here," Sarah said. With a grim smile, Annie raised her lantern and made the leap easily.

Sarah took Christine's free hand, and with Annie bringing up the rear, they began easing down the slick concrete footway, which sloped downward at the tunnel's pitch. It was close enough to the channel that the water—which frothed and raged more and more as it accelerated downward—leaped high enough that, within a dozen yards, their shoes and stockings were soaked through.

After ten minutes, the staircase seemed miles behind. And they noticed that the tunnel itself was narrowing, necking down, from more than ten feet in diameter back at the inlet to less than six. They now had to crouch slightly to keep from bumping their heads on the masonry arch. Every few minutes they shouted for Kendall and Stefan, but were met with nothing but silence and water for a reply.

Every twenty yards or so along the watercourse, in the very middle of the flow, was another stone pier just like the one serving as the foundation for the iron staircase, though much smaller. The churning water, now moving as fast as a river's rapids, pulled hard at the little blocks, as if trying to wrench them from the floor of the tunnel and hurl them downward toward the turbines.

"I think we have our answer on how to switch sides, if we need to, without retracing our steps," Sarah said. "We can use these blocks to cross the channel."

"Wonderful," Christine murmured. "Now it's two hops instead of one, with feet like blocks of ice."

However useful these little piers might prove, every one of them created a rolling wave on the upstream side that swelled up and then splashed back into the water on either side, creating a spray of cold rain that drenched them every time they passed a pier. Worse, every fifteen or twenty steps, they had to squeeze past a large ringbolt, driven into the tunnel wall and protruding a few inches—not much, but enough to make the already narrow pathway seem like an icy tightrope.

"What are these big rings for, I wonder?" Annie asked, as they edged sideways past one of them.

"For workmen, I'd imagine," Sarah said. "You've probably seen these things driven into the bricks lining the Erie Canal in Buffalo. Men who are making repairs or taking out obstacles tie themselves to them and then if they slip, it's not—" She made a motion with her hand to indicate that any such poor soul would disappear forever into the bowels of the earth.

The tunnel continued to squeeze inward, and they now had no choice but to ease sideways along the footpath. The roar of the water was almost intolerable now, reverberating off the tunnel's walls and creating a weird wheezing drone that they could feel vibrating in their teeth. After a while, the three stopped to catch their breath and relieve their cramping backs.

"Did I mention that I'm going to claw my father's eyes out when I see him?" Christine said, rubbing the small of her back.

"Leave me one of them, would you?" Annie said. "Sarah, how far have we gone, do you think? It seems like we've been down here forever."

"Has to be half a mile," Sarah wheezed.

"How much farther does it go?"

"The whole thing's almost a mile long. From what I've read, the tunnel will start to pitch downward more steeply when we get near the Long Drop."

"Now you tell me there's something ahead called the *Long Drop*?" Christine said. "What the *hell*."

"That's what they call it where the water falls freely, like a miniature Niagara Falls, into big iron tubes, which feed the turbines at the bottom."

"And I'm guessing we don't want to, say, accidentally step into the Long Drop," Annie said glumly.

"That would be best avoided. But we'll know before we get to that. We'd better get moving again, though. We've got to have enough strength to get back up this thing."

All three women were soaked to the skin, shivering, and desperately cold. They were deep under the city now, possibly even under the edge of the tourist district, as the pathway continued to narrow. After another ten minutes, they arrived at a fork, where the tunnel ahead split into two slightly smaller tunnels—each perhaps only five feet high—one going off to their right, one to the left. The bore was narrow enough now that the air rushing up from below, as the water surged down, was

INTO THE LABYRINTH

blowing a gale in their faces from two directions, and whipping the water into a frenzy.

"Stefan's a giant," Christine said. "Do you really think they could have come this far?"

"Until now, there's only been one way they *could* have come," Sarah replied. "They weren't outside, and we didn't pass them on our way, so they must be ahead."

Annie shined her lantern down both forks of the rapids. "Which way, though—that's the mystery."

They stood there where the tunnels diverged, getting a good drenching from the cold spray, but not knowing what else to do.

Sarah cupped her hands around her mouth. "Charles!" she shouted, as loudly as she could manage.

Christine followed suit. "Daddy! Are you down there?"

They stopped to listen. Nothing.

They took turns shouting again and again, until they were hoarse. Then Sarah squeezed Christine's forearm.

"I heard a voice!" she said. "From the right-hand tunnel, I think. Let's call again."

They did their best with exhausted voices, and then listened.

"There! It sounds like a man's voice saying, 'Down here.' Did you hear that?" Annie said.

"I did," Christine replied, forgetting the cold for a moment. "I think it was Stefan's voice. From the right-hand tunnel, definitely."

"Then we'll have to cross over," Sarah said. "That means we go back to the last stepping stone we passed."

The women shuffled back up the main tunnel, and soon came to one of the crossing blocks. Here the water was sending up a scallop-shaped plume of water where it collided with the block.

"Good night," Christine said.

Sarah looked her in the eye. "I know. But we can do it. We're almost there."

"I'll go first this time," Annie said.

Christine gripped her arm. "No. This time, I'll lead. Hand me your lantern."

Sarah nodded and gave it to her. "Be careful."

Christine eased herself to the edge of the walkway, and jumped. Her left foot landed squarely on the little pillar, but her wet shoe slipped, and she stood on tiptoe for a moment, trying to regain her balance, her bullseye lantern's beam flailing wildly over the dripping ceiling and walls. Sarah almost screamed, but caught herself.

"That felt better than it looked," Christine said, when she'd finally managed to plant her other foot. "Next step's easier." She hopped again and, this time, landed squarely on the pathway and grabbed ahold of one of the ringbolts protruding from the wall.

"Be careful," she yelled across the stream. "That thing is slippery!"

Annie nodded and pulled up her soggy skirt and coat, clutching them in one hand. "Here goes," she said, and jumped. Taking a lesson from Christine's near mishap, she jumped with both feet, and landed evenly on the stone block. Then she jumped to the pathway and joined Christine.

"You're trying to make me look bad," Christine said to her.

Annie smiled at her. "Now you, Sarah!" she called over, training her light on the stone block.

Sarah took a deep breath and made two graceful hops to rejoin the others.

"And you looked like a gazelle," Christine said, handing back Sarah's lantern.

Sarah brushed her dripping hair away from her face. "A fine gazelle I make right now."

"You *have* looked better," Christine said. "But still, not too bad."

They eased their way down the right-hand tunnel. The downward pitch of the narrow pathway was getting extreme, and it was more and more difficult to secure their footing.

"Look!" Sarah said, pointing ahead. "A light."

In the coal-blackness ahead, at the edge of a sharp turn, was a small flickering light. They began to shout for the two men again, but there was no response this time. The tunnel ceiling was terrifyingly low now, four feet at best, and the water channel broader and, presumably, deeper. In the near distance, they could hear a different sound—a deep,

338   *Robert Brighton*

booming rumble coming up through their feet: the sound of water free-falling 150 feet through the giant steel penstocks, relentlessly feeding the insatiable turbines beneath the High Bank.

"The Long Drop," Christine said.

"The light's just up ahead," Sarah said. "Around that bend."

They edged around the kink in the tunnel wall.

JUST AROUND THE CORNER, crouched by a lantern sitting on the concrete pathway, was Stefan. The big man blocked any view behind him, but when he saw the three women, he unwound his long limbs with surprising ease and came toward them, like a wolf spider in a funnel web.

"Hello, Miss Sarah," he called over the roar of the water. "Miss Annie. Christine."

Christine smiled broadly. "I don't think I've ever been so happy to see you, you big—"

"You shouldn't have come," he said, somewhat sadly.

Sarah played the beam of her bullseye lantern around Stefan, and saw the form of Charles Kendall huddled against the wall. She stepped toward the big man, perplexed. "Stefan, what's happened to—"

When she neared Stefan, the Cossack held out his hand. She reached hers out to grasp it, but he didn't take it. Instead, he grabbed the bail of her bullseye lantern and wrenched it out of her grip. He tossed it into the rushing water, where it expired with a sharp hiss, and disappeared.

"What in the devil!" Sarah said. "Have you lost your mind?"

Christine screamed, grabbed Annie's wrist, and trained the beam of her lantern past Stefan and onto her father. He was slumped against the wall of the tunnel, his bare feet dangling off the concrete walkway, and seemed to be prevented from falling in entirely by his hands, which were clasped together near his head and handcuffed to a large cast-iron handwheel.

Stefan reached past Sarah and tore Annie's lantern away, and it followed Sarah's into the roaring stream.

"All right, then," Stefan said. "All of you, over by him."

"What is the meaning of this?" Sarah croaked indignantly, as the three women sat on the pathway next to the unconscious man.

"Praise God, he's breathing," Annie said.

"Not for long," Stefan said, playing the beam of the remaining lantern over them.

Chrisine scowled. "I wish I could say the same about you, asshole."

"Did Brass put you up to this?" Sarah said. "If so, it's not too late, Stefan."

Stefan smiled. "*Brass?* Brass told me he wanted to work things out with your father, but I could not let that happen. So I told your father I could take him to the valve that controls his water. And now he can die a happy man, because—he's chained to it."

"I understand now," Sarah said. "You said you worked construction before Mr. Kendall hired you. You worked on this tunnel, didn't you?"

"Two years, digging in the dark. And it was in this tunnel of his"— he jabbed his finger toward Kendall's form—"that my brother died. He's still down here, somewhere, buried under tons of rock. He came with me to this country for a new life, and he ended up dead, a mile underground. So I must repay blood with blood."

"My father didn't kill your brother, and neither did we," Christine said.

"If your father hadn't been born, my brother would still be alive. And all three of you—you should be asleep in your soft beds right now, and this would have happened without any harm coming to you. Everyone would think Brass did it."

"You're going to leave us here to die?" Christine said. "Just like that? And to think I fucked you, you imbecile."

"I *am* sorry about that. But Fate has decided. So yes, I will leave you here, in the dark. But you three have a choice that he doesn't. He's going to take his time about dying. You can always jump in and end it quickly. Or," he said, pulling his big Colt revolver from his coat pocket, "I can shoot you now."

The women didn't reply, and the big man turned and began taking cautious steps away from them, back up the pathway.

"*Stefan!*" Sarah yelled after him. He turned and pinpointed them with his lantern.

"You don't have to do this," Sarah said. "You *know* this is wrong."

Stefan's huge form was a mass of shadow behind the bullseye

lantern, except for the glint of his teeth and sparkling eyes. "Goodbye," he said. "We're finished here."

"Not yet we're not," a familiar voice said from behind the Cossack. Stefan whirled around and his lantern flashed on the pale, pockmarked face of Harry Price.

Harry's arm was already in motion before Stefan had a chance to think. He brought his razor down hard on the wrist of Stefan's gun hand, severing the tendons and forcing him to drop the gun. Harry kicked the revolver into the channel and then, on one foot, launched an upstroke at the Cossack's throat. The arc of the razor threw Harry further off-balance, and he lost his footing on the slick concrete, going down hard on his back. Harry dropped his razor with a muttered curse.

Stefan threw down his lantern and descended on Harry like a thunderbolt. Even with one hand limp and useless, he was so much the larger and stronger man that in seconds he had his opponent pinned to the walkway. He pulled himself up to his knees and straddled Harry's chest, and then methodically began pummeling him with his good hand, working him toward the edge and the water flying by. After taking a half dozen hard blows, Harry managed to worm one arm free, reach up, and put his open hand over Stefan's face, as if to push the big man away.

But then Stefan screeched, an inhuman sort of wail, and reeled backward. His face passed through the beam of his fallen lantern to reveal that one eye socket was as empty and black as the tunnel. Harry had hooked out his eye with his thumb.

"You forgot something," Harry said, throwing the eyeball at Stefan and nimbly springing up into a fighter's crouch. "Why don't you quit while you still have something left to lose?"

Stefan growled and hurled himself at Harry, knocking the smaller man onto his back again. Harry's head hit the concrete with a thud. This time, Stefan would not repeat his mistake and get too close. He stood and loomed over Harry, taking up every inch of available vertical space, and raised his heavy boot to bring it down on the dazed man's skull.

Then there was a sharp, echoing report, and another, and another, and the big Cossack dropped abruptly to his knees, his remaining eye wide with surprise. Behind him crouched Sarah Payne, her nickel-plated Smith & Wesson glinting in the lamplight.

Harry shook off his stupor and tried to crawl past Stefan to Sarah, but the Cossack sat back heavily on his haunches, blocking the pathway and looking bemused. It wasn't entirely clear where he'd been hit, but he had most certainly taken three rounds somewhere in his big body, and he was getting weaker fast. He leaned forward, staring at Harry. Harry picked up the fallen lantern and trained it on the wounded man.

"Fucking nutsack," he said.

"*Cossack*," Stefan croaked.

"Not a red cunthair's difference, if you ask me," Harry said, approaching him.

Stefan managed to raise himself up on his knees, swaying. He extended his arms feebly, trying to grapple with Harry.

"Some fellows just don't know when they've been beat," Harry said and, with a swift kick, sent Stefan toppling into the water. Stefan made a gurgling yelp, his arms windmilled futilely over his head, but in a short second he was gone, rushing away down the dark tunnel toward the Long Drop.

"Thank you kindly, Sarah," Harry said, calmly replacing his hat on his head. "I may have to rethink my position about guns, after that little demonstration."

"I forgot I had the thing," she said, her voice shaking. "When Stefan produced his, that's when I remembered. I couldn't find a way to use it without hitting you, though."

"Glad you waited till the coast was clear," he said. "That was some fine shooting. Annie Oakley couldn't have done better."

They turned back toward Christine and Annie, who seemed stunned. Christine was rubbing her father's hands, which were purplish in the grip of the handcuffs.

"Thank God you're here, Harry," Annie said. "I've been wrong about you—"

"I don't care about that," he said. "Just don't any of you try to sneak out without me next time. It's really irritating. If Isadore hadn't tipped me off, I'd still be in the carriage house."

"I'm sorry, Harry," Sarah said. "You were feeling poorly, and I never thought it would come to this."

"No matter," he said. "Right now, we need to get him up

to the carriage and home. From the looks of it, he's been given knockout drops."

"But he's handcuffed to the wall," Christine said. "Should one of us go back up to get a hacksaw, or something?"

"Naw," Harry said. "These police cuffs are a joke. Same little lock, same little key." He removed the long stickpin from his tie, fiddled with the cuffs, and, in a few seconds, had them open.

"Spent my fair share of time in these things," he said.

"Well done," Sarah said. "But he's unconscious. And barefoot. Why in the world—"

"It was the nutsack did that," Price said. "I'm sure he chucked his shoes in there." He nodded to the raging water. "If you want a man to freeze to death slowly, take off his shoes. Even if he's got everything else on, he's finished."

"What do we do, then?" Annie said.

"I'm going to have to get him on my back and carry him up, like a sack of potatoes," Harry said.

"You can't possibly manage that," Sarah said. "All that way, uphill?"

"I carried bricks and timber for a lot of years," Harry said. "I reckon I can manage him, if you three can help me raise him up enough for me to get under him. Get on either side of him and hoist as hard as you can."

The women pulled Kendall to his knees, and Harry bent over and grabbed the man in a bear hug, and then half stood him up against the wall. "Try to lock his knees," he said to the girls, "until I can get under him."

Harry squatted and let Kendall's body slump forward over his back, then he struggled to gain his footing. "Sarah, you go on ahead with what's-his-name's lantern, because I'm going to need both hands to hold his arms," he said. "And mind your step, because just around the bend is my lantern. I left it there when I heard you up ahead. Miss Annie, you gather it up, because we can use two, just in case."

They started up the tunnel, Harry clearly straining under the weight of his burden. As they shuffled uphill, one dogged step at a time, at last the tunnel began to widen. The water, while still racing by, again became a little less violent. Now they could hear their panting, echoing off the masonry and the crystalline layer of ice that shattered sound as well as lamplight.

At a plod they retraced their steps upstream. Fighting fatigue, and slipping on the grade, each yard felt like a tiny victory, bringing them closer to the staircase and Isadore's carriage. It took the better part of an hour before, in the bullseye lantern's beam, the iron staircase reared up reassuringly ahead from the dizzying, endless water rushing past.

"Jacob's Ladder," Christine said, beyond the end of her strength.

"Just a few more yards, dear," Sarah said. "We're almost there."

When they arrived at the stairs, Christine sat down heavily on the wet, icy tread. "Let me rest here for a while. I'll be fine. You go on ahead. Get to the carriage."

"Nothing doing," Sarah said. "You're developing hypothermia." She knelt in front of Christine and began vigorously rubbing the girl's arms and legs.

"You're hurting me," Christine said through chattering teeth.

"Well, then, damn it, it hurts, but I'm not letting you rest until we get out of here," she said.

Harry was wheezing and running with cold sweat when he showed up a couple minutes afterward, with Kendall unevenly slung over his back and Annie following close behind. He gave the women a worried look.

"Mr. K.'s very weak," he said quietly to Sarah. "I'll take him up as quick as I can and come back for Miss Christine. She doesn't look too good."

"Why, thank you very much," Christine mumbled.

Taking a deep breath, Harry shifted Kendall higher onto his back and laboriously mounted the stairs.

"You go on," Sarah told Annie. "I'll wait here with Christine." She sat close to the shivering girl, trying to warm her. She realized that she was bone-tired, too, and thought briefly that she might start weeping.

She hadn't had time to become too morose by the time Harry returned. "Miss Annie's in the carriage with Mr. K.," he said, breathing hard. "Now you go, and I'll bring Miss Christine."

Isadore was waiting by the coach door when Sarah staggered out of the blockhouse and into the blizzard. The squall had become a full gale, sweeping off the river and pelting them with sharp pellets of ice. Isadore helped Sarah into the coach, next to where Kendall was lying pale and still as a statue on one of the bench seats, a couple of heavy blankets piled on him and only his face exposed. When Harry arrived soon after, he deposited Christine, who was quietly murmuring to herself, next to Annie. He closed the door and turned toward Isadore.

"Thanks, pal," Harry said to Isadore, sticking out his hand. "Obliged to you."

Isadore took off his glove and shook it. "Don't mention it. I'm just glad you didn't fall off the back, the way I was going downhill."

"You nearly shook me off a couple times, but it worked out."

Harry opened the carriage door wide enough to stick his head in, and said, "I'll drive the brougham back to Kendall House. Miss Annie, get Miss Christine under the other blankets. Sarah, you huddle up against Mr. K and keep him warm."

He shut the door again and rapped on Isadore's bench, and the big carriage started moving away from the blockhouse and toward the city again.

We're probably following the very same route we took underground, Sarah thought, feeling strangely warm in her sodden clothing. She put her arms around the inert form of Charles Kendall and, as she fell into some deep place, hoped that he could feel her heart beating.

46

FAMILY

SARAH JOLTED AWAKE IN THE PITCH DARK. "MAGGIE? MAGGIE?"

"Maggie's next door, Miss," a familiar voice said. "She's right as rain." A match flared, and Erin's face emerged out of the blooming lamplight.

Sarah looked around her. "Erin? Where am I?"

"You're in your bedroom, Miss," Erin said quietly.

"Bedroom? In Buffalo?"

"No, at Kendall House."

Sarah rubbed her eyes, tried to focus. "It seems like I've been dreaming."

"You've been asleep for a day and a half," Erin said. "Dr. Hindman has been keeping you on a sedative. He said the best thing for you was rest."

"Good heavens. He must have really put me under. Everyone's well?"

"Yes. Mr. Kendall is awake now, as is Miss Christine. Miss Annie, Isadore, and Mr. Price refused to see the doctor at all."

"That fits. I'm getting out of this bed right now. I'd like to see Maggie and then get on with things." Sarah swung around and put her feet on the floor.

"Wait—let me help you up," Erin said.

"I'm perfectly—whoa," Sarah said, finding her legs weak and wobbly under her. "Maybe I'll take you up on that."

"It's only about five thirty in the morning," Erin said. "Why don't you sleep a little more?"

Sarah shook her head. "I should think almost two days of sleep will be sufficient. But since it's early, I think I'll wash up and get dressed before waking Maggie."

"I laid out a change of clothes for you, Miss. Do you think you can you manage by yourself?"

"I'm feeling much steadier now, yes. You go and do as you please, and I'll get myself put together."

"WE'RE ALL LUCKY TO be alive," Mr. Kendall said later, at breakfast. "And I, most of all. Thanks to all of you. Sarah, Christine, Miss Murray, Mr. Price, and Isadore—for your bravery and loyalty—I am indebted to you in ways I can never fully repay." He raised a flute of champagne.

"I hope it teaches you a lesson. Pulling a stupid stunt like that," Christine snarled. "Half of me still thinks I ought to have left you down there."

"Christine," he said, "I could hardly have imagined that Stefan would turn on me."

"He screwed us both, in a manner of speaking," Christine said under her breath.

"Was it the cocktail, I suppose?" Sarah asked.

"Without a doubt," Charles replied. "Only a few minutes after I drank it, I felt stupefied. After that, I don't remember anything. I don't know if he carried me all the way down there, or if I walked and don't recall it. It seemed as though I was in a trance the whole time."

"Terrifying," Sarah said.

"And, Mr. Price," Kendall said, "I understand special congratulations to you are in order. For besting a fighter like Stefan, and while still not fully recovered from your ordeal."

"Don't think so, sir," Harry said. "Hate to admit it, but he was getting the better of me until Sarah filled him full of lead. Then we were in clover."

"Oh my," Sarah said. "I suppose that Stefan—"

"Utterly destroyed my Number Two turbine," Kendall said. "It'll have to be completely rebuilt. It's not designed to have something like—"

"We get the idea," Sarah said.

"Yes, of course. Sorry," he said.

"He got no worse than he deserved," Isadore chimed in. "To think I bunked with that man for more than a year."

"We have that in common," Christine said to Sarah out of the side of her mouth.

"Well, we all learned whom we can trust," Kendall said. "And better late than never. The problem turned out to be straightforward—presumably with Brass's encouragement, Stefan was going down there every few days and closing the valve a little bit each time. No one else would dare go down there, so he knew he wouldn't be caught. And it was you, Sarah," he said, raising his glass again, "who determined that the problem was in the tunnel, after all, and not in my factory."

Sarah cleared her throat. "You're far too kind. And I'd like to propose a toast of my own, if I may."

"Hear, hear," Kendall said.

Sarah raised her glass. "To Mr. Charles Kendall, for saving the lives of two of my dearest friends, and for putting his faith in the Avenging Angel Detective Agency, even when it didn't always make sense. To my partner, Annie, who wrapped up a second big case recently. And to Christine, Isadore, and everyone else not here for your kindness and hospitality here at your magnificent home. Maggie and I will never forget your generosity."

"You make it sound as if you were leaving us," Christine said, putting down her glass without so much as a sip.

"That was the arrangement, yes," Sarah said. "We'll be going back to Buffalo soon."

"Surely we can persuade you to stay a little while longer," Kendall said.

"That's awfully kind," she said. "But poor Annie has been holding down the fort alone for quite some time. And I'm afraid that staying longer would only make it harder for me to leave."

Christine suddenly jumped up from the table and threw her napkin down, hard. "That's—that's a—simply *cruel* thing to say," she stammered. "How could you? After—*everything*!"

Sarah was about to respond when Christine spun away from the table and ran out of the breakfast room, slamming the glass door so hard behind her that the panes rattled.

"Don't mind her," Kendall said to Annie, whose eyes were saucers. "She wears her heart on her sleeve."

"I'll go and talk with her," Sarah said, rising.

"Christine?" Sarah said, through the young woman's door.

"Go away!"

"Won't you let me come in?"

"No! I don't want to see you. Go. Run away to Buffalo, just like you ran away here. That's what you do, isn't it?"

"Now, Christine," Sarah said, "you know that I can't stay here forever. I came here to do a job, and the job is done. I have no choice but to go back."

The door suddenly flew open, and Christine was standing there, her eyes red and puffy. "You *always* have a choice. You can do as you please. Why not be honest about it? Don't say, 'I have to go back.' Say instead, 'I want to go back.'"

"Dear—"

Christine stuck her finger under Sarah's nose. "Don't start that 'dear' stuff with me. After all we've been through, you owe me the truth. Do you really *want* to go back to Buffalo? Do you *want* to leave us? Leave me? Leave my daddy? Can't you see how we both *need* you?"

"There are so many things, Christine, we might prefer—"

"So you don't *want* to leave!" she said triumphantly. "You don't want to go. You're going because you feel guilty."

"I don't feel guilty," Sarah said.

"You do. You feel guilty about leaving Annie to fend for herself—you said so yourself—but you know what I think you feel most guilty about? Deep down?"

"I'm sure you'll tell me."

"Well, someone needs to. It's not what you left behind that you feel guilty about. You feel guilty for wanting to stay. You feel guilty for loving us."

Sarah examined her feet for a few heartbeats, then looked up at Christine.

"I'll tell you what," she said. "I'll go and help Annie get Ruth settled in at home again. And there's a loose end with our other case I need to tie up in Buffalo. Then I'll come back for a nice, long stay."

"Do you promise?"

"Yes," Sarah said, "I promise."

Christine threw her arms around Sarah. "Oh God," she sobbed, "I'll have a mother again."

47

THE TRUSTEES

Five days later

DEEP BELOW THE VAST ELLICOTT SQUARE BUILDING WAS BURIED the Buffalo Safety-Deposit Vault Company, a windowless maze of identical concrete corridors lined with identical steel-fronted safety-deposit boxes, large and small. At the very back of this enormous bunker was a single office, belonging to the president of the company, Mr. Roland Park. In addition to standing guard over the secrets of Buffalo's wealthy, Park was also the chief trustee of Edward Miller's estate.

"This place gives me the willies," Annie whispered to Sarah, as their footsteps echoed down the dim grey hallway leading to Mr. Park's lair. "After that tunnel escapade, I'd rather stay aboveground."

"You and me both," Sarah said. "I don't like thinking that the world's largest office building is squatting on top of us."

"With any luck," Bert said, "this won't take very long. If they have any sense, that is."

"Never a certainty," Annie grumbled.

They were greeted at Park's office by a pale young secretary, whose large dark eyes seemed to have no iris at all, as though she and generations of ancestors had lived where the sun's rays never penetrated and had gradually adapted to the gloom. The secretary showed them into Mr. Park's office, where he and another man—a florid-looking fellow with a large ruby stickpin in his tie—were waiting.

"Bert, I believe you're acquainted with my cotrustee, Mr. Tucker?" Park said. Mr. Tucker deliberately rose from his chair with a reluctant, somewhat pugnacious air. He stuck out one large hand in Bert's direction, studiously ignoring the two ladies facing him.

"We've met, but it's been some time," Hartshorn said, shaking the man's hand. "And I have with me the Misses Payne and Murray from the Avenging Angel Detective Agency."

"I've heard about your agency, Miss Payne," Tucker said with a little smirk. "Lady detectives. Who knew there was such a thing?"

"There was such a shortage," Sarah said, "I thought I'd better do something about it."

Park laughed. "You're as witty as you are beautiful, Miss Payne. Oh, and pleased to meet you, Miss Murphy, of course."

"Murray," Annie said quietly, but Park was still looking, seemingly mesmerized, at Sarah.

"And where might your *friend* Mrs. Miller be today?" Tucker said to Bert, without any attempt to conceal his contempt. His Adam's apple bulged over his tight collar, as though he was attempting to swallow something especially large and dry.

"We thought it best that my *client* sit this one out," Bert replied. "Given her unhappy history with the trustees."

"Surely even *Alicia Miller* can't hold a grudge against the people entrusted with the fiduciary care of her children," Tucker said, frowning.

"We've no complaint against the trustees," Hartshorn said. "At the moment."

"What's that supposed to mean?" Tucker said.

"Now, gentlemen," Park interjected, "we'd best get down to brass tacks. Mr. Tucker and I have reviewed your report, Miss Payne, but we'd appreciate it if you'd walk us through your allegations."

"Miss Murray was our agent on the case," Sarah said. "I'll ask her to make our report."

Annie had brought with her a thick folder of her photographs and copies of the time records from the Miller Envelope machines. She explained her surveillance to the two gentlemen. Park nodded from time to time, while Tucker crossed his arms and looked out an imaginary window in the featureless concrete wall.

"As you gentleman can see," Annie said, summing up, "these allegations are supported by considerable evidence. Mr. Gaines has intentionally been sabotaging the business to get even with Mrs. Miller."

"Get even with her?" Park said. "For what?"

Annie looked nervously at Sarah, who nodded. Bert swallowed hard.

"For withdrawing her favors."

"Her *favors*?" Tucker said. "You can't be serious."

"She is being serious, Mr. Tucker," Sarah said. "I'm sure you'll agree that Mrs. Miller does have a certain magnetism."

Tucker sneered. "Rollie, wouldn't you think the magnetic Mrs. Miller would have had her fill of scandal by now?"

"The only scandal, sir," Sarah replied warmly, "is your obvious lack of respect for—"

"From a legal point of view, Mr. Gaines's motive is irrelevant," Bert interrupted, putting his hand gently on Sarah's forearm. "Simply put, he is in breach of his contract with the estate, and he must be removed from his position immediately."

"He's right about that," Park said to Tucker. "Legally speaking."

"Another reason I thank God I'm not a lawyer," Tucker said. "Because to me the *why* is far more important than the *what*."

"Rollie," Bert said, ignoring Tucker, "we submitted our report a week ago. You've had ample time to study it. And now the agent in charge has gone through it personally, as you requested. So at this juncture, I think it's only fair for the trustees to take action and remove Mr. Gaines."

"Only *fair*?" Tucker said. "That's rich. Hartshorn, your *client* has already received far more than her own husband thought was *fair*. You know better than I do that Ed Miller didn't want her to have a red cent—for God's sake, *you* drew up the man's will. And now she wants more. She wants to wrest control of Miller Envelope away from the majority owner." He shoved the folder over toward Annie. "And worse, to do so by smearing the man's reputation."

"If I may," Sarah said. "I knew Ed Miller rather well—as I'm sure you'll both recall from the newspaper accounts. And I can attest that he was very fond of Mr. Gaines. But I can also state with complete confidence that Mr. Miller would never condone Mr. Gaines's actions in this matter. Whatever ill feeling there was between Mr. and Mrs. Miller, Ed would never have wanted to see his business damaged—and his children's fortunes reduced—for the sake of settling a score."

"Well said, Miss Payne," Mr. Park said.

"Well said, well said," Tucker said, rolling his eyes. "We can talk past one another all day, if you like. But if you think that we, as trustees, are going to vacate Mr. Gaines's shares in favor of Mrs. Miller, Bert, you've got a screw loose."

"Bill," Park said. "There's no call to be uncivil."

"Sticks and stones," Bert said. "Which doesn't change the fact that Mr. Gaines has shown that he's unfit to be—essentially—an agent of the trust. He must be removed immediately."

"You said that already. Removed in favor of whom?" Tucker said. "Mrs. Miller, I presume?" He shot a look over at Mr. Park. "Now listen to this, Rollie."

"Perhaps I can take a slightly different tack," Hartshorn said. "How much is Miller Envelope worth? The entire enterprise?"

"What does that have to do with anything?" Tucker asked.

"Because, sir, when we are talking about Ed's trust, we are talking about money, and I would like to know how much of it we are talking about."

Mr. Park scratched his neck. "When the transfer of two-thirds of the company to Mr. Gaines was effected, the company's value was assessed at $300,000."

"So Mr. Gaines's share was worth $200,000?"

"That's what he borrowed to pay the trust, so at the time of the transaction, yes."

"And you've seen that the business is making approximately ten percent more envelopes now than it was at the time of the transaction. So let's assume for a moment that all of Miller Envelope is therefore worth $330,000. In round figures."

"Are you coming to a point sometime today?" Tucker said.

"I am," Bert said. "If I could produce a buyer willing to pay off

Gaines's note, plus a generous additional sum—I would presume that
the trustees would be acting within their fiduciary duty in vacating Mr.
Gaines's ownership?"

Tucker leaned back in his chair and looked at the concrete ceiling.
"Is this merely a hypothetical? Do you have a buyer, Hartshorn—or are
you just stalling for time?"

"I have a buyer."

"What's he willing to pay?"

"Before we get to that," Hartshorn said, "I trust you've seen the copies of all the new sales contracts that Mrs. Miller—acting on her own
as the company's sole salesman—has closed since she started taking an
active hand in the business?"

"Yes," Park said. "And, in all fairness, she's done an admirable job,"
he added, which made Tucker's face go red again.

"Then here's what my buyer will offer. But only if you decide today.
Here and now."

"This is going to be good," Tucker said. "Drumroll."

"We established—roughly, I understand—that Mr. Gaines's shares
are likely worth about $220,000 now. Two-thirds of $330,000, ten percent more than the value at the time of the transaction. I think that's
being generous, but that is neither here nor there. He owes $200,000."

"Correct," Park said.

"My buyer is prepared to offer double that amount—$400,000, in
cash—to repurchase all of Mr. Gaines's shares—*today*. But only if I leave
here with a signed purchase agreement."

Park's eyes opened wide. "What sort of buyer would propose
such terms? The whole company's not worth $400,000, let alone two-
thirds of it."

"Money is less important to my buyer than is securing a toehold
in the envelope business," Bert said. "He has great hopes for the future
of Miller Envelope, and he's willing to pay a premium to get in on the
ground floor."

"And if we don't accept this mysterious offer today?" Mr.
Tucker asked.

"In view of the generous financial consideration—and Mr. Gaines's

documented malfeasance—if the trustees do not accept my buyer's proposal today, I will immediately file a lawsuit for breach of fiduciary responsibility. It will be against the trust, and against you as trustees personally. And it will be brought by Mrs. Miller."

Tucker came out of his chair and jabbed a finger in Bert's direction. "You can tell that bitch that if she thinks she's going to blackmail me—"

"That will be enough, Bill," Park said, his voice reverberating in the concrete chamber. "This man's an officer of the court, and a friend of mine. And there are ladies present."

"Lady detectives," Sarah said. "To be precise."

"Now, Bert," Mr. Park said, "we've known each other a long time. There'd better be no funny business that your buyer is neither Mrs. Miller nor a straw purchaser working on her behalf. If so, that would be a legal battle I'd be willing to fight."

"You may rest assured that the purchaser is neither Mrs. Miller nor an agent purchasing the shares with any intention to transfer them to her. Indeed, he so stipulates voluntarily in his contract, which I have here for your review." Bert reached into his briefcase and took out a thin stack of paper.

"Let's see it," Tucker said, motioning with his fingers.

"You'll see in the contract that there is only one other small condition," Bert said.

"And that is?" Park asked.

"Whatever increase in value the company has enjoyed since the transaction with Mr. Gaines—and we've said that's roughly ten percent—has been entirely due to Mrs. Miller's sole effort in sales. Thus $40,000 of my buyer's $400,000 consideration is to be transferred directly to Mrs. Miller, but without increasing her ownership share. That will satisfy Ed's intention, I'm sure you will agree. And it leaves $360,000 net to the trust—on a $200,000 investment, and in only a little more than a year."

"Of course. He's saved the best for last," Tucker said. "I told you, Rollie, that—Mrs. Miller's behind this. She's gone and found some sucker willing to put his name on a contract for her benefit. Probably in exchange for her occasional—"

"I'm sorry to say it, Mr. Tucker, but you might want to read the signature page before you start making accusations," Bert said, sliding the papers across the table toward him.

Tucker slid the pages over to Mr. Park without so much as a glance. "Rollie, you're the lawyer here. I'm only a moneyman. I can't object to the dollars, as much as I might like to."

Park read through the first page, then the second, nodding and murmuring to himself. "It's all in order. Very straightforward." When he got to the signature page, he smiled.

"I didn't know you ran in these circles, Bert," Park said.

"What's that supposed to mean?" Tucker said, leaning over to peer at the signature page.

"What it means," Park said, "is that Charles Kendall—that would be *the* Charles Kendall—just bought himself two-thirds of an envelope company." He dipped a pen into an inkstand and signed the document, blew on it, and slid the contract over to Tucker. "Read it or don't read it, Bill, it doesn't matter. Just sign it."

48

TIME WILL TELL

"A MR. CHARLES KENDALL IS HERE TO SEE THE TWO OF YOU," Abby announced, poking her head into Gaines and Alicia's office. "Should I show him in?"

"*Charles Kendall?*" Gaines said to Alicia. "What's he doing here?"

"I couldn't possibly say. Of course, Abby, you may see him in."

A moment later, the door creaked and Charles Kendall stepped in, wearing an immaculate grey suit with a white-chalk stripe. Gaines stood and extended his hand. Kendall didn't shake it, and Gaines slowly lowered it again, rubbing it on his trouser front.

"To what do we owe this unexpected pleasure, Mr. Kendall?" Gaines asked, taking his seat.

"I had business in the city," Kendall said, pulling up the guest chair, "and I thought I'd drop by for a word about the recent inconsistency in your supply of my envelopes."

"I've been meaning to pick up the phone and call you myself about that," Gaines said.

"Is that right?" Kendall said. "Then my timing is indeed fortuitous."

"Indeed it is. What I wanted to explain to you, with all due respect to my partner here—Mrs. Miller likely wasn't aware of the limitations of our machines when she promised you the delivery schedule she did."

"What kind of limitations?" Kendall asked.

"Mechanical limitations," Gaines said, leaning back. "It's quite complex."

"I'll take your word for it. Well, then, what do you propose? Something needs to change, Mr. Gaines. I'm sure you'd agree."

"I do, I do, Mr. Kendall," he said, smiling. "I'd suggest that—if Mrs. Miller won't mind—I take over the management of your account personally. I'll see to it that we deliver."

"But I like working with Mrs. Miller," Kendall said. "What can you do for me that she cannot?"

"I'm a machine-man, Mr. Kendall. I know how to fine-tune our machines, and she doesn't."

"Would you call this an example of fine-tuning?" Kendall asked, reaching into his bag. He removed a folder containing Annie's photographs and a transcript of time clock records. He tossed them onto Gaines's desk.

"What is this all about?" Howie said, riffling through them and going almost purplish.

"I was going to ask you the very same question."

Gaines glared over at Alicia. "You're behind this, no doubt?"

She shrugged. "I had to do something to keep you from ruining me."

"Ruining *you*?"

"That's right. This company was almost stolen from me by my own husband, and I wasn't about to let it be stolen a second time."

"I didn't steal a thing from you," he said. "Why, I welcomed you into this business. Taught you the ins and outs!"

"Interesting choice of words," she said, and Kendall blushed.

"To think I fell in love with you," Gaines spluttered. "And all the while you were faking—"

"Now, Gaines, that's taking it too far," she said. "I wasn't faking anything. As God is my witness, I will freely admit that you just about blew the top of my cranium off that time you—"

At this, Kendall cleared his throat and shifted in his seat.

"Sorry, Mr. Kendall," she said. "I'd hoped you wouldn't hear that part, but the proverbial cat is out of the bag now, so I suppose it doesn't matter."

"No," Kendall said. "It's quite all right, Mrs. Miller. Go right ahead."

"I was only saying that I wasn't going to let Gaines here rob me of my rightful place in this company."

"Rightful place?" Gaines said. "The trustees sold me—not you—the majority of this business."

"Funny you should mention the trustees," Kendall said.

"Mrs. Miller won't find it so funny, sir," Gaines shot back, "when I have a little talk with them." He gestured at the photographs. "As long as I'm majority owner of this company, I will *not* be spied upon."

"Do I have a say in it?" Kendall said.

"With due respect, sir, if you don't like the way I run this company, you may take your business elsewhere. And Mrs. Miller may depart for the firm who wins your business."

Kendall nodded. "I considered that alternative. And for a while, it seemed like a sensible option, but you know—it felt like losing. And I *hate* losing, Mr. Gaines. So I decided to go a different direction." He threw over a carbon copy of his contract. "I bought you out."

Gaines picked up the document and leafed through it, skepticism turning to astonishment. "What? The trustees would never—"

"Yet they did. Mr. Park and Mr. Tucker have already agreed to the sale. You'll see their signatures on the last page."

"They can't do that unless they pay me off," Gaines said. "This company is worth far more than what I paid for it. The trustees told me so when I borrowed the money."

"I thought as much," Allie said.

"And you're correct, Mr. Gaines. We compared production volumes from this year to those of a year ago," Kendall said, "and the company is producing about ten percent more now than when you took out your loan."

"Then I want that gain in value—in cash," Gaines said, jabbing his index finger into the desktop.

"I'm terribly sorry, but as a condition of my purchase—and in recognition of Mrs. Miller's singlehanded sales efforts—that imputed gain goes to her. You may consider yourself fortunate that I didn't press to have your $200,000 debt increased by the amount you impaired the company during your term of majority ownership."

"What sort of game do you think you're playing? Don't think you can simply take away my company and leave me with *nothing*."

"I assure you that it's not a game, Mr. Gaines. True, you *get* nothing. But look on the bright side—at least you *owe* nothing. You're free as a bird."

"You do realize I'll pursue this in court," Gaines growled, his face an impossible shade of crimson.

"Be my guest. As you've seen, we have ample proof that you put your own company at risk, Mr. Gaines," Kendall said, "for your own selfish reasons. Oh, and I recommend you hire a very good lawyer, since my general counsel used to be the lieutenant governor of New York State."

Gaines's entire head had gone so red that it looked like a perilously overripe fruit. "You *need* me," he said in a choked voice. "Do you think *she's* going to be able to run this company? Run those *machines?*"

"You're welcome to stay the rest of the day, if you wish," Kendall said. "I'll pay you three months' severance, which should give you plenty of time to find another position. Now, if you do choose to sue me, I'll see that your severance is clawed back—every penny of it. You may take my word for it."

"I'm leaving," Gaines said, standing up and knocking over one of the teetering piles of paper on his typewriter table. "I'm not staying another goddamn second. Good luck with that—*sorceress*," he said to Kendall, pointing at Alicia. "You'll find out soon enough how she operates."

When he was nearly to the office door, Gaines turned back toward Alicia. "I *curse* the day you ever darkened my door. And if there's a God in Heaven, one day you'll get your comeuppance for making me love you." He yanked open the office door, and Abby almost tumbled into the room.

"Abby," Alicia said calmly, as the girl regained her balance, "would you mind showing Mr. Gaines out?"

Abby nodded, and they could hear Gaines cursing and ranting as he disappeared down the hallway. Alicia and Kendall stared silently at the open doorway for a moment.

At last, Kendall turned around in his chair to face Alicia, pursed his lips, and raised his eyebrows.

"I really do seem to rub people the wrong way sometimes," Alicia said.

Kendall laughed. "You have a wonderfully dry sense of humor, Mrs. Miller. It was bound to be ugly. That's why I didn't want the trustees here."

"I can't possibly thank you enough, Mr. Kendall."

"No thanks required," he said with a shrug. "It was a simple business decision. And a small investment."

"If you call $400,000 small," Allie mused.

"To protect my envelope supply, and retain my star copywriter?" he said.

"Good point. Come to think about it, perhaps I ought to have held out for far more."

He smiled. "It was also the principle of the thing. When Sarah told me about your call, and all that her agency had uncovered—and what Gaines put you through—frankly, it made me sick to my stomach. I hate blackmailers, Mrs. Miller. Whether they do it for money or—"

"I know. You don't have to say it," Alicia said.

"Thank you. My point is that I would have been quite content with this investment on that basis alone. Yet since then, I've begun to think there's gold to be mined here. Between your sales ability, your writing skills, and my connections and capital resources, I see no reason why this can't become a leading national company."

"I'd like nothing better," she said. "I will need another so-called machine-man, though."

"That won't be a problem. Two excellent ones will be here first thing tomorrow. Believe me, if they can run the machinery at my factory, they'll put these ones in shape in no time."

Alicia gazed down at her blotter, speckled with ink from the contracts she had secured and the advertising she'd written. "And the *name*?" she asked quietly, without looking up. "Is it to be Kendall Envelope now?"

"Unless you object, I see no reason to change the name. I'm an abrasives manufacturer. I don't need people thinking I've lost focus on my main business."

"I understand," she said, suppressing the urge to jump up and throw her arms around Kendall. "Thank you. I'd like it to remain Miller Envelope Company."

"Then so it shall. That leaves only one other thing I feel duty bound to bring up. Perhaps a slightly sensitive subject."

"Please. Whatever you like."

He shifted in his seat. "It concerns you and Miss Payne."

"How so?" Allie said warily.

He coughed slightly into his fist. "I recognize—as Sarah put it from the start—that things between the two of you have been *complicated*. And now, they're even more so. You and I have a business to run, and she and I have—well, I don't know what quite yet. But she has agreed to stay in Niagara Falls for a while. Only time will tell."

"So they say," she said. "But I wonder . . . does it always tell the truth?"

Kendall looked perplexed. "In any case. What I wish to say is that you and Sarah are both important to me, if in different ways. And so I am hopeful—"

"Sarah and I were once great friends, you know," Alicia offered. "It's only recently that she and I haven't exactly seen eye to eye. We both have our pride, I suppose."

Kendall seemed relieved. "And it wouldn't do for me to ask either you or Sarah to swallow it. What I might ask, though, is to look at this fresh start as Sarah's way—I will tell you that she argued your case quite forcefully, and with great feeling, after you made your proposal—of holding out an olive branch. I do hope you'll accept it in that spirit."

"Mr. Kendall," Alicia said, "I would like nothing more than to let bygones be bygones." She paused. "And who can say? In time, Sarah and I may end up becoming closer than we were before."

"That would be wonderful. Thank you for being so receptive. And by the way, I think it's time you began calling me Charles. Or Charlie. We're partners now."

"That we are, Charlie," she said, holding out her hand. "And I hope you'll call me Allie. Or Miller, as the mood strikes you."

"Done," he said, shaking her hand. "It's going to be my pleasure to have you as my partner, Allie."

"Time will tell," she replied, with a wink.

COMING TO TERMS

"YOU HAVE TO LOOK AT IT PHILOSOPHICALLY," AARON BRASS said to the small group of men lolling around the ABW office. "It almost went our way."

"We should have known the Cossack had his own agenda," Utting said.

"Nah, it was Kendall's lady detective who spoiled it," Mars said. "We couldn't have seen that coming."

"I wouldn't give the girl too much credit," one of the other men said. "The tunnel plan was too obvious from the start. Someone would have figured it out eventually. Believe me, there are other ways to cripple the man's production. And much subtler ones, at that."

"Now is that so?" Brass said.

"Yes, it's so. And ways to hurt him personally, too. In ways he'll never forget."

"Do tell."

"As soon as you and I agree on terms, I will. You can have Kendall's factory for your union—I don't give a good goddamn about that. I have a more personal score to settle."

"Let's talk turkey, then," Brass said, opening his cigarette case and holding it out. The man selected a likely-looking smoke from the gold case, and stuck it in his mouth.

"Going to need your help with this," he said, the cigarette wagging between his lips.

"Of course," Brass said, striking a match and holding it out over the desk.

Jeremy Horn leaned forward and touched the end of his cigarette to the little flame. "Thanks," he said, sitting back and exhaling at the ceiling. "Now let's get down to business."

The End

ROBERT BRIGHTON'S
AVENGING ANGEL DETECTIVE
AGENCY™ MYSTERIES

THE DEVIL'S
BUSINESS

THE NEXT AVENGING
ANGEL DETETCTIVE
AGENCY™ MYSTERY

© Ashwood Press, LLC

Acknowledgments

As I've said to any number of people over the years, authors don't write *books*. They write *manuscripts*. It takes a host of people to help an author turn a stack of pages into a real book, and this one was no exception.

The Library of Congress in Washington, DC, is one of my favorite places on earth, and if you are serious about doing research—or simply learning something new in beautiful surroundings—it will quickly become one of yours, too. The librarians in the Newspaper & Periodical and in the Science & Business Reading Rooms deserve special note for their very capable assistance.

To everyone along the labyrinthine path that leads from manuscript to printed book—artists, cover and page design and layout, printing, and fulfillment—I offer my most sincere thanks and admiration. I hope my books read well, but in any case, I know they *look* and *feel* great because of all of these sometimes unsung heroes.

I cannot fail to thank my friend and steadfast supporter, Judge Penny Wolfgang, who is both a fine jurist and an even finer human being.

Special thanks go to my editors on this project, Kimberly Laurel and Adrienne Pond, who both did so much to improve my words.

And as always, thank you is simply not enough for my wife, Laura, whose contributions to my work (and my life) are far too numerous and profound for words.

Robert Brighton
February 2024

About the Author

A NATIVE OF BUFFALO, Robert Brighton is an authority on the Gilded Age, and a believer that the Victorian era was anything but stuffy.

When he is not sniffing out unsolved mysteries, Brighton is a wanderer. He has traveled in more than fifty countries around the world, personally throwing himself into every situation his characters will face—from underground ruins to opium dens—and (so far) living to tell about it.

A graduate of the Sorbonne, Paris, Brighton is an avid student of early twentieth-century history and literature, an ardent and relentless investigator, and an admirer of Emily Dickinson and Jim Morrison. He lives in Virginia with his wife and their two cats.

For more information visit:
RobertBrightonAuthor.com